Praise for *Echoes of Betrayal*

"Moon's pacing is as leisurely as a snowball rolling down a mountain, and it leads just as surely to catastrophe; every crisis solved reveals two larger ones, and the intriguing characters must frantically build strength and courage to survive."

—*Publishers Weekly*

"[Moon's] military acumen ensures convincing battle scenes while her talent for character building makes for sympathetic and believable heroes and villains. Fans of epic fantasy with an emphasis on military strategy should enjoy this series."

—*Library Journal*

"Excellent . . . highly recommended!"

—BookLoons

"Highly rewarding . . . [Moon] has a deep concern with the moral issues created in her world, one that gives her characters a seriousness many of the successors to Tolkien have been unable—or unwilling—to bring to their writings."

—*Asmiov's Science Fiction*

Praise for the Paladin's Legacy series

"Elizabeth Moon makes a triumphant return to the fantasy world she created in her first trilogy, The Deed of Paksenarrion. . . . No one writes fantasy quite like Moon and—amazingly after so long—her characters feel exactly the same, as if the last book had been published a year ago. . . . Hopefully we won't have to wait another twenty-odd years for the next book, but if it's as good as *Oath of Fealty*, it'll be worth the wait."

—*The Miami Herald*

"Through her characters, Moon makes the world breathe and come alive."

—SFF World

"What sheer delight! *Oath of Fealty* is an engrossing new adventure returning old friends to us in the first of more books in the Paksenarrion universe. It's quite simply a smashing story, and I am panting to read the next install-ment from this consummate storyteller. Hurry up, Eliza-beth!"

— ANNE MCCAFFREY

"More than worthy to stand alongside the earlier tales of the Paladin Paksenarrion and her companions, set in a land that ranks alongside Andre Norton's Witch World and Tolkien's Middle-earth for invention, deeds of valor, and battles of good against evil."

—JACK CAMPBELL,
New York Times bestselling author of the Lost Fleet series

"Has just what I look for in an Elizabeth Moon fantasy: magic, action, damned fine swordplay, and characters who hold honor and loyalty higher than life itself. An epic win!"
—JODY LYNN NYE, author of *A Forthcoming Wizard*

ECHOES *of* BETRAYAL

PALADIN'S LEGACY

ECHOES of BETRAYAL

PALADIN'S LEGACY

ELIZABETH MOON

BALLANTINE BOOKS • NEW YORK

Echoes of Betrayal is a work of fiction. Names, characters, places, and incidents are the products of the author's imagination or are used fictitiously. Any resemblance to actual events, locales, or persons, living or dead, is entirely coincidental.

2013 Del Rey Books Mass Market Edition

Copyright © 2012 by Elizabeth Moon
Excerpt from *Limits of Power* by Elizabeth Moon copyright © 2013 by Elizabeth Moon

Published in the United States by Del Rey, an imprint of The Random House Publishing Group, a division of Random House, Inc., New York.

DEL REY is a registered trademark and the Del Rey colophon is a trademark of Random House, Inc.

Originally published in hardcover in the United States by Del Rey, an imprint of The Random House Publishing Group, a division of Random House, Inc., in 2012.

This book contains an excerpt from the forthcoming book *Limits of Power* by Elizabeth Moon. This excerpt has been set for this edition only and may not reflect the final content of the forthcoming edition.

ISBN 978-0-345-52418-8
eBook ISBN 978-0-345-52481-2

Printed in the United States of America

www.delreybooks.com

9 8 7 6 5 4 3 2 1

Del Rey mass market edition: May 2013

For Richard, best of husbands, and for Michael, best of sons:
you have enriched my life and made the work possible

Dramatis Personae

Fox Company (formerly Kieri Phelan's mercenary company)
Jandelir Arcolin, commander, Lord of the North Marches
Burek, junior captain of first cohort
Selfer, captain of second cohort
Cracolnya, captain of third (mixed/archery) cohort
Stammel, veteran sergeant of the Company, now blind

Tsaia
Mikeli Vostan Kieriel Mahieran, king of Tsaia
 Camwyn, his younger brother
Sonder Amrothlin Mahieran, Duke Mahieran, king's uncle
 Beclan, his younger son and Duke Verrakai's squire
 Celbrin Konhalt, his wife
Selis Jostin Marrakai, Duke Marrakai
 Gwennothlin, his daughter and Duke Verrakai's squire
Galyan Selis Serrostin, Duke Serrostin
 Daryan, youngest son and Duke Verrakai's squire
Dorrin Verrakai, Duke Verrakai, formerly a senior captain in
 Phelan's Company, now Constable for the kingdom
Oktar, new Marshal-Judicar of Tsaia
Sir Flanits Clannaeth, commander of Royal Guard unit,
 Harway
Vossik, veteran sergeant of Duke's Company, now with Duke
 Verrakai training her militia

Lyonya
Kieri Phelan, king of Lyonya, former mercenary commander
 and duke in Tsaia
Sier Tolmaric, member Lyonyan Council

Aliam Halveric, commands Halveric Company, Kieri
     Phelan's mentor and friend
Estil Halveric, his wife
Sier Halveric, Aliam Halveric's older brother
Garris, senior King's Squire
Arian, half-elf, Kieri's betrothed
     Elves
Orlith, Kieri Phelan's tutor in elven magic
Flessinathlin, the Lady of the Ladysforest, elven ruler of this
     elvenhome kingdom, Kieri's grandmother
Dameroth, Arian's father
Amrothlin, the Lady's son and Kieri's uncle

Pargun
Torfinn, king of Pargun
     Elis, his daughter

Kuakkgani
Ashwind, itinerant Kuakgan, Tsaia
Oakhallow, grovemaster Kuakgan, Tsaia
Larchwind, itinerant Kuakgan, Lyonya
Pearwind, itinerant Kuakgan, Lyonya

Adventurers
Arvid Semminson, Vérella Thieves' Guild
Dattur, kteknik gnome and Arvid's companion

ECHOES *of*
BETRAYAL

PALADIN'S LEGACY

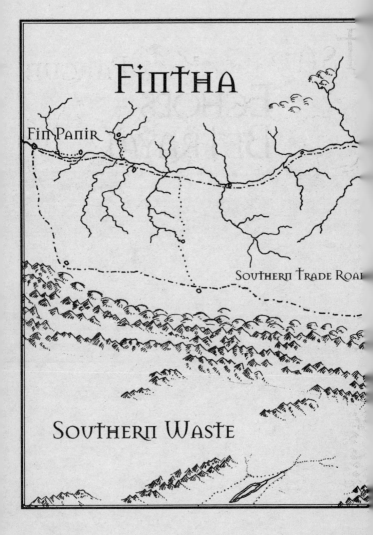

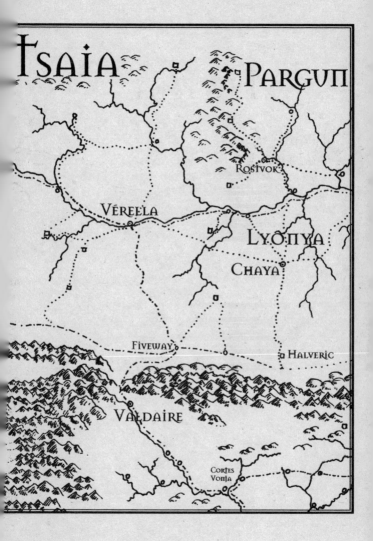

CHAPTER ONE

Aarenis

Arvid Semminson, lying naked, bound, and bruised on the cold ground somewhere in northwestern Aarenis, reflected that honor among thieves was a myth. Valdaire's Guildmaster had taken everything he had: clothes, weapons, gold, his Guildmaster symbol, and that very damning—in the Guildmaster's eyes—letter of safe passage from the Marshal-General. In return, the Guildmaster had indeed found a room for Arvid, as he'd offered: Arvid had spent several very unpleasant days in the Guildhouse cellar before his kteknik gnome companion Dattur, worried by his absence, had tried to rescue him, only to be captured himself.

After some additional time in the Guild's cellar, they'd both been dumped into the lower compartment of a trade-wagon and driven out of the city—several days out, in what direction Arvid had no notion—in the untender care of journeymen enforcers who intended to pry every detail of information from them both before killing them.

Now the journeymen tossed dice for first choice of his weapons, all the while loudly discussing what they intended to do with him. Certain tools were, they'd said, heating in the coals. He would be warm then, one jeered, throwing a hot coal that bounced off his back before he felt more than the sting.

He heard the fire crackling somewhere behind him. Smoke fragrant with the scent of roasting meat curled past his nose, but where he lay only cold wind caressed him, and his belly cramped with hunger.

He should have stayed north of the mountains once he was sure the necklace had already gone south. He should have realized that his long absence from Vérella had given his second in command—Harsin, with his false smiles—a chance to seize power and proclaim him a traitor to the Guild because he had gone to do the Marshal-General's bidding.

He would have Harsin's liver roasted on skewers if he got out of this alive, which—at the moment—seemed unlikely. What he needed was a rescue, but who in all Aarenis knew or cared about him? His gnome servant, maybe, but Dattur was trussed up as tightly as Arvid himself, and gagged as well.

You could ask for help.

Arvid had heard that voice before, and it was not a voice he wanted to hear. Nor the chuckle that followed. He was not a Girdish yeoman; he had respect for the hero-saint, but . . . it was not for him. Besides, it was Gird's Marshal-General's letter in his pocket that had put him in this mess. If not for her—

You'd have been hanged long since for the thief you are.

He was *not* a thief—he *had* been a thief, but that was years ago, and anyway—all right, yes, the Marshal-General had saved him from those Girdish who were sure he'd stolen the necklace, but he hadn't. And it was being seen as too friendly with the Fellowship that had turned the others against him.

Would you have let her die?

He knew which "her" that was, of course. Paksenarrion. Of course he would not have let that vicious jealous bitch Barra kill her after all she'd suffered—

And the gods healed.

Well, yes, that was true, too. But now, here . . .

You are almost as stubborn as I was, lad.

Arvid felt a gentle hand on his bruised head and then the sting of something cold on his bare shoulder—one and then another. And another.

The fire hissed. The men swore and stood, their weapons—some of them his—clanking. "What about them?" one said. "Let 'em drown or freeze," said another. "Take the meat inside." Arvid heard the door of the hut—hardly more than a shed—creak open and then slam shut. Cold rain, the winter rain of Aarenis, pelted down on him, harder every moment. He shivered; his teeth chattered. Cold water ran into his face, melting away the blood that had glued his eyelids shut in the last beating. Under his nose he saw a stretch of dark earth speckled with pebbles glistening in the rain.

Wet leather stretched. Arvid remembered that even as his hands twisted . . . but it had to be really wet, and he was chilling faster than the leather softened. He struggled on. Hair by hair, the leather thongs stretched. Enough? It had to be enough.

You could have sent a paladin, he thought into the dark sky. *She has her task. You have yours.*

It did not seem the right moment to tell that sort of voice that he was not in service to that sort of voice. It was the right moment to escape, if he could. He worked one stiff hand loose, then the other. He could scarcely move his fingers and fumbled at the thongs tying his knees, his ankles. All the time the rain pelted down, hard cold drops—some of them ice pellets now, it felt like. He needed a knife, a sharp— His hand knocked against something, a loose rock—and he saw the glassy scalloped edge of broken flint as if outlined by the sun.

He wanted to say, *You could have sent a knife,* but what if the rock disappeared? By repute, the gods were big on gratitude. He clutched the flint awkwardly, sawed at the thongs, pulling and sawing together, and finally his knees were free and then his ankles. He tried to stand, but the blows he'd taken, the hunger of two days trussed and gagged in a wagon, prevented it. He crawled instead, the flint in his mouth, bruised hands splayed out on the cold mud, bruised knees gouged afresh by the stones, until he reached Dattur, who was himself struggling with his bonds, but unsuccessfully. They had bound the gnome upright to a tree, using a length of rope—and rope did not stretch in the wet, but shrank.

Arvid sawed away at the rope. One strand then another parted. The gnome finally got free and pulled the gag from his mouth.

"Master—"

"Shh . . ." Arvid was shuddering with cold.

"Give rock." The gnome reached for his hand and pried the flint out of it. Arvid collapsed against the tree trunk. Leafless though it was, it broke the wind and some of the rain. The gnome hopped off the boards the men had placed to keep him from touching the rocky ground; Arvid had a moment to think *rock-magery*, and then the gnome touched the flint to one of the exposed rocks between the tree roots. The rock opened silently as a mouth, and the gnome and Arvid slid into the gap, out of wind and rain alike.

Still cold, still wet, still shivering, but alive, for which he should, he knew, be thanking the gods . . .

Yes.

He muttered a shaky *Thank you* in a voice he scarcely recognized as his own, and scrubbed at his arms and body, trying to warm them. Dattur, he realized, had moved to one side of the hole they were in and had begun chanting at the rock. Arvid wanted to ask what he was doing, but as a dim blue-gray light spread from the gnome and his working, he could see for himself. The rock opened without sound or mess . . . The light brightened as if rock were transmuted into light. Did the light show outside? Would the robbers, should they discover him missing, find them by the light coming out a crack in the rock by the tree?

Arvid forced himself up and staggered to the foot of the hole they'd slid down; a wet cold draft touched his face, and a snowflake kissed his nose. He moved back into the tunnel and huddled near one wall. Their captors wouldn't see anything through snow.

Under his feet, against the curve of his back, he felt a faint warmth. Was the rock warming up? He flattened one hand against it . . . warmer than he was, at any rate. Dattur was ten full paces away now, chanting in words Arvid did not know; the space in the rock grew distinctly warmer but did not extend. The warmth gave Arvid strength; he pushed himself up and started to walk forward, but a jerk of Dattur's head was a clear signal to stay back.

Now he could see that the rock was disappearing *upward*. Arvid tried to calculate direction and distance . . . could it be that Dattur was making a passage into the hut where their captors lay sleeping? That would be disastrous—the two of them, naked and unarmed, could not deal with four armed thieves—but Dattur had proved no fool so far. Arvid leaned back against the rock, felt its warmth drying the hair on the back of his aching head. Just as he finally remembered the rockfolk talent for bringing cold sleep to humans, the entire contents of the hut fell into the gap Dattur had created: walls and roof landing on the packs, pallets, weapons, and men still wrapt in rock-magery. Snowflakes whirled down through the opening, and the cold wet met the tunnel's warmth, melting instantly. Even the fall did not wake the men. Before Arvid could reach the mound of debris, Dattur had burrowed into it, snatched up his own sword, and sliced four throats.

Without a word, he dropped the sword and held up both hands; stone flowed up and over to close the gap as the light dimmed. Then it strengthened again, and Dattur finally turned to look at Arvid. "It is between us no debt owed for this," he said. "Without my master freeing me, it could not be done. Without my doing, it was no chance."

"I—thank you anyway, Dattur," Arvid said. "Does it not tire you?"

Dattur shrugged. "Not this little." He frowned then. "No human should see rockmagic at work. No human should see rockfolk unclothed. I know you have a good memory, master, but . . . do not speak of this."

"I will never speak of it," Arvid said. Having said that, he had a powerful desire to look, to commit to memory the differences between gnome and human anatomy. Instead he looked down and turned to the heap before them. "I will look for what we need."

In the end it took both of them to untangle the mess. Finally, clothed in a mix of the thieves' garments and what remained of their own, he and Dattur built a small fire at the end of the tunnel near the tree and ate what food they'd been able to salvage from the dusty pile: two skewers with hunks of half-cooked meat still on them and a loaf of coarse bread. They didn't care; the fire burned off the dirt, or so Arvid told himself.

"It would be well to leave while falling snow covers our tracks," Arvid said after picking a string of meat from between his teeth with the bodkin he carried. "Surely the Guildmaster will send someone to check on those four."

"They will never be found," Dattur said. "When I leave, I will close the stone, all of it."

Arvid shuddered at the thought of men encased in stone, even dead men, but he knew it was best. He looked out the opening—dark now and still snowing. Madness to start when they could not even see. "We'll have to wait until morning," Arvid said. Surely they would be safe until then.

He woke when daylight—dim enough through falling snow—returned. Dattur was awake and already smothering the coals. Arvid clambered up, wincing at his various bruises, cuts, and burns, and gathered up the little clutter they'd made. Then Dattur began filling the space behind them. Once more Arvid watched stone behave as no stone he had ever seen, finally rising up beneath their feet and lifting them to the surface.

Snow still fell; the ground was covered with it. As they looked around, talking softly, a horse snorted. Arvid found the team hitched to a line between two trees, ragged blankets tied on their backs with cord. The wagon's arched cover had shed the snow, and the space inside was dry, if not warm . . . but travel with a wagon would slow them. And surely the Guild had placed secret marks on the wagon—he felt along the rim of the sides, where the cover was pegged down. Yes, there.

The horses, however, were not marked. Dray horses didn't matter that much—any horse would do, and these two thick-coated, thick-legged beasts of middling size were nondescript brown, one lighter than the other. Arvid found the nearly full sack of oats and a pile of hay in the wagon and filled their nose bags. Bridles and harness were in the wagon, too. He checked the bottom compartment where he and Dattur had been carried. A small chest, with a stack of parchment scraps, an ink-stick, a small stone bowl, a lump of wax, and a seal . . . He felt the seal. A Guildmaster seal. So the Guildmaster expected his men to send reports? Arvid added the seal, wax, inkstick, and four or five scraps of parchment to his pack. He found a bag of coins, enough for four men to supply themselves for almost a quarter-year. Payment? Or just for supplies? A small keg of coarse meal, a sack of onions, and another of redroots.

He tossed the harness out of the wagon, and he and Dattur spent some time unbuckling sections until they could strap the blankets to the horses' backs as pads to sit on. The tugs made reasonable stirrups, and on these beasts, which showed not the slightest concern for anything but food, they needed no more complete saddle.

"It's better if you ride," Arvid said to Dattur, who was eyeing the preparation of both horses with obvious concern. "We want this to look like human thieves came along and stole both the horses and everything out of the wagon. If the snow doesn't cover our tracks, yours would reveal that a gnome was here, and they'd know we'd escaped. With the hut gone and their people gone, they just might think it was wizard work."

Dattur agreed to ride if Arvid would lead the horse. Arvid put the half sack of oats across its back, making sure the sides balanced, and then lifted Dattur—surprisingly heavy—atop.

He had no idea where they were or who they were likely to meet, but at least they weren't tied up and left to freeze, and they could survive for a few days on meal and onions and water if they found no other source of food. He had no intention of being captured again.

Snow stopped by what Arvid guessed was midday. By then they had crossed a creek and followed a trail upstream and around several bends without finding any sign of habitation. The clouds lifted slowly, letting in more and more light. Now he could see mountains rising above the slope they climbed, higher, snow on their sides. Which mountains, those to the west or those north of Valdaire? The pass to the north? After the blows to his head and riding in that closed wagon, he had little idea of direction. He glanced at Dattur and pointed. "The pass?"

"Dwarfmounts. Dasksinyi," Dattur said. "We cannot cross until spring."

"I don't want to go north now," Arvid said. "I want to kill that man and get the necklace back. And my horse." The shaggy beasts they were on had the short plodding stride of a typical farm chunk and jolted his bruises and strained joints.

"You think he has the necklace?"

"I think he knows where it is," Arvid said. "And if I'm beaten up, robbed, starved, and left to die in a cold rain because I'm running errands for the Marshal-General of Gird, then I intend to finish the job." He rubbed his cold nose. "And

I want my own Guildmaster medallion back." That treacherous scum Mathol, the Valdaire Guildmaster, would have it locked safe away.

"Are you sure?" Dattur asked. "You don't act much like a thief, really. Maybe you will reform—"

"Of course I am . . . well, not an ordinary thief . . ."

"You're a liar—I've seen that—but I've never seen you steal."

"I used to," Arvid said. "When I was a lad; we all had to. But stealing . . . it's boring, mostly. And when the Guildmaster asked me to check on some businesses we had a contract with, he found my insight into accounting most useful." He sniffed. Was that a hint of woodsmoke? A current of air brushed his left cheek. He looked at the gnome. "Do you smell smoke?"

"Aye," Dattur said. He pointed. "Upslope and ahead. It'll be woodsfolk, I don't doubt."

In the north that would mean woodcutters on some lord's estate. Here he had learned to be wary of his assumptions. "Do you know anything about them?"

"Sly. Dirty, thieving, mischievous—" Dattur looked disapproving, not frightened.

"My brethren," Arvid said, grinning. "Apart from 'dirty,' though right now we qualify there. I wonder if they're under the Guild, though . . . We could be walking into danger."

"I don't know," Dattur said. "If you help me down, stand me on a rock, I can find out more."

The horses had shambled to a halt; Arvid slid off, then lifted Dattur down to stand on one of the many snow-capped boulders. He himself was stiff, cold, and still very hungry. One horse snuffled hopefully at the sack of oats across the other's withers; Arvid led them a length apart, tied Dattur's to a small tree, and considered whether to give them a handful of oats. Might as well. It wasn't the horses' fault that his stomach felt glued to his backbone.

By the time he'd untied the sack and put oats in both nose bags, Dattur had finished whatever gnomes did with the rock and hopped down. "They're not Guild connected," he said. "Woodsfolk." He sniffed.

"They have a fire and maybe a cooking pot, and we have meal, onions, and redroots." Which would be better for being cooked in a pot. When the horses finished munching, Arvid lifted Dattur back onto his horse and mounted his own.

The horses told him where the woodsfolk were before he could see them, ears pointing at both sides of the track. Arvid could see the drift of smoke through the trees now and smell baking bread. His mouth watered. He reined in.

"I would share," he said loudly. For a long moment, no one answered, then a stocky man wearing a dirty sheepskin as a crude cloak stepped out from behind the very tree Arvid had picked as most likely. He had a short bow in his hands and a wicked-looking arrow to the string.

"You not us," the man said in Common so accented that Arvid could barely understand.

Arvid's horse flicked both ears backward; Arvid glanced back and saw that another man had stepped into the trail behind them, also with a bow. In the distance, another horse whinnied; Arvid's horse whuffled.

"Friends for food," Arvid said. "We share."

"You give. Us eat."

"No." Dattur launched into a language Arvid didn't know, sounding more like quarreling cats than words. The men answered in the same language, and finally the one in front removed the arrow from the string of his bow and stuck it in a quiver by his side.

"Share," he said, and gestured. Arvid slid off his horse and lifted Dattur down. The gnome stamped three times with his left foot and twice with his right. Arvid had no idea what that meant but hoped it would mean supper and a safe night's sleep.

THE FIRE THEY'D smelled lay in a slight hollow; four wagons surrounded it, brush piled on the windward side to break the wind. Their two horses joined nine others tied to a picket line; Dattur took their sack of redroots and onions to the fire. Arvid took off the bits of harness while Dattur jabbered away with the woodsfolk, then filled the horses' nose bags with oats and spread the tattered blankets over their backs. When he bent to pick up a hoof, the man watching him grunted.

"You care horse?"

"Horse needs foot," Arvid said. Without a word, the man passed him a hoofpick made of horn. "Thanks," Arvid said, and went to work. By the time he'd finished both horses, he was trembling again with cold and hunger.

As he came to the fire, the dancing light picked out details he had not noticed before: men, all in rough sheepskins with the fleece turned out; women in layers and layers of long shirts and skirts. All the women wore a string of blue beads across their foreheads. In the north, blue would mean Girdish. Did it here? Children, legs wrapped in strips of sheepskin with the fleece in.

A man brought him a round of bread and held it out. Arvid looked at Dattur. "Share?"

Dattur nodded at one of the several pots on the fire. "Cooking."

Arvid bowed, hoping it was the right thing to do, and tore the round, handing the larger piece to the other man. He tore it again and offered the larger to Dattur, but Dattur shook his head and took the smaller one.

The bread was warm; Arvid could hardly wait until the other man tore off pieces and handed them to the oldest man and woman and then bit into his own piece. At last he could eat, and he sat with a thump, his legs betraying him, and stuffed his mouth with warm bread.

"Who hit?" asked the first man, pointing at Arvid's face.

"Thieves," Arvid said.

"You thief!"

"Not same." A woman handed him a bowl of something that steamed; Arvid nodded his thanks and sniffed. Onions and redroots and whole peppers as long as his thumb. Something else . . . he looked up. The woman's eyelids were almost closed. Without taking a bite, he turned to the man. "I don't steal from fire-friends."

The man blinked, looked away, looked back. "Only give little sleep. You need."

"Not fire-friends," another man said. "No gaj is fire-friend."

"Is fire-friend," the first man said. "One night. Give me bowl, fire-friend." Arvid handed it over; the man dipped his bread in it and ate. "I could sleep better. Ajai, give him only the plain." The woman turned back to the fire. "Is insult to refuse food from woman. Woman angry causes trouble."

"I meant no insult," Arvid said. "But I have had a bad several days. Makes trust hard."

"So face shows," the man said.

The woman brought him another bowl; she widened her eyes at him. Arvid dipped his bread in and ate it. If it was drugged . . . he would be robbed, but he did not think they'd leave him naked in the rain or snow. The stuff burned his mouth so he gasped; tears ran down his face. The women laughed at him; the men grinned.

"No peppers so hot in the north," Arvid said when he could.

"No," the first man said. "But is good for many things. Makes sweat."

"I can tell," Arvid said.

Across the fire, a man began to pluck the strings of a fat-bellied instrument, and another tapped sticks . . . or bones, Arvid saw on second look. A woman began a song in a high nasal voice, words Arvid could not follow. It would not have passed for music in any city tavern in Tsaia, but here in the snowy woods, as more voices joined in, that human resonance had a similar effect. He did not know the tune or the song . . . and it stopped abruptly. Another instrument was passed from hand to hand toward him until he took it and tried to pass it to the man on his right, who shook his head.

He looked at it more closely. Flatter than the other; when he plucked a string, it had a strong sound. "I once played a small one something like this," he said, plucking one string after another and feeling out the sounds it could make. "As a boy, my father bade me learn." There . . . and there . . . and there . . . he could find a half dozen notes, four or five combinations that sounded good. "I do not know your songs, but here is one of my people." A drinking song, common in all the taverns of Vérella because it was easy to make up more verses. He started with the ones that came first to mind:

"A pretty girl in springtime
Sweet and fresh as the air
Is like the wild-plum flower

But only for an hour . . .
A handsome lad in springtime
Is like the Windsteed's foal
Quick to dance and fight
His pride is his delight . . ."

One of the men beat a rhythm, this time with a stick against a box, and a woman shook a gourd with pebbles. Two men started the next verse with him.

"A pretty girl in summertime
Working in the sun
She ripens like the grain
But harvest brings her pain . . ."

Feet stamped when he finished. Arvid could not tell if it was courtesy or actual pleasure. He held the instrument out; this time his neighbor took it. He was handed a bowl of something that smelled of strong drink. He pointed to the lumps on his head, shrugged, and passed it on. They seemed to understand. After more songs—mostly long, plaintive laments—one of the older women said something in their language, and the men got up slowly.

That night, Arvid set himself to sleep lightly despite the supper he'd eaten and the exertions of the day. No matter what the woodsfolk said, he knew they still regarded him as a target. He guessed that their laws required him to prove himself worthy of their friendship; it could not be bought with redroots and onions, a song, or even gold. Residual soreness from riding bareback, from the bruises and cuts, helped him stave off deep sleep.

Soon he heard the faint sound of steps approaching, pausing, the creak of a knee joint as someone bent down to him. Arvid lay still, aware of every probing finger, every stealthy shift of his cloak. He did not tense at the slight tug before the thongs that held the sack to his waist were cut away, but as the thief settled back, letting the cloak fall, Arvid rolled, sprang, parried the cut aimed at his head, and tripped the thief.

As they rolled together, trading blows, others awoke and lit torches from the banked fire. No one interfered, though Arvid heard mutters that sounded suspiciously like bets being laid on one or the other. Finally he managed an elbowstrike to the other man's head and then rolled him into a choke hold, held until the man dropped his long knife.

"Mine," Arvid said, snatching the sack of coins as he released the man and shoved him aside. He stood.

Those watching all nodded; the man felt his neck, nodded, and left his knife on the ground, looking from it to Arvid.

"Yours," Arvid said, making a pushing motion. The man grinned, thrust it into his belt, and stood. The women made a peculiar sound, a fluttering whistle, thin and high, and then one of them threw her arms up and whirled around, skirts flying.

THE BRAWL MADE them all friends, even the one he had fought. "You did well," the man said over and over, nodding and grinning. "No gaj lie so still, breathe so sleep. You one of us, Torre's childer."

"Torre?"

They went off in a mix of Common and their own speech Arvid could hardly understand, about Torre Bignose, a poor shepherd, and Dort the Master Shepherd. Was this the same Torre as in the legend of Torre's Necklace? And—as he was following the trail of a necklace—did he have, Simyits save him, *another* legendary figure interested in his fate? Gird and Torre working together? He shuddered.

He asked about the way to the pass; they shook their heads. "Too late. Much snow."

They were stuck in the South for the winter, then. Dattur agreed . . . no one took the Valdaire pass in deep snow; it would be worse on the other side. Despite repeated invitations from the woodsfolk, Arvid had no mind to spend the winter with them. For one thing, the Guildmaster in Valdaire needed a lessoning, and for another, he wanted to redeem his reputation by coming north with the necklace in hand. They stayed with the band through another snowstorm, then refused an invitation to stay through Midwinter. Arvid knew he would learn nothing more of the necklace here; he needed the city. Arvid could not walk the streets of Valdaire as himself, Arvid Semminson, but his beard had grown in, his hair was unkempt, the woodsfolk happily traded their typical garb—more colorful than he'd worn in years—for one of the horses, and two men guided him within sight of the city walls. No one, he was sure, would recognize him now.

CHAPTER TWO

VALDAIRE, APPROACHED FROM the northwest on one of the minor roads that fanned out toward the Westmounts, looked as dour as the winter day: clouds hung low on the mountains, lifting only to reveal a longer trail of snow. Arvid trudged along, feeling the perfect oaf in a blue-striped shirt, a blue-and-red knit two-tasseled cap, fleece-in sheepskin shoes like shapeless blobs, and a sheepskin cape over all. He was warm enough, but he knew he smelled just like the woodsfolk: smoke, sheep, and dirty human. Dattur, beside him, wore much the same, but in different colors. He seemed content.

Arvid had to show coin at the city gate to gain entrance, but it took only five copper serfs—fumbled one at a time from different pockets—to prove his solvency. The guards did not search the sheepskin cape, where he'd hidden the gold, or Dattur's, where he'd hidden his weapons, though they looked into the horse's pack. A small sack of oats, a few onions and red-roots, a couple of round hard loaves of bread, plus a dirty blanket offered no threat.

"What's your business here?" one guard asked.

"Sell horse," Arvid said as gruffly as he could. "Eat much."

"Go along, then," he was told. "Horse market's across the city."

He had thought long about coming back to Valdaire. It would be easy enough to kill the Guildmaster. Easy for him, anyway. But to do it and get away safely—that would be more difficult. And to do it in a way that the Guildmaster—and the others—knew who had done it, and still get away safely, that would be nearly impossible.

Perhaps he should just kill the man. Perhaps he should just get the necklace . . . if he could figure out where it was . . . and kill the man on the way back north. But first—he dragged his mind to the immediate present—they needed different clothes and a place to stay. And they needed to get rid of the horse.

The horse market in Valdaire was busy even in winter. Their nondescript dray horse sold to the second horse-coper for less than its worth but with no questions asked. Arvid pocketed the nitis and started looking for a used-clothes dealer, avoiding the streets near the Thieves' Guildhouse.

"YOU KNOW YOUR companion is a kteknik gnome?"

Arvid grunted. He was hungry and tired and longed for civilized food and a bath, which he could not get in these clothes and smelling as he smelled. One shopkeeper after another had turned them away. It was almost dark, the markets closed, and they had found this shopkeeper just closing up. Arvid hadn't liked the look of the shop or the man, but he had run out of choices.

Now the shopkeeper poked him, hard. "You hear me? I said your companion is a gnome . . . did you know?"

"Knew," Arvid said, in as woodsfolk an accent as he could manage. "Don't care."

"You're not woodsfolk," the man said. "And you travel with a gnome. I know someone would pay to know more." He smirked and rubbed his fingers.

"I know someone who would *die* to say more," Arvid said, and grabbed the man's sword wrist, slamming it to the counter. Under his grip, the man's wrist twisted, but Arvid had the correct angle and used it. The man cursed and reached for his dagger with his other hand, but Arvid was faster. "That was a mistake," he said as the man stared in surprise and then slowly slumped onto the table. "True or not, you set your own fate."

"A bad mistake," Dattur said from behind him. "They will know who killed him."

"They won't care," Arvid said. "And they won't know if we change clothes fast enough." As he spoke, he rummaged through the assortment of secondhand clothes in the shop, tossing Dattur a green wool jacket to replace his sheepskin and then an oiled-leather hooded cape. Arvid pulled off his own motley assortment, shivering in the cold shop. When they were dressed, Arvid put the sheepskins and other woodsfolk items into a pile of other rustic clothing at the back of the shop.

Outside, the snow still fell; the narrow street was empty. Arvid found a cash box with "Gallis" carved in the lid under the counter, then used the shopkeeper's chalk to draw a Thieves' Guild symbol on the table—"Didn't pay." He took what he thought would be a likely Guild fee from the box and replaced the box under the counter.

They left, unseen and unheard, Arvid hoped, in the dark and silent snowfall. Thanks to his experience and the tools in his own black cloak, he found a likely lock to pick, behind which was a small stable providing a bed of hay and the company of two stocky, warm, and very calm cart horses.

When they left well before dawn the next morning, Arvid fluffed the hay, brushed the snow over their tracks to the gate, and relocked the gate from the outside. By late afternoon, he had visited a money changer and changed a few of the gold Guild League natas into less noticeable silver nitis and nis, replaced his clothing, and visited a barber to have his beard trimmed. Now he presented the appearance of a somewhat travel-stained but respectable merchant, and felt ready to look for comfortable lodging for a few days.

Cheaper lodgings were full, he was told, as the city was full of wintering soldiers. Nobody questioned his identity or purposes as he inquired at one inn after another. Finally, he found a room at the White Dragon, a substantial inn in the northeast quarter. Here, near the winter quarters of several mercenary companies, streets teemed with traders, crafters, and off-duty soldiers. The innkeeper gave the two of them a piercing look, but a gold nata changed his expression. He sent them up to his remaining empty room with a boy to lead the way.

When the boy had left, Arvid sniffed. The room smelled reasonably clean; empty clean chamber pots stood at the foot of each bed. A thick blanket of undyed wool and—amazingly—a pillow were on each bed. Arvid turned the pillow over and smacked it; nothing ran out. Better and better. Dattur would have preferred a ground-floor room, but he himself liked being upstairs, without windows . . . it felt safer.

CHAPTER THREE

Chaya: the Palace

KIERI PHELAN, LYONYA'S king, paused at the top of the steps down to the palace courtyard. Despite all he had said to hearten his Council and the small guard he would leave in Chaya, the cluster of Siers and palace servants gathered near the palace entrance looked scared. He could understand that. Beyond them, the fifty Royal Archers on their horses and his half dozen King's Squires looked nothing like an effective army: too few and too new. He did not doubt their courage, but he would have been very glad of a cohort of his former Company. For the first time in his life, he was going into battle without any veterans, with nothing but his own ability to mold these novices into a fighting force by sheer strength of will.

And that meant hiding his own concerns—not only about his troops, but about the whereabouts of the elves who had promised, not two days before, to bend all their powers to aid him. Since then he had seen or heard nothing of them. Were they doing anything to heal the taig or repel the Pargunese, or had they withdrawn yet again into their own protected world? And the dragon: could it really prevent more scathefire attacks? The Pargunese troops: how many had landed, how many more were crossing the river even now? How close were they to Chaya? And how many more days until Aliam Halveric, with the rest of Halveric Company, arrived from his steading in the south? Had he even started yet?

He smiled at those waiting and came down the stairs briskly, demonstrating his confidence, but though they bowed as he passed, their faces did not relax. Only Arian, her gaze steady as ever, her expression resolute, reflected his own feelings. He had convinced her to stay behind, to wait for Aliam; she had understood his reasons and agreed without protest.

"A Lyonyan king has not gone to battle in generations," Sier Belvarin said. He had led the Council's argument against Kieri's commanding in the field.

"A Lyonyan king has not been needed in battle for generations," Kieri said. "The war is not over, even though no more scathefire has come. Pargunese invaders are on this side of the river. There's no one else to take command. I'm needed." He signaled the groom who held Banner, his gray charger; the man led the horse nearer. He clasped Belvarin's shoulder. "It will be well, Sier Belvarin, if we all do our duty. You have your orders." Orders he had to hope Belvarin and the others would carry out, *could* carry out.

He ran his hand down Banner's head, checking the bridle, then the girth, as if for any ride. At least he had this familiar, war-experienced mount. Banner flicked his ears and snorted. "Easy," Kieri said; the horse stood quietly as Kieri mounted and picked up the reins. He nodded to the groom, who stepped back. Between his thighs, he felt the horse tremble with eagerness, and up from the ground, through the horse, surged a plea from the taig itself. Whatever the elves had done, the taig had not fully healed. He had a vague impression of elves busy on or near the upriver scathefire track, but this call had come from downriver.

"We will survive," he said to the worried faces tilted up to watch him. "I've done this before." No change in their tension. "After all," he said, forcing a grin, "we have a dragon on our side." That didn't help, either. "And the Lady approves." That did; their faces relaxed. He felt a wave of pity . . . most of them did not know yet how she had been involved in the disaster that had befallen the realm, how fallible she was, and it was not the time to shake their confidence further. To them, she was the great, the beneficent, the all-powerful elven queen who could do no wrong, whose desire was law.

"Let's go," he said to his Squires with a last glance at Arian. She nodded: understanding and trust and hope all in that gesture. He turned Banner's head to the gate. Outside, a crowd had gathered. He lifted his hand in greeting, smiled at them, exchanged greetings with the mayor and Council members.

"What if they get past you?" someone called from the crowd.

"Then you stop them," Kieri said. He waved a hand at the new, small, city militia, their weapons in hand. "You are brave, and you have the will." Most of them stood straighter at that. He hoped their fragile confidence would not be needed.

They rode northeast from the city, heading for the near end of the eastern scathefire track. Even though he had explained the marching order before the invasion ever started, and the reasons for it, the small force fumbled its way into formation, taking almost twice as long as the entire Phelani Company would have. If he'd had just one cohort of Phelani, under an experienced captain—! But he didn't. He pushed that wish aside. He'd started his military career with fewer than this. At least he'd managed to convince Arian she should stay behind in Chaya.

He set a brisk pace; he wanted to meet the invaders as far from Chaya as possible. If their force was as large as Torfinn had said it might be, he could not hope for a clean victory, but he could delay them, perhaps until Aliam brought up the rest of the Halverics.

When they came to the scathefire track, Kieri's heart clenched at the sight of so much anguish for the taig. Nothing but ash remained where the dragonlet had gone, and the blackened sticks and stumps of trees on either side. The others' faces looked the way he felt—shocked, horrified, heartsick. Whatever the elves had done here, he saw no healing, though the taig no longer seemed as anguished.

They moved down the track, making better time on that fire-hardened surface; wind blew the soft ash away from the horses' hooves. Kieri thought the Pargunese troops were also likely to use this open track instead of the narrower, meandering forest trails.

Toward evening, one of the forward scouts reported that he'd made contact with a wounded forest ranger on his way south to Chaya. Kieri pushed forward with his Squires and a squad of Royal Archers, leaving the supply train behind, and found the ranger, one arm wrapped in a bloody bandage, slumped against a tree.

"Sir king," the man said, struggling to stand.

"Be easy," Kieri said, waving him back down. "I need your report, not formality." He squatted down beside the man.

"Yes, sir king. A large body of Pargunese troops marching this way on the fire trail, only a day away, if that. They got across just upstream of Blackmarsh, following that magical fire; it burned out the Halveric camp there. I was in Blackmarsh, close enough to feel the heat of the fire, but escaped."

This close, Kieri could see that the ranger's eyebrows had burnt away, leaving his face looking peculiarly blank and shiny.

"How many, and what arms?" Kieri asked.

"The Pargunese? Maybe five hundred at first, but now maybe two to three hundred foot—pikes and crossbows—and twenty horse. We rangers harried them along the way, sir king, as much as we could."

"Rangers only? What about Royal Archers or Halverics?"

"Not many Halverics left—a few showed up, right after the fire, then more trickled in. Seven hands of them altogether, under a sergeant, but some wounded. They've helped. The Royal Archers to the west weren't sure they should leave their camp—they'd been fighting the first wave, from before the fire, and expected more to come. They did lend us ten of their fifty. When I was hit and couldn't bend my bow, I came south as fast as I could, hoping to reach Chaya and give warning, but—" He paused; Kieri could tell that despite the food he'd been given, he was exhausted. "And our supplies are low, sir king. I hadn't eaten in two days when I met your scout."

Kieri cast his mind back over thirty years of war and could imagine every miserable hour of the defense . . . outnumbered, confused, leaderless, hungry and cold and tired.

"There's too many of 'em, sir king," the ranger said. "We've tried, but—"

"Be at ease," Kieri said again. "You and the others have done very well; I honor your service. Now I am here, and the Pargunese will not know what happened." The ranger's jaw dropped a little. "There are ways for a fox to eat a bullock . . .

not in one gulp, but one bite at a time." Kieri stood. "You need a surgeon's care and rest and warmth," he said. "My supply train is coming, and you'll be taken care of."

"But there are so many—" the man said. "And that fire—"

"The fire is gone," Kieri said. "It will not return." He hoped and trusted that the dragon would prevent that, though he would have been comforted to have the beast itself at his side, ready to flame a formation of Pargunese.

Would you really?

The thought in his mind bore a tang of smoke and hot iron. Kieri's thoughts stumbled for an instant, and then he thought, with all his might, *Yes*.

We are not tools of the lateborn. I have my work; you have yours.

Not hostile, not friendly: commanding.

Kieri gave a mental shrug and turned back to his task. Dragons and elves, both uncanny, but dragons—in this war—far more useful than the other. Once more the tang of a smithy, the ghost of a chuckle, and then it was gone.

He glanced at his Squires, their faces sober. One, in that interval, had taken off his cloak and laid it on the ranger, over the bloodstained cloak that had been ripped short to make the bandage on the man's arm. Kieri nodded. "Indeed, that is well thought of." Then he touched the taig and called a little warmth into the soil under the ranger. The man's face relaxed as the warmth touched him.

"Sir king—the taig needs—"

"Needs all of us. You have given your life and blood to the taig; accept a gift in return."

Kieri stepped back, motioning the Squire who had given his cloak to stay close to the ranger. "Here is what we will do," he said. "I believe that the main force of the Pargunese is this group—and perhaps one on the other scathefire scar. Arian said the dragon killed Pargunese soldiers there, but I don't know if it killed all of them. More could have come across later. The smaller landings, that we heard of before the scathefire came, may have been diversions only, and may have joined with the larger groups—or not. But we must get the Royal Archers out of their camps and into action."

He looked at his Squires. "Which of you knows this area well?" Three hands went up. "Excellent. Each of you will partner with someone who does not—"

"But that will leave you with only four—"

"I'm not going to stand in front of the Pargunese army yelling insults," Kieri said. He turned to Banner and dug into his saddlebags for his writing materials. "Four will be plenty for the plan I have. Now: two pair will go east of the scathefire track. One will head for the Royal Archer camps we expect between here and the border. You will give them my order to proceed to the scathefire track, with rangers you will find as guides, and parallel the Pargunese, harassing them in the flanks and rear but not joining open battle until further orders. The other will parallel the scathefire track until even with the Pargunese and stay even with them as they move. The pair to the west of the track will go directly to that Royal Archer camp this ranger mentioned, bringing any rangers or Archers found to join the harassing teams on this side." He squatted down, bracing the writing board on his knees, and wrote the orders. "When you reach your assigned locations, one of each pair will act as courier; the other will stay with whatever forces you have found, to receive and transmit my orders. Be alert for Pargunese flank scouts and any stragglers—they'll be desperate, trying to reach their main party, I've no doubt. Evade if possible; kill them all if not. We're in no state to care for prisoners."

"What about steadings?" Kaelith asked.

"Warn them," Kieri said. "Any within a few hours' march of the scathefire should leave—they might be discovered. If we had just a few more troops, we might set up an ambush. The Pargunese may be low on supplies, and faced with an easy source, like a steading with animals and stored grain, they might start looting—might even get drunk and fall asleep. But we don't have enough troops—yet."

As the Squires rode away, Kieri considered what to do next. Fifty Royal Archers and a few Squires couldn't meet the remaining Pargunese head-on any more than the rangers and Halveric remnants could—unless he could get them all collected, and that would take days.

For a moment anger flared. This was the situation he'd hoped to avoid: little groups of defenders, disorganized, demoralized, uncoordinated, fumbling about in the forest while a well-trained force invaded. But anger now would do no good. What he needed now was a plan ... a specific plan for this specific band of Pargunese. Break them into separate groups, each vulnerable to attack ... yes, the obvious but perhaps not the only course of action.

Short of supplies, the ranger had said. How short? What would they do for a royal supply train? Would they be fool enough to attack the obvious?

"I need to look at the maps again," Kieri said. "We won't try to move at night—" Difficult enough with experienced troops used to night maneuvers; these were at the limit of their ability in daylight. "—and it's darkening. We'll camp off the scathefire track and build a barricade."

It should not have taken as long as it did, but the camp was finally reasonably secure, though as the snow ended, the marks of their passage on the scathefire track were clear enough.

Kieri was still awake, poring over the maps and his guesses about the location of the Pargunese, when he heard sentries outside his tent.

"Come on," he said to the Squires on duty. "Let's go see what we have."

"Sir king, you must be careful—"

"I am always careful," Kieri said, wrapping his sword belt around his waist. He set his helmet on his head. "Don't call me by name."

At the north side of the camp, he found the sentries—Royal Archers—bows drawn, arrows pointing at a group of soldiers in a curious mix of uniforms.

"They say they're Halverics," one of the sentries said without looking away from his target. "But they could've stolen what Halveric gear they wear."

Kieri looked at the faces, indistinct as they were in the flickering torchlight. Glints of ornaments—Halverics wore none on duty—but he felt no menace through his taig-sense. He had seen all the Halveric cohort once, before they had left for the north—but these troops were clearly exhausted and cold and had come through hard fighting. "Who commands?" he asked.

"I do, m'lord," said the one in front. "Vardan, second sergeant."

The name was right, and her accent was pure Lyonyan, but her face was so streaked with ash and blood that Kieri didn't recognize her, and she wore a wide neck ring over the leather gorget with the Halveric stamp. "What happened to your uniforms?" he asked.

"Burned off, m'lord," the woman said. "There was that fire—purple-white, it burned—"

"Scathefire," Kieri said. "And you *survived*?" He could scarcely believe it.

"A few of us, sir. In a ditch of water, near our camp—coming back from patrol."

"That's a Pargunese crossbow you carry," Kieri said. "How did you come by that?"

A flash of white teeth in the grimy face. "Surprised a patrol of Pargunese—killed 'em all. But m'lord, there's a crowd of Pargunese on the fire's track. We've been sniping at them—"

"I'll want your report," Kieri said. "But first I'll see you fed and warm. Good work, sentries, but these troops are what they claim."

Vardan went with her troops, as he expected, to see them fed and settled—however much they might get that night—and then came to Kieri's tent. She had scrubbed the grime off her face and hands but still wore the neck ring. In the brighter light in his tent, he could see that the design looked foreign. Kieri recognized the woman now that her face was clean—she'd been a corporal in one of Aliam's cohorts that last year in Aarenis.

"I knew you, sir king," she said, bending her knee. "But I didn't like to say, out there in the woods, if one of them Pargunese was about."

"Good thinking," Kieri said. He pointed to a chair on the other side of the table where he'd spread the map. "Have a seat. Do your troops need anything more?"

"No, sir king."

"Tell me what you know, then."

Vardan began to talk, pointing out on the map where her unit's encampment had been, where they had patrolled, and the location of the ditch. "Days go dark so early. We were past sunfall coming back, but once we had our feet on that dike, we had naught to worry about, I thought. Out of the swamp, firm ground. Then . . . then this light came. Not any natural light—"

"I saw it, too," Kieri said.

"Well, we went on, to make it to camp, we hoped, but it was faster—it rose up, the trees burning before it—and I felt the heat and ordered 'em into the water. We were in it up to our necks, staring as it came down on us, then we dived—most of us—but it burned off the top handspan of the water and whatever was that close—my cloak, for one thing. Four of us didn't go deep enough."

"Good thing you had the water to jump into," Kieri said.

"Aye, that it was. I owe Falk an offering for that, when we get to a Field. And thanks to our captain, Falk hold his soul, for making us dig that ditch." Vardan paused; Kieri poured her a mug of water. Vardan took a gulp, then went on. "When we got out, there was just the scar, nothing but ash, and fires burning along each side of it. Nothing left of the camp or the ten who were in it. And all of us wet, cold, with no supplies. If not for the rangers, we wouldn't be here."

Kieri let her tell the rest of it without interruption. She had done what he would have expected from a Halveric sergeant or one of his former troops. Between the terse sentences, he easily imagined the struggle it had been—and the years of experience that had given her the skills and character to save so many and use them so effectively.

"So this morning," Vardan said. "The ranger with us said he knew by the taig the king was coming, and I said we ought to go to meet you—you'd find a way to use us better than skulking behind trees and giving a volley now and then."

"And how far away are the Pargunese, do you know?"

"The rangers harass them, and they have a few Royal Archers, too. They are on both sides, and it slows the Pargunese down. We made them afraid of the woods—lured them to a steading a day—a day and night ago—" Vardan shook her head; Kieri realized the sergeant was near total exhaustion.

"We passed them early this morning; they did not notice, because the rangers were shooting at them. I think we must be a half-day ahead."

"Will they march at night?"

"No. They try to barricade themselves at night. I don't know if they found another farm, but it did not go well for them last time."

"You have bought us time, Sergeant," Kieri said. "If you had done nothing more than delay them, that would have been valuable. But bringing trained archers, already armed—" Twenty-eight Halverics plus the fifty Royal Archers with him . . . nearly a cohort, all trained to shoot in volleys. "I sent messengers to that Royal Archer camp you mentioned, ordering them to make haste to meet us, but that will take them a day at least, even mounted."

"What about Captain Talgan?" Vardan asked. "The Halverics we found saw another fire to the west—but he was at Riverwash—"

"Riverwash burned," Kieri said. "Scathefire." The woman's face paled under its southern tan. "As far as I know, no one in the fort there survived. I have heard nothing from there . . . Assassins preceded the attack, disrupting the courier system for several days."

"So all we—you—have—"

"Is here or scattered through the forest, so far as I know. And though the dragon—"

"Dragon!"

"Yes, dragon. A witness, one of my Squires, saw the dragon destroy a troop of Pargunese near Riverwash, but I have no assurance that the dragon killed all the Pargunese who landed there . . . or that none have landed since." Kieri nodded his thanks to a servant who brought a jug of steaming sib to the table. He gestured to Vardan's mug. As the man poured, he said, "Aliam's on his way with the rest of Halveric Company, but he won't have reached Chaya yet. We need to hold the Pargunese away from Chaya and the King's Grove until he can reinforce us. With your contingent, I now have eighty archers—"

"We're almost out of bolts and arrows, sir," Vardan said.

"Plenty with us," Kieri said, grinning. "That's one thing I managed, to boost the production of arrows this past half-year. I can supply your troops with good blackwood bows and plenty of arrows." He asked a few more questions, learned that no more Pargunese had landed after this force, and then sent Vardan to rest.

KiERi WOKE in the predawn darkness, aware of a stir in the camp. Two small groups of Royal Archers—seven in one group, nine in the other—and some twenty rangers had arrived, having marched through the night. That brought the number of archers up to a full cohort, but they had not ever maneuvered together. And these last were all tired, having had no sleep. Kieri ordered the newcomers fed first, then the other troops, as he considered the best way to use this combination.

As the light grew, he began to get reports from his forward scouts—the Pargunese were still moving warily south along the scathefire track and at their present rate would reach him shortly before or after dark. They did not have scouts out at a distance—having lost many to the rangers' superior woods skills—but were still a compact and dangerous fighting unit. They had taken another farmstead—from which the owners, warned, had fled—and obtained some food there.

"We'll go to meet them," Kieri said. "I want daylight for that. Are there tracks both east and west on which we can move fast?"

"On the west, yes," one of the rangers said. "But on the east, the only track bears away—it's not that useful. What we did was let 'em get past and then cross behind them, work up close enough, and then snipe from there."

"Here's what I plan to do," Kieri said, and motioned to the maps still spread on the table. "If they move at yesterday's speed, we can be in place here"—he tapped the map—"well before they reach it. That will let me place archers on the east side as well. Our harassing archery will slow them enough to give the supply train time to set up the second ambush here." He pointed again. "We want it to look as though we started to build a barricade across the scathefire track, didn't have time for a good one, and fled. They're more likely to go over it than over the burnt-brush tangles at the sides." He looked up to be sure they understood. "They'll see a climbable barricade with plunder on the other side; they'll be exposed as they try to get over it. Then we attack through the gaps beyond the barrier, where this burnt stuff was used for the barrier itself."

THE PARGUNESE MADE enough noise to hear before they came in sight: stamping boots, jingling mail, hoofbeats, creaking leather. Kieri peered between the tree boles for the first sight of them. Banner uttered a soft fluttery sound; Kieri laid a mailed hand on his muzzle.

He had a hundred archers now, well supplied with arrows but unused to fighting together . . . against two hundred and more, short of bolts—they must be—but trained and experienced in formation fighting. The Pargunese knew they were in trouble, moving ever deeper into hostile territory, knew they were losing men constantly to sniping.

Why were they still coming? Why had they not retreated? What was behind them worse than what they were facing? Whatever the reason, they would be angry and ready for a battle. Would their discipline hold?

The Pargunese appeared, still marching in straight ranks, their dark blue cloaks almost black against the snow, their helmets rising to a spike. The outer rows all around the formation carried their tall, narrow Pargunese shields to the outside. Heavy shields, with a spike on the bottom to let them be braced on the ground during an engagement. On this side, the west, that meant shields hung on the sword-hand shoulder, their pikes in the left hand . . . unless they had that many heart-handed men, they'd find it hard to fight that way, though it gave them some protection from sniping.

Behind the main formation rode their mounted troops, now down to eleven from twenty, all in heavier armor, all with a longer spear braced upright in a socket and a shorter pair of javelins. Although they outnumbered his troops, they looked surprisingly small against the backdrop of the forest across the gap. He could see the entire formation at once.

Once again Kieri wondered why they were still advancing. They had to know they were marching away from reinforce-

ment, away from their supplies . . . losing troops daily. Most
armies lost heart when their numbers dropped so far. These
looked almost—almost enchanted.

Kieri reached out to the taig and felt the malice of the Pargunese but no more than that. He could not tell if that meant
no enchantment or if it was the taig's own suffering that
clouded its communication.

When the front line reached the mark he'd set, one of the
rangers blew a horn. The Pargunese faltered a moment, but
one of their officers yelled, and they marched on.

A second horn call. Fifty archers on the west side—Royal
Archers and Halverics both—rose and sent flights of arrows
into the Pargunese formation. The formation shrank visibly
as men fell. The Pargunese officers bellowed: "Hold, you
fishbait! They've clumped—we can take them if we stick
together—shields—form for charge!"

Exactly what Kieri had hoped. The Pargunese were all yelling now, insults only Kieri and a few others understood. They
faced right, held their shields up at an angle, and charged at
the woods. Frustrated, tired, hungry men in a foreign land,
after days of being picked off by ones and twos, they wanted a
fight.

A third horn call now, as Kieri signaled. From the east, the
far side of the scathefire track, his other fifty archers emerged
and shot directly into the Pargunese rear. Kieri could not
see how many fell but knew that most of the rear rank and at
least some of the next would be sorely wounded if not killed.
The compact Pargunese formation—originally ten files of
twenty-four—had now lost almost fifty of its original strength.

"Reform! Pin-pig!" It was the only workable formation for
a unit beset by archery in multiple directions. Kieri watched as
the Pargunese struggled, losing more every moment, to back
and turn into the circle, bristling with pikes, shields locked
together for protection. The officers had all dismounted, turning their horses loose, and were in the center of the pin-pig,
their long spears sticking up like flag standards. After a moment of stillness, he saw the covering shield quiver, opening
small holes near the center of the formation.

"Dropping volley," he said to the nearest Royal Archer. "Cover." They knelt and put up their shields.

Kieri looked past the clumped Pargunese and saw that his unit on the far side was still standing in the open, bows bent. "Back!" he yelled. "'Ware volley." But the bolts were already in the air, including those rattling on branches overhead. Kieri looked down, trusting his helm and shield to protect him. Only one of his people was hit, the bolt piercing his helmet and killing him instantly. The Pargunese shields overlapped again, clattering like shutters.

"They're short of bolts," Kieri said.

"Or they want us to think so," one of his Squires said.

"Can they use stray arrows in those crossbows?" asked one of the rangers.

"Yes, but not very accurately," Kieri said. "Some of the units in Aarenis use a compound bow—not as long as the blackwood bows—and shorter arrows as well, but even those don't fly well from crossbows except in a dropping volley. I think if they had plenty of bolts, they'd have fired another volley. Look—they're moving."

The Pargunese, closely hidden under their overlapping shields, were creeping slowly along the scathefire track, still heading south.

"How do they do that?" one of the Squires, Panin, asked.

"Training," Kieri said. "But it's hard, exhausting work to keep those shields tight and carry their weapons. Those in the rear are having to walk backward." He looked around. "We'll keep pace with them; it won't be hard."

"And when they reach the barricade?"

"They can't get past it in that formation. They may even break open before then. And then—we hit them again."

"It seems . . . unfair," Cern said. Kieri recalled that he was only five years out of Falk's Hall.

"War's not fair," Kieri said. "We want to hinder them—kill them in the end—losing as few of our own people as possible." He had said this before, but these Squires had not seen even one pitched battle. "Their invasion wasn't fair; the scathefire wasn't fair."

The Pargunese would expect a hostile force to be pacing

them . . . they would be, even in the cold, sweating and miserable under their shields. Someone's arm would get tired; someone walking backward would stumble. Fury and panic both would be stalking their minds even as the Lyonyans stalked their flanks. After a while, the Pargunese began to relax their formation, as he'd expected. They did so cautiously. Blinded on the flanks by the protective shields, with no more mounted fighters to keep a lookout, they could not see Kieri's forces. First their ankles, then their shins . . . a gradual lowering of the interior shields . . . those in the rear swung around to change places with the next forward rank . . . and then the leaders saw the barricade. They halted.

Kieri hoped they would see it as he intended: a crude, hasty barrier of logs and tangled brush bracing some sharpened stakes reaching across the scathefire track. Beyond it, a wagon on its side, barrels and bales spilled out onto the snow, traces cut where the team had been freed, signs of panicked flight. Would they take the bait or suspect the trap?

Suddenly, the tight cluster opened out; from his height, Kieri could see a man in armor in the middle of the cluster, space opening around him . . . and then the transformation he had never expected to see again, as the man's armor seemed first to melt into his body and then split apart . . . his shape changing from human to the spider-like form of one of Achrya's servants. Kieri felt the taig's revulsion at the touch of the thing's claws. The Pargunese soldiers kept a careful distance. The thing chittered, audible even at this distance. Another Pargunese yelled; the soldiers opened a lane to the front.

"You have to hit the eyes," Kieri murmured to the ranger at his side. "Or underneath . . ."

The thing paused at the barricade, head lifted, turning from side to side. Kieri felt a chill run down his backbone. It was Achrya's, and Achrya could see what mortals could not. The dragon had said Achrya would soon have no power, but this was Achrya's servant. "Now!" he said. Bowstrings twanged; arrows split the air, some sent high and some lower . . . but the thing was over the barricade in a blur of speed before the first arrow arrived. Pargunese men fell instead; those unwounded did not re-form or return fire—as he'd expected—but rushed forward to the barricade as if compelled to follow the spider-thing.

"What *is* that?" Vardan asked; Kieri heard others asking as well.

"Achrya's creature," Kieri said. "And we must kill it—if we kill all the men and leave it running loose, we have lost." Kieri mounted Banner and lowered his visor. "Come on," he said. "And you," he said to the Halveric sergeant. "I need a ten-squad."

The Squires scrambled to mount and catch up as Kieri urged Banner past the end of the barrier in the trees and turned toward the scathefire track, where the creature had clambered onto the overturned wagon and now waved its front legs at its followers. A dozen Pargunese had made it over the barrier; the rest of the Lyonyans were picking off the others as they tried to climb the brush, their shields askew. Kieri glanced back, calculating angles and odds—his remaining Squires, a squad of Halverics commanded by that sergeant. Plenty, if they were fast.

Banner charged; behind him, Kieri heard other hoofbeats and the Halverics' running feet. He knew the others were coming, outflanking the barrier. Then two more of the Pargunese soldiers shifted into the great spider shapes. Kieri felt a familiar wave of chill calm sweep over him. *Holy Falk, Lady of Peace . . .* He'd known there could be more than one—was that all? No, for another two Pargunese stopped short and seemed to shiver.

Kieri shifted his weight; Banner responded instantly, shortening stride and bringing Kieri directly to one of them in mid-change. Kieri's sword-stroke took the creature across the middle, splitting a still-soft carapace. On the backswing he took the second. Even as he looked back, Banner snorted and changed leads, swinging his hindquarters around.

Where were the Squires? Cern's mount was just leaping one of the things Kieri had killed, ears pinned, eyes wild. Cern grabbed for mane as the horse bucked on landing, but he managed to come up on Kieri's shield-side. "Sir—"

"Quiet," Kieri said. The two lesser creatures faced them, forelegs raised and the vicious spinnerets he remembered

pointing at them. How far could the venom go? Did they have
other weapons? The first to change, the largest, was still
crouched atop the wagon, facing the other Squires and
Halverics, who seemed to be unable to move. It must be the
commander.

"I can shoot one," Linne said. She had caught up with them
and nocked an arrow.

"The eye, the underside of the abdomen," Kieri said. "The
rest is armored." He glanced back at the other soldiers who'd
made it over the barrier and were advancing again in a straight
rank. Another three had made it; none seemed to be changing,
and none had crossbows. It should be easy to avoid them . . .
pikes were too heavy to throw far. He distrusted "easy" when
his own supporters were on the other side of the enemy and
immobile.

Linne and Cern both drew and released; the arrows sang
through the air but stopped short of the creatures as if they had
hit an invisible wall.

So much for easy.

Then he heard Sergeant Vardan. "Get moving!" she yelled at
her squad. She took a step forward, slow, as if she were pulling
herself free of deep mud, but she moved. "What are you, raw
recruits in your first skirmish? Halverics! Pick up your feet,
you lumps! Falk's Oath in gold! That's our *king* over there.
Move!"

Behind her, the others began moving—older veterans first
and then even the newest. The spider-demon he thought of as
the commander leapt at the Halverics; Kieri spurred Banner
even as Linne's next shot hit one of the others—once, twice,
and then it was down. The third wavered, spurting something
from its spinnerets but missing both him and Cern as Kieri, on
his way past, swung and cut a deep gash in the carapace. He
was just aware that Linne had paused to engage it.

Banner swerved to miss the wagon, then lunged ahead;
Kieri had nothing but his sword, and the thing had reached the
Halveric sergeant, seized her in its clawed forelimbs. She
hacked at it with her sword, but it would not bite on the thing's
carapace. Kieri saw other Halverics coming to her aid—and
then Banner reared, striking the thing's abdomen from behind

with iron-shod forehooves. Kieri leaned down, stabbing, but
Banner's hooves skidded off that hard carapace, and his stroke
missed. The thing whirled, dropping Vardan's body; Kieri had
his sword up again and swept it side to side across the array of
eyes. Banner jumped sideways as a gout of venom spurted at
them, then in again, and this time Kieri managed to lop off its
head.

With that, the Pargunese stopped. He heard the clatter of
their dropped weapons, their shields, and looked around to see
them all fall to the ground, as if only a spell had kept them
upright. With a triumphant yell, his own troops ran forward,
ready to kill.

"Wait," Kieri said. Across the scathefire track, his troops
were gathering, moving nearer. He spoke to Cern. "Tell them
not to kill anyone who does not resist. Most of these men were
not willing." He looked down. Almost under the spider-thing's
body, Vardan lay still, with a cluster of surviving Halverics
around her. Blood soaked the trampled snow. "Does she live?"
he asked. "She saved my life and perhaps the kingdom."

"Not much longer," said one of the older Halveric veterans.

Kieri dismounted and knelt by Vardan; one of the Halverics
took Banner's reins. She bore deep wounds in her body; he
could not understand how the beast had done so much damage
so fast. But her eyes were open and recognized him. Two of the
Halverics were trying to staunch her wounds.

"Sir . . . king?"

"It's dead. We won. You saved us, Sergeant."

"Is . . . good."

He put his hands on her shoulder and closed his eyes, reaching for his healing magery, but nothing happened.

"No," she murmured. "Not now. Let me . . . Falk calls me."

Kieri opened his eyes; Vardan's face was peaceful now, and
much paler.

"Tell m'lord Halveric . . ." she said, and then with no more
words, she died.

"Falk will honor you as you have honored Falk," Kieri said.
He bent and kissed her forehead. "For all your deeds this day,
you will be honored both here and there, above and below, and
songs will be sung and your bones laid to rest in all ceremony."

When he stood again, he saw that all was quiet, but the day was not over. He gathered his Squires and went to look at the Pargunese, now huddled in a group under guard. He had said they had no facilities for prisoners; he had planned to offer no quarter, but he could not in all conscience kill them now they were disarmed and obviously had been forced by enchantment. The old compact he had lived by for so many years, that he and Aliam and Aesil M'dierra had imposed on most of the others, held him now in his own heart.

He gave his orders: march the prisoners to Chaya, kill only those who try to escape or resist. It took longer than he'd hoped to right the wagons, hitch the teams to them once more, and transfer the wounded—his own and the Pargunese—into them.

Next morning at dawn he was away to Chaya with his Squires.

CHAPTER FOUR

WHEN KIERI RODE back into the palace courtyard, he saw Arian coming down the palace steps to meet him, back in her Squire's uniform. His breath came short . . . in his mind he clothed her in a queen's robe and then wondered if she would be comfortable in it. The rest of his Council, following Arian down the steps with worried expressions in stark contrast to her smile, pushed that question out of his mind.

"The Pargunese force is gone," Kieri said. He dismounted and arched his back, stretching. "Our forest rangers, a squad of Halverics who survived, and some Royal Archers mounted an effective defense—all praise to them. They cut the Pargunese numbers by more than half, and the Pargunese came on only because their officers were all servants of Achrya, who held them in thrall. The survivors, no more than thirty, are prisoners now until I decide what to do with them. They'll be here tomorrow or the next day."

"Surely you'll kill them," Sier Halveric said. "They invaded—they killed—"

"They were spelled," Kieri said. "Until I know their true intent, I am not eager to kill men who had no will of their own."

"Send them back to Pargun?" asked Sier Davonin. "If their leaders are dead, maybe they won't make trouble."

"We can't possibly know they won't," Halveric said.

"Siers," Kieri said a little more loudly. They fell silent. "We will meet in Council when I have had a chance to bathe, change, and eat something. I will tell you my thoughts then. At the moment—" He let out a big sigh. The Siers moved aside, and Arian fell in behind him as he entered the palace.

"Food, sir king?" the steward said from just inside the doors.

"Yes. Anything hot, please. I rode straight through. I'll bathe first and eat in my chambers." He glanced at Arian and Harin. "You two, come with me. Garris, dismiss those who rode with me; they need at least a full day off duty."

Upstairs, he found his bath already waiting.

"We saw your party coming," Harin said. "We knew you'd want to bathe."

"I chose the right Squires," Kieri said with a grin.

By the time he had finished his bath and dried himself, he could smell food in the other chamber. His chamber robe, soft and warm, felt so comfortable he decided to eat before dressing for the Council meeting. He padded barefoot across the bedroom carpets to the table laid for him near the window. Arian stood there, ready to serve him; Harin had gone to the door, and Devanyan had joined him there.

"Sit down, Arian," Kieri said. "We have things to talk about."

"Yes, sir king." She sat on the edge of a chair, tense as a drawn bowstring.

"The first is this—do you still want to marry me and be my queen?"

"Yes! Of course!"

"There's no 'of course' about it," Kieri said. "We've both been in mortal danger—you with the dragon fighting scathe-fire and me with the Pargunese and those servants of Achrya. And then finding that the Lady was not coming to our aid because she was trapped underground—that's enough shock that a change of mind could be understandable."

"She put a glamour on me," Arian said. "That's why I left; I didn't realize it then. She made me blind to the taig until I got far enough away—and I thought it was my fault, that the taig rejected me for my love of you. That was not right; I was angry with her then, and again for getting herself in a situation where she did not come to your aid at once. It wasn't fair."

"No, it was not."

"And I *am* of the same mind, and I do love you and want to be with you. I hope I can be a good queen for you." She frowned a little as she said that.

"I am sure you will." Kieri took a spoonful of soup.

"I do worry," Arian said. "Your sister, even as a young

woman, knew so much more than I do. She would not have let the Lady control her as the Lady did me. She had known she would be queen; she had trained for it. I have learned much being a King's Squire, but I am not sure it's enough. I hadn't been to court before except at her coronation, and now I've seen Siers and their families, and some of what being a king requires. It's so complicated." She looked away. "I'm sorry . . . you're tired and hungry, and you saved the land."

"Alyanya's true daughter," Kieri said; she looked back at him and smiled. Before he could say more, he heard Harin, from the door, say, "Arian? The rest of the food—"

Arian went to the door and came back with a tray of dishes.

"I don't really need more—" Kieri began.

"You do," Arian said. "Especially since this hot-pot was made especially for you." She set out the dishes—the steaming pot topped with a flaky crust, the basket of rolls, the smaller pot that smelled of apples and spices, a jug of cream.

"If I eat all this, I will start snoring in the Council meeting," Kieri said around a mouthful of the hot-pot. Chunks of ham and venison mingled with redroots, onions, mushrooms . . . it was almost gone before he realized he hadn't stopped eating to answer her fears. "I was hungrier than I thought," he said. Instead of stuffed and sleepy, he now felt wider awake. He eyed the apple dessert and the jug of cream, then looked at Arian and grinned. "There are two spoons," he said.

"Indeed there are, sir king, in case you drop one." Her mouth quirked; the indecision and worry of a few minutes earlier had vanished.

"I know you like apples."

"Yes . . . and if that is an invitation, then I accept."

Eating from the same dish, across the table from each other, reminded him so of those private meals with Tammarion . . . his eyes stung, and he looked up to find Arian with an expression even more like Tamar's. "Is something wrong?" she asked.

"No," he said. "Nothing. It is . . . a homecoming." He swallowed that bite of the dessert and said, "And now for the second thing."

"I am listening."

"Remember what I said when you arrived with the elves: when we are alone, I am not 'sir king' to you but 'Kieri.' If you wish to continue as King's Squire until we wed—"

"I do, of course," Arian said. "And after, as well."

"Well, not after. You will have Queen's Squires of your own then."

"But I want to be with you—"

"Of course, and you will be. But not guarding me. You will be my queen, worthy of your own protection." Now she looked troubled; Kieri put his hand on hers. "Arian, what bothers you about that? You will still go armed, as I do; if it's about keeping your sword—"

"Not that, sir . . . Kieri. It's . . . what I was saying before. I know how to be a ranger or a King's Squire. I don't know how to be a queen. It's so different."

"Are you sure this is not a fear the Lady put into you, Arian? Or is it about . . . having children?"

"No, not that. I promise. And it's not you, anything about you. I want to be with you, at your side. It's my own ignorance. I don't have any idea what a queen does—your sister, I imagine, did what you do, but a king's wife . . . what would I *do*? I asked Sier Halveric while you were gone, and he said queens are more decorative than anything else—I should wear the right clothes and be gracious to people. It sounds like standing around smiling all the time."

"He's wrong," Kieri said. "Some queens have been like that—in Tsaia, anyway, and Torfinn of Pargun seemed to think of his queen as a housewife in fancy clothes—but we can make our own rules. I can't imagine you doing nothing but that. I'd rather have you as co-ruler than the Lady, if that were possible. Your good sense, your courage, your warm heart, your taig-sense: all fit you for being Lyonya's queen. The rest is . . . is all surface and things you can learn with more experience. You say you haven't traveled much—well, as a queen, you can. You can be my ambassador where rank is needed, as Elis is Torfinn's."

"But she grew up a princess—"

"And I did *not* grow up a prince." That, he could see, startled her. "Arian. Trust me in this: you have everything it takes to be a queen but the experience, and you will get the experience by being a queen. You will make mistakes—I have made mistakes, this past year, as a king."

"No—"

"Yes. I should have sent my own couriers to Torfinn and Ganlin's father, asked them before I sent those girls to Falk's Hall—"

"Elis and Ganlin wouldn't think so."

"Maybe . . . but it nearly got me killed, and may have gotten Torfinn's wife and children killed, when the war started. I have made many mistakes in my life, Arian, and you will make some as queen, but that is not important—what is important is your willingness to take the chance." He thought a moment. What story would help her and not increase her worries? "When I had the chance to escape from captivity—though I had wished for the torment to stop—it was terrifying to make that leap for freedom. And it was a leap—down out of a window onto a roof, and then running, running, as fast as I could. And then in the town, hiding and running, down to the harbor, jumping again, to grab a rope slung from a ship and hang on. I was scared the whole time. I had no idea what would happen, if the people would take me back to him. So I understand how frightening this change can be for you: new tasks, a new role."

"But you were only a child—"

"And change is daunting for adults, too. But I promise you, Arian: I will help you with every skill and every knowledge I have. Think of it—" He paused a moment. "Think of it as a new horse—a Pargunese Black, for instance, tall and maybe not well trained. Snorting and plunging . . . you would ride it, wouldn't you?"

"Oh, a horse—yes, certainly."

"You would train it—you would teach it?"

"Of course."

"Then think of the tasks of a queen as that kind of challenge. You have made friends among the other Squires, I know. Now make friends among the courtiers—and others who are not courtiers. Travel—make friends for Lyonya abroad. Start with Tsaia, where I have friends and you already know Dorrin Verrakai. After we're wed, make a visit to Vérella—"

"With you?"

"No—I can't leave yet. With . . . um . . . Sier Davonin, perhaps. That would be a compliment to their court. Estil Halveric, if she has the time."

She looked serious, but beneath that he could feel a change, a healthy change, in her mood. "I would like to see more of Tsaia," she said. "And Dorrin Verrakai."

"The third thing to settle is our wedding," Kieri said. "Now I know you still wish it . . . the sooner we marry, the better for the realm. My reasons are those of state: this realm was in mortal peril and is still wounded. Lyonya needs its king to provide an heir. I know that seems like valuing you for breeding alone—"

Arian laughed aloud at that. "I know a better reason to marry soon," she said. "Do you not recall I said I loved you— loved you from the day I first saw you and have had trouble keeping my hands off you? My worries were of being good enough at the tasks of a queen . . . not fear that you cared only whether I would bear healthy children."

"Oh . . ." Kieri felt heat rising in his cheeks, but he also laughed before going on. "In Tsaia, announcements of engagements on the day of Midwinter Feast are considered auspicious enough . . . but no one marries in winter. Do you know the customs here?"

"You could ask the Seneschal," Arian said. "Or your ancestors may have wisdom for you."

"If that suits the Seneschal, then it suits me. And I think we should tell the Council today and plan to make Midwinter Feast the formal celebration of the engagement." Kieri pushed himself up. "And now I must dress and visit the ossuary before the Council meeting. Come with me there." She looked startled; he smiled at her. "They won't hurt you."

"I'm not afraid, sir—Kieri. My mother's family had a bonehouse, and I visited it with her as a child. But this is the royal ossuary—"

"It is where your bones, as well as mine, will someday rest. You need to meet them. Tell the Council I must visit there first and then go let the Seneschal know I'm coming—I won't be long."

After she left, he dressed, belted on his sword, and went into the hall. Harin and Devanyan fell in behind him. The Siers were milling about downstairs, but Arian had been there and they only nodded as he passed them.

The Seneschal met him at the outer entrance to the ossuary. "Sir king—they will be glad you are home safely. And your lady awaits you within."

"She told you?"

"No, sir king. I knew from her face. I am happy for you both, and so will they be." He led the way inside. Arian, he saw, had already taken off boots and socks and sat on the bench, looking around with interest. Kieri sat down and pulled off his house boots.

"It's not what I expected," Arian said.

"It's not what you'd expect inside, either," Kieri said. The Seneschal led the way with one of the big candles and set it on a holder for them, then bowed and withdrew. Kieri felt that ancient peace enfold him. He heard Arian's little gasp of surprise.

"They're . . . like the others only . . . more."

"My father," Kieri said with a gesture. "And my sister, on the women's side."

"What is that—oh—it's writing. At my mother's family's bone-house the oldest were painted with pictures in certain colors, but no writing."

"Can you read it?" Kieri asked.

"No . . . at least . . . it says something about beloved son, doesn't it? Here?"

"Yes. I did not know the script at first, and then I could read it."

"I hope they like me," Arian said.

"You can read the script—I think that proves they do." They were shoulder to shoulder now; Kieri felt a pressure from those bones, from all the bones. Did Arian feel it? She moved across the aisle to his sister's bones.

"And this was her child . . . I came to her coronation, you know."

"I didn't—" Kieri's throat closed. That others had known his sister as an adult, and he only as a tiny child, barely able to walk steadily . . .

"All the Knights of Falk were summoned, and the senior knights-candidate. She was beautiful. And gracious, very gracious. It grieved us all when she died."

Kieri felt the faint touch he had felt before, his sister's presence, but this time not full of anger and warning . . . this time a caress, a blessing. *She was gracious, too. As she is now. Be happy.*

Moved by impulse, he reached out and took Arian's hand and lifted it high. "This is Arian, who will be my wife and my queen," he said. "Make her welcome, for my sake."

Light bloomed in the ossuary, far brighter than the candle, bright as summer sun and carrying the scent of ripe fruit and roses. The pressure he had felt before increased, inexorable, and in a moment he and Arian were joined as they had not been before, embracing. Then joy and the light faded back to the candle's glow.

"They made us welcome indeed," Arian said, in a shaky voice.

"They believe you are a queen," Kieri said. "Remember that, when you doubt it." The chamber felt quiet again, the presences withdrawn. Kieri sighed. "And now for the Council."

KIERI LAID OUT the situation as best he could. "Our troops defeated the Pargunese army in battle; survivors of the scathefire attack on the Halveric camp, forest rangers, and Royal Archers stationed in the area had much depleted their numbers before I got there." Faces relaxed; a murmur rose. Kieri went on.

"What we know now is that the Pargunese were befooled and then led by Achrya into moving above the falls—into land the rockfolk had denied them, land containing two hills in which dragons had laid clutches of eggs, supposedly guarded by gnomes."

"But there are no—" someone said.

Kieri held up his hand for silence. "Under Achrya's urging, the Pargunese took some of those eggs and broke them, releasing an immature form of dragon. In a later change, the immature dragons became a form of fire, uncontrolled and uncontrollable by humans. The Pargunese thought they had a weapon—thought they could control it—but they had released what Achrya wanted: chaos and terror that only the gods—or a dragon—could control. That is what burned Riverwash and a Halveric encampment; that is what we saw the other night."

"If the Pargunese have them, they could send more," Sier Halveric said. He looked more angry than frightened.

"They do not," Kieri said. "The dragon—and yes, there is a dragon; Arian and I both met it—will prevent that; the dragon means us no harm." He paused, but no one spoke. "That is good news, but I have better: King's Squire Arian has consented to become my queen, and the ancestors and the taig and the Lady of the Ladysforest have all agreed."

Stunned silence, then a burst of applause that ended when Kieri held up his hand. "Because of the perils just past and the uncertainties of the future, I believe it wise to marry sooner rather than later, and Arian agrees. We will celebrate the engagement formally on the day of Midwinter Feast, and the wedding will be on the half-Evener."

He had thought that would make them happy, but disappointed looks went back and forth.

"You could wait until the Evener," Sier Hammarin said. "Half-Evener—it could be storming; snow won't have melted. It's a royal wedding; there'll be guests to invite who must travel a distance. Evener, or even Midsummer, if you wanted, would be better. Now that you've found someone . . ."

"We don't want to wait," Kieri said. "And oaths given on Midwinter are unbreakable, as you know."

Hammarin chuckled. "Young folks are always in a hurry, but you surely know, sir king, the custom—no need to wait the way *you* mean."

It took Kieri a moment to understand that; he felt his face heating up. "That wasn't what I meant," he said. No one laughed. "But you may be right—" Hammarin *was* right, he realized. Next to the coronation, his wedding was the most important state occasion, requiring time for planning and consideration of the guest list. "Arian?" he said, turning to her. "What do you think?"

"Spring Evener's better," she said. "Especially after the war, you must invite the other kings as well as our own people."

"And just enough planning time now," Sier Belvarin said.

"I SUPPOSE," GARRIS said after the meeting, "you're going to appoint another King's Squire to replace her? We've lost enough that you might well hold another examination anyway, especially as she'll need her own Squires once you marry."

"Arian will stay with the Squires until we marry, as she wishes," Kieri said. "But no dangerous assignments, Garris. She can serve in the palace." He pushed away the memory of the two Squires who had died in the palace . . . no more Pargunese assassins, at least. He yawned.

"When did you last sleep?" Garris said.

"Um . . . I'm not sure. Not last night; I wanted to get back here and reassure . . . people."

"Arian." Garris smirked.

"And the Siers." Kieri grinned. "But of course Arian most of all."

"I'm glad for you," Garris said. "But go on to bed and let me send out my messages. If you yawn in front of me anymore, I'll fall asleep myself."

Kieri fell asleep almost as soon as he lay down, only to wake in the dark of night. He stretched, then wondered why he'd wakened. No sound disturbed him; coals still glowed in the fireplace. He felt no menace. So . . . what? Arian? No, of course not. The Council? No, they were as content as they could be, knowing he would wed. Squires, Royal Archers, forest rangers . . . nothing came to mind that would wake him up.

Where were the elves? He blinked, trying to clear his mind. They had been there, at the end of the scathefire track, that first day after the attack. The Lady had sworn her aid to heal the land. He had ridden back to Chaya, leaving the elves behind, thinking they would defend . . . but when he returned, the Pargunese had come, hindered only by that mixed force of humans and a few part-elf rangers.

Where *were* the elves? He had seen no healing of the scathefire track, no new growth. Had they but awaited his departure and then gone back to the Ladysforest? Surely not, for the taig had calmed . . . He reached out for it and tried to trace its fabric all the way to the river. Here . . . and here . . . were the rents the scathefire had made. And there, on the other scathefire track, he felt . . . not the elves, but the effect of the elves. Pain lessened. Fear calmed. And it was winter, he reminded himself: not the time for new growth.

So they had not deserted completely. But why had they left the place where he'd found them? He tried to use his taig-sense to reach them, to find his grandmother, but met only fog . . . or so it felt.

He rolled to his other side. So now he knew where the elves were . . . why had he wakened? He didn't feel sleepy now, nor did he feel menace near. He pushed the covers aside, fumbled his feet into fleece-lined slippers, and went to the window above the courtyard. He pushed the curtains aside and let the night air, frigid as it was, roll in. The clouds had blown away south; starlight glittered on the snowy roofs of the lower buildings—the stable, the smithy, the storehouses. Kieri leaned out into the cold air. He could just see sentries moving silently where they should go and the loom of the King's Grove trees, streaked with snow.

So still a night . . . He breathed in deeply and then looked up at the stars. Nowhere near morning, just after the turn of night. A touch of warm air on his face startled him; he jerked back. Nothing. But not nothing . . . her. "Tamar?" he whispered. Another touch of warmth. Joy flooded him—her joy, he realized—and then a buffet to his shoulder that knocked him into the window frame hard enough to dislodge a chunk of snow frozen there. And she was gone.

The snow fell onto the swept stones below—a small sound, but one of the sentries turned and came across the courtyard, peering up at the wall, alert.

Kieri leaned out. "My fault—I was stargazing."

"Sir king! Is all well?"

"Very well," Kieri said. He could not see the expression on the man's face, but he could imagine what he thought: the king, up in the middle of a cold winter's night, leaning out the window. "I woke, and it was so quiet, I wondered if it snowed."

"Shall I tell someone—"

"No. I'll go back to bed." Kieri stepped back and pulled the curtains closed. He slid into the covers that still held the warmth of his body and lay for a time thinking of Tamar. That she approved of Arian did not surprise him, but the buffet? What had that meant? She used to do that when she thought he'd been foolish . . . What had he done this time? Laughter ran through his mind, then faded. She was gone. She had given him a buffet when he left, if he lingered in farewell . . . he understood, and with that he fell asleep.

Next morning he was in the salle when a servant brought word that a courier had come from Aliam Halveric. "Bring him here," Kieri said.

The courier was Cal's son Aliam, about the age Kieri had been when he himself had come to Halveric Steading. "Sir king, Lord Halveric will be here in another two days, if the weather holds. He asks that you send word where you want his troops to camp or if you want them to march straight on to join up with Captain Talgan in Riverwash."

"Captain Talgan was lost," Kieri said. The lad paled. "Riverwash . . . burned."

"The—the whole *town*, sir king?"

"Yes. The strange fire weapon the Pargunese had threatened. I wrote Aliam about it."

"How—did you stop it?"

"I did not. What they called scathefire is instead dragonspawn . . . and a dragon stopped it."

"A dragon? I thought there were no dragons anymore."

"So did I," Kieri said. "But there are, and I have spoken with one. Tell me, young Aliam, have you breakfasted?"

"No, sir king. Granfer—Lord Halveric—said stop for nothing on the way. Don't you eat or sleep, he said, until you've seen the king."

"Well, you've seen the king, and if you can wait while I finish exercise, you can eat breakfast with the king as well."

Aliam looked around the salle and grinned. "Can I play?"

"Lad, you've ridden all night, haven't you?"

"Yes, but that's—Granfer and Father both said that's nothing."

"True, but I'm not minded to see your grandfather's face if

I put you against rested fighters twice your size. Maybe after breakfast I can find you someone suitable to spar with. And maybe you'll see something here you don't see at home."

Concentrating on the boy, Kieri had ignored his Squires. The boy's eyes widening a little was his only warning; he lunged sideways just as someone grabbed for his shoulder and knocked him off balance. He fell on his side, rolled, avoided the kick. Arian, of course. She shifted sideways as he came up to one knee and then pounced, but he was ready with a strike to the back of her knee. She fell, already rolling away, and he made it to his feet. "Enough," he said. "Our guest needs his breakfast, as do we."

THE BOY HAD never been to Chaya before, let alone the palace. Kieri ignored his startled reactions and trusted that the arrival of food would overcome any shyness. He had long persuaded the palace cooks that he needed a heartier breakfast, and platters of sizzling sausage, stirred eggs, and hot breads disappeared as the Squires joined in.

Garris came into the room. "Courier's ready to go—anything else?" Then he noticed the boy. "Is that—"

"Yes. Aliam sent him ahead to tell us: two days. But I still need to send word of the attacks and the present situation."

"I could go," young Aliam said.

"You probably could," Kieri said, "but your king wants you here for the time being. I have a courier available who slept last night and has already eaten, and I have questions for you when we're done." He and Garris left; when he returned, Arian sat with the young Halveric, who was eyeing the basket of honeycakes.

"Go ahead," Kieri said, taking two for himself. "Do you like sib?"

"Yes, sir king."

Arian poured for all three of them.

"Do you always have King's Squires with you?" the boy asked.

"Yes, that is what they do."

"Could I ever be a King's Squire?"

"Not until you're a Knight of Falk," Kieri said. "After that, we'll see. You may not want the job. It's not all living in the palace, you know."

"I saw them—you, Lady Arian, too—back home last fall. I thought then, if Granfer isn't going south again, and Father doesn't want to, then being a King's Squire would be exciting."

"It's not a second best," Arian said sharply.

"I didn't mean it that way—only it's been our family tradition to go south and fight there. But Granfer's old now, and my father doesn't want to go again."

"I wanted to ask you about the rebuilding," Kieri said. "How is that coming?"

"Oh, it's almost like it was before. We all worked on it, of course, and the elves made wood join even better than old Sosti, that Granfer said was the best he'd seen. The elves didn't like having our Old Halveric's skull up in the attic, but Granfer insisted and so did Gram. She said it belonged there. The elves wouldn't touch it, but when the roof framing was up, I put it back in. Gram is happy. I wanted an indoor salle, like the one here, but Granfer said wars aren't fought indoors."

"He's right, and he said the same to us when I was his squire," Kieri said. "I kept thinking I'd build one when I had my own Company, but instead we used the dining hall if the weather was really too cold."

The boy yawned suddenly, then blinked and widened his eyes. "I'm not really sleepy," he said. "If there's something you need—"

"I need you rested for later," Kieri said. "Sleep now."

"But it's daytime. And I'm in Chaya."

Kieri chuckled. "And Chaya will be here when you wake up again. Come now, don't argue with your king."

When the boy was well away, following one of the palace servants to a guest room, Arian said, "I hope our sons are like that."

"And I."

"You didn't tell him about us—"

"No. He's Aliam's grandson and should have learned prudence, but he's at an age to blurt things out anyway. I want to tell Aliam myself."

"Ah. I have little experience with boys that age."

Kieri went on, "We need to send word of our announcement and the wedding date to all the kingdoms—today or tomorrow, at least."

"Already?"

"Yes. It will be slow going—winter weather—and though we are not waiting until summer, I do not want it to seem a hasty, careless affair. Duke Verrakai will be in Harway, I'm sure, in defense of Tsaia. She could not come to my coronation, but I hope she will be able to come to the wedding."

"She's . . . remarkable," Arian said.

"Yes. And she is in a difficult situation, as the only Verrakai not attainted and thus not proven in the royal courts to be free of evil magery. Mikeli had to trust someone and trusted her on my word, but she must know others suspect her, especially as they know she has magery. It was well she used it to save the king's life, but many Tsaians will still have their doubts."

"That crown will not have helped," Arian said.

"No, indeed. I wish I knew more of that," Kieri said. "She has been sparing in her letters to me, saying the king does not wish it talked of. I have not asked Mikeli, in case he took offense that she had mentioned it to me. But it seems to me such regalia would be a reason for someone to seek it—it's an unclaimed crown, and it must belong somewhere."

"Well, it's safe in the Tsaian royal treasury, at least. All but the necklace."

"The necklace?"

Arian told the little she knew, what Dorrin had told her about the necklace. "And then it was stolen from Fin Panir, she heard."

Kieri shook his head. "Worse and worse. Rumors of a lost crown being found . . . a necklace from the same suite of jewels on the loose . . ."

"Duke Verrakai says she told the king it would draw trouble."

"As honey draws bees, yes. And I'm sure she's thinking of the same trouble, from the south."

"But that's Tsaia, isn't it?"

"No. It's everyone. What touches Tsaia touches us—and

Fintha—and Pargun and, through all of us, the rest. What I learned from Pargun's king is that Pargun and Kostandan trade all the way to Aarenis." He felt a sudden chill. "And I hadn't thought—there wasn't time—but Alured the Black doesn't have to invade through Valdaire—he could sail up the river. I must tell Mikeli that. Ships can't get past the falls, but land an army on the shore below, and . . . here I thought our danger might be over for at least a few years."

"Well," Arian said, "you've thought of it now. So we can plan a defense, and surely he won't show up this winter."

"No, I think not. But he had been a pirate on the Immerhoft—the sea down there—and he will have ships and men who know how to fight from them." He ran his hands through his hair. "What a day! I must write those letters, to Mikeli and the Marshal-General as well. And still there's the rest of the Pargunese invasion to deal with."

By late afternoon, the letters announcing his engagement and—for Tsaia and Fintha—his assessment of the new danger from the south were on the way, along with a letter each to Dorrin and Arcolin. The party he'd left to follow him had arrived with the prisoners—bedraggled and tired, but no more injuries or deaths.

Kieri went down to the courtyard to look them over. Chaya had no large prisons. Smaller than Vérella and more orderly, it had small jails meant to house the occasional violent drunk until he or she had slept it off. He could not leave them in the courtyard, without any shelter, in winter. They were a dispirited lot anyway, pale and pinched with hunger and exhaustion, most with at least one bandaged limb.

His Council had sided with Sier Halveric—these were dangerous enemies. They had killed Lyonyans and tried to burn the kingdom down. They deserved to die. If Kieri had not fought so many years in Aarenis and argued for the Mercenary Code against so many who saw no reason for it, he might have felt the same way. But though enemies, these were military prisoners, and the code was bone-deep.

He had a chair brought out and set before them. All around, Royal Archers stood with arrows nocked. He sat down in the chair and set the great sword in its scabbard across his lap.

Then Kieri spoke to them in Pargunese, as he had to Torfinn. "For your attack on my land, your lives are forfeit. But you were ensorcelled by evil, and for that reason alone I will not kill you here and now. You will be fed and housed, to be returned for judgment to your own king, if he wills." He waited a moment; all those pale eyes stared back at him, and none moved. "You will give me your parole, one by one, to attempt no violence on those who guard you or those who bring you food and other needs until such time."

"Why?" asked a man in the front, tall, burly, with bandages on his head and sword arm.

"Why not kill you? Blood shed in anger harms the taig, the spirit of the land. If your king judges you must die, that blood is on his hands, not mine. Why feed you and house you in the meantime? Because that is the code I live by—the code we mercenaries swore to in Aarenis."

"We'd of killed you if you was our prisoner."

"I do not doubt that, but my way is not your way. Though if you choose to die, you may."

The man scowled. "A hard death, I'll wager."

"You lose. If you would rather die than give your word to abide my commands until you return to your king, you will have a sword-stroke to the neck."

"You would give war-honor?"

"Yes."

"And we return to Pargun . . . when?"

"When I have word of your king and meet with him to learn his will in this."

"But Einar is dead."

"Not Einar. Torfinn, your true king."

"Torfinn has no honor," another man said. "His daughter—"

"Is Pargun's ambassador to this court," Kieri said, raising his voice. "But that is not to the point. Here it is: you will give your parole to me personally, each one of you, or your life is forfeit. When my messengers find your king, or his legitimate successor, you will be sent to him for his judgment of your rebellion. I cannot say what he will do. I have said what I will do. What say you?"

The first man who had spoken looked back over either

shoulder, first heart-side, then sword-side. Then he shrugged and nodded. "I say you speak truth like a man. How do I swear?"

The old mercenary ritual of surrender and parole would not suit this occasion; Kieri's observation of the Pargunese lords at his earlier meeting had given him a better idea.

"You will kneel and kiss the scabbard of my sword. If you intend falsehood, this elf-made sword will tell."

"I do not swear falsely," the man said. He took two steps forward and went to his knees. Kieri led him through the oath, in Pargunese, and the man kissed the sword.

"Now go over there," Kieri said, pointing. The man stood, bowed, and walked off to the area Kieri had marked off for those who had given parole.

He was halfway through taking the oaths—so far all had sworn—when a small party of horsemen rode into the court. One was a King's Squire, and one was Aliam Halveric himself, flanked by his son Caliam and the Knight-Commander of Falk. Kieri took the oath of the man kneeling before him, then held up his hand to forestall another coming forward. He stood, peering over the heads.

"Did you marry her yet?" Aliam yelled in a voice that could have carried to the Tsaian border.

Kieri laughed. The prisoners shifted uneasily. In Pargunese he said, "That is an old friend, from my days as a mercenary. Do not fear." To Aliam he said, "Get over here, man of war: I need your advice."

The group dismounted and made their way around the remaining prisoners and the Royal Archers. "We made better time than I thought we would," Aliam said as he came close enough to speak in a normal tone. "Cal wanted to be sure the sprout had made it."

"He did; he had breakfast with me and is somewhere inside, in care of a King's Squire."

"And Estil said to ask you first thing if you'd married her."

"Who?" Kieri said, but he could feel himself reddening. "And no, I haven't married yet." He looked closely at Aliam. Kieri had worried after leaving Aliam's steading that he might relapse. Now it was clear that the friend he'd known was—

though a little balder and grayer—healthy in mind and body. "I'm glad you brought Cal," he said. "When I've taken these oaths, I have something to show you. Go on inside, see if you can find young Aliam. I'll be with you when I can."

He finished taking the rest of the oaths and then explained what he would do. "We have no great prisons here—nor even empty granaries, not in this season. For the present, you will be housed in the outbuildings here—some in the stables, some in the other spaces, as we can make room and contrive bedding. You will keep your own spaces clean, and fetch your own food from the kitchens, and return the cleaned pots and dishes. Now, is there one among you with more rank whom you consider your leader?"

Eyes shifted back and forth, and finally one said, "Makkar." Others nodded. The same man who had spoken first turned and looked at them.

"You want me?" He sounded surprised. Some nodded, some didn't. "Who else?"

"Bladon!" someone called.

"No," another man said. To Kieri he called, "I am Bladon; I should not be leader. I vote for Makkar."

Much stamping of feet and muttering, and then Makkar said, "Give hands!" and arms shot up. "Agreed?"

"Aye."

"They call me leader," Makkar said. He came to Kieri and bowed again. "My neck stands between them and you. What now?"

"First you will eat," Kieri said. "Then you divide the men among the places to rest, as you think best. You will tell this man"—he indicated the captain of the Royal Archers—"who needs a surgeon and what supplies you need. The Royal Archers have my command to treat you fairly."

"It is well," Makkar said. He turned to the prisoners. "Oathbrothers together." The group shifted around; Kieri could now see what looked like fives—hands—in clumps, though some had only three or four.

"Captain," Kieri said to the Royal Archer captain. "Take these men to the mews and see them settled. Place a guard, and when you have a report of the wounded and any other needs, see to their care."

"Yes, sir king." He saluted and turned; Kieri entered the palace, where he found the Halveric trio in the main passage, young Aliam reporting on everything he'd seen since he left them, with a bemused King's Squire standing by.

Cal glanced up, saw Kieri, and tapped the boy's shoulder. "Show respect, son."

They all bowed, murmuring, "Sir king," but Aliam had a glint in his eye that Kieri recognized.

"I'm glad you're all here," he said to them. To the Squire he said, "Ask Garris to come to my office, if you please, and Arian as well."

"What is it?" Aliam asked, this time with no hint of mischief.

Kieri shook his head and led them into his office. The Halveric sword, wrapped in a green cloth, stood in the sword rack. He said nothing until Garris arrived. Garris glanced at Cal, then the sword rack, and his eyes widened. Then Arian came in. "Close the door, please," he said to Arian. "This is a private matter concerning Halveric Company and Caliam Halveric."

"What—" began Aliam; Kieri shook his head.

"You may remember something I mentioned when I visited in early autumn. I will not dwell on the circumstances," he said. "But in the third year of Siniava's War, a Halveric sword was lost in Aarenis and never found. By good chance, Captain Arcolin found it this past campaign season, recognized the style and then the mark—"

Caliam had gone pale. "Sir king!"

Kieri went to the rack, retrieved the sword, and unwrapped it. He held the sword in its new scabbard flat across both hands. "It has been blessed by a Captain of Falk, Cal, and carried by hand from Aarenis by Arcolin, who sent it by royal courier from Vérella. I did not have it when I came down earlier, or I would have brought it—but here it is, *your* sword, safe once more from any evil. Take it now, and joy with it."

"I never thought . . ." Cal reached out slowly and picked it up. "I never thought to see it again . . . I hoped it had been lost

in the river or . . . or somewhere it could not be used wrongly."
He ran a hand down the scabbard and fingered the grip. "It is
certainly mine. Where—how did Captain Arcolin find it?"

"Hidden in the bottom compartment of a trader's wagon
with many other weapons not listed on the manifest. Some
were evilly enchanted, and that is why Arcolin had it ritually
purified and blessed, in case of any contamination."

"And you're sure it's harmless?" Aliam said, scowling.

"Yes," Kieri said. "I felt no evil in it and had another Captain
of Falk check it as well. Although 'harmless,' as applied to a
sword, is hardly the right word."

Cal had regained his color; his eyes glittered with unshed
tears. "Sir king, I have no way to thank—"

"It is Arcolin, not I, who found and brought it back, Cal."

"But you thought to have us all here, and—" Cal shook his
head, unable to say more.

"And now to something as cheering, I hope," Kieri said.
"Aliam, you asked if I had married 'her' yet, but you seemed
to have no idea who 'she' might be. In fact, you have met
Arian before, and we will celebrate our engagement this Midwinter Feast and be wed at the Evener."

Aliam grinned. "So Estil is right again! She thought so! You
remember, Kieri, after your coronation, with the horses—"

"I wasn't listening then," Kieri said. "But I would have you,
my oldest friends, know Arian better. Here—we've been standing too long—I have chairs in this room for a reason. Garris,
we might as well have a private supper in here, don't you
think?"

"Of course," Garris said. "I'll tell them," and he went out.

Cal still held the blade a little awkwardly; he had another at
his hip and no place to hang that one. "Give it to your son for
now," Aliam said. "Unless the king objects to having a rash
youth armed in his presence."

"Not I," said Kieri. "In fact, it's time he learned to manage a
blade at his side indoors." He rummaged in his desk drawer.
"Here's a hanger. Let's see how he does."

The adults racked their blades before sitting down and tried
not to laugh as the boy strutted up and down, occasionally
catching his father's sword on the chairs and tables.

By the time supper arrived, the boy had settled down. After several unsuccessful attempts to fit himself into one of the chairs with the sword, he put the sword in the rack with the others. As they finished supper, Kieri said, "Aliam, I do have bad news, which I have not sent you on the road."

Aliam nodded.

"You lost a lot of people. The Pargunese did have an un-quenchable fire; it burned two swaths through the forest down to rock, as they'd threatened. Riverwash is nothing but ash, including Talgan and your troops there."

"Dear gods!"

"Talgan had posted half his command in another place—also attacked with fire—and most of those died, but some were out on patrol."

"What was it? Are there more?"

"You will find this hard to believe," Kieri said. "It was living fire—dragonspawn—and Arian killed them with the aid of a dragon."

"A *dragon*! But—but there are no dragons anymore!"

"There are," Kieri said. "Moreover, this dragon can take man's shape. I was as surprised and disbelieving as you, until I saw it myself." He went on to tell what the dragon had told him, what he had seen himself, and what Arian had done with the dragon.

"You rode a dragon?" Aliam said, staring at Arian.

"No, Lord Halveric. It carried me in its mouth." Arian grinned. "It was a comfortable ride, like being inside a feather bed." She told the rest briefly.

"And . . . I do not question your courage, Lady Arian, but was that not . . . dangerous?"

"I knew the dragon intended me no harm," Arian said. "I had seen it kill Pargunese. But yes, I was frightened the first time. How could an arrow kill a creature of fire? But arrows tipped with a dragon's own fire can. It must be much like the way stone-tipped arrows kill daskdraudigs."

"Your surviving troops are here," Kieri said. "I assigned them the Royal Archer barracks—many of the Archers are still out in the field."

"I want to see them," Aliam said, pushing himself up.

"I'll take you," Kieri said. "They should be well rested by now, but they're not all in good uniform; they had to borrow from dead Pargunese."

"I'm not going to scold them," Aliam said.

"Your Sergeant Vardan held her patrol together, found other surviving Halverics, and harried the Pargunese force all the way to where we defeated and captured them."

"Linnar? I'm not surprised."

"Alas, she died in the final battle with the Pargunese—killed by one of Achrya's creatures," Kieri said. "Her body's here, and if you want to use part of the river meadows for burial of your people, be my guest."

"You stay here, Ali," Aliam said to his grandson as he and his son belted on their swords again. Kieri led them across the courtyard.

The Halveric troops looked better than they had on arrival, but Kieri knew how Aliam's heart must ache to see so few, and so many of them wounded. He went to each one, greeting them by name and praising them.

CHAPTER FIVE

Tsaia: Verrakai Estate

DORRIN VERRAKAI CALLED her steward Grekkan into her office. "Pargun invaded Lyonya," she said. He stared, eyes wide. "I expect at least some Pargunese will make a diversionary attack on Tsaia. There's a Royal Guard unit in Harway, but I must leave and organize Tsaia's defenses."

"The king—" Grekkan began.

"The king named me Constable; he gave me this task, and he will send orders, I don't doubt, as soon as he hears of it. Now, I do not know how long I will be gone. This may be the time my remaining relatives choose to cause trouble, so be vigilant."

"You can leave some troops here, can't you?" Grekkan looked around as if he expected Pargunese to pop out of the walls.

"Not more than a handful. I'll send someone after Beclan, telling him he must come back, gathering troops on the way, and bring them to Harway. A groom—he won't be needed once I leave with Daryan and the others; all the horses will be gone but the one he rides."

"My lord—Squire Beclan is a Mahieran."

"I know. That's why I'm asking him to gather troops: Beclan's of the royal family, and he has that presence. And they'll be protection for him."

"Yes, my lord," Grekkan said.

"I must write letters to the other nobles," Dorrin said. "Daryan should be in today or tomorrow; I must be ready to leave the day after. Do your own planning for the household and let me know if there's anything I should send back from Harway when I get there."

"Yes, my lord," Grekkan said. He bowed and left her, heading for the back of the house.

Familiar lists ran through Dorrin's mind: what was packed for any campaign, plus what would be needed in winter. Heavier clothing, shelter, more fodder for mounts . . . Verrakai lands, unlike the Duke's Stronghold in the north, produced abundant hay and grain, so that would not be a problem. She stopped by the kitchen to let Farin Cook know there'd be a flurry of activity in the next day or so and more troops to feed later.

"Your meals today, my lord?" Farin asked. When Dorrin said nothing, she frowned. "You're not going hungry, my lord, not if there's a war to fight. You've not an extra finger of flesh on your bones; we don't want you taking the cold sickness."

"I leave it to you," Dorrin said. "Tell me when it's ready, whatever it is."

She had finally moved into the traditional ducal office after clearing it of all traps and dangers. On the broad worktable, she spread maps of eastern Tsaia. Arcolin would guard the northern border with Pargun. South of him, but north of the river, two different counts held border land. When she'd asked them, back in the summer, they'd claimed to have the required number of troops.

Her own levy would be short, as she had warned the king— so many Verrakai vassals had died in that abortive attempt on Kieri's life that she had not yet found enough able-bodied who could be trained to make up the number. Three Marshals had come late in summer, but neither they nor the Squires had found the remaining vassals apt at martial skills. Verrakaien had always scorned the use of women, too. It would be a year or more before those now in training could be really useful.

She looked at the notes she'd made after talking to the other nobles, the recommendations she'd made at Midsummer. At Autumn Court she'd learned that most had been ignored. Their vassals were busy; their local Marshals assured them joint training wasn't necessary; harvest had been heavy—or too light—or they'd been busy with something else. Duke Marrakai, who'd actually experienced war against the Pargunese when he was kirgan, had done the most, but only about half what she'd proposed. And his lands were west of Vérella; they would be among the last to arrive.

If they had continued their sluggish response after Autumn Court—which she suspected in spite of the scolding the king had given them—the realm might gather a bare third of the muster on the king's rolls. Only a few of those—the house militia of the various lords—had drilled regularly with their lords. What could she do with that motley and ill-trained force? What would the king expect her to do?

All dep¯ ided on what the Pargunese intended. Were they really determined to attack Kieri? Could they be deflected by a small but stout defense at the border? Surely they did not intend a long campaign in winter, across a river that might freeze and trap their boats.

She began her correspondence with a suggestion to the Royal Guard commander in Vérella. Not orders, as the king had not given her authority over the Royal Guard; she could only hope the commander would pay attention. A third of the light cavalry and half the heavy cavalry should be sent to the east to guard the border; a third of the light and the remainder of the heavy should stay with the king. The other third south, to watch the Valdaire road and patrol the southern trade route. She laid out her reasoning carefully, knowing the king would read it as well. Then she wrote orders to one lord after another, based on her latest knowledge of their resources and readiness. Despite the king's comments at Autumn Court, she was not sure any of them would obey promptly.

She ignored the sounds of the children and servants until Farin Cook said, "My lord, lunch. I called twice. I can bring it here."

"No . . . no, I should come." She had stiffened in the chair; she shook out her hands and stretched as she came into the passage. "Kitchen?" she said.

"No, my lord," Cook said firmly. "I'm making trail rations for the troops. There's no room. Small dining room's best."

"Fine. Has Grekkan eaten?"

"No, my lord. Do you wish him to join you?"

"Where is he? I can fetch him—stretch my legs."

"Out in the storehouses counting something, I don't doubt." Cook sniffed. "Don't you be standing talking; the food's hot now."

"I'll be quick," Dorrin said.

Grekkan came out of one of the storehouses carrying a slate as Dorrin crossed the courtyard. "My lord, the weavers have been working steadily, but we still don't have as many blankets as you said."

"That's all right. Come eat with me; Farin doesn't want it to get cold." They walked across the courtyard; Dorrin thought of ducking into the stable to find the farrier, but Farin had opened the kitchen door and was looking at them. Later, then.

"We haven't gone over the estate accounts since just after you came back from Autumn Court," Grekkan said. "I'd like you to see them." Grekkan had spent the first quarter of his tenure as steward bringing them up to his standard.

"We'll have to do it quickly," Dorrin said. "I have much to do this afternoon."

"Yes, my lord. I'll make it brief." He looked at the ceiling. "The quarterly grange-set for all the granges and the estate contribution to the royal purse will have to come partly from your holdings in Vérella. Harvests were good throughout despite the late start in some vills, but you remitted the estate's share for all who had lost a family member in the battle."

Holdings in Vérella . . . Dorrin was only too aware how little she had on credit with the bank there. "I still have the jewelry confiscated from those attainted," she said. "I'll take that with me to Harway and sell it there. Can you give me an approximate value?"

"I can try," Grekkan said.

"Good." It would keep him busy while she finished her letters. Dorrin found the box in which she'd put all the rings, bracelets, necklaces, jeweled combs, and the like, now all clean of poison and any taint of evil.

DARYAП ARRÍVED WÍTH his troop after dark, the distant sentries signaling his arrival with their torches. Dorrin came out to greet him when he rode up to the stableyard gate. He dismounted and bowed.

"Greetings of the night, my lord. I report all well when we left our area."

"I have urgent news," Dorrin said. "There's war: Pargun and Lyonya." She shot a glance at the troop sergeant, Piter Arugson, once in her cohort. He nodded slightly; he knew how to prepare them. "Dismiss your troop and come inside."

Daryan did so in correct form, handed his reins to his sergeant, and followed Dorrin inside.

"There's supper kept warm for you," Dorrin said, sending a maid to fetch it. "Come by the fire and I'll explain." She'd had his fleece-lined slippers brought down, and as he warmed himself by the fire and then began to eat with all the appetite of a fast-growing young man, she told him about Arian's visit, the invasion, and what she must do.

"I could send you back to your father," she said at last as he wiped his plate with another slice of bread. "You are a year too young to be required to ride into danger—"

"But I want to," he said, dropping the bread. "Please, my lord—don't send me home like a naughty child. Roly—"

"Your brother's what, four years, or five, older than you? Yet, I won't send you home if you want to chance it."

"I do, my lord. And Gwenno's gone—"

"And Beclan will be behind us."

His jaw dropped. "You're not taking Beclan? Why? Will he guard the household here?"

"No. He was outbound before I knew of this; he's at least several days away. I'm sending a messenger to him, telling him to raise troops on his way in, then follow us. Our troops will be the first levy to reach Harway, so we will be first in combat if the Pargunese do invade."

Daryan said, "Will you command us, then, my lord?"

"Initially, yes," Dorrin said. "But if there's a prolonged war and many different units, I must find a field commander for my own militia. None of you squires have the experience for that."

"Even Beclan?" He sounded surprised.

"Even Beclan. Kieri Phelan felt it took at least two full seasons of campaigning under experienced commanders for a squire to develop the skills. More for some. Captain Selfer was Kieri's squire for three years, then junior captain, and now he's a senior captain." Dorrin looked at Daryan and did not ask if he had imagined himself leading troops in battle. Squires all did, one time or another. Daryan, as the youngest and smallest, with an older brother who had saved the king's life, would want to prove himself.

Daryan, slightly flushed, shoveled in another mouthful of buttered redroots, as if to stop himself saying anything.

"I have dispatches for the king and Council, and orders to send as well, when we arrive in Harway," Dorrin said. "I'm certain I'll need to meet with the Royal Guard commander there. You and Gwenno will manage your combined squads for the time being—"

"She's senior," Daryan said.

"Yes. But there'll be plenty for both of you to do. One of you will need to visit the grange and let the Marshal know that I've arrived, for instance. We may meet a courier on the way; I'm surprised no one's arrived yet. So your task for this evening is to prepare your own gear—you'll need three suits of clothes at least—and see that your squad is ready to leave by noon tomorrow. Your sergeant will have done most of it, but you must check. How are the horses' shoes?"

"Two lost a shoe, my lord, and one is lame. Three need to be reshod, besides the two that lost shoes."

"Well, then. How will you plan what needs to be done?"

Daryan told her; she had thought before he had the most organized mind of her squires. She grinned at him. "Well done, Daryan. See to it you're abed by four glasses from now, and tell your sergeant the same."

"Yes, my lord."

THE NEXT MORNING, Dorrin woke to find all busy with preparations. Farin Cook had rations for the squad packed and ready to carry by breakfast time; the farrier had a roaring fire in his forge; servants scurried back and forth loading the supply wagon—not needed for one squad but essential if this became a long campaign. Rations, blankets, tents, braziers, spares of everything from stirrup leathers to swords. Dorrin finished the last of her messages, tucking the one for the king into a stiff tube of blue leather with the Verrakai crest on it. Then she went out to the kitchen garden with its apple trees. Could she do what Arian had tried to teach her?

She laid her ungloved hand on the old tree's cold bark. At once—so fast she almost pulled away—it warmed under her hand, and she felt the *something* that Arian called the taig. Still strange to her, and unsettling, but she felt welcome in it, too. She wanted to know how Kieri was, but though she tried to ask the tree—feeling foolish even as she did so—nothing came of it but that warmth, that welcome.

One of the servants opened the garden door. "My lord? Cook says lunch is ready."

Dorrin stroked the tree's gnarled limb and came inside.

"Can we make the shelter by nightfall, my lord?" the sergeant asked.

"No . . . but we don't know how bad the situation is." Was it Arian's worry tugging at her or something more? "We can make it by turn of night, even riding in the dark, and if they've sent a courier, we'll be that much closer to Harway."

"Well, then, we're ready."

They set off against a steady north breeze under a thin skim of clouds that flattened out shadows. The marks of yesterday's travelers showed clearly, though, and by dark they were well into the forest. The blazes Dorrin had ordered cut to mark the way for traders now helped them find the way, shining pale in the torchlight. Shortly after the last light died in the west, they heard someone coming and a hail.

"Go on, Daryan," Dorrin said. "See what we have."

Daryan signaled his troop, and two of them rode forward with him while Dorrin held the others still. She heard the voices: challenge, response, surprise, but no alarm, and then Daryan came back, his horse high-stepping with the squire's excitement. "It's a royal courier, my lord. For you."

Dorrin rode forward. The man wearing a courier's tabard over his Royal Guard uniform looked pinched with cold and tired in the wavering torchlight. As well he might, she thought, if he'd ridden straight through from Harway.

"You knew?" the man said. His tone was almost accusing, but Dorrin could imagine the frustration of riding hours through the cold without need. "That girl said, but I wasn't sure."

"My squire, Gwennothlin Marrakai," Dorrin said, nodding. "Of course I called in the nearest militia, and more are coming. What does the Royal Guard know?"

"I left as soon as the Lyonyans told us there was trouble," the man said. "I don't know more than you do." He spat to the side. "I guess I'll go back now."

"Do you have a message for me? Written?"

"Oh. Yes, my lord."

"Then let's get to the shelter and I'll read it."

"How far's the house, my lord?" His voice held a faint whine.

"The house?" Dorrin scowled. "You've no reason to go on: I'm here, the person you came to see."

"Well, but . . ." He spat again. "I been riding all day, and yesterday, too. It's a long way back to that shelter and no fire there, neither."

"It's as far to the house as back to the shelter," Dorrin said, nodding at the nearest marked tree. She felt a vague uneasiness. The man was a royal courier—had to be, wearing that uniform—but she could not imagine anyone in that service expecting to travel on to a duke's residence for a night's rest when the duke was there, on the road, headed somewhere else. It made no sense.

"If you say so, my lord," the man said. He looked away, once more spitting to the side of the trail.

Dorrin felt cold down her spine. He had never actually looked straight at her, she realized. He had looked down or away, using the need to spit as a reason to keep his gaze averted. Was he a traitor? Was he—worst of all—a Verrakai in a loyal man's body? She shifted both reins to one hand, let the other drop to her side, and flicked a hand signal she knew the troop sergeant would understand.

"When did you leave the shelter?" she asked, riding another horse-length closer to him. If he'd left early, he should have reached the house by nightfall, not this halfway point.

He spat yet again. "Oh, well," he said. "M'horse was that tired . . . I thought the house was closer, so I didn't leave until . . . maybe near nooning."

Time enough, if a Verrakai magelord had been hiding in the woods, to attack . . . but he should have been delirious with fever, not already invaded. The invasion must have happened before. So why had he waited to start for the house?

To catch her on the way. He would have known—his powers were ample for that—when she set out.

Would he attack her, or one of her party? Behind the courier, false or true, Daryan sat his horse watching them. Too close to the courier; too close to her.

"Ride on to the shelter," she called to Daryan. "Start a fire for us. Be swift."

"Yes, my lord." Daryan wheeled his horse and booted it to a canter.

The courier whirled at the sound, and Dorrin's next flick of the hand sent five crossbow bolts into the man's torso. He gave a hoarse cry and slid from the saddle; the bolt of mage-power he'd sent missed Daryan by a scant armslength.

"You . . . you killed a royal courier!" one of her Verrakai militia said.

"I killed a traitor," Dorrin said. "*If* he's dead. Sergeant: perimeter guard. There may be more. Do not approach him; he's still dangerous."

Why hadn't she recognized his magery instantly? she wondered.

She dismounted, drew her sword, and walked over to the fallen man. Still alive but mortally wounded, too weak to raise an effective attack of magery. She barely felt the malice he flung at her shield, but she saw in his eyes undying hatred. "How long?" she asked.

His lips twisted in a sneer. "Not long enough; you should be dead."

"And I am not, and you are dying. How long were you in that body?"

"Guess," he said. "Or if you have the courage, bend closer; I will tell only you, not those scum."

"I think not," Dorrin said. Arcolin's experience warned her. She backed away.

"Coward bitch!" he said; blood spurted from his mouth. His body convulsed, and a mist formed over it though the body still jerked. Dorrin spoke the words she had spoken when she expelled the Verrakai spirit from Stammel, but the mist did not disperse. Instead, it drifted toward her on the current of air from the north, hardly visible in the wavering torchlight.

"My lord?" The sergeant's voice was shaky.

"If I cannot dispel the mist—if it enters me, if I act differently—kill me at once."

"My lord!"

"At once." Dorrin backed away from the mist a step, then stopped. She would not lead it closer to her people. They had no protection; she had her shield of magery. She must lure it to her alone. "I must not become what that was; this realm has had enough evil Verrakaien." She stepped forward.

If Verrakai command words would not work on this one . . . what did that mean? Could it penetrate her mage-shield? Who had it been, and how many years had it lived, to have so strong a hold on life unbodied? And what would work?

Kieri's words, the remembered words of the man who had freed him from torment, came to her: *There is a High Lord above all lords; go to his courts and be free.*

The mist reached her shield, thick enough to dim the torchlight and spread like a stain on glass. She felt a mental itch, a high thin keening like a fly trapped in a corner. The first touch on her skin was like fire. The noise in her head grew.

"Falk's Oath in gold," Dorrin said, "and the High Lord's justice oppose your evil. By this ruby, by the High Lord's rule, as Falk's knight and the High Lord's loyal servant, I banish you. Begone, foulness, and be born no more." With her sword, blue now glinting from its blade, she drew the sigils for Falk and the High Lord on the mist; the mist brightened, condensed, and for a moment she felt engulfed in chaos. Then it was gone—the pressure, the sound, the mental itch, the burning pain.

The sergeant, sword drawn, stood near her, eyes fixed on

hers as she turned. "It touched you," he said. "I saw it pause and then—"

"My shield held it off briefly, then it got through. But I am unchanged," Dorrin said. She saw doubt in his face. "I have no relic of Falk to prove it by, but I do still wear Falk's ruby." She touched it; it glowed to her touch. "And see the blade of my sword—you saw it flare when it touched the mist, and now when I touch my bare hand to it—" She pulled off her glove with her teeth and laid her hand on the blade. "Nothing."

"How did you destroy it?"

"I did not," Dorrin said. "It ignored my commands as lord of Verrakai. But Falk and the High Lord destroyed it. Did you hear my prayer?"

"No, my lord. Your lips moved, but we heard nothing. That's why we thought . . ." His voice trailed away; he still looked worried.

"Watch me closely," Dorrin said. "And by all means, when we reach Harway, tell the Marshal—as I will—and the Royal Guard commander what you saw and how I have behaved since. I'm going to get the courier's seal ring and the messages he carried, if any." Nothing happened as she touched the body. She found the message case, the seal ring, pulled off his gloves.

"Why's that?" asked the sergeant, standing near.

"Look," Dorrin said. On the inner wrist was a tattoo, barely visible in the torchlight, but the horned circle was evident. "He must have killed the real courier and taken his clothes; there's no way a Royal Guard soldier could hide that mark." She touched his chest and felt something lumpy. She ripped open tunic and shirt with her dagger, and there it was—Liart's emblem.

The sergeant whistled. "That's bad."

"We'll have to take his body and keep watch for the body of the man he killed. And we need to follow Daryan quickly. Get this loaded on his horse." She glanced aside; the horse he'd ridden was gnawing on a lichen-covered limb.

She turned away, tucking the message case and ring into her doublet, and mounted her horse. She felt—different. But not different in a bad way.

When the body had been lashed to the horse, the sergeant told off three to stay with it and follow at a slower pace, and then with Dorrin set off at a hard gallop. The track was open now, unobscured, after the work she had done on it; even at night she could see the way, the snow seeming almost to glow in the starlight.

Dorrin hoped to catch up with Daryan before he reached the shelter, but he'd had a good start and she'd told him to hurry. She wished she could see the hoofmarks on the track more clearly. In daylight, she'd have known which were those from Gwenno's party the day before, which were the courier's, and which were Daryan's, but in the starlight that was impossible. Still, the rumpled trodden snow should keep Daryan from getting lost.

At last they came out into the clearing around the shelter. Dorrin stared. No fire. No horse. No welcoming call from Daryan.

"Where is he?" asked one of the militia.

"I don't know," Dorrin said. "In trouble, I expect." She kept her voice calm with an effort; her thoughts sped. If the one she'd killed had not been the only one—if others had lurked nearby, had seen Daryan ride away— She tried to put that aside.

The shelter had a supply of dry wood and ready-made torches; by their light they found the body of the real courier, his hands charred, his eyes gouged out, wounds all over his body, his blood darkening the snow and ground around him.

"Blood magery," the sergeant said.

"Yes." Dorrin could scarcely speak. She touched the ruined eye sockets, the charred hands. "Falk's welcome for him and great reward for his service." To one side she saw footprints leading into the woods. "Bring a torch nearer." Three sets of footprints coming toward the shelter's unwindowed north side from the woods . . . two going back. So the mage had had help subduing the courier, just as she'd feared.

And Daryan might have found two—or more—with mage powers when he arrived. Or they might have ambushed him along the track.

"Who's best at tracking?" she asked the group.

One hand went up, one of the Verrakai vassals. "M'lord, I can read sign."

"Did you see any indication that Daryan had veered off the track we were on?"

"No, m'lord, but we was riding too fast. I can look now."

"We'll start at this end," Dorrin said. "Five of you—it's not safe with fewer—and you nontrackers stay back, don't confuse the marks. We need to find the trace of Daryan's horse. Is there anything distinctive about it? You were on patrol with him."

"Hisn's got bigger hooves, m'lord. And more width at the heel than any of ours. I know it well, m'lord."

"Do you think he's captured?" the sergeant asked.

"I don't know," Dorrin said. "It cannot be good, whatever it is."

THEY SOON FOUND where Daryan's horse had left the trail; the tracks were easy enough to follow. In a short time, they saw light ahead, flickering light that glittered on the snow, and as they neared, they could see torches burning on stakes, forming a rough circle. The stumps of saplings showed where the stakes had been cut. In the center, bound to a larger sapling from which limbs had been cut, Daryan: alive. Light and shadow danced over his body, his face; it was hard to see how badly he was injured.

Or if he had been invaded.

One of the militia started forward. "Stop," Dorrin said. "It is a trap."

"But the boy—"

"We shall see." In the light of the torches, she could not see into the trees beyond; the glade had been ringed by quick-growing firs, and now all she saw was a wall of darkness. Enemies could be—almost certainly were—hiding there, ready to shoot into the clearing. But she had to risk it. "Daryan," she called. "Squire!"

His head lifted. "D-don't c-c-come!" he said. "T-trap!" His voice shook; he must be perishing with cold. "D-don't."

"Can you tell us what?"

"C-crossb-bows. In t-trees. All around." A pause, then: "My lord."

"Back twenty paces and start looking," Dorrin said to the troops. "They'll be set with trip cords, like hunters' traps." It was easy to set up a crossbow to shoot that way. And it was proof the trap had been planned; they would have guessed another party would be using the trail to Harway. "The cords will be out there"—she gestured at the glade—"and run back to the individual trees, then up the trunks to whatever branch they tied the crossbow to. If we're not careful, the arrows will kill Daryan; if we don't find them all, they'll kill one or more of us as well." She could not feel any magery at work.

"Daryan, where are you hurt?"

"Th-they cut off—my-my thumbs." A pause and then, "And . . . my—my heel-cords."

Rage and horror filled her, then grief. She had let this happen to the lad, and now he would be a cripple the rest of his life. If he lived. She wanted to run to the boy, but no one could outrun a crossbow bolt. He would have to wait—whatever additional harm that did him—until they could get to him without killing him or themselves.

It seemed to take forever to clear all the trees—twelve bows in all they found, and she hoped that was all. Finally, she led the way across the snow, catching her feet twice on trip cords. They had brought the torches nearer; now she could see the little pool of blood at his feet and realized that only the rope binding him to the tree held him upright. His skin was cold as the night itself, but his eyes still had the spark of life. She leaned close, wrapping her cloak around, ready to catch him when those cutting the ropes behind the sapling freed him.

"My lord, I was stupid."

"Hush, Daryan . . . I have no blame for you."

"I saw lights. I thought I should see if it was trouble—"

"The man you saw before I sent you away was not a real courier," Dorrin said. "The real courier is dead."

"If I had done what you told me—"

"You might well have run into the same ones at the shelter—that's where we found the body. How many were there?"

"Three. Th-they—I think they—" He moaned as the others

freed his arms, and his wounded hands fell forward. Dorrin put her arms around him, holding him upright as best she could as the others worked on the lower ropes.

"You're a brave man, Daryan Serrostin," she said quietly. "Keep talking—it will help you stay awake, and right now we need you awake, even though it hurts."

"It wasn't so bad after . . . after I got cold enough." More of his weight came onto her. One of the others put his own cloak over Daryan's back and helped support him as the last bonds yielded to daggers. "Th-they put snow . . ."

They had wanted the boy to live until Dorrin and her party arrived, wanted him alive and in pain and frightened, and wanted his rescuers to see that they had killed him with their attempt at rescue. As if her relatives spoke directly to her, Dorrin could see their reasoning: the injury or death of a squire would discredit her, even if she was not killed herself, and would impede Tsaia's defense.

"I—I don't know what—what I can do," Daryan said. "My hands—"

"You are a man of courage and ability," Dorrin said. "You will find a way."

"But—but I can't be your squire—"

"We don't know that yet," Dorrin said. "Lie still now—we're going to carry you to the shelter."

With poles quickly cut and blankets, they made a litter for him and before dawn had reached the shelter. Dorrin let her sergeant bandage his hands and ankles and forbore to say he was lucky not to have been gelded as well.

"I tried to fight, but it was all a dazzle," Daryan said, sipping the mug of sib she held for him. "Like the light you make, my lord, but flickering. I couldn't move after a bit." He winced at the bandaging. Dorrin would have given him numbweed, but he was still too cold, and she dared not.

"My lord, what next?" That was the sergeant.

What next indeed? The attack had changed everything again. Knowing there were more Verrakaien in the woods—that they knew she was away from the house—could she justify being away? Leaving the defenses to Beclan, the king's cousin, inexperienced as he was? And yet to send a messenger back was to risk that messenger. Her magery had not detected her relatives . . . she could not detect them now. They could be anywhere, just out of sight or on their way to Verrakai Steading, but what they meant was clear—malice.

CHAPTER SIX

FOR A FEW moments, Dorrin could hardly think. A youngster entrusted to her care crippled for life . . . two others isolated, vulnerable. More Verrakai killers on the loose somewhere. Had Gwenno even reached Harway? And Beclan, the king's cousin—a logical target for the other Verrakai. Her duty to her king and her duty to her people . . . so closely balanced and calling for such different actions.

Daryan himself decided her. "My lord, go on. I know what my father would say—you must care for the kingdom first."

Confusion settled into the familiar patterns of command. She had, indeed, no choice: the king had named her Constable, war-leader, for the kingdom. With invasion imminent, she must go on.

"We're not leaving you, Daryan," she said. "You'll come with us." He looked a little better now; she knew his injuries, though crippling, were not life-threatening. Cold had stopped the bleeding.

Next morning, the tracks of the earlier party, Gwenno and Arian and their escort, showed clearly. Daryan, clothed, insisted he could sit a horse; the steadiest rider in the militia rode double with him. Nothing untoward happened on the ride to Harway except that Daryan could not stay balanced at any gait faster than a strong walk. They reached Thornhedge Grange by midafternoon; it was empty but for the junior yeomen set there as a watch.

"Marshal and them's over along the river," one of them said. "Royal Guard set them to guard there, case them Pargunese try to come over."

"Where's a surgeon?" Dorrin asked. "My squire's hurt."

The boys stared curiously at Daryan, at his bandaged hands.

"There's Master Llasstin, down Market Street," one said. "But us Girdish, we ask t'Marshal. I know just where he's stationed—want me to get 'im?"

"Daryan?"

"He's—on—duty," Daryan said. "Could I just—stop? Here?"

"Help him down," Dorrin said to her militia. "You lads—is there a litter in the grange?"

"Yes . . . but it's not but a few steps," the boy said.

"He can't walk right now," Dorrin said. "One of you, run ahead—find the Royal Guard commander and tell him I'm here. And one of you go tell the Marshal."

Daryan gasped as the Verrakai soldiers helped him off the horse and into a litter.

"Daryan, I'll send someone to bring the surgeon to you. I'm sorry, but I must go."

She met the commander of the local garrison in the main street, riding toward her. On the heart-shoulder of his rose-and-white tunic he had a knot of Clannaeth yellow and rose.

"I'm Duke Verrakai," Dorrin said. "Currently Constable—and you are?"

"Sir Flanits Clannaeth," he said. "Local Royal Guard commander. Didn't you bring troops?" He looked past her. "Your squire—that girl—said you would."

"I brought all who were nearby," Dorrin said. "Then we were attacked on the way. One of my other squires is hurt—he's at the grange, and I left those troops with him. What's the situation?"

"I sent a courier for you—he should have told you—"

"He's dead," Dorrin said. "Killed on the way; we found his body." She told the rest as quickly as she could; his expression reflected her own shock and horror at Daryan's maiming. "So tell me—what's the situation?"

"No Pargunese have come here, but they hit Lyonya hard. I hear tell Riverwash is gone—some kind of magical fire. We saw a glow from here," Sir Flanits said.

"The whole town's burned?"

"Aye. Something like white fire, hotter than any fire ever seen. We had Lyonyans fleeing to our border, of course; one of them claimed to see it, Riverwash vanishing in flames. Third

night of the invasion, that was, same night your squire arrived
and that Lyonyan woman with your squire went back over the
border."

"Arian," Dorrin said. Should she mention that Arian was a
King's Squire? No. "One of their forest rangers," she said in-
stead. "She told me of their rangers killing some renegade
Verrakai that had come into their forest."

"Ah. I wondered what she was doing here." Sir Flanits gave
her a searching look. "Do you think you'll ever catch them
all?"

"I hope so," Dorrin said. "But the ones who hurt Daryan got
away. Two, maybe three. The lad thinks he wounded one."

Sir Flanits nodded, then went on with his report. "I'd already
sent word to the king, when we first heard of invasion. We put
more guards at the border, and I asked the Marshal to send his
yeomen to watch the riverbanks. There's a Field of Falk here,
too, and the Captain's people have moved south, along the border." He paused. "Ardli's dead, then? The courier I sent?"

"Yes. It must have been more of my damnable relatives
who did it. And we—or you—have another problem. My other
squire, the one who was to follow me with more troops, is
Beclan Mahieran, the king's cousin, second son of Duke
Mahieran. Royal family and a natural target for those Verrakai
who attacked Daryan Serrostin. You know I must remain here;
I expect the king will send more troops this way, and other
peers should be sending their levies. The king expects me to
command them in case of invasion. You must take at least a
tensquad of your troops—more would be better—and go to
my steading, find Beclan."

"My lord!" Sir Flanits drew himself up, chest out. "I know
the king sent word that you were to take over as field commander if anything happened . . . but he also said the Royal
Guard remained under *his* command. You can't order me—"

"Your duty is to protect the royal family," Dorrin said. "The
king *and* his heirs; Beclan is close in succession. More, if he
were taken over by one of the Verrakai, he would be a positive
danger to the king—a trusted relative in appearance but within
a deadly enemy. That must not happen. I can't prevent it, having to stay here, but you can."

"But only the king gives me orders," Sir Flanits said. "I am a Knight of the Bells; I am a count's son—"

And he was an idiot, Dorrin thought. Saying so would not help. "Sir," she said, letting those decades of command stiffen her tone. A pause, then: "Your duty is to the king and his family. A member of his family, close in succession, is in deadly peril. I told you renegade Verrakai—traitors, under attainder— are loose in the forest."

"But they're your—"

"What do you think the king will say when Beclan Mahieran is killed, or captured and tortured, or worst of all invaded and made into an enemy, because you, sir, would not move one finger to help him?" She did not pause for another interruption. "Beclan is a brave lad, but he is not yet of age. He has no battlefield experience, nor have most of the household troops with him. He has *no* protection against magery." She paused then, and when she saw a more thoughtful expression on the commander's face, she went on more quietly. "I am not ordering you; I am reminding you of the king's orders that you protect not only the king but his close relatives. From what you say, between the Girdish yeomen and my own troops, I can take over here in Harway, and you can take your troops to help Beclan."

"I was sent here to watch the border," Sir Flanits said. "That was the king's last command."

"I understand," Dorrin said. "And your dispositions, so far, have been those I'd have made. But now that I'm here, your primary duty—"

"Is directly to the king. Yes. But you have so few troops."

"I will have the yeomen from Briarhedge Grange and the soldiers of the local field as well," Dorrin said.

"You expect them to come under your command?"

"Yes. And as you were told that I am Constable, so also were granges and fields, as well as other lords whose troops may be sent here."

This time he nodded. "Very well, then. I don't know this boy. What's he like?"

"A handsome young man, like that whole family, but privilege had gone to his head. However, he has matured since

Midsummer and I've found him energetic and quick to learn once he admits he doesn't know everything. Did you see his brother Rothlin at court?"

"Yes. Yes, I did."

"Then you'll recognize him. He's much the same, just a few years younger and his hair is a shade or so lighter. Beardless. He'll have the Mahieran colors on his shoulder, of course." Now that he was listening and seemed more cooperative, Dorrin let her voice relax to a warmer tone. "If it were just leading some troops from the steading to Harway, I would not be so worried," she said. "But with the attack on Daryan—knowing some Verrakaien are loose in my domain—that's not something Beclan has the experience to handle. And my own people are in peril as well, especially the young children, but I know that's not your duty."

"If we were at the house . . . is it defensible? Do you even know how many Verrakaien we might face?"

"No. The former duke deliberately falsified the family rolls: I know his records are untrustworthy and have no way of knowing how many more Verrakaien might be at large. The house is not designed to be defended by force but by magery. The biggest danger is not recognizing the Verrakaien for what they are. At the house—if they've taken over other bodies—" Who could resist best? "If she's alive, trust Farin Cook. She rules the kitchen and would be hard to invade. If Beclan's not there when you arrive, then he's still out in the southwest of my domain, trying to gather troops. My advice—not an order—would be to leave half your troops at the house, with orders not to trust visitors, and send half to find and guard Beclan. My steward, Grekkan, has maps; he can show you Beclan's patrol route." If Grekkan had not been taken over. Dorrin pushed that thought away. "For now, I must find an inn."

"The mayor here, that's Saldon Rennit, he said you could have the Council meet-house. It's got tables and maps and things, he said. I can show you the way. And since I'm taking my troops away, you're welcome to barracks space for your militia."

* * *

Once dismounted and inside the warm Council meet-house, Dorrin felt the fatigue of the past day and night weighing on her shoulders. Her eyes felt gritty; she wanted at least a few hours' sleep, not a conference with civilians, but it could not be helped. She refused the offered mulled wine and accepted sib instead.

Gwenno arrived, looking bright-eyed and excited. "The Guard commander said something happened to Daryan. Where is he? My lord," she added a moment late.

"At the grange," Dorrin said. "He was ambushed and injured." No sense in hiding it; Gwenno would find out soon enough. "They cut off his thumbs and cut his heel-strings."

Gwenno paled. "Holy Gird!"

Before the girl could start asking the questions Dorrin knew were coming, she said, "Right now, Gwenno, I want you to go to the grange here. Find out if the Marshal has arrived, if he is able to heal Daryan, if the surgeon has come. Do not try to talk to Daryan even if he is conscious. Report back to me if I have not come to the grange by then."

"At once, my lord," Gwenno said.

Dorrin had just completed her first briefing to the mayor of Harway when Marshal Berris himself arrived with Gwenno, looking grim.

"Marshal Berris," she said. "How is my squire?"

"Not dead yet," he said. "Asleep. The surgeon and I are sure the wounds are cleaned, which is all we can do."

"In the Duke's Company, we had a surgeon who once reattached a cut heel-string," Dorrin said.

"Perhaps he could, but Llasstin can't. And his thumbs— nothing to be done there, either." He shook his head. "This will do you no good, Duke Verrakai. A duke's son, come to such grief in your service."

"Worse for him. A brave lad. I thought perhaps since he's Girdish—"

"Marshals, alas, do not have the healing powers of paladins. And even paladins . . . I never heard of one being able to replace thumbs. You helped heal Duke Marrakai, I heard."

"With the Marshal-General," Dorrin said. "I assumed it was mostly her."

"Possibly. But did you try a healing with your own magery?"

"No," Dorrin said. "I have no idea how thumbs grow . . . no . . . no mental image to work from. Of course I prayed for his life, but then I was more concerned to get him warm; he was perishing with cold. His heel-strings pulled up, didn't they?"

"Yes. Master Llasstin said that to find the upper end he would have to cut the boy's leg more, and he advised against it. Said wound-fever was already a possibility and that would make it worse."

"Our military surgeons said opening a wound made it safer, if it was cleaned and packed properly. One of them, if he found a clean cut, would sew the string back together. Sometimes it failed, but a few times it healed sound."

"Well, Llasstin won't touch it. If you can't heal it, there's no one else."

"I can try, but I don't have the training or the knowledge of herb-lore to prevent wound-fever. Is there anyone . . . ?"

Marshal Berris scowled. "Hedge-witches claim to. Or Kuakkgani, but we don't have a Kuakgan nearby. Your predecessor hated them even more than Girdish. There's a wizard in town, claims to have healing potions, but I'm sure that's nonsense."

"We had one with the Company—he and the surgeons were always arguing, but his potions did work. He saved Paks's life when she was a novice."

Berris blinked. "Saved a paladin?"

"She wasn't a paladin yet—she was a green soldier in her first battle, wounded. The wizard gave her his healing potion."

"It was Gird, I'm sure, who healed her," Berris said a bit stiffly. "But if you want to try the wizard—"

"I'd try anything to give that lad back his thumbs," Dorrin said. She turned to Gwennothlin. "Find the wizard and ask him to come to the grange." She looked at Berris, who nodded, but with his lower lip tucked in. "I'll come now and do what I can."

"And I'm off to bring the Captain of Falk's Field to the grange," Berris said. Dorrin nodded.

DARYAN LAY LIMP and pale in a bed in the spare room of the grange; Dorrin knew the look of someone drugged with numbwine and the smell of surgeons' poultices. The surgeon, bald and stooped, glanced up as she came in. "Ah. Duke Verrakai?"

"Yes," Dorrin said. "And you're Master Llasstin?"

He nodded. "There was nothing I could do but poultice the wounds. Made with a sharp blade and no indication of poison on it. He'll live, no doubt of that, but crippled." He shook his head. "Pity, in one so young."

"We had a surgeon in Phelan's Company who had some success with heel-strings," Dorrin said.

"Never seen it. Don't know it." The surgeon shook his head. "Lad's a cripple. Nothing to be done. Family won't thank you." He turned away.

"Excuse me." That voice from the door brought her around, hand on sword-hilt, but the man at the door was no threat. Tall, dark-faced, in a hooded robe patterned in the colors of a summer forest, greens and browns, this was clearly a Kuakgan. The same one she had met? She could not be sure but thought this one was younger.

"Don't bring any forest filth in here!" the surgeon said sharply.

Peaked eyebrows rose. "Forest filth? Do you not yourself use plants from the forest to brew your healing potions?"

"I know you hedge-witches," the surgeon said. "And I've seen wounds go bad from having dirt packed into them."

"Ah, but I'm not a hedge-witch," the Kuakgan said. He looked at Dorrin. "You are Duke Verrakai?"

"Yes," Dorrin said. "And you?"

"I am Master Ashwind, a traveling Kuakgan who has no settled Grove. I know Master Oakhallow, whom you met."

"All the same," muttered the surgeon.

"No," said Master Ashwind, not looking at the surgeon. "Though I respect the hedge-witches for their knowledge of herb-lore, the lore of Kuakkgani is different and comes from a different source. I came to tell the Duke of dangers in Verrakai domain and what I have done about them."

"I will return to change his bandages in the morning," the surgeon said, nodding at Daryan. "When he wakes, he can have a bowl of meat broth and then a dose of numbwine. Unless this . . . Kuakgan . . . persuades you to some other treatment." He stalked out, taking the door into the grange itself instead of going past the Kuakgan to the outer door.

Master Ashwind smiled at Dorrin. "I would not have stayed but that you need to know the word I bring. What is wrong with the boy?"

"We were attacked on the way from Verrakai Steading to Harway," Dorrin said. "Last night, it would have been." It felt like days ago. "He was captured by renegade Verrakai. They cut off his thumbs and cut his heel-strings."

Ashwind hummed, a sound like a hive of bees; the room warmed. "What did the surgeon say?" he asked after a moment.

"That he could do nothing but bandage the wounds," Dorrin said. "I sent for a wizard—there's one in town, they tell me. In the Duke's Company we had a surgeon who once or twice sewed up heel-strings and a wizard whose potions could restore blood, but neither could restore a missing limb. I have none but herbal healers in my domain. I should have—"

"You have been busy enough," Ashwind said. "May I approach the boy?"

"Certainly," Dorrin said. She watched as Ashwind put back his hood and crouched beside the bed where Daryan lay. He put his hand on the boy's forehead, then lightly on his chest.

"You are Falkian, and they say you have the old magelord powers. Have you yourself tried to heal the boy?"

"No," Dorrin said. Was everyone going to ask her that? "I prayed for his life last night, but I do not know enough. Our surgeon said that it was easy to go wrong and make things worse."

"True, if a healer comes with arrogance and does not listen . . . but I think that is not true of you. Your land tells me it is not." He looked up at her, his eyes glinting green in the lamplight. "I would like to see his wounds."

"Can you heal him?" Dorrin asked.

"I don't know until I have seen the wounds," Ashwind said. Dorrin nodded; Ashwind folded the blankets down and lifted one of Daryan's bandaged hands. He held it between his as if it were a fragile, precious ornament.

Someone banged on the grange-side door. "Lord Duke!"

"I must answer," Dorrin said.

"Of course," Ashwind murmured.

"Lord Duke, Marshal Berris and the Captain said to tell you they're ready." An excited voice.

"Just a moment," Dorrin said through the door, and then turned to Ashwind. "I'm needed," she said. "I must speak to the Captain of the Field and Marshal Berris."

"Before you go," Ashwind said, "you need to know what I came to tell: Oakhallow told me of Verrakai to the north of him—sensed through the trees of his Grove. I came north, following their trail from deep in Konhalt lands into yours. I did not go as fast as I might, having slowed to give aid to wounded trees. As I went, I raised the forest against them so they could not get past me to the south. I came upon them—it must have been but a few hours after you had passed. They were indeed heading southwest. They thought to attack me with their magery, believing me to be a mere wanderer at first."

"How many?"

"Three, one of them injured. When they realized my nature, it was too late for them; they were trapped. They are penned there in your forest, and to my knowledge no magery will free them."

"You didn't kill them?"

"My powers are not for death," Ashwind said. "I intended to ask you to come and render your judgment, as you are the lord there."

"I cannot," Dorrin said. "My duty to the king holds me here. If you can help this lad—Daryan, his name is—please do so and I will return here when I can."

"You are tired," Ashwind said. He laid Daryan's hand down carefully and came to her. A breath of the summer forest seemed to surround her. "Permit me." Without waiting for an answer, he cupped her face in his hands and blew gently onto it. All the scents of a healthy summer woodland filled her nostrils, and she felt at once awake, alert, and rested. He stepped back and turned to the bed once more.

"Thank you," Dorrin said, and went out to face a grange full of men and women, some in Girdish blue and some in Falkian red. She put Daryan out of mind for the time being and explained to them what they must do.

"What if the Pargunese break through?" asked a Girdish woman. "Who will come to help us?"

"Couriers have already ridden for the vills and domains west," Dorrin said. "Some will already be preparing to march here."

"But that fire we saw—"

"If fire comes, we will move aside and let it pass—we cannot stop it," Dorrin said. "That is why I said all must prepare their households to leave in an instant. But what I heard from a King's Squire from Lyonya is that the Pargunese had a quarrel with the new king of Lyonya, and the attack would fall heaviest there. I daresay the Pargunese hope we will stay out of it—they will not want to fight here again, having been defeated so recently."

"Will you be at the border yourself?" the woman asked. Marshal Berris shot her a furious glance; she ignored him.

"Not all the time," Dorrin said. "I must meet with the commanders of any new forces that arrive and organize supplies for all of you. If the Pargunese do come, I will be there. Otherwise I will be at the meet-house, here at the grange, or at the field."

The Marshal and the Captain dismissed their people, then asked, "How is the boy?"

"Did you know a Kuakgan had come?" Dorrin asked. Marshal Berris shook his head. "A Master Ashwind, he says, a wandering Kuakgan without a settled Grove. I thought they all had Groves."

"I've heard of wandering Kuakkgani," the Captain said. "I'm Selyan, by the way, Captain of the local field." He and Dorrin exchanged the Falkian greetings, then he went on. "Marshal Berris tells me it's Duke Serrostin's son."

"My lord Duke." That was Gwenno, at the grange door.

"Yes?"

"The wizard says he has no healing skills that would help. He works with the judicar, he says, with truth spells and such-like."

"Thank you, Gwenno."

"How is he?"

"We're still working, Gwenno. Go back to the meet-house and be ready to bring me any messages."

"Yes, my lord."

"I'd like to meet this Kuakgan," Captain Selyan said.

"Come, then," Dorrin said. "I suppose there are more Kuak-kgani in Lyonya." She led them back to the room where Daryan lay.

"Not in Lyonya, no," Ashwind said, turning from the bed. "The Great Lady of the Ladysforest likes us not, for the old quarrel with the Tree. We travel through, avoiding the Ladys-forest."

"Can you heal him?" Dorrin asked again.

"I am not sure," the Kuakgan said. "My skills work best outside, in the trees, but that would be too cold for this lad right now. And I am a guest in this house—this grange. It is your rules, Marshal, that must be honored here. Duke Verrakai invited me in; I must have your leave to stay."

"If you can heal that boy, you have my leave to do whatever you must and stay as long as you like," Marshal Berris said.

"Time is against us," Master Ashwind said. "The sooner it's done, the better for all these injuries, and already it is almost a full day-span. But the lad is young and not yet full-grown—his own body wants to go on making and knitting up sinews." He looked at Marshal Berris. "Do you have a lad who could gather branches for me?"

MARSHAL BERRIS AND Captain Selyan rolled Daryan onto his stomach and unwrapped the surgeon's bandages. On Daryan's marble-white legs the gashes looked like red mouths with the surgeon's horsehair stitches black across them.

"We must open the wound," Master Ashwind said. "I must find both ends of the heel-strings, and you must hold one while I hunt the other."

Dorrin had watched the Company surgeon reattach a heel-string; she thought she knew what to expect. The spruce twigs steeping in water by the hearth gave off a sharp aromatic steam that cut through the meat-smell of the wound. Her task was simple: hold the slippery lower piece of heel-string firmly in the tongs while the Kuakgan found and pulled down the piece connected to the calf muscles. She expected him to do what the surgeon had done: make an incision up to the bunched muscle, then find and pull down the heel-string. Instead, he leaned close and began to hum. Slowly the muscle relaxed, the hard bulge softening, lengthening, until the tip of the heel-string showed in the wound. Without ceasing his hum, he gestured to Dorrin to pull the piece she held in tongs up to touch the other. With slight moves of his fingers, he directed her to move it a little more—and sideways—and hold. Then, looking up at the Marshal and the Captain, he nodded.

Dorrin felt her own power itching in her fingers but dared not do anything without direction. Master Ashwind waved to the yeoman-marshal by the hearth, and he brought the can of spruce twigs. Master Ashwind's hum changed to a singing murmur Dorrin could not understand. He took three needles of the spruce and laid them across the cut ends, as if they were stitches, then carefully positioned more, all aligned the same. He ran his hand down her arm, and she understood he wanted her to use her magery as well. She released her power, as she had for Duke Marrakai, for the Kuakgan to direct. Though she felt no real connection to the wound, the spruce needles sank into the heel-string. For a moment she could see the green lines of them beneath the glistening white, and then they disappeared. Still singing, Master Ashwind touched her arm again, pointed to the tongs, and mimed opening them. Dorrin did so, and the heel-string now showed unbroken beneath the cut skin. Ashwind sprinkled water from the can of twigs into the wound, then held the edges of skin together, and slowly, from one side to the other, the skin rejoined. Then he sat back on his heels and shook out his arms.

"It's—it's healed!" Marshal Berris said. "Will it—is it strong enough for him to walk on?"

"Yes. But there are three more wounds, and I may not have

strength for all of them in the time remaining. I am thinking, a lad with one lame leg and one thumbless hand is better off than a lad with two sound legs and no thumbs. I must try for a thumb next, but it is a longer and harder healing, though I need no assistance but the Tree's for that. I must go outside now and draw strength from the taig."

Dorrin looked at the Marshal and the Captain, and they stared back. "Well. That was . . . I don't know what."

"Was your magery involved, Duke Verrakai?" Marshal Berris asked.

"I'm not sure. I willed it so, but whether it actually took part in the healing, I don't know."

"One of us, at least, needs to be at the meet-house and ensuring that the militia understand their role," Captain Selyan said.

"I must go," Dorrin said. "Marshal Berris, will you stay in case Daryan wakes?"

"Certainly."

"And if Master Ashwind thinks my magery of assistance for the other heel-string, if he can manage that, I will return at once. Captain Selyan, if you'll accompany me, I can explain what should be done if I must return to the grange."

DORRIN RETURNED TO the meet-house after her last visit to the grange that night in a state of confusion, exhaustion, and amazement. She offered prayers of thanks for the kindness of the gods, that Daryan had now two whole heel-strings and one thumb.

"It will not be strong yet, nor the size of what it was," Master Ashwind had said. "I could not expend the power to grow it out to full size and still mend his other leg. And the other thumb . . . it is too late for the graft."

"I thank you, Master Ashwind," she said.

"Will you now come with me to judge the Verrakaien I have the trees holding?"

"I cannot," Dorrin said. "I told you: I must stay here."

"The boy will do well," Master Ashwind said.

"It is not that," Dorrin said. She thought he had understood.

"I am here at the king's command, because of the Pargunese. I cannot leave."

"Then I must go," Master Ashwind said. "I must return to the trees . . . and you should know that I cannot herd the men closer to a town."

"Does that mean they will go free?"

"I am not sure I can overpower them, and I would have no way to move them," Master Ashwind said. "So they will go free if they have survived so far." He paused. "You could send some of your soldiers with me to take charge of them."

Dorrin shook her head. "I cannot. None of them could withstand the magery. I'm the only one, and I cannot go." As he stood looking at her, she tried to think what argument would convince him to do something different, but she was so tired . . . "Will you return here after you've eased the trees? Since you have no settled Grove?"

"I could, if you wish, but I would rather go where the trees need me." He bowed to her, and then he was out the door and gone, into the darkness.

Gwenno was already asleep on a pallet when Dorrin came into the small room set aside for sleep; she did not wake as Dorrin took off her sword and boots and lay down, still dressed, on the simple bed the mayor had provided.

WHEN SHE WOKE, it was to find the mayor and his Council stirring about the meet-house, waiting for her with fires lit and food ready. Gwenno, already awake and dressed, was halfway through a bowl of porridge, but jumped up when she saw Dorrin and went to fetch another from the hearth.

"The news is good, my lord," the mayor said. "No troops have attacked our borders, and no more of that strange fire has been seen. The Captain asks that you meet him at the border post when you can."

"I will do so as soon as I've cleaned up and eaten," Dorrin said. "I was up late last night."

"Yes, my lord. And the Marshal sent word the lad's doing better and he himself has gone out to make sure the yeomen are in their assigned places; a yeoman-marshal is with the lad."

"That's a relief." Dorrin sat down; Gwenno set a bowl of porridge and a mug of sib in front of her.

"Would you like me to warm water for a bath?" she asked.

"If you'd just bring a can of hot water upstairs, Gwenno, I'll take a bucket bath—it's all I have time for. I thank you, Mayor, for your hospitality. Please, while I'm eating, tell me what else you know."

"No word yet from Sir Flanits and those Royal Guards you sent off to find Beclan, my lord. But I suppose there wouldn't be."

"No—I pray Sir Flanits finds Beclan unharmed and does not stumble unawares on the renegades." She was not at all certain that the Kuakgan's power with the taig could overcome magery.

And when would reinforcements come? Mahieran troops should be starting now, if the Duke had mustered them at the first alarm. She'd sent word to the domains just across the river to move their troops east in case the Pargunese attacked there. So far, two boatloads of ten, a mere twenty, had shown up.

CHAPTER SEVEN

BECLAN MAHIERAN PUSHED ahead through the blowing snow. Behind him, his little band of Duke's Company and Verrakai militia continued to crunch along, making no complaint. He was their commander, and the Phelani soldiers had enforced appropriate discipline on the Verrakai. Two tensquads instead of the three hands the other squires were allowed to command. Despite Duke Verrakai's occasional scoldings, Beclan was sure his extra troops showed she knew he was the most senior, the most qualified. This was his third patrol with them and the farthest west; he felt that he now had their full respect as both Duke Verrakai's squire and Duke Mahieran's son.

True, this morning his sergeant had suggested they might wait a day, that the Duke would not mind if they were back a day late because of weather that she would have experienced herself, but he had nodded respectfully when Beclan insisted. Vossik always showed proper courtesy, and Beclan was glad Duke Verrakai had assigned the man to his group, another clear sign that she considered Beclan first among the squires.

Now, however, Beclan was less sure of his decision. The snow had thickened; the trail so easy to follow from Deerhollow to Woody Ford was now deep in snow. There was—there should be—a way shelter coming up in the form of a sheep pen, but he could not see it. He wasn't lost—he was sure he wasn't lost—but in the storm it was impossible to judge time or precise direction; the sky was impenetrable cloud.

His father's last letter, in answer to his enthusiastic report about being given more men to command than the other squires, had been more warning than congratulatory. "I think it's the best thing she could do for you, but don't be cocky, boy.

Not with winter coming. You've got some experienced troops, you say, and they'll have campaigned in winter. You've never done more than ride in to Vérella from home, and even then not in a bad snowstorm. Listen to them. This is not like being squire to Marrakai or Serrostin; Verrakai can teach you things about the military none of the rest of us know."

He couldn't argue with his father, not through letters. But Duke Verrakai had said the squires must make decisions, learn to command, not just lean on the experienced veterans. She'd also said not to ignore their advice. When Gwenno Marrakai had asked if they always had to take that advice, Duke Verrakai had said yes if danger was imminent but otherwise no. But, she had also said a squire who refused advice would be responsible for the outcome.

Beclan scowled at the memory. When he'd left home the first time, his father and his cousin Mikeli had both given him a special mission: to watch that new Verrakai Duke and report anything indicative of treason or abuse of magery. He'd been excited about that, alert and ready to find out her secrets . . . and, over time, disappointed to find that she had none. Or she was cleverer than he'd thought. When she had first assigned the squires to take patrols out, he had tried to enlist the other two to keep watch in his absence—usually at least one would be at the house—but Gwenno and Daryan both had refused.

And his father had forbidden him to use the king's name to persuade the others.

He didn't dislike Dorrin Verrakai. If not for her, he'd have been squire to Marrakai or Serrostin—the one entirely too enthusiastic and the other too plodding for his taste. He'd enjoyed being the tallest and by a quarter-year the oldest of the three. He'd enjoyed meeting Paksenarrion, though something in her clear gray eyes made him uncomfortable.

But he wasn't making a name for himself, stuck over here in a domain mishandled for generations by its former lords. None of the little steadings and vills were as prosperous as his father's; the people were poor and dirty and ignorant. They hadn't even recognized the colors of his family knots, and he wasn't sure they even knew a Mahieran sat on the throne of Tsaia.

He sank ever deeper into his thoughts, trying to ignore the way his face felt, the snow building up on his left side.

"Sir! *Sir!*"

The shout from behind roused him. He turned to look. His sergeant was just behind, pointing. "What is it?" he asked.

"The shelter, sir. Just there. We might stop, give the horses a break."

Shame flooded him. He hadn't seen it. He, the leader, hadn't seen it. "Yes, of course," he said. He turned his horse's tail to the wind and followed the sergeant. The others were already in the enclosure, which he could see now had dry-laid stone walls and a low building that looked hardly big enough for them all. His horse stopped, head down, inside the gate. One of the others came up to hold his horse while he dismounted. The sergeant met him.

"You go on in, sir; we'll take care of your horse. You been breaking trail. We'll have something hot in no time."

Beclan brushed off as much snow as he could before stooping through the doorway into darkness. Out here in the southwest of Verrakai domain, none of the improvements Dorrin had planned and begun nearer the house had taken place, so the hut was not only dark and cramped, but flakes of snow had sifted through the roof and the packed dirt floor stank of sheep droppings. No one had thought to store dry wood for the next arrivals; only a couple of very dirty rough-tanned fleeces lay in one corner, visible when one of the troops finally got a torch from their baggage mule alight. For a wonder, there was a crude fireplace in one corner. Beclan leaned on the wall as the Phelani soldiers badgered the others into finding wood and starting a fire.

When the sergeant came in again, Beclan said, "I think we'd better stay here the night."

"Very good, sir," the sergeant said. Beclan was sure he wanted to add, "We'd have been better off to stay in the vill," but he didn't. Instead he organized the work parties and set one team to cut branches from the pines and spruces to make a rough shelter for their horses.

Nonetheless, it was a miserable afternoon and night: what fuel they found was wet, and in the end only the dried lumps of cow and sheep dung would burn. The little fireplace smoked, and melting snow on the thatch dripped cold here and there. The shelter became crowded, smelly, and smoky though never comfortably warm.

Beclan knew he should not feel sorry for himself—he was too old for that and a royal besides—but he did feel sorry for himself. Here he was, in a filthy stinking hut, with only trail rations to eat and nothing to sleep on but dirt and sheep dung, while other people—other squires, even barons' squires—lounged in houses that didn't leak, warmed by fires that didn't smoke, eating real food hot from kitchens, looking forward to sleeping in warm beds and putting on clean clothes in the morning. His brother Rothlin and the king were probably having a jolly evening with their friends. When he finally slept, he had bad dreams he did not quite remember when he woke, but their dark mood stayed with him.

In the morning, the snow had stopped, though it lay deep on what had been their trail.

"We'll make Deerhollow by nightfall, sir, no doubt," the sergeant said. He looked entirely too cheerful, Beclan thought.

"I mistook which side of the trail," Beclan said.

"Easy to miss in the storm, sir," the sergeant said. "Now the snow's stopped, shouldn't be a bad day if it doesn't start again."

The sky was still covered with furrowed clouds, but higher and a different gray than the day before. Beclan's horse kicked out a couple of times, then settled to a steady pace in the knee-deep snow. Deerhollow, with the promise of real fires and better quarters, straddled both sides of the trail, so there was no missing it when they came near.

He was the more astonished to see a man he recognized as one of the grooms at the steading come out of one cottage.

"Squire Beclan!" he called, staggering and slipping in the snow as he hurried forward. He waved a message tube. "The Duke says you must hurry. She's gone—she needs you."

Beclan stared. "What?"

"She says it's war, Pargun invading Lyonya—"

Beclan threw himself off his horse. "Let me see!" His fingers, stiff with cold, fumbled at the ties that held the tube closed; he finally got it open and tipped out the curl of paper. Dorrin's handwriting was clear, and her orders plain:

> *Beclan: Pargun has invaded Lyonya with a new weapon of magical fire. I am gone to fulfill His Majesty's command that I take charge as Constable of all forces defending the realm. Daryan and all I could muster from the immediate vicinity are with me—not above twenty. Gwennothlin went ahead with the Lyonyan King's Squire who gave us warning. Gather what troops you can, from every vill and steading and grange on your way, and bring them to Harway. Be alert for spies the Pargunese may have sent ahead. Do not engage a superior force but evade them and report here.*
> *Dorrin, Duke Verrakai*

The seal looked the same as every other time he'd seen it.

Though it was cold, Beclan felt as if fire tingled in his veins. He had never felt so alive in his life. War. Here. Now. His chance to show what he could do, his chance for glory. Was this what the king had felt that night when he first learned of Verrakaien treason?

And . . . was this another Verrakaien treason?

He handed the paper to his sergeant. "Do you think this is the Duke's writing and signature?"

"Yes, no doubt at all. Why?"

Beclan chewed his lip for a moment. "I must be sure," he said. "I must not raise a troop if this is some enemy's plot . . . I mean, there was no hint of this when we left."

"Enemies don't give warning, sir, when they mean to attack. The Pargunese would not stand on the farther shore and say please."

"Very well, then." Beclan looked around. This village, as he knew from having passed through before, had only three able-bodied men of fighting age, thirteen having fallen or been crippled in the attack on Phelan. He pulled out the village roll from his saddlebag and called the names. No one answered.

"That Dunnon, he's away," the groom said. "Left at day-break, he did, on account of some boy come in with word of sheep straying."

"Did you tell them what the Duke said?" the sergeant asked.

"Well, o' course I did," the groom said. "I mean, they wondered who I was and why, and I had to say."

"You'll not find a one of them, sir," the sergeant said quietly to Beclan. "They'll be hiding out somewhere they know and we don't. We could spend days and not find them. Best we go on."

"But—they're bound to serve. And the Duke told me to muster them."

"Sir, think a little. Three men trying to do the work of sixteen so their families will live through the winter. They've got no reason to love Dukes of Verrakai out here. The Duke doesn't expect you to make bullocks of calves overnight. Bring what you can, any who come willingly, and leave the rest. If the war goes bad . . . well, it hasn't yet."

It made sense; Beclan, looking around, could see no sign of healthy men lurking about. But it was sense he did not want to see; he had a responsibility to the Duke, and he would look better if he came in with fifty or even a hundred than making excuses why he had so few.

"We could make it to Thistlemead today if we get on," the sergeant said.

"Yes, Sergeant, I hear you," Beclan said. "Fine, then. Come with us," he said to the groom. "I suppose you told everyone along the way what the Duke said."

"Well . . . o' course I did. Didn't see nothing wrong with it." The groom looked worried now. Beclan was glad of that. The man should have known not to tell the Duke's business to everyone. Half the muster might be running into the woods as soon as they heard his troop approaching. Though maybe, closer in, the villagers who had actually met the Duke would be more loyal.

At Thistlemead, four men stood by the way as Beclan's troop rode in. "There should be six," Beclan said, consulting the muster roll. Not to his surprise, one was reported too sick to rise from his bed and produced hacking coughs when Beclan went into his smoky little hut. The other simply wasn't there.

"A bad time of year," the sergeant said. "I would say four

out of six, this season, with the fever going round, shows this village well, sir." His expression dared Beclan to say anything critical.

The men had no mounts and hardly any equipment. Beclan considered the difficulty of transporting twenty men on sixteen horses and one pack mule through fresh snow. He looked at the sergeant, who looked back. "We'll need to—" he began, and started to swing a leg over the saddle.

"No sir," the sergeant said. "You're breaking trail, sir." He turned to the troop. "You four," he said. "Time to stretch your legs. Let these men ride a bit."

The men looked alarmed; Beclan wondered if they'd ever been on a horse, but remembering what the Duke had said about sergeants, he kept quiet and put his foot back in the stirrup. Soon they were on their way, and every so often the sergeant changed out another four to walk.

That hadn't gone so badly, Beclan thought, but at the next two villages, none of those on the muster roll showed up. Beclan could just imagine himself reporting to the Duke with a mere four.

He called the sergeant aside. "The groom's put the fright into all the places he visited, just as you said. But he followed our route out from the steading. What if we go back north another way? There's that trail Daryan was sent on, west of Kindle and Oakmotte, seven or eight vills along it. They won't be expecting us. It shouldn't take us any longer than going by that more eastern route, and it's farther from the border with Lyonya, so if the Pargunese do break through, we're more likely to evade them."

"That's good thinking, sir, except the Duke said come directly. She knows what your route was on this trip; if she needs you, that's where she'll expect to find you."

"But she's gone to Harway. What she needs are reinforcements—and I don't see us getting them on the route the groom took, do you?"

"No, sir, I don't. But sir, with all due respect, you're the king's cousin. The Duke wants reinforcements, but she wants you safe even more. We know what's on the route we came out, and the groom followed. We don't know what's on this other trail."

Beclan's frustration of the past few days nearly overwhelmed him, but he fought it down. "If it was safe enough for the Duke to assign Daryan to it, it's surely safe enough for me—for us. And it's farther from the border, so the Pargunese are less likely to have come that far if they did cross the border."

"Sir . . . with respect . . . it's always best to let senior command know where you are."

"We can send the groom back to Verrakai Steading and on to Harway," Beclan said. "But we'll be there before he is."

"Yes, sir," the sergeant said. Beclan could tell he didn't approve, but after all . . . the Duke had put him in charge. And he had twenty-four soldiers and himself, twenty of them armed.

Two days later, the next villages had yielded a total of twenty-three men. They had no arms or horses, but they were able-bodied, and each had a sack of food for the journey. They were also slow, since it was no longer feasible to switch off horses with only twenty horses and forty-two men. Besides, they needed the extra pack animals.

"We could split them off," Beclan said to the sergeant at one of the rest breaks. "You could take them, with an escort, and I could go on to the villages."

"No, sir," the sergeant said. "With all respect, sir, the Duke charged me to stay with you, as she did one of us with each squire. Your life and limb are my responsibility."

"But I'm not a child," Beclan said. He knew the moment he'd said it that it was a childish thing to say; he hated himself for that hint of whine.

"No, sir, but you're not Duke Verrakai, neither, and it's to her I've pledged my oath. She bade me obey your orders up to a point, and leaving you to take another route by yourself is that point. Where you go, sir, I follow."

Beclan had no doubt he meant it: Vossik had been a sergeant in the Duke's Company . . . he had been a soldier longer than Beclan had been alive, and he had chosen to stay with Dorrin Verrakai. Beclan understood such loyalty, but he still felt annoyed at the slow progress they were making. Somewhere things were happening, and he wasn't there.

"Well, then, why not send most of them on east to the improved road—you were right; this trail is slower with so many. You and a hand of others can stay with me. That's surely enough."

"We could all go east now, sir. We've surely got most of the muster that's left along this route."

"We could . . ." Beclan thought about it. He would be coming in with more than he'd left with . . . but a round fifty would be so much better, a full half-cohort. "But the Duke may need every body we can dig out. I can't justify holding up all these to slog along on a narrow trail when I know the need is urgent, but two more villages—if we get but five from each, we'll be contributing a full half-cohort."

"I suppose Voln could command these," the sergeant said. He chewed his mustache. "It's risky, sir—risky for you. Most of us old-timers will have to go with the larger bunch, be sure none of 'em get the idea to slope off home without you there. At least they're a day away from their homes. But you promise me, sir, if something does happen and I say go, you will go— no matter what."

"Is that what the Duke said?" Beclan said.

"Yes, sir, it is. It's my honor, you see. Your safety."

Beclan felt a cold chill down his back. As a boy, he'd expected protection from his father's vassals—adults protected children anyway. But for years he had not thought of anyone literally dying to save him. Yet there the sergeant was, the same unemotional quiet man who had been assigned to him . . . and he would send Beclan away, to save him, and die holding off pursuit.

Until that moment, he realized, he had not really grasped the commander's dilemma, though Duke Verrakai had spoken of it to the squires more than once. *We send those who trust us to their deaths*, she'd said. *That is what battlefield command is. When someone gives you an oath, you are responsible for your commands, so think before you command. If you are not able to accept this, you are not fit for it.*

War had come, and the Duke would be doing that now, as she had done before. He must try to do the same. Out of a dry mouth he said, "Well, Sergeant, I so promise. And I also swear not to lead us into trouble—if it comes to us, I cannot stop it."

"Very well, sir." The sergeant stared into the snowy woods for a moment, then smiled. "I don't expect there's much to worry about after a storm like that the other day." He gave over command of the muster to Voln, then named the five Verrakai militia who would stay with him and Beclan.

"T' young lord's not comin'?" asked one of the men from the last village.

"We're going to Thornapple and Oakmotte," Beclan said. "Then on to Harway."

"But—" the man began.

Two others shushed him; one said, "He's the king's cousin; he can do what he wants, Tam."

Beclan felt a tiny glow of pride that he had not told them and one had recognized him.

He and his smaller escort, all mounted, passed through Oakmotte—no muster there—and were most of the way to Thornapple along the crest of a hill where the snow was not so deep when Beclan heard someone calling for help off to the east. He turned his horse off the trail, into deeper snow.

"Sir, stop—"

"Someone needs help. Didn't you hear?"

"Yes, sir, I heard a yell. But there's a war, the Duke says. It might be an enemy."

"And it might be one of the Duke's own people in trouble. We have to find out." He reined in just as his horse lurched, snorted in alarm, and then slipped down the slope, steeper than it had looked under its concealing blanket. "I can't stop here," he yelled back up to the others. "He's sliding."

The sergeant's curse was eloquent and complex; Beclan spared a moment to admire it while he tried to help his horse balance. They ended up in a hollow, the horse belly-deep in snow. Beclan looked back up to the trail; they had left an obvious track that looked very difficult indeed, ice patches visible under the disturbed snow. "Sorry," he said to the horse and to the sergeant. "I'll see if we can get back up."

"Leave the horse," the sergeant said. "You might make it."

"What about the horse?" Beclan asked. He did not relish the

idea of dismounting in snow that deep, and he noticed that the "sir" had disappeared.

"It'll do better without you on top."

That made sense, yet he wanted to find a way to ride up. "Maybe there's a gentler slope a little way back—or along."

"And maybe it's worse."

Beclan's horse, clearly uneasy, snorted repeatedly, stamping one hoof after another. Beclan slid off on the uphill side and found himself uncomfortably close to his nervous horse, in snow over waist deep. It would be really stupid to slip and fall under the horse.

He pulled the reins over the horse's head, untied his saddlebags to relieve the horse of more weight, and slung them over his shoulder. He felt unbalanced but, on the sergeant's direction, turned the horse in its length several times, hoping it would trample out a space from which to scramble up the slope. Gradually, he and the horse together made a space where the snow was no more than halfway to his knees.

Then he tried to climb up the slope, digging his hands into the snow and kicking at it to make steps. He had gone up a little more than his own height when his feet slipped out from under him, and he slid back down as if he were playing a child's game. He tried again, furious with himself for looking silly—though the men above weren't laughing—and again slipped and slid, this time almost all the way to his horse, which snorted and feinted a kick at him.

"This won't do," he heard the sergeant say, but he flung himself at the slope once more, and once more failed. "Sir, we're coming down," the sergeant said. "You nor your horse can make it up. Put those saddlebags back on him and mount, so you can get clear if one of ours falls." To the rest he said, "You two—back down that way—at least three lengths apart—and you others, come forward with me. Don't start downslope until I give you the signal, and remember: point 'em straight down and sit back. Whatever you do, don't yank 'em to the side."

Beclan tied the saddlebags on again, put the reins back over his horse's head, and mounted. Once he was up, he glanced up the slope and saw that the sergeant had positioned them all facing the slope and separated enough that one horse falling wouldn't trip another. He heard the sergeant say "Now!" and the other horses started down. The sergeant, Beclan saw, leaned right back and his horse seemed almost to swim down the slope, snorting with every stride, until he had gone past Beclan's level. One of the other men lost his balance and yanked sideways on the reins as he slipped; his horse, twisting, fell to that side and then rolled, legs thrashing in air for a moment. A sound like a branch breaking came from underneath; the horse squealed.

There was nothing to be done for rider or horse. The man was dead, his body a horse-length from the horse, his skull crushed, the horse with a broken leg. Without saying a word, the sergeant cut its throat; the blood spurted out onto the snow. The men looked at Beclan; he could scarcely meet their eyes. If he had not been stupid . . . but he hadn't meant to slide down . . . he hadn't known the slope was that steep.

"Sir," the sergeant said. "With all respect, it is my advice that we go east, over to the other road, and go straight to Harway."

"I'm sorry," Beclan said through stiff lips. He felt like throwing up. "What about . . . him?" He could not think of the man's name.

"*Hadrin,* sir?" The sergeant's slight emphasis made it clear he was aware Beclan didn't know the name. "We'll take him along, of course. Can't leave him out here in this." Quickly the sergeant set the other men to work as Beclan eased his horse down to their level. One cut the girth of the dead horse's saddle and pulled it free, then opened the saddlebags to find Hadrin's spare shirt to wrap around that ruined head. As Beclan came close, the sergeant said, "If you'll just hold the horses, sir," and handed him the reins in a bunch.

The call for help came again, this time clearer. Beclan looked in that direction but could see nothing; the sergeant and men were using the dead man's cloak to wrap his body, tying it closed; they didn't seem to hear. He did not know what to do; he felt wrong, sitting there just holding the reins while they worked . . . and none of them now would meet his eyes, not even the sergeant. Was it because he hadn't used Hadrin's

name? Did they know he'd forgotten it, or did they think—
what did they think?

You must know your people, the Duke had said. *You must
know their names and their faces, their families and their
hopes and fears.* He had known their names—at least he had
learned them once—but . . . but they were just Verrakai serfs,
really, with so thick an eastern accent he could barely understand them, and anyway, all they ever talked about was . . . he
couldn't even remember. What did he know about Hadrin?
Married . . . yes. An ugly wife with a scar on her face that
pulled up one side of her mouth; he'd wondered why anyone
had married her. Children? He didn't know.

He should know. He should know all those things the Duke
had said, and . . . he hadn't bothered. Gwennothlin had. Daryan
had. He'd heard them talking about their patrol groups.
What had *he* been doing, those times he might have been
learning? Thinking of his rank. Thinking of what he would tell
his father, his brothers, when he came back to Vérella.

And now he had led these men into danger, and Hadrin had
died because he himself couldn't climb up the side of a hill in
the snow, and it was all his fault.

The call came again. "Help! Help!" This time all the men
turned toward it; the sergeant shook his head, then gave Beclan
a hard look that Beclan interpreted as contempt. He dismounted, still holding the reins he'd been given, and looked
the remaining horses over. His own had a scrape on one knee;
one of the others had a jagged but shallow tear on its neck,
probably from a branch. The other four were apparently unharmed. He dug into his saddlebags for the jar of ointment he
carried and smeared it on the injuries.

"We'll put him on your bay, Efrin," the sergeant said. Beclan
looked up and saw two of the men carrying the cloak-wrapped
bundle toward him. "You can ride double with Pedar; we'll
rotate the riders." There were two bays; Beclan couldn't remember which one Efrin rode, and the reins were all tangled
in his hand. The sergeant moved past him, saying, "Just drop
them," and grabbed the right set, leading the unmarked bay
forward. Beclan scooped up the reins again, watching as the

men heaved Hadrin's corpse over the saddle and lashed it on; the horse snorted, but the sergeant soothed it.

Finally they were all mounted again.

"We'll be going through woods without a clear trail," the sergeant said. "Easy to get off our aim that way. I should break trail." He looked at Beclan; Beclan nodded. He still felt sick to his stomach. "While it's day and the sky's mostly clear, it'll be easy going east, but picking a way in this snow won't be. If it looks like a gentle slope down, could be a drop-off under it. So follow single file. If I go down—" He chewed his mustache longer than usual. "I'd best not," he said finally.

Beclan rode second, feeling the gazes of the others as if they were made of cold steel chilling his back. The sergeant's progress through the snowy woods was not straight; Beclan wondered, the first time he went around a low hump in a sort of opening rather than straight across, but the ragged root-end of a storm-felled tree, visible as they came even with it, proved the sergeant had seen danger where he himself had seen only an easier route.

He looked ahead, past the sergeant, trying to see what the sergeant saw, trying to anticipate where he would turn and which way.

"Help! Help!" Closer now, and he could tell it was a man's voice for certain. Ahead and to the heart-side, where the trees were thicker. Beclan could not help noticing that the sergeant's head did not so much as twitch in the direction of the call. He wanted to get his young fool of a squire to the Duke, that was it, and others would die because he would not risk Beclan's skin. Because Beclan had proved himself stupid and one had already died of his stupidity. It wasn't fair.

He felt his shoulders hunching and tried to sit straighter, but the denser woods made it necessary to bend and twist to avoid being knocked in the head or swept off the saddle entirely. He tried to fix the faces of the men with him to their names, to their horses: Efrin usually rode the plain bay now carrying Hadrin's body, Pedar rode the chestnut now carrying double, Vidar rode the bay with a blaze and a hind sock, and that meant Simi-with-spots rode the roan.

"Help! Help! Please!"

The sergeant angled slightly away from the call and the thicker trees that hid whoever had called. "Sergeant," Beclan said. "Shouldn't we at least look?"

"I'm not risking you, sir. And there's something uncanny about these calls. They don't come from the same direction all the time."

"They're always on our heart-hand—"

"Yes—and we've been turning back and forth to get through the forest. I'm not even sure we've been making as much eastward as I wanted. From what we first heard, we should've passed the calls by now, be hearing them behind . . . but the last three times they've been abreast of us."

The woods had thickened again, what seemed a large area of dense pines and spruce with barely room for the horses to pass between them. No wonder this area had never been farmed, Beclan thought. It seemed colder and dimmer here; the crisp tree shadows that had lain on the snow earlier, making it obvious which way was sunward, were gone. When he looked up, the sky had hazed over; the low winter sun could not be seen at all for the height and density of the trees.

"We should turn south," the sergeant said. "Sword-hand, and sharply."

"Help! Help! Please help!"

Beclan glanced back at the others; all were staring into the trees on the heart-hand side, their faces, in that shade, pale and pinched. He shuddered, suddenly afraid, ashamed of that fear, but still . . . "Yes," he said to the sergeant. "Sword-hand, and now."

The sergeant nodded and reined his horse to the right . . . but there was no space between the trees that way. He gave a hard kick; his horse took two nervous steps forward, then snorted and threw up its head, backing quickly.

"Let me try," Beclan said, but his horse, too, would not push through the snow-covered branches no matter how he kicked. Nor could the others. Behind them, the trees had closed, a solid mass of green.

"Magery," the sergeant said. "It has to be. We got in and can't get out—it's a trap of magery, with tree magic. Means a Kuakgan, I'll be bound. We must have stumbled into a Grove.

But a Kuakgan who could do this wouldn't be calling for help. Happen it's another trespasser. If we find the Kuakgan and explain, we'll be safe."

Beclan's heart hammered in his chest, as the skim of clouds overhead thickened and it seemed darker every moment. "But if we can't find a way . . ."

"We can probably go onward. Kuakkgani tree magic shapes Groves to maze trespassers and prevent them doing harm to the Grove itself. If the Kuakgan's gone visiting somewhere, we might be stuck here several days, but in winter they usually stay close to their Groves. Funny that a Kuakgan settled on Verrakai lands . . . I'd have thought the Verrakaien would drive one out."

"Could they?"

"Oh, enough of them, probably. But there's a feel of Kuakkgani magic about this, now we're in it. A friend of mine, back in the Duke's Company, was kuakgannir and told me a lot about what a Kuakgan does. However, whoever's calling for help won't be a Kuakgan and could be dangerous, so best be alert." He had raised his voice so the others could hear; they all nodded. "If we're lucky, the Kuakgan will find us soon and give us a meal and a night's shelter even before setting us on our way."

As they rode on, it was clear that the opening in the trees now formed a narrow trail that curved more and more, so they could not see far ahead or any opening to either side. Gloom deepened, but although the clouds now formed a solid gray lid overhead, no wind stirred the branches. Another cry came, sounding a little closer, but still off to the heart-hand side.

"It's a spiral," the sergeant said over his shoulder to Beclan. "Leads us in, won't let us out. We could stop, camp here overnight, have better light to meet whoever's in there."

"Do you think there's an open space ahead?"

"Almost certainly. What Kolya said was that these Grove traps led to a clearing."

"This trail's narrow," Beclan said. "We'd be separated, each with his horse, and no clear sight from back to front, if we camped on the trail. Wouldn't it be better in the clearing?"

"That's true, sir. It's just that we don't know what we'll meet."

They came out of the trees suddenly, into a clearing perhaps ten horse-lengths across, surrounded by dense trees; Beclan's horse pricked its ears and trotted a couple of strides, then stopped. Beclan felt dazed, as if he had come out of a cool house into hot sun. Was that the Kuakkgani magic?

Across the clearing, two men crouched over a third beside a makeshift shelter of old branches and leaves. They looked like most winter travelers, bundled into heavy clothes and winter cloaks, not like Pargunese soldiers. Beclan relaxed; his sergeant did not. "Who are you?" he called.

"Travelers in distress," one of the men called back. "And I see that you, too, have had trouble—is that not a man's body on that horse?"

"The horse fell with him," the sergeant said. "Broke his neck and back."

"We're trapped here," the other man said. "Can you help us? We're out of food now, and our friend's hurt."

Beclan realized that the man had not needed to shout. They were closer . . . he didn't remember walking closer . . . he looked at Sergeant Vossik. Vossik stared ahead, his body rigid. Beclan glanced behind; the other four were walking forward slowly, their gait awkward and their expressions blank. He touched his sword-hilt and drew it out slowly.

Even as Beclan thought *magery,* Vossik drew his sword and lunged forward, stopping as suddenly as if he'd run into a wall, shuddering. Then he turned slowly, jerkily, and Beclan saw that his face was contorted.

"Run, lad," he said in a hoarse voice, as if he had been hit in the throat. "*Run!*"

Beclan stared—remembered his promise that he would run—remembered also Sergeant Stammel, met at Dorrin's city house. Was Vossik being invaded and resisting? He could not leave Vossik to that horror . . . he had to help him.

As he hesitated, Vossik lurched closer, his eyes desperate. "Go!" Then, as if realizing Beclan would not or could not, his expression changed to determination.

"Kill me," he said.

"No!" This could not be real—not so suddenly. Beclan looked around wildly—there must be someone, somewhere, to help.

"Do . . . it . . . save . . . you . . ." Vossik said. He dropped his own sword and staggered close enough to grab Beclan's blade with his gloved hands and pull it toward himself. "Better die, lad," he said. "I know you're brave enough. Like this."

Hand by hand, he forced the blade into his belly while Beclan, horrified, stood and watched, unable to do anything, even let go the grip.

"Gird . . ." Vossik said at last, and fell; the blade dragged free, and Vossik's blood reddened the snow.

"We still have four," one of the men said. "Enough for all . . ."

That horror broke Beclan's immobility; he could at least save the other men from that fate. With a cry he whirled and cut down the others of his patrol. They did not resist much; the magery slowed them, made them clumsy, and it was like killing calves or pigs. He wanted to throw up, scream, cry . . . but he could no longer deny the reality: he was trapped with three killers who wanted not just his life but his body, his self.

He sent frantic prayers to Gird. *Help me! Save me! Don't let them!*

But already a honey-sweet voice in his head crooned to him, stroking his panicked mind to near stillness.

He had heard of magery and its evils all his life, but he had not seen the former Duke's magery at work; even his brother had not seen it, for Rothlin had not been in the room. He had not seen Dorrin Verrakai's use of magery in the courtyard; he had been deemed too young to ride in the procession and had spent that part of the day with his mother and younger siblings. He expected pain, struggle, terror . . . not this . . . this *gentleness*.

"You are the king's cousin . . . but why is *he* king and not your father? Why should not the crown come to you in time? It would be easy, young lord, if you have the courage and the wit . . ."

A voice as sweet in his mind as honey in his mouth, telling

him everything he had ever thought about Mikeli and Camwyn, soothing him with every dream he had imagined for himself.

"Kings should have power—power in themselves. Your cousins have none, were chosen to have none, to be weak rulers in a realm that needs strength. You are strong and could be stronger yet . . . if you have the courage. You could return power to the Mahierans, power they should never have given up."

Beclan could scarcely see, now, for the crowding visions . . . himself on a great charger, sword held high, himself in the Hall at Vérella, striding down the center, ranks of nobles on either side bowing low, trumpets blaring.

"Mikeli the weak cannot even open the box in which that other crown lies, but *you* could. You could have both crowns; you could restore the ancient lineage to its heritage of power; you could be the king . . . and in your heart of hearts you know that."

He struggled to speak and croaked, "How?"

Silky and sweet that voice, gentle and coaxing. "How? You need but let us help you. Help you discover your powers, help you understand yourself better, help you achieve what you dream . . . what you deserve . . ."

But magery was evil. He'd grown up knowing it was evil; he'd been told to watch for any sign that Dorrin was misusing it . . . he had seen blind Stammel, Vossik's struggles . . .

"*Your* life. *Your* power. *Your* crown . . ."

All those times, as a boy, he'd thought his older brother weak for deferring to Mikeli just because Mikeli was the prince, and even his father—a duke of the realm, a grown man— deferred to Mikeli . . .

"You are the strong one, Beclan Mahieran. You are the one chosen . . ."

Chosen by whom? he wanted to ask, but he could not speak now. In his mind's images, he was even taller, stronger, more handsome, more powerful. Again the crowds bowed; light flashed from his fingers, and in front of him the crowns glittered . . . ruby and gold and pearl . . . sapphire and silver and diamond . . . He moved his hand, and the crowns rose, hovering in the air before him.

He opened his eyes, and there before his feet lay Vossik. Vossik dead, Vossik's blood staining the snow. When had he moved back here? He could not remember.

"Taste that blood and see . . ." the voice said. "Your first kill—taste it!"

Before he realized it, he was kneeling in the bloody snow, staring at Vossik's dead face. Without his will, his hand reached out to the wound, the blood . . . and there, bloody but gleaming a little in the dimming light, was a medallion. He knew it, and his hand rose to his own Gird's symbol. As he touched it, his mind cleared a little. The stench of Vossik's death rasped along his nose; Vossik's courage and honor . . . Beclan blinked back tears.

"Taste the blood," the voice said. "Take the crown you deserve . . ." Its seductive murmur continued as he tried to resist. *Help me! Don't let me give in!* But his hand was already moving back to the bloody wound. He concentrated, forcing it to reach for Vossik's medallion. Light sparkled briefly; the medallion came off its thong as if he'd cut it, and he quickly scrubbed it in the snow, then rubbed it on his cloak. It gleamed brighter. His hand wanted to open, drop it, he longed to taste the bloodstains on his fingers, but he fought that impulse. *Kill me if you must,* he prayed. *Don't let me—*

All at once, as if someone had closed a window, the voices in his head were silent. He rose to his feet, unhindered by compulsion. He put Vossik's medallion safe in his cloak pocket. Two of the men now stood, swords in hand, almost in reach, watching him. The third lay still, and Beclan was sure he was dead.

"Little virgin," one of the men said, grinning. "Did you even know you had the power?"

"I . . . am not a magelord," Beclan said. "It is Gird's power—Gird saved me!"

The man laughed. "There's nothing like the innocence of that first time," he said to the other, who nodded. Then to Beclan, "It would have been easier on you the other way, but we can still overpower you, boy. And we will."

At a nod, both of them came at him, one on either side. Beclan fought with all his skill—with skill he did not realize he had, with frantic prayers for help and the wish that he could slow them the way they had slowed the others—for a time that seemed impossibly long. He could not get breath enough into his burning lungs; his arms felt heavy as logs. Surely they would tire, too—and finally one missed a parry and his own blade slid home. He yanked it out as the man cried out, dropped his sword, and fell. Beclan turned, off balance, saw the other's blade sweeping at him, tried desperately to get his blade across for the parry, knowing he was too slow, and in-stinctively *pushed* with the hope it would miss him. The blade hung in the air, twisted aside; he could see the man's surprise, rage, horror as the sword slid from his grip. Before he could pick it up again, Beclan hit him—once, twice, and again, wild blows. When the man finally fell, Beclan could scarcely be-lieve he himself was still alive and darkness had not fallen.

Shaking with exhaustion and terror, Beclan cut the Ver-rakaien throats with his dagger, all three of them, dead as they were. Then he fell to his knees, emptied his belly on the stained and trampled snow, and cried until it was truly dark. He roused from tears to horror worse than before.

He was alone in the night, still trapped in the clearing with all these dead men, men he had killed. Who knew what their spirits might demand? Across the clearing, he could hear the horses stamping, snorting, their tack jingling and creaking. Wind moaned and hissed like angry ghosts through the ever-greens that closed the trap; in the distance, a branch broke and fell with a resonant thump.

His hand strayed to his Girdish medallion, and he tried to think. If the Verrakaien had not invaded him while alive, surely Gird could protect him against the dead. The horses . . . the horses' saddlebags held food for them and·for him; he could build a fire. He pushed himself up and walked toward the sound of their hooves.

At first they bolted around the clearing, squealing and buck-ing, saddlebags coming loose from several, but finally they quieted, let him get close. He soothed them, dug out handfuls of oats from one saddlebag, and gave each a small portion.

They snuffled at his hands for more. Then he strung a hitch line by feel, tied the horses to it, and lit a fire, using the sticks the Verrakaien had used for a shelter. By its light, he dragged the bodies of his patrol, naming them as he did so, into a neat row. The enemy he left where they lay. He gathered the fallen saddlebags, removed the rest from the saddled horses, pulled out the nose bags and oats, and fed the horses. The sound of their munching comforted him.

By then he was hungry and rummaged in the saddlebags for food for himself. He crouched by the fire, chewing trail bread he barely tasted, staring at the row of men who had died because of him. He was afraid to sleep. He sat the night through, holding the two Girdish medallions, one in either hand.

Surely it was Gird's power, not his own, that had saved him—had twisted that sword from a man's hand, moved it aside from the killing strike aimed at him. He could not be a magelord; no Mahieran had the power. He did not feel different than before, the way he thought magelords must feel. He felt infinitely older and more ashamed. He could see every wrong decision he had made as if painted in bright colors on a page. He longed to be back home, once more a child in his father's house, a child who would grow up better and not make those mistakes. He longed to be with his father now, kneeling before him, telling him, asking his forgiveness . . . not here alone with the bodies of men who had died because of him.

When dawn came, he tried again to leave the clearing, but he could not. He gave the horses another nose bag each of grain, melted snow for them to drink from the leather bucket among the gear, and led them around the clearing before tying them again. Though he was sure the forest was empty, he called out and then blew a blast on Sergeant Vossik's horn. No response to either.

He had food for some days yet; he could use the other supplies to make himself a little shelter, but the thought of being trapped there quickly escalated into "forever," and he imagined himself starving. He looked at the horses and shuddered. He did not want to kill again. Surely the Kuakgan who had made this trap would return. Surely someday he would see his home again, his family. The life he had found so confining and boring, before he became Duke Verrakai's squire, he now remembered with longing. He promised himself, and Gird, and his father that he would never, ever, be so stupid, so selfish, again.

CHAPTER EIGHT

Sir Flanits arrived at Verrakai Steading with his troop to find Beclan had not yet returned. Duke Verrakai's steward made the Royal Guard troop welcome and said no visitors had come since the Duke left for Harway. The next morning Flanits led his troop on, following the route Verrakai's steward had given him.

Several frustrating days later—snow obscuring the track he was supposed to follow and no sign of the young Mahieran—his scout reported fresher marks of both foot and horse heading north away from the trail they were on. Was that the squire and his escort? If so, why had they turned instead of coming straight back as they'd been told? Flanits mentally cursed Duke Verrakai for sending him on this hunt for a boy who was probably perfectly safe when there was a war where he might actually be useful. However wicked renegade Verrakai lords might be, surely they could not overpower so many. At least with some of the men on foot, they would not travel as fast as he with his mounted troop.

The track led to another village, where more men had joined the muster, and another. Most were on foot now, no doubt slowing down the march, and he should be catching up with them. Then the track split. A larger number, mostly on foot, had headed east, back toward Verrakai Steading. A smaller number—all mounted, by the hoofprints—continued north. Sir Flanits had no idea what lay between where he was and where the Verrakai Steading was—or what was farther north. The sketch the steward had given him covered only the route Beclan was supposed to take. Had Beclan gone back east? That would have made sense, but who had continued north?

The stupid boy and his equally stupid escort had not bothered
to leave any clues. Flanits chewed his mustache in frustration.

Though he had seen nothing threatening so far, he could not
push worry aside completely. The very silence and emptiness
of the hills, the distance between the little clusters of poor
huts, made it clear how easily a group of renegades could pass
unseen. Beclan, the king's cousin, fourth from the throne, was
somewhere out here. Anything might happen.

Flanits looked again at the tracks. A king's cousin wouldn't
walk—he'd ride. He'd be with riders. Perhaps he'd gotten bored
with the slow pace of the others and was trying a shortcut to
Harway. "We're going north," he said. He hoped he was right.
A mounted party on the trail of a mounted party lacked the
advantage of speed.

The tracks, he was sure, could not be more than a day old,
and all showed a walking pace. He lifted his reins, and his
mount broke into a trot. As they rode, he noticed that the broad
ridge on which they rode narrowed little by little.

WHEΠ ΤΗΕΥ CAΠE to the next change of direction, Flanits
could not repress an oath. He could not tell who had skidded
down the unexpectedly steep slope of the hill first, but the
dead horse at the bottom, its blood staining the trampled snow
around it, was evidence enough of the danger. He looked up
and back: six horses had gone down in flurries of snow, and
one had tumbled. One first—the little beaten-down oval suggested that its rider had tried to clear a space for an attempt
back up the slope—and others had come down after, in support. That argued for the Mahieran boy to have been the first.

"What now, sir?" asked one of the troopers. "That's a bad
slide."

"Obviously," Flanits said. "Though the others got down
safely." Their tracks were clear, leading away into the trees.
"Jen, ride on a little and see if you find a better place to get
down. I saw none behind us for the last glass or so. We'll rest
the horses." He dismounted, as did the rest, and gave his horse
a handful of oats. He disliked the look of the slope as much
from the ground as from the saddle. A hard freeze overnight

had put a crust on the snow; the ice he could not see would be even more slippery.

Jen came riding back and reported. "Sir, there's no good place. Ridge gets narrower and then drops hard into a cut for a stream, steeper than this and as sharp up again on the other side."

"Must have realized that from a map and decided to go down. Gird grant it wasn't the squire on that horse—" He nodded downslope. "Though I think not. I think he went down first, typical bravado. We'll have to do the same. Not a problem with any of *you*." He grinned at his troop, ignoring the cold in the pit of his stomach. It didn't matter what danger lurked below—slippery ice, rocks, some enemy—they had to go on.

No one fell. At the foot of the slope, he looked briefly at the tracks of the other horses and men's boots. All the tracks led away; the dead horse wasn't his concern.

He led his troop on into the forest, following the obvious track. Apparently, the Mahieran boy—or the sergeant—had chosen to angle almost straight east. Perhaps their map showed another obstacle. After a time, the track curved gently north again. Flanits hoped that meant it headed for a ford or bridge across the stream his own scout had seen. It would make sense to cross the stream farther from the ridge.

When the trees closed in, Flanits stopped and looked around. "This won't do."

"Sir?"

"Unless that stream you saw, Jen, turned due north to the Honnorgat, we should've reached it by now, with the angle of the trail. For that matter, we should've reached the stream that must run between these ridges. Get in among these trees, where we can't see the sky, and we could be lost. That may've happened to them. We'll get back to that little rise and try a horn call from there. Surely they'll have a horn with them."

The trees behind looked thicker than they had, but Flanits had grown up in forested country. Trees and their way of looking completely different from the other side didn't fool him. He set his horse's head to the tracks they'd made coming, and confusion ceased when they rode up onto the little rise cov-

ered with leafless pickoaks and beech instead of dense conifers.

"Now, Medlin," he said. The hunting horn sent its long
sweet call out across the snowy woods. Once. Twice. Again.
They listened. No wind stirred the few pickoak leaves still on
the tree. Then a harsher, slightly deeper tone, one long note,
came back. "Again," Flanits said.

Medlin blew again, this time the Royal Guard Assembly
call. Once more they listened, and once more that single note
came from a distance, this time broken in the middle with a
blat that made Medlin grin.

"Not a good hornist, sir. Bet they were trying for another
note."

"Give them the same call again, Medlin." If it had been a
Royal Guard group, they'd have started for his when they first
heard Assembly. Flanits found he had his mustache between
his teeth again. What would a Mahieran squire do? He should
know at least some of the standard horn signals, including
Assembly, but what about that former Phelani sergeant? They
had their own signals. Who was in charge over there?

Once more the answer was a single long note, this time fading out in a sort of stutter. It didn't sound any closer.

"We'll have to go to them," Flanits said. "Though then we'll
be as lost as they are." Despite his words, he felt better. He was
sure in his heart that Beclan was somewhere near—he had
found the boy in all this empty forest, and that made up for
missing the war.

"Follow their tracks?"

"No. If we can get them to keep blowing that horn, we can
go straight. I think they began to circle the way lost people do.
Once more and everyone point where you think it's coming
from."

Medlin blew Assembly again, and once more the answer
came. Flanits pointed his horse toward the sound, at an angle
to their earlier track. As they came off the rise, the conifers
once again thickened before them, but Flanits turned a little
more north, hoping to skirt the conifers. Heading north should
shorten the distance.

He tried to estimate time passing in his head and, at his best guess of a quarter-glass, told Medlin to blow the horn again. This time the answer was quicker and sounded closer, though no more skilled. Still just one note and not a pure one. They rode on, and after stopping again, Flanits heard running water somewhere ahead. Good—if they found the stream, they could follow that north to the River Road . . . once they found the Mahieran lad.

"We'll go on to the water," he said. "Then blow again." The stream, when they came to it, tumbled noisily over rocks, ice along its margins. Downstream, it curved sharply north. As they watered the horses, Medlin blew Assembly again; this time the answering horn was quicker and almost directly to their sword-side, perhaps a little behind. Flanits felt relief.

They set off again, following the stream until it turned north. They had not gone twenty lengths beyond that when one of the troopers said, "Sir—stop."

"What?" Just when things were going better, Flanits thought.

"I feel something."

Flanits prayed for patience. "*What!*"

"Sir . . . there's a Kuakgan spell around."

"What do you mean? A Grove?"

"Not exactly. It's something they can do . . . like a trap."

"And how do you know this?" Flanits booted his horse back down the formation to face Terfol, one of the replacements he'd been sent a few tendays before, when those who'd won the toss had gone back to Vérella to celebrate Midwinter Feast there. "Are you telling me you're not Girdish?"

"My family's kuakgannir," Terfol said. "I grew up that way. But Girdish, too."

"You can't be both," Flanits said.

"That's not what the local Marshal said, sir. He said Gird didn't hate the kuakgannir, because Gird was an old human and they mostly were."

It was not the moment for a theological argument. "So . . . you're part kuakgannir. Fine. Tell me what you feel."

"A Kuakgan's set a snare, sir. Remember when it seemed like the trees were closing in?"

"Yes—you're not going to tell me they were."

"They might have been. A Kuakgan can herd them, you know. And they can make snares to catch people."

"Why didn't you tell me this back then?"

"Because I didn't feel it then. We were on the fringe of it, I guess. But now we're closer in."

"So . . . are we in the trap itself?"

"No, sir. They're usually laid in a spiral, like a snail shell." Terfol drew the shape on the air. "We've gone the other way around, so it's not catching us. But if we go straight for the horn sound now, we'll meet the strongest walls."

"And likely our squire's caught in it," Flanits said. "Is that what you think?" It made sense to him.

"Maybe, sir. And if he is, he can't get out, and we can't get in—not without going back and entering by the right door."

"So we need to find the Kuakgan and tell him to open it, is that it?"

"Yes, sir. Or her. But I don't know where the Kuakgan is."

"You don't have a *feeling* about that?" Flanits knew his tone was unfair, but he was tired of the endless pursuit, and Terfol's plaintive tone eroded his patience.

"No, sir. But if the lad's in a Kuakkgani trap, he won't come to harm. He's not a criminal or anything; when the Kuakgan comes, he'll be released."

"And we can all go back to Harway, maybe even in time for Midwinter buns," Flanits said. He didn't believe it. When things started going wrong, they usually kept going wrong. "It's cold; we don't know what supplies his group has; we don't know where the Kuakgan is or how long the trap will be shut." He looked at his troop, and they looked back. No one offered any ideas. "Is this as close as we can get?" he asked Terfol.

"I think so, but I don't—I never tried to get into a Kuak-kgani snare, sir."

"We can at least give another signal, can't we?"

"Yes, sir."

Flanits waved to Medlin, who blew Assembly yet again. Now the answer came—slightly closer, he thought—from their sword-side directly. They had turned a corner when they met the stream; that made sense.

"We'll try a hail," Flanits said. He turned in the direction of the horn call and bellowed as loud as he could. A blurred yell came back. "Someone," he said. "Human, and responsive, so not part of the trap." He tried again: "WHOOOO?"

The answer had two syllables, that was clear, but not what it was. Further experimentation with the horn proved that whoever was in the trap knew only a few of the horn signals—not, for instance, the stutter-code for spelling out words. Nor could he blow more than one controlled note.

Frustrating. Flanits chewed his mustache again and told his troop to set up a temporary camp. Could they risk entering the trap? Even some of them? If the cub needed help . . . He was still pondering all this when a hail came from across the stream. A figure in a long, dark green robe with a staff hurried toward them. A Kuakgan.

Master Ashwind wasted no time opening the trap; Flanits wasted no time on thanks but took his troop straight in on the line he had determined. Now the sounds were clearer, and soon they emerged into the clearing to find the Mahieran cub standing alone amidst the bodies of his patrol and three strangers. Blood stained his clothes, but he did not appear to be injured. And his story, which he poured out to Flanits as if he were a criminal trying to excuse his crimes, made the hair on Flanits's body rise in horror.

All the others were dead, and dead by Beclan Mahieran's hand. He admitted it. He looked guilty; he kept saying how sorry he was. Fourth from the throne and a murderer? Or a traitor, concealing a Verrakai who had taken him over?

"We'll take care of you, young lord," Flanits said. He tried to sound soothing, encouraging. "Get you out of this and back with your father—"

"Duke Verrakai—"

"She's busy," Flanits said. "She was concerned about you; that's why she sent me to find you. She'll be glad to know someone so close in succession is safe away from the war." Something flashed in the boy's eyes then, and Flanits suspected the worst. "Let's be going and not waste the daylight," he said.

The Kuakgan was able to tell them the quickest way north to the River Road, and Flanits elected to head for it instead of back toward Harway. He did not trust either Duke Verrakai or the Kuakgan entirely, and he had in his flask enough numb-wine to render the lad helpless as soon as he was safely away.

CHAPTER NINE

Valdaire

ONCE SETTLED INTO the inn, Arvid set about gathering the information he needed as unobtrusively as possible. Dattur stayed upstairs most of the time, mending their clothes and keeping the room clean. Arvid had agreed that showing themselves as a pair in the common room was risky. In the common room downstairs a few days after their arrival, Arvid listened to the conversations around him, signaling for a refill of his mug just often enough to avoid being asked to give space to another.

Soldiers in several uniforms crowded the room, gambling and drinking. A servant explained, when he asked, that it was payday for several of the mercenary companies, the best of times for all the inns in Valdaire.

Arvid found himself wondering how Paksenarrion had fit into such rowdy situations. At the next table, a wiry redheaded man in a maroon tunic and a husky brown-haired woman in blue were arm wrestling, with a noisy group betting on the outcome. The bettors included those in both uniforms. Arvid recognized the maroon as Phelan's Company—or whatever it was called now—from the north but not the others.

Most were betting on the woman, who certainly looked to have the advantage at first, but Arvid, out of a memory of Paks, hoped the redheaded man would win.

One of the bettors in blue said, "Heard that scumbag Gallis got hisself killed t'other day."

"About time. Cheated everybody, Gallis did." The woman who answered, also in blue, spat to the side. "Who did it?"

"Thieves' Guild, is what I heard. Didn't pay his safepass, supposedly."

"Didn't pay his dues, more like," the woman said. "I always thought he was a thief himself. Who's got his shop?"

"Dunno. Don't care. Heyyy!" The man shouted as the match reached a climax—the woman gaining a half finger and then the redheaded man slamming her arm down flat. The Phelani soldiers roared their approval; those in blue growled their disappointment. Coins chinked as the Phelani swept their winnings off the table. Another challenge came, but the soldiers in maroon dispersed to the bar and tables, pounding their champion on the back and offering him as much ale as he could drink.

"Same as ever, damned Foxheads," the woman who had lost said, shaking out her arm. "Cocky bastards. We should've had those barracks. We'd been promised—"

"I heard it was because their captain thought we'd treated Captain Arneson badly."

The woman scowled. "It wasn't our fault. It was the commander's—" She stopped abruptly and glanced around; Arvid, not looking at her face, saw the grip the other blue-clad soldier had on her wrist. They moved away; other soldiers took over the table, and in moments the rattle of bone dice was added to the noise.

Arvid ordered a plate of cheese rolls and settled in for a longer session. That Gallis's death was being attributed to the Thieves' Guild pleased him; that no one cared pleased him more. A busy tavern like this was exactly the place to pick up the information he needed. He filtered out friendly insults, gossip about who was bedding whom, complaints about losing a bet or having extra duty.

The next voice that caught his attention was male, with a strong north-Tsaian accent.

"The Captain don't remember, either."

Arvid strained his ears to hear through the other voices.

"But you—"

"We both know it. We come through that mountain on the gnome road, and we come out a hole that didn't close behind us. I could find it. Bet you could, too."

An inarticulate grunt, then: "Stands to reason somebody else knows. Besides gnomes, I mean."

"Somebody north? Or south?"

"Has to be south. North side's the gnome princedom; anybody gets off the trade road and they've got gnomes all over 'em, just like those that stopped us. But on this side—they just let us out and sent us away."

"With no memory of it, or so they thought."

"Right. Only *we* remember and the others don't. So I'm thinking we should tell the Captain."

"And I'm thinking we shouldn't."

Arvid had located the speakers now, two men in Phelani maroon uniforms, faces brick-red from years of campaigning here in Aarenis. Both broad-shouldered, both—when he shifted in his seat so he could see their hands busy with tankards and food—with callused, scarred hands. One almost bald, his short beard mostly gray; the other with curly dark hair silver-streaked on the sides. Automatically, he marked them for later recognition. Baldy with a broad face, pale eyes, wide crooked nose, scar from brow to jaw, just missing one eye. Curly with a long face, dark eyes, peaked eyebrows, no scars there, but a wide deep furrow in his right forearm.

He also saw the rigidity of a pair of shoulders facing away from those two . . . the rigidity of someone listening as closely as he himself was listening but without the skill to conceal it. Whoever that was did not wear a uniform but, like himself, wore civilian clothes with a weather-stained dark cloak over them and a broad-brimmed leather hat, obviously wet. A traveler just in, or someone who wanted to be thought a traveler just in? Certainly, Arvid thought, someone with intent to gather information and thus most likely a spy or a thief of the Guild.

A bar frequented by soldiers would be ideal for spying, of course. Or thieving. Which was it?

Arvid signaled again, and the server came over. "I'm hungry, after all," he said, "but I need to visit the jacks. Can you hold this table while I go and then bring me one of those?" He pointed to a deep earthenware dish topped with a pastry crust.

"Indeed I can. That's what we call a hot-pot; your choice of ham or mutton. It's a niti, with bread and a side of winter greens." A tiny pause, then the server leaned a little closer. "We're almost out of the ham, and it's the best."

"Ham, then," Arvid said. "And the jacks?"

"Through there," the server said.

Arvid pushed back his chair and stood; the server took a long strip of white cloth and laid it over the chair back and table. Down the indicated passage, Arvid found an arrangement he'd never seen before: a long room with a row of little stalls on either side and running water showing in the channel below.

His trip to and from the common room gave him a better view of the two Phelani veterans but only a glimpse of the eavesdropper's face, a shaven cheek, the gleam of an eye between the hat's shadow and the cloak's upturned collar. Whoever it was wore a long blade that poked out the back of the cloak. Arvid contrived to stumble over it. In a flash the man turned: for an instant, Arvid saw more—no beard, strong teeth, face wider than he'd supposed, angry expression. "Get away!" the man said. Arvid apologized with a bow; the man grunted and turned away quickly.

When Arvid glanced at the table where the two Phelani veterans were seated, they were both watching, alert now to something that might prove dangerous. He smiled at them. "You're in Phelan's Company, aren't you?"

"Yes," said the bald one.

"Did you know a yellow-haired woman named Paks?"

"Do you?"

"I've met a Phelani veteran named Paks, yes," Arvid said.

"Where?" asked the other one.

"Up north," Arvid said, with a tip of the head. "Town on the south trade road; you wouldn't know it."

"Try us," the bald one said, his voice edged.

"Brewersbridge," Arvid said. "Good ale there. Better here, though. Stand you a jug?"

"You're a gambler," the bald one said.

"No. I watched that match and hoped your man would win, but I didn't bet—" A blow caught him in the back; he staggered forward, and then a gloved hand yanked on his shoulder.

The man standing at the bar, hat still pulled low, said, "You ran into me and didn't even offer a mug, and you're buying strangers a jug? What's your game?"

"No game," Arvid said. He shrugged his shoulder out of the man's grip. "I did not wish to annoy you further."

"You do annoy me," the man said. "You come between me and them I'm—" He stopped short, pulled his cloak tight, and strode from the room.

"You!" the barkeep yelled. "You owe—" But the man was out the door, into the cold dark night.

"I'll pay," Arvid said. "I annoyed him." He pulled a coin from his pouch. "Will this cover it?"

"Yes, sir. Thank you." The barkeep smiled. "You're lodging here, aren't you?"

"Yes," Arvid said. He glanced back at the two veterans. "That jug of ale suit you?"

"Aye . . ."

"And a jug for these soldiers," Arvid said, putting down another coin. As the barkeep turned away, he leaned closer to the men. "That man was listening to your talk. I even heard a few words from where I sat—there." He glanced toward his table with the cloth still protecting it. "If this matter you spoke of is private, a more private place to talk would be advisable. It is noisy here and hard not to raise one's voice."

"You heard—"

"A little. I am not asking for more, merely giving warning that the man was listening to you with full attention—I could tell by his stance."

"And you created that diversion—"

"To interrupt, yes. For my acquaintance with your former soldier Paks, I would not see her comrades spied on in such a dangerous time."

The two men glanced at each other, then the bald one nodded just as a serving wench brought a jug to the table. "Thank you, lass," the curly-headed one said. Then, to Arvid, "And thank you for your diversion and your warning. Do you know anything of that man?"

"Nothing, and he took good care that none could see his face too clearly. When he turned on me first, I saw only a broad face—big teeth, no beard. I could not even see the color of his eyes."

"Hmmm." The bald-headed man had picked up the jug but now set it down again. "I think we won't drink more ale this night. But there's plenty to share." He looked around. "Vic! Come over here—we've a jug of ale to share." The redheaded man who'd won the arm wrestling came with several of his friends; the bald-headed man passed him the jug. "Congratulations—but don't drink too deep. We may have trouble on the way back, and we'll stick together. See that everyone understands."

"Of course."

"If you'll excuse me," Arvid said, tipping his head toward his table, where a serving wench was setting down a platter.

"Of course, of course," the bald man said.

Arvid finished his dinner just as the Phelani troops, with much laughing and jostling, paid up and left in a group. When they were all gone, one of the blue-clad contingent began a song that had the others thumping their mugs on the tables:

"Fox in the henhouse,
Fox in the byre,
Fox on the run with 'is tail on fire:
Run, fox, run. See the fox run.

"Fox-red hair and
Fox-pale eyes
Might be the Duke or a king in disguise
Run, fox, run. See the fox run.

"Foxhead troops
Take all they can
If it's gold or glory, they're the man
Run, fox, run. See the fox run."

Arvid realized that it was a jest on the Phelani and wondered what the Phelani sang about those in blue. He went upstairs, where he found Dattur curled up on one bed, seemingly asleep, and his own cloak, mended, folded neatly on the other.

He thought of waking Dattur to ask him about what he'd heard, but he knew his companion was tired. Their bedroom, right above the common room, carried the stamping of feet and banging of mugs right through the floor as if it weren't there. Arvid replaced his knives in the cloak pockets, hung the cloak on a hook, and lay down, falling asleep to "Cedars of the Valley."

The next morning, while dressing, Arvid told Dattur what he'd heard the night before.

"They used gnome road?" Dattur had slept in his clothes as always; though Arvid had promised to turn his back, the gnome was unwilling to show his skin again to a human. Now he stopped in the act of putting on his shoes.

"That's what I understood," Arvid said. He checked the set of his knives. "That would be unusual, wouldn't it?"

"It would be fatal without permission," Dattur said. "And it is not given. Not that I ever heard. So they must have done something for the prince, and it must be something important."

"They were Phelani soldiers," Arvid said. "Older men. What could Phelani do that gnomes would reward like that?"

Dattur shook his head. "It is not sense to me. That princedom is powerful. That prince will not need their service. Information, maybe. But what information?"

"The necklace?" Arvid said. "But I don't see why—I was told gnomes knew it existed but had disclaimed knowledge of it or its jewels."

"It would not be the necklace," Dattur said, tying the laces of his shoes. "And the men should not remember."

"They said no one else did." Arvid ran a rag over his shoes and put them on.

"Should be no one. And they think they know entrance?"

"If I heard them right," Arvid said.

"Many want to know that," Dattur said. "Entrance to the halls—"

"But you said it would be fatal to enter uninvited. Guards always there, I'm guessing."

"No." Dattur stared at the floor for a long moment. "It is . . . it is that . . . it is rock, my lord, and I cannot say more than that. Not in a language you know." He muttered something Arvid couldn't quite hear that sounded like the clatter of pebbles rolling down a slope. Then he looked up. "Do you think they will tell others what they remember?"

"I don't know," Arvid said. "Will you come down, or shall I bring you morning food?"

"They must not," Dattur said, without answering Arvid's question.

"I agree," Arvid said. "Many would want to know, and if they are known to have such knowledge, some will seek to force it from them."

"Do you know anything of the man you saw listening?"

"No, except he was trying to hide his face and had a surly temper. I suspect he was a spy, most likely in the Guild or working for the Duke of Immer."

"Who is said to seek a crown."

"Yes. And would no doubt take the necklace if it came near him." Arvid sighed. "I'm hungry, Dattur, and while I am hungry and have money, I find it good to eat."

"Go, then, my lord," Dattur said. "I will eat later. We must not be seen together, even in the morning. Not after that. And you should change your cloak."

"You did an excellent job mending it."

"Do you not think another thief would recognize it? Black—with those pockets—and while they do not show on the outside by any bulges, the way it swings—"

Arvid spread his hands. "What would you have me do, Dattur? Go unarmed into a city full of enemies?" And yet, before Dattur spoke again, he realized it would signal "thief" to another in the Guild. "No, you're right," he said. "I thought, over colored clothes—and many wear black."

"But not that kind of black cloak," Dattur said. "Why not blue?"

"Girdish? But I'm not Girdish."

Yet.

Arvid shivered but turned his mind from the voice.

"Green, then," Dattur said. "I could sew pockets in that—take them from your black cloak if you cannot find the right skins and cloth. The hang would not be so noticeable in a colored cloak. And, if I may say so, a padded doublet under it, so from behind you look . . . heavier."

Arvid went down to breakfast without his black cloak. When he came up with a bowl of apples and nuts for Dattur, the gnome had already cut the cloak two handspans shorter, making it look more like a merchant's city style, not a traveler's. Arvid put it on; it did not reach his knees, and he knew it would give him a different silhouette.

He already knew where to find tailors in that quarter of the city and knew, too, that they kept a stock of ready-made cloaks. Arvid forced himself to choose one as far from his own taste as possible: blue, green, and brown plaid with an edging of dyed rabbit fur around the hood, the whole lined in green. But the cut would lend itself to his purposes. He bought a blue quilted-velvet winter tunic cut to fit over a doeskin doublet dyed green; the tunic laced with green cords.

He changed into the new clothes, resigned now to looking like any other respectable but not wealthy merchant. At a glover's, he bought a pair of long black gloves "for winter riding" and some glove leather dyed to match to make pocket linings for his new cloak. Well before noon, he was back at the inn, upstairs. Dattur nodded his approval.

"I have to admit I'm warmer," Arvid said. He loosened the tunic laces. "And I'm sure I look heavier." He sighed. "But we should leave in case that fellow last night reports on me. I didn't see recognition in his eyes, but if he's good at descriptions—"

"Where?" asked Dattur. He had laid the new cloak, spread wide open, on the bed; the cut end of Arvid's old cloak lay on his own, along with its shortened top, and he was marking where to attach the pockets on the plaid one with a bit of chalk.

"That I don't know," Arvid said. With the beds covered in cloaks, he could not lounge on one; he pulled a stool from the corner and sat down. "I would like to leave my regards with the Guild—"

"You should leave them alone," Dattur said. "My lord," he added. More and more he forgot to say it; Arvid preferred the informality.

"Do your people ignore insult and unprovoked attack?" Arvid asked.

"No, but . . . my lord, you are but one man, and the Guild here has many members. And you came here on the trail of the necklace . . ."

"I wish I'd never seen the damned necklace," Arvid said. "It's been nothing but trouble for me since I gave it to Paks."

"Indeed?" Dattur leaned back. "Was it not because of her that you became head of the Guild in Vérella? And because of her that the Marshal-General herself sought you out and asked you to come to Fin Panir?"

"Yes . . . and look what that got me."

"It saved my life, so I'm not inclined to think it was the gods' ill will," Dattur said. "But if you regret it—"

"Of course I don't regret it," Arvid said. "But—" He stood up and strode back and forth around the small room. "I feel . . . I feel a trap closing in on me. Not the Guild assassins or whoever that man worked for . . . There's a . . . a pressure inside."

Dattur's small black eyes seemed to glitter for a moment, then he looked down. "It might be," he said, "that in all this there is a god seeking you."

"I was happy as I was," Arvid said, louder than he meant to. His voice sounded querulous to him, not the suave faintly amused voice he had cultivated so long. "I was," he said more softly. "Dattur, you're kteknik and I've never asked why." The gnome said nothing; he might have been stone himself. "I'm not asking now," Arvid went on. "But surely you felt . . . felt more free once you were cast out and yet also bereft."

"To a gnome, the Law is the greatest comfort in life," Dattur said. "We rest in the Law as men rest in their beds on a cold night: around us is chaos and evil, but in the Law we are safe." He looked up, straight at Arvid's face, and Arvid could not turn away. "To be cast out of the Law—to be forced to live without it, even to the matter of clothing, forced to live among strangers as well—is the greatest pain. It is no pleasure. What it is that you humans call freedom is to us like . . . like sleet and fire together on bare skin."

"I am sorry," Arvid said. He wanted to ask why, then,

gnomes ever broke their Law, but the misery in Dattur's face stopped the words in his throat, unsaid.

"My lord, I come near saying what must not be said to one who holds my life," Dattur said. Still he stared, as if willing Arvid to understand.

"I do not ask what you do not wish to say," Arvid said.

"My lord, you have been courteous to me in all things," Dattur said. "You have taken care for me, as if I were your . . . your son and not your servant. It is harder for me to do what I must to repay you what I owe when you are so . . . I forget and take liberties. And yet I see no end to this. I have not completed my prince's punishment, and I have not come nearer repaying you—"

"Your saving my life twice is not enough? I deem it so and would free you if you would accept my word."

Dattur shook his head. "You were wounded saving mine, and wounded with my blade. I make no complaint, my lord, and I serve you willingly, but . . . it is not easy."

"What could I do to make it easier?"

"Nothing."

Arvid felt simultaneously a cold chill down his back and a warm pressure, as of a friendly hand, on his head. He shuddered. Whatever was happening would change him—had changed him—and he had been as comfortable in himself before as Dattur within the gnomish Law. Dattur bore that without complaint . . .

"I cannot see a way to revenge myself on the Guildmaster here, who so disrespected me and sent me to torment and death, as he thought, and also to regain my position in Vérella without risking you, who are not of this quarrel. And the necklace—I have no idea where it is by now. Could it have reached that Duke of Immer? Would the Marshal-General want me to go there?"

"Do you want to be always a thief in Vérella?"

That was not a question he expected. "I want to be—" *Who I was,* Arvid thought, that confident, sophisticated, witty man who had been so certain of his superiority. He could never convince the gnome he was not a thief, yet the gnome felt bound to him. "I cannot abide the thought that I might never be what I was before," he said finally. "As you cannot abide the thought that you might never return to your prince."

"Ah," Dattur said. "My lord, I am bound to your service, but within that I am able to perform any service you require. Perhaps my lord will permit me to suggest that a little more knowledge of the Law would be helpful?"

"I don't want to be a judicar," Arvid said.

"No, you have not the temperament," Dattur said. "But like many humans you misunderstand the purpose and use of Law. I could teach you."

CHAPTER TEN

Valdaire, day before Midwinter Feast

BUREK, JUNIOR CAPTAIN of Arcolin's cohort in what was now widely known as Fox Company, arrived back in Valdaire from Cortes Andres with an escort of Phelani a day before Midwinter Feast; he had told none of them of his new status. If it was status. He could not imagine himself using the Andressat name, especially in the current political situation. Troops were just finishing drill in the winter-quarters court-yard when he and his escort rode in; the mountains rising above and behind the compound were lit by the westering sun, the snow there rose-gold.

"Welcome back," Captain Selfer said. "You're just in time for Midwinter Feast."

"Is Lord Arcolin here yet?" Burek asked.

"No," Selfer said. "I wouldn't expect him until spring; the pass is closed."

Burek dismounted and handed the reins to one of the men assigned to stable duty, giving the horse a pat on the rump as it was led away. "I have word he should hear," he said. "Can couriers get through?"

"Not now," Selfer said. "We're on our own until his return."

"Well, then, I must tell you," Burek said. Selfer nodded and led the way to the officers' quarters, a corner of the compound fitted out for their use.

"What is it, then? Are you not fit for duty?"

"Oh, that—yes, though the surgeon in Cortes Andres told me to avoid blows to the arm for another six hands of days. I am doing exercises daily to strengthen it again." Selfer handed him a cup of sib, and Burek took a sip. "What it is—you know what I thought of my parentage."

"Yes."

"It's true. Andressat acknowledged me, wanted me to stay and take my place as his grandson."

Selfer's eyes widened. "So you're leaving us?"

"No. No, I told him I bore no rancor, but this is my life now—a life that suits me—and though I am glad to count him friend and respect him as my grandfather, I am not . . . I don't belong." Burek took another swallow of sib. "He introduced me to his sons. One of them left rather than speak to me as family. I do not want that burden on my heart."

"But surely—to be acknowledged—and you would have a home—"

"Would you leave this Company to go home—wherever your home is?" Burek asked.

"Well . . . no. But my home is a tiny barony in a badly managed dukedom; my father had eight sons, of which I'm fifth. It's not big enough for us all, not that we quarrel . . . it's just not enough. So I left to become Duke Phelan's squire, and others left as well. If they needed me . . . but they don't."

"So you understand."

"Yes, but I have a name and family—I have always had a name—"

"And so have I," Burek said. "Burek is a good name; it was my foster father's."

"You don't mind—"

"I don't. I honor the old man for acknowledging me—I had thought him so proud he never would, but though he has a great sense of honor, he is not arrogant. I admire him. To know that he would bring me into the family openly—that is a comfort, I admit, but I am better here."

"I'm glad to hear that," Selfer said. "Your troops respect you, and I need the help. I'd hate to have to break in another who is new to the Company."

"Another?"

"Yes. I was Captain Dorrin—now Duke Verrakai's—junior captain and took over her former cohort. Cohorts are meant to have a senior and a junior captain; Count Arcolin's message sending me here authorized me to hire a captain, subject to his approval in the spring. I might have waited, but with you injured and no certainty you'd return, I went to Golden Company for advice—they had recommended you, after all. M'dierra had no recommendations this year, so I went to the hiring hall and found a former Clart officer who'd retired but then found it boring. It feels odd to have a junior captain older than I am, but I felt I could not wait."

"How is Sergeant Stammel?" Burek asked.

"Arcolin said he was blind," Selfer said. "I was in Lyonya, and then with Captain—with *Duke* Verrakai in that domain, until Count Arcolin sent for me. And his word met me in Vérella, so I never saw Stammel. It is hard to believe—he was always so—" Selfer spread his hands. "I don't know what he'll do."

"Did Lord Arcolin tell you about the Blind Archer?" Burek asked. Selfer shook his head; Burek recounted that story.

"So . . . he's going to stay in the Company and fight as a blind archer?" Selfer said.

"I don't know. The troops want him back, but there's more to being cohort sergeant than that. He knows that, surely. Sergeant Devlin was beginning to talk about Stammel not returning . . . but it's up to Lord Arcolin in the end, I suppose."

"And Stammel himself," Selfer said.

They ate early in the last evening light, and Burek met the other captain, Harnik. Short and wiry like many cavalry troopers, he might have been made of rawhide thongs burnished dark by long usage as much as the southern sun. Though some cavalry favored long hair, Harnik had gone almost bald and had trimmed the remainder of his curly gray hair close to his neck.

"I hear you saved old Andressat's life," Harnik said after they'd been introduced. "I remember seeing him in Siniava's War, when we fought with the Red Fox—arrogant old fellow, isn't he?"

"Perhaps he's mellowed," Burek said.

Harnik snorted. "And perhaps rock melts in the sun. But he is older, and sometimes it happens old men go soft."

Burek glanced at Selfer, but Selfer did not look up from his plate. What would Arcolin have done? Let the man talk, learn from him what his talk yielded about himself. Burek reached for the pot of honey and dipped some onto his bread. After dinner, Harnik had the early watch and went out to inspect the line of sentries.

"I'm glad you said nothing about Andressat's mission to the north," Selfer said.

"Do you think Harnik is a spy?" Burek asked.

"No. I think he is a man who says what he knows, or what he thinks he knows, which can be worse," Selfer said. "I did ask Clart's man of business—Clart himself is away somewhere—but was told only how long Harnik had served and that he'd retired. Not a word against him, and I imagine he's brave in a fight. The problem is . . . I know he talks—and loudly—when he's in his cups. What you and I know about Andressat must not be talked of."

"Well, I'm not supposed to drink much for a quarter-year," Burek said. "So if there are things to be done that should not be let out, send me."

"I will," Selfer said. "And I'm glad to have you back, someone who knows our ways. Harnik's a willing worker, but he still uses 'near' and 'off' for 'left' and 'right' half the time in drill. Our people are learning—but also he knows nothing about standard sword drill. And on top of that, though Devlin's experienced and doing well as senior sergeant of your cohort, my senior sergeant stayed with Dorrin in the north. Both of us have short cohorts and less experienced junior sergeants and corporals. I hope Arcolin brings us plenty of new troops to fill in."

The nightlong Midwinter vigil did not include Burek; the Company surgeon insisted he go to bed. The next day, as observed in the northern tradition, was a day of games and revelry for the troops. Burek took the first watch, carrying up a basket of warm honeycakes and fried snow to share with the sentries on the wall. Watches were short, so everyone had a chance at the fun. Burek spent his off-watch in the afternoon reading the Company logbook.

Next morning, Burek was out early to relieve Selfer and begin the day's drill. His own cohort grinned before settling to work; Selfer's did not, but they did not know him. He told their sergeant to warm them up with close-order drill, and then he spoke to the armsmaster about his arm and what the surgeon had said.

"With respect, Captain, you young men always want to hurry a healing, and healing won't hurry. If your surgeon says no hard work for that many days, I don't want to see you out here with even a hauk in that hand."

"I need to be fit by campaign season—"

"And you will be, if you follow orders. I'll stretch it out for you twice a day, and we'll go from there. And no formation drill. Sure as there's snow on the mountains, someone'd hit a shield into it and you'd be back where you were, or worse. You can do longsword work with another captain, but no shield or dagger."

Burek had expected that but felt he'd had to ask. Selfer had gone to a late breakfast; Harnik was going over supplies with the quartermaster, Maia. Swordplay would have to come later. "When was your last hill march?" he asked Devlin.

"Maybe ten days agone, Captain," Devlin said. "I wouldn't say we're really stale yet . . ."

Burek looked over the north wall at the mountains rising above. "See those clouds? We're due another storm. Load 'em up; we'll be back before dinner, but we need to use the day the gods give us for the work that needs doing."

"Yes, sir," Devlin said, and turned to the cohort. Selfer's sergeant did the same. Burek went to the mess hall and alerted the cooks that the men would all need a pack meal. Selfer, who had just finished his late breakfast and lingered in the mess hall with a third mug of sib, grinned at him.

"You're taking mine, too, aren't you?" he asked.

"Unless you say no," Burek said. One of the cooks offered him a sweetcake; he shook his head. "I had enough riding on the way here, and I need to walk out the soreness. Besides, did you look up at the north sky and the mountains?"

"Storm tonight or tomorrow," Selfer said, nodding. "Back before dark?"

"In time for supper," Burek said. "Gods willing. Taking full packs, so if we aren't, we should be all right." The first troops were already filing in to pick up the bread and cheese and sausage they would eat on the march; Burek took his and jogged across the courtyard to his quarters, stuffed an extra pair of heavy socks in his tunic, and then packed his own pack. By the time he had it on and his winter campaign cape over it, the cohorts were ready, four abreast in their column of march, fox-head pennants already uncased and fluttering in the breeze.

"You riding, Captain?" Sergeant Devlin asked.

"No," Burek said in a tone that brought a chuckle from someone. "I rode all the way from Cortes Andres. The last thing I need is a cold saddle under me. No, I'm walking to get the kinks out. That's all we do today—a nice easy walk in the hills." This time it was a dramatic groan from two or three. Burek ignored them and led them out the gates, around to the left, and up the rising ground north of their winter quarters. Directly ahead of them, brown hills patched with snow in the hollows lifted toward higher, steeper hills with much more white and then to the mountains themselves, snow-covered trees below and snow punctuated by the jagged edges of rocks to which no snow could cling.

The snow-covered hills were too far away for them to reach and return by supper, but the brown ones would have snow on their north sides. Burek led them at a brisk pace up the first rise. Sure enough, not far below the crest the sheep trail they were on was covered with snow all the way down to the bottom. He turned west a little, following the crest of the hill, looking for an even more challenging trail he remembered from the previous spring. As he went, he kept an eye on the clouds; he had no mind to have them caught out in the storm. When he came to the trail he remembered, he changed his mind. The rough tumble of rocks with a web of sheep trails would indeed make a good exercise, as would the climb up the opposite slope, but he did not trust the weather. To his left, on the southward slope of the hill, they had ample room to practice keeping formation on a slope, across it, down it, and back up it.

By the lunch break, they were all sweating freely; Burek had spotted a lambing hut, and they squatted in its lee, munching rounds of bread and hunks of cheese and sausage.

"Didn't figure you'd be ready for an exercise like this, Captain," Sergeant Devlin said. "Heard you were bad hurt."

"I was," Burek said. "Nearly lost the arm, the surgeon told me, but being young and fit is what saved me. So as soon as they let me, I thought I had best get fit again. I'm not allowed to risk the arm until after the half-Evener, but there was nothing wrong with my legs." He grinned at the sergeants. "Except those days horseback, when I hadn't ridden since I got to Cortes Andres."

"So," Devlin said, looking at his sausage, "we're out here working up sweat just to loosen your legs, Captain?"

"And yours," Burek said. "Captain Selfer said he hadn't had you out on the roads lately."

"He thought we had enough of that coming across from Verrakai lands to Vérella and then down here," Selfer's sergeant said. Devlin opened his mouth and shut it again.

Burek finished eating and looked around. The jacks trench, well away from the lambing hut, was still in use, but most had finished. He used the jacks himself, then nodded to the assigned team, who filled it in. Then he led them to the foot of the slope, next to a dry streambed, and told them of the final challenge he'd planned.

"Open out along the streambed," he said. "It's a race to the ridge trail; pick your own routes. Winner from each cohort is off jacks duty for two tendays; winning cohort is off for a hand. First cohort to assemble in formation, ready to march back, wins. Sergeants, go on up—you'll be giving us the signal to start and judging the winners at the crest."

"You, sir?" Devlin asked.

"I need the exercise, remember?" He grinned at them, and they saluted and started up the slope. He waited until the sergeants had reached the crest and turned to face him, then said, "Ready." The sergeants waved their arms, and the cohorts charged the slope. Burek had the first part of his own route planned and scrambled up it, bent almost double. On either side of him, the others did the same, some silently and some grunting with every stride.

Burek had been good at hill running as a lad, but he had not done it—not like this—for years. Off to his left he saw someone already a horse-length ahead of the uneven line. He reached for a clump of grass to help himself up a steeper place and remembered in time he must not strain that arm. Two steps instead of one and then a quick three strides on a gentler slope before he was faced with a low ledge of crumbling rock, just too high to step up easily. Someone, trying to leap up it, caught a toe and fell, rolling in front of someone else so they both slid an armspan down the slope, cursing.

Burek made it over that obstacle and spared no more glances aside . . . the hill demanded all his breath and both eyes open to avoid tussocks and rocks and patches of snow. His chest burned; his legs felt heavy as sacks of grain. At last the slope eased; he looked up and saw that the clouds hid the upper mountain slopes to the north and to the west poured through the pass. Someone yelled from the crest trail—a winner, no doubt. He still had a bow-shot to run. On the easier slope, he gained on those ahead of him, and when he came level with the sergeants, he saw that perhaps a third of both cohorts had already made it, moving into their assigned files. Others ran into position even as he walked over to the sergeants. Everyone was most of the way up, only two still on the steeper part of the slope.

Burek looked north again, gauging how near the clouds were and how fast they were forming. The nearest mountain slope . . . He stared. Something was moving just below the clouds . . . a line of tiny dots against the snow, dark, moving as if along a trail. Wild animals? But the gait was wrong—more like men. Could there be a trail there? And where were they going with a storm coming? The line shortened . . . Were they going behind a rock? Into a cave? The last disappeared just as the clouds would have blotted it out, and a gleeful shout rose from Selfer's cohort. The last two soldiers bolted for his own cohort.

Burek congratulated Selfer's sergeant, then turned to Devlin. "I see we need more such exercises," he said. "But not today; we'll do our snow marches closer to the city."

He led them back faster than they'd come; the first snow

flurry left cold wet kisses on his face just as they reached the back side of the winter quarters. He reminded Devlin that his cohort would have all the jacks duty for the Company for the next hand of days—all but the lucky overall winner, who was freed of that for twenty.

At supper that night, he asked Selfer about any trails along the mountains themselves and tried to describe what he'd seen.

"You must have hawk's eyes," Harnik said. "But I never heard of any trails that high. There's one in the pass itself, heading east, but it only goes to a flattish meadow where you can camp if the caravansary is too crowded."

"I've been there," Selfer said. "But there's nothing else. It must have been dwarves you saw—or maybe wild goats."

"Didn't move like wild goats," Burek said. "But it was a long way off."

The next day, snow fell steadily. With Burek's cohort having all the jacks duty for the next hand of days, Selfer's had the courtyard—usually the easier, but not with snow forming a new blanket as soon as they'd cleared off the first. Checking on the cohort work details, Burek heard one old veteran say to another, "So you saw 'em, too?"

"That I did. But nobody'll see anything in this storm." Then the man looked up, nodded to Burek with a polite "Morning, Captain," and said nothing more.

The two were in Selfer's cohort, and he had not learned all their names yet, but they carried all the physical signs of long service. Well, he would learn them all soon enough. Thinking about that, he went to check on the stables, where work parties from both cohorts were finishing up the morning mucking of stalls and grooming. Harnik was talking to the farrier.

"Well, young Burek," Harnik said, "I hear your cohort lost the challenge yesterday." His voice was a little loud; Burek wondered if he was going deaf.

"They did," Burek said. "But they probably won't next time. It was a near thing."

"I wondered if you'd get them back before the storm. Once or twice, when we Clarts rode out that way to practice skirmishing, a mountain storm came down on us."

"Did you see much game?" Burek asked.

"Nothing but sheep," Harnik said. "And angry shepherds if we rode too near. They say the high mountains have rare and magical creatures, but I've never gone far—it's not horse country once you're above the trees. You like to hunt?"

Burek shook his head. "Never had the time. I thought I saw some goats on the mountain yesterday, but it may have been staring too long at snow."

"That would be it," Harnik said. "There was a time we went out in winter—sunny day after snow—and my eyes burned for the rest of the day."

That evening, Harnik was off duty. Burek and Selfer ate supper together. "What do you think of him?" Selfer asked, nodding to the empty place.

"I'm not sure," Burek said. He was not sure how much to say. "Is he a little deaf, maybe?"

"Maybe. I don't know if I made the right choice—what Lord Arcolin will think. It's clear to me that Harnik thinks he's senior—he is older and more experienced, I don't dispute that. But I feel as if he expects to be made senior captain when Arcolin comes."

"Captain Arcolin wouldn't do that."

"No, but Harnik's always giving me advice, telling me what I should do. And he talks on and on about what they did in Clart Company. Clart's a good cavalry company, but they're not infantry and it's not the same. And Lord Arcolin's Company has its own traditions already."

"And yet Harnik is one of us now, until Captain Arcolin comes down, so—"

"So we must get along with him. Yes, you're right. But I have orders directly from Lord Arcolin, and so do you, from before he went north. I worry that Harnik may step beyond those, present himself to merchants or even potential employers as having more authority than he does."

"Surely he wouldn't—"

"The day before you came, we got a load of fodder from a supplier this Company doesn't use. Harnik had authorized it rather than asking me who our suppliers are. I had some on order, and that's why the stable lofts are stuffed. Our usual supplier wasn't happy; I hated to make Harnik look bad . . .

I'm not sure what to do, Burek. This is the first time I've had a separate command down here. I was junior to Dorrin Verrakai."

"Did you tell Harnik not to do it again?"

"Of course. He puffed up a bit but then apologized . . . only in a way that convinced me he thought my objection silly."

"What do you want me to do?" Burek asked.

"What you did yesterday—just make it clear that you're in charge of your cohort. They like you, it's clear. Mine will come to know you—they've heard good things from yours already. I made a copy of the muster for you, with some notes, today; it's in your quarters."

"Thanks," Burek said. "That will help. By the way, who are the older veterans—one bald with gray eyes and a scar from brow to jaw and the other with graying dark hair, dark eyes, and a big scar on his right forearm?"

"Bald Laris and Gannin," Selfer said. "They're old friends— same recruit cohort. Never made corporal, either one of them, but good soldiers in their place. They haven't given you trouble, have they?"

"Not at all," Burek said.

"Good. I was a little surprised that they stayed with me after Duke Verrakai left the Company. We lost three hands who were senior enough to make that choice. I think they're the oldest who stayed."

"What is Duke Verrakai like?" Burek asked. "You know I had a year with Golden Company—was she like Aesil M'dierra?"

Selfer shook his head. "I'm not sure. I saw M'dierra only from a distance, back when I was the Duke's senior squire. Dorrin Verrakai was the next senior captain to Lord Arcolin. To look at, tall, dark. A better fencer than Lord Arcolin— almost as good as Kieri Phelan was, if not as good. She's a Knight of Falk—absolutely honest, strict but fair. I didn't know she was a Verrakai at first—she never used the name, and the family had repudiated her. As her junior captain, I learned so much—but that was in the north, not on campaign. You're actually more experienced than I am at that, Burek. I was here last as a squire."

"But I never fought in Siniava's War," Burek said. "Even as a squire."

"Well . . . she's a noble now. The king attainted her whole family for treason, except her, and gave her the family title and lands to administer, with the assignment to capture her fugitive relatives and turn them in."

Burek shivered.

"She hired her former cohort—and me, as acting captain— from then until after the Fall Evener, when Lord Arcolin was confirmed Count and wanted us back with the Company. We trained her people as much as we could in a half-year or so, and I thought we would go back to the stronghold in the north, but Lord Arcolin sent word to Vérella that we were to go south. So we came, escorting Count Andressat . . . and you know the rest."

"It was late to come through the pass," Burek said.

"So the gnomes said," Selfer said. "But they knew the Duke's Company and let us through."

THEY PASSED THE rest of the evening planning exercises for the next few days, assuming the snow held. Selfer had the early watch and came back from each round to report that snow still fell. "The first really big snow of the winter," he said. By the time Burek took over for the second watch, Harnik had not returned. Selfer shook his head. "I hope this won't be a habit now that you're back."

Harnik reappeared while Burek was making rounds for the second time, his voice a little slurred. "Well, lad, it's no night to be coming up that hill from the White Dragon into the face of the wind. I almost turned back and begged a bed there, but I knew you depended on me. Can't leave you two young bravos without a graybeard to back you up."

So. This was near insubordination, but what could Selfer do with a half-drunken older man in the middle of the night? "Captain Selfer has tomorrow's schedule posted in the guardroom," Burek said, in as neutral a voice as he could manage. "You'll be taking both cohorts for a march after the morning chores."

"In a snowstorm? He can't be serious."

"I believe, Captain Harnik, that Captain Selfer has done this before."

"We'll see what the morning brings," Harnik said, and stumped off to his quarters, muttering to himself. Burek could just hear a phrase or two . . . nothing flattering to Selfer. He continued his rounds without waking Selfer, making sure that the sentries had their sib in shelter every second turn of the glass.

Selfer came into the guardroom before the end of the watch, carrying a pot of sib with him. "He's snoring loud enough to hear in the courtyard," he said. No need to give the name. "What time did he come in?"

"My second round," Burek said. "And he'd been drinking. Said he'd almost decided to spend the night at the inn."

"Um." Selfer poured sib for both of them. "Anything else to report?"

"No. I thought perhaps some enterprising thief might think we didn't man the walls on such a night, but nothing happened." Burek stretched. "I have one more round—better get to it."

"Go on, then. I must think what to do."

What to do about Harnik . . . Burek thought about that as he went from sentry to sentry. Did he and Selfer really need a third captain with both of them healthy? But Captain Arcolin had told Selfer to hire one for the winter. In those few days he couldn't tell how much help Harnik actually was. For himself, the older man's condescending attitude was not a problem. Harnik was Selfer's second and Selfer's hire; he himself, having sworn his oath to Arcolin and clearly second to him, did not care how Harnik treated him. He would have command only over Selfer's cohort.

Yet . . . if the man was a drunkard, if he could not do the work for which he'd been hired, if he continued to show disrespect for Selfer as his commander and Burek as a fellow officer, they would be better off without him. He wondered what kind of contract Harnik had signed. His own had been provisional, as he'd expected, but Arcolin had confirmed him as a permanent hire, with an initial two-year contract, at summer's end.

It was light enough now to see the steady fall of the snow, the smoke from the kitchens disappearing into it, the shapes of the buildings and the piles of snow covering roofs and ground. Burek loved the silence of snow and the smell, so clean and pure; he stood a moment in the middle of the north wall parapet and let the snowflakes land on his face until they caught in his eyebrows and chilled his eyelids. Then, laughing at himself, he turned his back to the slight breeze, blinked the snow away, and looked down into the courtyard. One of Selfer's corporals for the first round of daytime sentries, out of the mess, looked up, spotted him, and called, "Relief ready, Captain!"

"Relieve the posts, Corporal," Burek called back. He retraced his steps to the first post and waited until the corporal and his little troop were up on the parapet, then walked along with them as each post changed shifts, and led those relieved down the steps by the front gate.

He expected to find Harnik and Selfer at breakfast in the mess hall, but only Selfer was there; he waved Burek over. "Guard changed, Captain Selfer," Burek said. "Nothing to report on my last round, either."

A cook's helper came over with bowls of porridge and a basket of hot bread. The captains' table already had a pitcher of honey and box of salt. "Here, Captains. Ham next."

Burek poured a stream of honey into his porridge and sprinkled salt on it. "I thought Golden Company's mess was good, but this is better."

"Wait until you rotate up to the north," Selfer said. "There's a pastry cook at the stronghold as good as any you'd find in a Valdaire inn."

"I've never seen the north at all," Burek said. He ate rapidly, glancing now and then at the door, expecting to see Harnik.

"He's still snoring," Selfer said. "I banged on his door, and he grunted; I thought he was awake. But then, when I got my boots on and walked past his room on the way out, he was snoring again."

Burek grinned. "We could give him a snow bath."

Selfer thought about it, then shook his head. "Bad for discipline for the troops to see a captain dumped in the snow. But we could take a bucket in if he's not up by the end of break-fast."

"I can take care of the morning chore details," Burek said. "The jacks detail is all out of my cohort anyway." A server arrived with a platter of ham steaks; Burek stabbed one and pulled it onto his plate.

"You've been up all night," Selfer said, cutting his own. "He should do it."

"Yes, but if you need time to settle things with him, I can be out of the way and ensure the others are." Burek wondered what was holding Selfer back. They really did not need a third captain, and if Harnik was going to cause trouble, better to let him go now.

"I wish I'd at least seen Arcolin before coming down here," Selfer said. He ate two bites of ham steak before saying more; Burek finished his own and took another, raising his brows in question. "It's complicated," Selfer said. "This is the first time I've been on detached duty like this. I know I had Arcolin's permission to hire someone temporarily, but I've never—I don't know how to dismiss an officer. What if Harnik considers I do not have authority?"

"You hired him," Burek said through a mouthful of bread. "Surely that proves your authority."

"It should, but . . . Harnik has hinted that he thinks he should be senior—you've seen that, I'm sure."

"Yes," Burek said, thinking of what Harnik had said when he came in. "Insubordination?"

"Well, it may be. But if it comes to a court—down here—"

"It will not come to a court," Burek said. "Have you talked to Count Arcolin's banker or man of business?"

"Not about this, no. I didn't think of it."

"He accepted Count Arcolin's letter, giving you authority to draw funds, didn't he?"

"Yes, but—"

"Here, Guild League laws prevail . . . What you must show is the authority to make a contract, the contract itself, and non-fulfillment of a contract. You did have Harnik sign a contract, didn't you?"

"Yes, of course. But he didn't swear an oath." Selfer sliced open a small loaf and pushed a slab of ham in it, then tucked it into his tunic. "Without that oath, the contract isn't valid if Harnik challenges me."

"That's not Guild League law," Burek said again. "If the banker has accepted Count Arcolin's letter, then your right to make a contract is clear."

"Is that really—? I thought, because the Company was oathbound—"

"That matters to Count Arcolin and to you. But not to the merchants and courts of Valdaire. What do they care of the laws of another kingdom except when trading there?"

Burek remembered something Andressat had said in one of their long talks before he left. "If it worries you, why not talk to Count Arcolin's banker? He will be discreet; bankers do not gossip. He can advise you on the law."

Selfer nodded. "That is well, Burek; that is very well."

They started out of the mess hall only to meet Harnik coming in. "Sorry I'm late, lads," he said. "Something wrong with the ale last night, I think. Burek, can you take the work details this morning? I've got to get ready for the main exercise." Without waiting for an answer, he went in to breakfast.

"Take a patrol into the city; I can stay up longer," Burek said. Selfer gripped his arm. "I will."

Burek walked the rounds for a glass, checking each work detail, but as usual the sergeants had all in order. He could not help yawning now and then and wondered when Harnik would come out and relieve him. He assembled the troops in the courtyard, ready to march. Finally, he went to Harnik's quarters and knocked. "They're ready, Captain Harnik."

The door opened; Harnik's face was even more flushed, and Burek could smell the drink. "Is my horse ready?"

"Your horse?"

"Of course. I'm not going to slog through the snow like a—" He stopped and peered past Burek. "It's snowing too hard. We can't go out in this." He shut the door in Burek's face.

Burek stared at the wooden planks for a moment, trying to think how to handle this. He did not want to leave Harnik alone in the compound, not after what Selfer had told him. He turned to face the troops.

"Change of plan," he said to Devlin. "Captain Harnik thinks it's snowing too hard to go out on a march. So: weapons practice, here in the courtyard. Hauks instead of swords, though, in this wet snow."

Between hauk drills in formation and close-order drill, Burek kept them busy until Selfer returned. Harnik did not reappear. Selfer arrived near midday with four other riders. Burek stared: Aesil M'dierra of Golden Company, Nasimir Clart of Clart Company, a Gird's Marshal, and the hard-faced one-armed man he remembered as head of the mercenaries' hiring hall. Selfer, when he dismounted, had an expression Burek recognized with relief: the senior captain had come to a firm decision.

"Captain Burek," Selfer said. "Would you dismiss the troops to lunch, please. And then come to the Company offices."

"Yes, Captain," Burek said. By the time he turned around, the sergeants had their troops back in formation, and the dismissal took only a moment. Then he followed Selfer and the others into the large room where the Company records and maps were kept. The others stood in a row; Burek wondered why they were there and what Selfer planned. Selfer introduced the visitors—Marshal Steralt was the only one Burek had not met. They nodded at him but said nothing.

"Captain Burek, where is Captain Harnik?" Selfer asked.

"In his quarters," Burek said. "He said it was snowing too hard to take the troops out."

"And yet he had the duty to supervise today's exercises, did he not?"

"Yes, sir." Selfer knew that; it must be for the benefit of these witnesses.

"Was he drunk?"

Burek hesitated. "He—he looked flushed and smelled of drink when I knocked on his door to tell him the troops were assembled."

"What did he do after he said it was too snowy?"

"Shut the door in my face," Burek said.

"You mentioned something to me earlier today about insubordination," Selfer said. "Please tell us about it."

"I don't remember his exact words," Burek said. "It was

when he came in last night—he said he'd thought of staying the night in the inn but felt we were too young to be left in charge without an older man—him—here."

"I see." Selfer went to the door and spoke to the soldier posted there. "Go tell Captain Harnik to come to the office at once." Then, to Burek, "I'm sorry—you've been up all night and done his duty this morning as well, but what I learned in the city was too serious—it took time."

Burek was far too curious now to feel sleepy. "I'm fine, Captain," he said. He looked at the others while they waited for Harnik to appear. M'dierra, his former commander, gave him a brief approving nod. Nasimir Clart he knew by sight but had never spoken to; the wiry dark-haired man with a neat pointed beard looked him up and down and then transferred his gaze to Selfer. Gaster Teraloga from the hiring hall gave him a brief smile then looked away. The Marshal stared at the wall. Why had Selfer brought them?

They heard the soldier knock—once, then again, and again—and then a furious blurred voice yelling. Selfer took a step toward the door.

"Best not," M'dierra said. "One of your sergeants, maybe?"

"I'll just see," Burek said. Selfer's senior sergeant, Pedar Mattisson, attracted by the noise, was already coming; Burek signaled him and explained. Mattisson nodded.

Moments later he returned. "Captain, if I could have a word."

"It's not a secret, Sergeant. What's his condition?"

"Drunk and incapable, Captain," Mattisson said. "Roused enough to yell at the sentry, but when I went in, he was sprawled on his bed and there was an empty jug on the floor beside him. We can carry him in here if you want."

"No," Selfer said. "These witnesses must see him in his present condition."

They all went to Harnik's room; Harnik lay sprawled on his bed, a jug on the floor beside it, and did not respond to voice or shaking.

"Did you see a jug with him last night?" Selfer asked Burek.

"No, Captain," Burek said. "He could have hidden it under his cloak, though. It was cold and snowing; we exchanged only a few words, and then he went into this room. I went back out as I had the watch."

"Drunk, incapable, and insubordinate," Nasimir Clart said. "And no surprise. And he told you he'd retired, Captain Selfer?"

"Yes. Said he'd left Clart Company to join his brother on a farm or something like that, and then the brother died . . ."

"And I was away, so you could not check what he said with me," Clart said. "I say here, before witnesses, that this man was discharged from Clart Company for drunkenness and suspicion of theft."

"Why did you not bring him to court?" asked Marshal Steralt.

"He had fought well enough in Siniava's War," Clart said. "He promised to go home to his family, and I saw no need to shame him." At the Marshal's sharp look, Clart shook his head. "I'm not Girdish, Marshal, as you know, nor yet a gnome to worship the law. That war changed many men." He turned to Selfer. "But if I had known, Captain Selfer, that he presented himself as he did, I would have told you even if you had not come to me. I hope you believe that."

"Certainly," Selfer said. "I know Duke Phelan and Lord Arcolin always considered Clart Company honorable. I wish Lord Arcolin were here—"

"No need," Marshal Steralt said. "There's no doubt you have his authority to act in his place, and there's no doubt this man lied when you hired him, exceeded his authority in purchasing fodder without permission, showed lack of respect for you and Captain Burek, and is now drunk when he should be on duty. His former commander speaks against him. It only remains to wake him up and finish this."

Burek had never considered what it might take to discharge an officer from command, but one of the books in the Company offices laid out the specifications and procedures. Harnik, finally roused with a bucket of snow dumped on his face, had been half carried to the office where Marshal Steralt sat as judicar; Harnik paled when he saw Nasimir Clart. Burek and Selfer each gave his evidence again, as did Guildmaster Teraloga from the hiring hall and Clart.

Harnik first blustered, attacking Selfer for his youth and inexperience and suggesting—as Selfer had said he feared—that Selfer had no right to command. Then, confronted with his own lies and his obvious drunkenness, he wept, pleading for mercy.

"It is mercy Captain Selfer does not have you whipped in front of the troops," M'dierra said.

When it was done and Harnik back in civilian clothes, out the gate into the swirling snow, banned from the mercenaries' hiring hall, Clart said, "You have offered no blame, Captain Selfer, but I feel some responsibility. I have a young officer I could lend you until you find someone qualified—no cost to you but his board. He won't give you trouble, I'll stand for that."

"And I have a nephew who came this past autumn," Aesil M'dierra said. "It would be good for him to be under another's command for a time. He's eager to show himself capable."

"I thank you," Selfer said. "That would be a help." When the others had left, he turned to Burek. "You're just what I needed, Burek. One last thing: we should both tell the sergeants before the rumors get any wilder and make it clear we stand together. Then you're to bed, if you'll take my order."

"Willingly," Burek said, yawning.

CHAPTER ELEVEN

ARVID HAD NOT planned to stay in the same lodging too long, but the snows that now came to Valdaire every day or so made the comfort of his inn too appealing. He knew everyone's name from Jostin Psedann, the innkeeper, all the way down to Pidi, the boot-boy. Jostin greeted him cheerfully each day—it was all due to Arvid's continued signs of prosperity, he knew, but still welcome. When a ground-floor room became available where Dattur could put his feet on stone, Jostin offered it to him first.

Dattur continued to act as Arvid's servant, keeping their room spotless, mending and polishing anything he could find to mend and polish. In addition, he went out on his own, finding a rockfolk tailor for whom he could do contract work.

Arvid himself had a keen eye for value and soon learned which of the city's markets and shops offered the best possibilities for small-scale trading . . . and the most gossip that he hoped would eventually lead to the necklace. His story—that he was a northern merchant who had not realized how early the pass over the mountains closed—brought nods and chuckles. Stranded northern merchants were nothing new. He and Dattur together made almost enough to cover their expenses, so he was sure the gold he'd taken from their abductors would last until spring.

They were still careful not to be seen much together; Dattur usually ate in their room or in one of the cookshops near the tailor's where he worked. Gnomes were uncommon in Valdaire but not rare enough to excite comment, and a gnome working in a dwarf's shop would likely be taken for a young dwarf, not a gnome at all. Arvid ate in the inn's common room at least once a day, sitting alone. They left the inn and returned to it separately and never walked together in the streets.

At some point, Arvid knew, the Thieves' Guild would find out that their journeymen had disappeared, but the amount of gold sent with them suggested that a long absence would not trigger suspicion. The longer they weren't recognized, the more likely they would not be. A slightly thickset merchant in a green-and-brown-plaid hooded cloak stumping about on foot should not call up memories of the lean, black-clad, black-hatted man on horseback with pointed beard and mustache and a gnome companion at his side.

He still could not think of any way to take his revenge on the local Thieves' Guild, secure the Marshal-General's letter, find and obtain the necklace, and make his way back to Vérella.

On this snowy afternoon, Arvid came back to the inn before his usual time and, after taking a meal to Dattur in their room, settled into what was now his favorite table—against the wall, small, perfect for one person—with a pot of sib and a mug of soup to warm him while he waited for his supper.

The tables filled quickly; he was congratulating himself on his decision to come in early when the door opened again and a red-faced man he knew he'd seen before stumbled in. For a moment, he could not place him . . . but then remembered the man had been in Fox Company uniform with a captain's knot on his shoulder. Now he was wearing civilian clothes and had a pack slung on one shoulder. Interesting.

The man demanded a room in the blurred voice of someone a little drunk or very upset. Arvid carefully did not stare but managed to notice every detail of the man's appearance. He was not surprised that the innkeeper demanded prepayment for a room, or at the man's attempt to bluster and use his position with "Fox Company up the hill there" to avoid payment, or that it didn't work. The innkeeper was firm: he wasn't in uniform and thus could not use his position as surety.

"But you saw me in here yesterday."

"So I did, and you were in uniform. And you still owe me for that jug."

"Damn you!" The man fumbled a coin out of his pouch and

slapped it on the counter. "There's your jug and deposit on a room, too."

The innkeeper, lips tight, took the coin and led the man upstairs. Jostin was, Arvid thought, more patient than he himself would have been—but then, he made his living by accepting paying guests, not turning them away. He listened. By the sound of it, Jostin had led him to one of the rooms directly above. Arvid lingered over his supper—a generous helping of roast goose with vegetables and a bowl of steamed, spiced grain—and wondered if the man would come down to eat. He did, finally, looking over the now-crowded room where Arvid had the only single table. He pointed; Grala, Arvid's favorite serving maid, shook her head but finally made a "wait" gesture to him and came to the table.

"Sir, that man wishes a seat, and this is the only table with room. He could wait until you finish—"

"I am nearly finished," Arvid said. "It will not bother me to share, and you are full tonight."

"Thank you," she said, and beckoned to the man to come.

Close up, the flush was clearly from drink rather than cold, and the man immediately demanded a jug of ale.

"The water here is foul," the man said. "I'm Harnik, retired cavalry officer. You?"

"Ser Burin," Arvid said, giving the name he had chosen for his merchant persona. "Merchant, as you see."

"Traveling?"

"At times. Not in winter," Arvid said.

"Well, if you're looking for an experienced guard-captain for your caravan next season, I'm for hire."

"I thought you said you'd retired."

"From the cavalry. Old wound. Fit enough to do caravan work." The ale came; the man drank half a mug at one swallow. "Or if you need personal protection . . . never a bad idea with the city full of soldiers and those who prey on them. You merchants—always have gold in your sleeves—need somebody with blade skills to keep off the riffraff."

Desperate for work, then. Arvid could add up scores as well as anyone and was sure the man had just been cashiered, probably for being a drunk.

"Not at the moment, thank you," he said, as meekly as he thought a merchant should, and applied himself to his dessert, spiced apples baked in custard. His earlier hatred for the south was weakening under the influence of southern cooking.

Harnik took another swallow of ale, hooked one arm over the back of his chair, and glanced around the room. Arvid had already noticed that no Phelani uniforms were in the room. Harnik leaned forward. "Wouldn't advise you to deal with Fox Company," he said.

Arvid raised his brows but said nothing.

"Couple of young fools up there, making a mess of things. No respect for experience. It'll all come to grief, you mark my words."

A different servant appeared with a platter of bread and cheese, which Arvid recognized as the cheapest choice for supper. Harnik took a bite of cheese. Arvid scraped out the last bits of custard in his bowl. As if someone had touched him with a fork, he was suddenly aware of interest somewhere in the room. He'd never seen that other man again, the one who had tried to keep his face hidden. He leaned back, sighing with obvious satisfaction, and twisted his head from side to side as if he had a cramp in his neck. There. Heart-hand, table for four—the man facing them looked down just too quickly. Round-faced, blue-eyed, freckled, gray roughspun shirt, brown vest, hands Arvid classified as "outdoor work." Arvid looked down at his bowl and licked his lips, as if thinking of ordering another.

"Can't trust 'em," Harnik said, washing down the cheese with another swallow of ale. "Need someone to guide 'em but won't listen. Not bad lads, but—" He put a slice of cheese on one of bread and took a huge bite. He almost choked but got it down with more ale. "They imagine things, you know. Being that age. One of 'em even thought he saw someone up on the mountain, going into a hole. Told him it was goats—had to be—but you could see he didn't believe it."

Attention at the next table might as well have been a spear, Arvid thought.

"I'm thinking about another apple custard," Arvid said to Harnik. "Join me?"

"No, I don't eat too much. Got to stay fit. Fact is, I won't finish this. It's enough for two meals for someone like me."

In addition to the ale. Arvid smiled and excused himself. Across the room, he saw Jostin watching him and mimed bringing payment. He gave a tip to Grala.

"Was he a problem to you?" she asked.

"Not at all," Arvid said. "A man with a grievance, I think, but no trouble to me. Though I don't plan to hire him." He went back to the room, thinking. Had the two veterans talking about some trail into the mountain been with the "young fellow" who thought he'd seen a hole in the mountain and someone going into it? Was that all one story or two? And was it true or made up?

He told Dattur about the man at his table, and Dattur had his own information about him. "When I went to the cobbler's to pick up those short boots, mercenaries were there, too. Cavalry, by their boots and spurs and blades. They talked of one who had claimed position in their company, lying, to be hired by Fox Company, and how angry their commander was."

"Did they say who they were?"

"No, but the cobbler did after they left. Clart Company. They said their commander found out only today."

"I'll take your tray out," Arvid said. "They're busy; it would be awhile before someone came."

In the common room, he saw at a glance that the round-faced man now sat where he had been, talking to Harnik. No surprise; that was what he'd come to see. The question now was what to do about it. It wasn't his business . . . it hadn't been his business before, when he'd warned the two soldiers someone was listening in. Only because of Paks . . .

And me.

Arvid's heart skipped a beat and started again, faster. He handed the tray over the bar. "Has the snow stopped?"

"I doubt it," Jostin said.

Arvid pondered. He could walk up to the Fox Company compound, but it would break the pattern he'd established for Ser Burin, and he doubted the mercenaries would let him in the gate to talk to their commander. Legitimate merchants did not come to do business in the dark.

Yet he felt he needed to do something. Tomorrow, in day-light, when the mercenaries might listen to him and he wouldn't be as vulnerable on the way there . . . that should do. Across the room, his former tablemate—Harnik, that was his name—rose unsteadily; the round-faced man tossed a pile of coins on the table and then helped Harnik toward the stairs that led up to the second-floor rooms. So, drunk as he was, Harnik wouldn't get far by morning. Arvid went back to the room he shared with Dattur and slept the night away.

CHAPTER TWELVE

THE MORNING AFTER dismissing Harnik, Selfer paraded his cohort and took their proxy oaths right after breakfast. Both cohorts worked to clear the courtyard of snow, and in the midst of that, the captain Clart Company had promised them arrived. Ivats was as different from Harnik as could be imagined, a cheerful, bright-eyed, red-haired young man.

"It's my fault," he said to Selfer. "I kept bothering the others, asking what I could do, so they sent me over here. You're supposed to make me sorry, I think."

"How are you afoot?" Selfer asked. "We're infantry, you know."

"I joined the cavalry, didn't I?" Ivats said, laughing as he said it. "I don't mind foot-slogging in the cold; it's heat that bothers me, and I'll be back with the Clarts by the Evener, if not sooner." He looked around. "This place is so big—how many troops do you have?"

"Two cohorts, both a little under strength right now, but Lord Arcolin will be bringing down replacements in the spring and possibly another cohort."

"You're lucky. We're all crammed into an inn on the far side of Valdaire, with our horses scattered through every livery barn in the city."

"What I need most from you," Selfer said, "is backup to whichever of us is taking out both cohorts at once. One of us should be here in quarters."

"Better than that inn," Ivats said. "Where do I sleep?"

"Officers' quarters here," Selfer said, leading the way. "Lord Arcolin has the one adjoining the Company offices; then me, and you can have this one, between Burek and me."

"A room to myself? This is luxury indeed!" Ivats said. He

tossed his pack onto the bed. "What do you want me to do first?"

"We were going to have a skirmish out on the hill beyond our wall," Burek said. "You and I can do that. M'dierra said she was sending a nephew over to act squire."

"To get the bur out of her own saddle blanket," Ivats said. "He's following her around like a puppy."

"You've met him?"

"Not to speak to. Just seen her with a wide-eyed, excited boy tagging at her heels. He looks a likely lad, but he's at that age—you know."

"I do. Well, if you're ready, I'll get the troops together and we'll go."

"Did you want me to wear your uniform?"

"No," Selfer said. "You're a guest of sorts."

Burek took the cohorts out with Ivats beside him. "You'll take my cohort—Devlin's a long-time veteran, and he'll see you right. Our commands may be different from yours, but you'll catch on. I'll take Selfer's—I don't know them as well, or they, me, so it makes it more even."

Soon the open ground just north of the compound was a trampled mess as tensquads and half-cohorts maneuvered, closed, and drilled with hauk and shield. Ivats, Burek decided, was everything that could be hoped for. He seemed tireless and enthusiastic. Near midday, a slender youth in a Golden Company tabard came into view around the corner of the compound, marched up to Burek, and gave a Golden Company salute.

"Captain Burek, Captain Selfer asks that you return to the compound."

"Who are you?" Burek asked, though he was sure it was M'dierra's nephew. That bone structure certainly fit her family.

The lad flushed. "Sir, I am Poldin M'dierra, assigned to this Company as squire."

"Thank you, squire," Burek said. "Please tell Captain Selfer we will be on our way immediately."

Ivats followed the cohorts into the mess hall, and Burek went to report to Selfer. He found Selfer in the Company office, talking to a merchant.

"I'm not surprised he was drunk," Selfer was saying. "But I don't understand what your concern is, since he's no longer with this Company."

"It is not his being drunk but some of the things he said," the man said. "And the interest what he said provoked." He was tall, lean-faced, dark eyes and hair, with a neatly trimmed beard in the southern style, and something about him did not fit "merchant" to Burek's eye. "And it connected, in my mind, with something I heard in the same inn some nights ago, which also provoked interest, though from a different listener."

"Other than yourself," Selfer said. He looked at Burek. "Captain Burek, this is Ser Burin, resident for the winter at the Dragon. He says he has information that concerns us."

"About Harnik?" Burek asked.

"That was his name," the man said. He had an easy, skilled voice, clearly a man used to persuading others. "Some days ago, when I was newly arrived at the Dragon, a number of soldiers were gaming there. One of yours, a redheaded fellow, won a wager on his skill at arm wrestling. It was after he won that I noticed two older men in your uniform talking at the next table. And beyond them, standing at the bar, someone listening."

"What were they talking about?" Selfer asked.

"A journey they remembered that they said others in your Company did not. It had to do with gnomes and a short way through the mountains—that's all I know. I recognized that the man listening to them was a spy of some kind, so I . . . caused a disturbance, and that gave me a chance to warn them."

"Why?" Selfer said.

"It's difficult to explain," the man said. "Look here, Captain, if I share something with you, can you keep it between us?"

"Depends what it is," Selfer said. "If you're going to tell me you're picking pockets at the Dragon, I'm not going to keep that secret. Best you know I'm a Girdsman—we don't tolerate that kind of thing."

"Not at all," the man said. "I'm not a thief."

"Well, then, if you trust my judgment, I will hold my tongue."

"Very well. I am known in the north by a different name and

came south on an errand for the Marshal-General, on the trail of a certain . . . item. And some years ago, I knew the paladin who was once of your Company. Paksenarrion."

Selfer scowled. "Do you have any proof—are you Girdish yourself?"

"No. Although both Paksenarrion and the Marshal-General seem determined I shall become Girdish. At any rate, you knew Dorrin Verrakai, did you not?"

"Yes," Selfer said. "Most recently, I had a contract with her after she became Duke Verrakai."

"So I had heard. Then you surely know of items she found and took to Vérella to give the king, and perhaps you know of the gossip surrounding them."

"Yes . . . but how did you hear?"

"Gossip, as I said. I was asked to report what gossip I heard and from whom. I was . . . uniquely placed, you might say, to do so."

Selfer's expression changed. "You! You're the . . . you *are* a thief!"

"No. I was a member of the Thieves' Guild, but not a thief. Just as you have persons in your Company who are not themselves soldiers, do you not?"

"Yes, but—you're the one who got Paksenarrion out of that place?"

The man inclined his head.

"Then you're the one who gave her a certain—" Selfer stopped as the man laid a finger to his nose.

"*Item.* An item, yes, that she took to Fin Panir and gave to the Company of Gird and that—most important—was stolen from under their noses last summer."

"I suppose not by you?"

"Not by me; that is correct. I was in Fin Panir at the Marshal-General's invitation to tell what I knew of Paksenarrion to their archivists. However, she was aware that the item might become a target for thieves; there was concern about the other items as well."

"I knew that," Selfer said.

"Alured," Burek said. "It would be Alured wanting it."

"Quite so," the man said. "I foiled one set of thieves, but

another got the . . . item. The Marshal-General thought perhaps I could trace it, but I left Fin Panir too late; I had been
injured. I found what I believe was the successful thief's body,
with Thieves' Guild marks on it. I wasted more time going
back to Vérella to see if it had gone that way. Instead, I believe
it came south."

"Did you contact the Thieves' Guild here?" Selfer asked.

"Unfortunately, yes. I had been here before, on business for
the former Guildmaster, but this time—this time I was betrayed by the Vérella Guild, and the Marshal-General's letter
explaining me to Marshals fell into the Guild's hand. I was
taken and nearly killed but escaped and returned through several changes of identity to become, as you see, Ser Burin."

"But you have no proof."

"No. But I have a kteknik gnome companion at the inn who
will corroborate what I have said. As you know, gnomes follow their Law and even when cast out do not lie." When Selfer
said nothing in answer, the man went on. "Your soldiers spoke
of a secret way across the mountains, or through them, and my
gnome companion, when I told him, became frightened. I saw
no more of the man who had listened that night, and I do not
know how much he heard or what he understood of what he
heard. Last night, however, your former captain spoke of another captain here who had seen a line of men—or beings,
anyway—moving along the mountain away from known trails
and entering a hole. Harnik was convinced it was not so and
ridiculed the man as young and inexperienced, liable to imag-
ining things. But the fellow listening to him—the fellow who
came and sat with him to drink after I left, which I saw when I
came back into the common room—was clearly interested. It
is none of my affair if you have a secret passage through the
mountains, but others think it theirs . . . and if you asked me
who might have such interest, I would say—"

"Alured," Burek said again. "A way to take an army secretly
into the north, unseen by those at the pass."

"But we have no such secret way," Selfer said. "It is true we
met gnomes on the way south because it was late in the year
to cross the pass." He looked puzzled. "I don't remember

much . . . We made better time than usual with their guidance."

"Your soldiers—at least two of them—think they remember that secret road," the man said. "You might ask them—they were boasting of their better memory and that others did not seem to know."

"Can you describe them?"

"Certainly. One was tall, stocky, balding, with a scar like this—" The man ran a hand down his own face. "The other had dark curly hair with a little gray in it and a wide scar on the forearm of his heart-hand."

"Bald Laris and Gannin," Burek said. "I heard something yesterday—the day before—they were talking to each other and I think meant not to be overheard, but the problem with Harnik put it out of mind."

"I would have your name," Selfer said to the man. "Your real name, if you please."

The man shrugged. "Arvid Semminson. I doubt you know it and hope you will not spread it about. That is the name my enemies here know, and they think me dead; it is also the name Paksenarrion knows, and the Marshal-General."

"Do you think she would have sent word to one of the Marshals here in Valdaire?"

"I doubt it. I think she thought I would either catch the thief in the north or go back to Vérella."

"Would your . . . gnome friend have heard the Marshal-General use your name?"

"Yes . . . but you should know he's not merely my friend. I saved his life, and he feels he is bound to me by debt, though I have tried to free him. He is kteknik, you see—"

"What is that? You said that before."

"A gnome who has displeased his prince and been for a time exiled; he cannot wear his princedom's uniform, and he is usually sent on a mission of some importance, which, when fulfilled, will restore him to his position. Dattur—that's his name—says it is painful to be apart from his people and those who understand the Law. Though I know he will not lie on my behalf, you may not be certain, and thus I tell you he considers himself in my service."

Selfer fiddled with a quill not yet trimmed to a pen, rolling it back and forth in his fingers. "What are your plans, then?"

"May I sit?" When Selfer nodded, the man—Arvid, Burek reminded himself—moved one of the chairs a little and sat down, flipping back the corner of his cloak as if to free the hilt of a sword that wasn't there. The cloak, however, hung as if something other than cloth were in its making. Burek sat in one of the other chairs, where he could watch Arvid's hands. "I am not sure," Arvid said. "When I survived the death they planned for me, my thought was to come back to Valdaire, take my vengeance on the Guild's local master, retrieving the letter the Marshal-General had given me, supposing it to be still intact, and then go in search of the item."

"And now?"

"The Guild knows that I traveled with a gnome . . . they captured us both. So it is necessary to go in disguise—these clothes—and we do not go about together. I would prefer not to be captured again."

"How did you escape?" Burek asked. "Did your gnome companion free you?"

Arvid explained. Selfer imagined himself in that dilemma and wondered if he'd have been able to get free. Certainly not without someone who could provide shelter: open the rock? It seemed incredible, and the man was, after all and despite his denials, a thief and no doubt a liar.

"It's a long story, how we made it back to Valdaire," Arvid said, "and since then, I've been acting the merchant and listening for word of that item."

"Have you heard nothing?"

"Nothing. I cannot go into places thieves frequent—as a merchant I would have no reason to do so—and no one's mentioned the item in the Dragon. I suspect it was transported past Valdaire quickly."

Selfer considered asking how a man and a gnome with no employment could afford to stay at the Dragon but decided against it. Instead, he said, "So . . . there's apparently some secret passage through the mountains, other than the Valdaire pass, known to gnomes . . . and this item in Aarenis that's been stolen. Burek, would the Count be likely to hear of it?"

"No . . . Andressat's off the Guild League routes. My guess is that if it's not still in Valdaire, it's already with Alured. I can't think who else would have sent thieves for it."

"I'm not sure that's accurate," Arvid said. "I handled the item myself, remember—it is beautiful and obviously valuable. Any professional or amateur thief might make a try for it just for that. So might a wealthy person. In my experience, wealthy merchants and nobles are not necessarily free of avarice." Selfer said nothing in response, and after a moment Arvid went on. "In addition, the item is connected to other items."

"So it was surmised," Selfer said.

"Yes. And did you also know that when the Marshal-General and Paksenarrion herself tried to move the other items from the king's treasury, they could not? And the chest sealed itself and would no longer open? I did not see this but was told by the Marshal-General."

"Where is Paks?" Selfer asked suddenly.

"I do not know that, either. She was expected to arrive with the Marshal-General in Fin Panir a day or so after I did, but according to the Marshal-General, one day she simply left, riding off to the south."

Selfer frowned. "I still do not quite see how this has to do with my command," he said. "The mystery of the secret passage, yes. We will need to talk to Laris and Gannin. If they did not merely dream it while dozing in the saddle, it means that something clouded my memory and that of all the others. Why would those two have knowledge?"

"Dattur says such ways are very secret and the gnomes would have cleared the knowledge from your minds; he was very upset when I told him what I'd heard. I believe his greatest concern was that they might try to find the opening again, perhaps only out of curiosity. It would be deadly, he said."

"If Alured found it and could get through," Burek said, "that would be a great advantage to him. Surely Tsaia has guards to the north of the pass—"

"Indeed, though not *at* the pass, as that is still in gnomish territory," Selfer said. "We need to know where both ends of the secret way are—and how strong the gnomes are. I know—

I think I remember—that we told the gnomes we met of possible danger from the south, so they will be alert, at least."

"But they're only gnomes—how big an army do they have?" Burek asked.

"*Only* gnomes?" Selfer said. "How can you—oh, you rarely see them here in the south, and then only the merchants. Burek, they are the hardiest of fighters, and it is from them that Gird Strongarm learned both law and warfare. It would not take many gnomes to defend an entrance to the underground, I'm thinking. But if such exists, and the location is known, they will not be pleased with us for having revealed it. If that is what happened."

"One of my concerns," Arvid said, "is the welfare of those soldiers who do remember. The spies' interest tells me that someone is looking for a secret way north—and if there's enough money behind such a goal, your people could be abducted and the information squeezed from them." He turned to Burek. "Even you, Captain, as Harnik mentioned a young captain having seen something that could fit with the earlier story."

"What do you want in exchange for this information?" Selfer asked.

"Nothing," Arvid said. "Or rather, your silence about my real identity and, should you hear anything about the item, perhaps that."

"Hmmm." Selfer leaned back in his chair. "Are you willing to stay while I talk to the two veterans you mentioned?"

"Yes," Arvid said.

"Burek, bring them here, please."

"At once," Burek said. Once outside, he wondered if he should have left Selfer alone with that obviously dangerous man. Arvid Semminson . . . a northern sort of name. And that cloak, though obviously made by a local tailor, hung like no cloak that tailor ever made. And the way he sat, in a way that would have cleared a sword-hilt if he'd worn one. Surely Selfer would realize there must be weapons hidden in that cloak or up a sleeve. He almost turned back to send someone else, but saw his targets coming out of the mess hall and called to them.

Back in the office, the two veterans showed no uneasiness at Selfer's summons.

"Did you ever see this man before?" Selfer asked, tilting his head toward Arvid, who turned to look them in the face.

Gannin nodded. "Yes, sir. Some nights ago, the time Vic won a wager against that big woman in the Blues, me and Laris here was talking, and he warned us of a spy. He was wearing black at the time—both of 'em, I mean, the man he said was a spy, and himself as well, and me and Laris thought maybe they was working something together, so we gathered up a group to walk back with and nothing happened. But if he's telling you we talked Company business, no sir, we did not."

"Laris?"

"Same, sir. This man went out to the jacks, and coming back he stumbled into the one he said was listening, he said to get a look at his face. Man was angry, tried to start a fight. This'un wouldn't, and t'other stomped out wi'out payin'. *He* paid for him and a jug for us, but we didn't drink it—shared it out."

"He didn't come to complain of you," Selfer said, tenting his fingers. "But to tell me about that spy and another, who was listening to Harnik last night. Harnik was drunk—"

"Wasn't the first time, sir."

"No. But my concern is something else. When we came down from the north, we met a party of gnomes as we neared the pass—it was late for caravans, you recall."

"Yes, sir."

Burek felt the tension that suddenly filled the room. He glanced at Arvid but saw no change in expression or posture. The two soldiers, though, were standing stiff now, faces too expressionless.

"You were heard—twice, once by this man and once by Captain Burek—saying something about a secret passage."

Laris reddened; Gannin paled. Burek tucked away those reactions for later use.

"I have no memory of passing through the mountain," Selfer said. "But apparently you do. Or so you indicated. And Captain Burek believes he saw something on the mountain that afternoon before the clouds came down and it started snowing.

Captain Harnik told him it must be goats, but I'm wondering—what *do* you remember?"

The two stared straight ahead, then Laris spoke. "Well . . . sir . . . we was just . . . like . . . it might not be real, after all . . ."

"Spit it out, Laris."

"Do you remember camping near the entrance to the gnome prince's hall? And you and Count Andressat going in to talk to the prince?" Laris asked.

Selfer looked shocked. "No. And you do?"

"Yes, sir," Gannin said, nodding. "'Twas our turn to fill jacks next morning, me and Laris, with them gnomes watching to be sure we made it all tidy, turf laid down and everything. We's told they was rewarding the Count by taking us a faster way. I thought, back to the Valdaire trade road, but it wasn't. Up the side of the mountain, in among rocks. Bad place for an ambush, I thought. But then straight into the mountain we went."

"Into the mountain?"

"Yes, sir. And all as quiet as quiet. Nobody talked. I could hear the horses' hooves cloppin' along, of course, and sometimes water trickling somewhere. We stopped a time or two to eat, but even then, nobody talked."

"Even us two," Laris put in. "Looking around, 'most nobody looked anybody in the eye. We drank, we ate, we got back on the horses and rode on. Easy to doze off, and I know I did—"

"And me, too," Gannin said. "But I kept trying to figure out which way we went in case something went wrong. Other ways led off of the way we went; I was trying to count shield-side and sword-side, the way we're 'sposed to. Laris was next to me; he was looking around some, too, when he roused."

"Couldn't tell time," Laris said. "No ladyglasses, no day and night. But for all we never went above a footpace, I'd swear it wasn't more than a day, day and a half, before them gnomes said get off the horses, almost there, and then we come out into darkness, but outside. With a bit of dawnlight way off east and the mountains behind us. Gnomes said follow that trail, and we did, and no one spoke until we were back on the trail we knew, over the pass."

"So when we got into quarters, and the chores done," Gannin said, "I said to the sergeant, how about that for a change, and he said what did I mean, and I said going right through the mountain, and he said none of your wild stories, Gannin, you were just sleeping in the saddle."

"Nobody remembers it but us two," Laris said. "At least—the first ones we asked about it didn't." He looked at Gannin. "And Gannin here says it's a way anyone might take if the gnomes weren't there."

"So it is," Selfer said. "And I don't recall a bit of it. But no more talk to the cohorts or down at the Dragon: it's too important to be gossiped about. You'll talk to me or Burek, or Lord Arcolin when he comes, so we can put down all you remember of the side passages, though I doubt we'll ever see the place again. Aside from that, it is Company business. Understood?"

"Yes, sir. But I'm not sure I remember all of them."

"Whatever you do remember. And be careful. This man thinks you may be in danger from those spies—might be taken and questioned by them."

"You mean we can't go down to the Dragon?"

"No. That would be punishment, and you've done nothing wrong. But go with a group and stay with the group. And no more talk. If anyone in town brings it up, however casually, report to me when you get back. Is that clear?"

"Yes, sir."

"Dismissed."

The two saluted and left the office. Selfer gave Arvid a long, thoughtful stare, then said, "I have a proposition for you."

Arvid's eyebrows went up, but he said nothing.

"You have done us—and perhaps Tsaia—a very good turn. Certainly I will not reveal your true identity abroad or to more than know it already, even in the Company. If I hear of the item, I will share that information with you. However, I would be interested in what you hear that might be pertinent to military actions. You are acting as a merchant, you say. What might you do in that line that we could use to give an excuse for coming here from time to time?"

Arvid smiled. "Thank you. Let me think . . . so far my commercial dealings have been small, as someone seeking to get a foothold in a new market."

"Pots," Burek said.

"Pots?" Selfer said. "We have pots enough."

"When I went to Andressat and we were attacked," Burek said, "some of our baggage had to be abandoned. Dort was killed, and a horse wounded. I remember now that I have not accounted for the smaller items left behind, including personal cooking gear." He grinned. "I could of course send one of the men to the city to look for such things, but that exposes them to risk and also wastes their time. If this merchant can run that errand—testing his skill, too, that would be—then perhaps we can think of others."

"How many?" Arvid asked. "And what size? New or used?"

Burek explained, and Arvid left shortly after.

"Did you really lose those pots?" Selfer asked.

"Yes," Burek said. "Hadn't thought of it until now. What do you think of him?"

"Arvid Semminson? Or Ser Burin? I'll tell you something odd, Burek. He's the one who got Paksenarrion out of the Thieves' Guild warren . . . and Paks told Dorrin something about him. Thought he was gods-touched, she said. And that item—"

"Should you name it?" Burek asked.

"Possibly not, though this must be the safest place in Valdaire. But there's trouble brewing on account of other . . . items . . . that the Duke found in the family house. That item Semminson followed is thought to be part of the set of those other items. And the Duke took those other items to the king's coronation, where they made a stir when she gave them to the king."

"And so Count Andressat goes north, worried about Alured. Does *he* know of this item?"

"He heard about it in the north. Wait—did he mention it to anyone while you were there?"

"I don't think so. He might have told his sons."

"Probably safe enough."

Burek thought of the angry third son. "I'm not sure," he said. "One of his sons seems to be the family troublemaker. He stormed off just before I left, angry that his father was acknowledging me."

"But surely he wouldn't go to Alured," Selfer said. "And anyway, the king and the Duke know that rumors about the items had already spread through the markets in Vérella."

"And might have reached Aarenis," Burek said, nodding. "If it was known at the coronation, then word would have reached here within two tendays, easily. From there to Cortes Immer, supposing he was at Cortes Immer, certainly before the Autumn Evener. Faster if Alured—Vaskronin as he calls himself now—had spies out as far as the north."

"Duke Verrakai thought he would," Selfer said.

"So whatever these items are, they're something he would want?"

"Oh, yes." Selfer got up and poured mugs of sib for both of them, then opened the door, looked out, and closed it again. "You might as well know so if you hear gossip you can report it. Duke Verrakai found a hidden crown and other royal regalia. She gave it to the king in proof of her loyalty. The other item is a necklace believed to be part of that regalia, separated from it long ago—no one can imagine how—but the box that holds the rest had an empty compartment."

"So . . . what would I hear about?"

"The necklace? I never saw it, but Paks described it to Phelan last winter—sapphires and diamonds."

"You're sure this Arvid didn't take it and just lie about it?"

"Not completely, no. But I do know the Marshal-General had invited him to Fin Panir because she said so when she was visiting the Duke."

"I suppose, if Vaskronin gets the necklace, he'll use the stones to make himself a crown."

"Maybe. But they think—the Duke, the Marshal-General—that he's after the rest of it, to gain legitimacy for the claim that he's the true heir to Old Aare—and thus Aarenis and the north both. That last year of Siniava's War, he started saying a priest had told him that years ago." Selfer took a long swallow of sib. "Ridiculous—it's been generations and generations since there was a king in Aarenis. Nobody knows who might be, if anyone is. And Old Aare . . . nobody lives there now but a few pirates on the coast. What good would it do to claim the throne of a pile of rock and sand dunes?"

A knock on the door, and Poldin M'dierra peeked in. "Captain Selfer, Captain Ivats sent me to ask what your orders are for the rest of the day."

"I'll speak to him," Selfer said. "Burek, I'll give the early watch to Ivats, the late one to me. You've got the night off, but I don't recommend a late stroll down to the Dragon."

"No, sir," Burek said. "I'll start an inventory this afternoon, if you'd like to brief Ivats."

"Good, then."

Burek spent the rest of the day with Maia, the Company quartermaster, preparing the inventory Count Arcolin would need when he arrived from the north. Supper that evening at the officers' table felt awkward until they were halfway through the hearty meal. Burek liked Ivats and the young M'dierra was eager to show himself useful, but Burek and Selfer could not discuss the topic that most interested them at the moment with the others present. Then Ivats sat back with a satisfied sigh.

"If I could borrow your cook to teach that fellow at our inn how to cook cut-legs . . ."

"Not a chance," Selfer said, grinning. "We know what we have."

"He makes wood out of meat over there, I'm telling you," Ivats said.

"My aunt M'dierra eats at inns, mostly," Poldin said. "But she says it's to do with business and makes me eat with her soldiers."

"So you should," Burek said. "Even captains eat with troops most of the time."

"I ate in an inn once," the boy said. "It was very good."

The men laughed, sharing a thought over the boy's head. He flushed.

"How far did you get with the inventory?" Selfer asked Burek.

"One room," Burek said.

Ivats pushed back his chair. "Near time for my watch, I think."

"Can I come?" the boy asked.

Ivats looked at Selfer, brows raised. Selfer nodded. "You can carry the lantern," Ivats said.

Burek yawned in spite of himself.

"Go to bed," Selfer said, grinning. "You've earned it."

Walking across the court, Burek felt much older than he had when Arcolin hired him. He wasn't sure when it had happened. The hard campaign the year before had been part of it, but having the cohort to himself when Arcolin rode to the north and left him in charge and then taking that patrol to escort Andressat home and all that happened there. Himself, Burek . . . Andressat. He grinned into the cold dark and then pushed open the door to his quarters. A lamp burned there; a brazier had warmed the room a little, and a bucket of water stood beside it. His bed, with its woolen blanket, stood along one wall; clothespress and pegs and an armor stand easily held everything else he owned.

For a moment only he compared this simple room to the elegance and luxury of his grandfather's house, where he might have had an apartment, fine clothes, the deference of servants, the companionship of his noble relatives. Filis's angry face came to him. Not companionship alone but enmity as well. He took a deep breath of pure satisfaction. This was his: this room and his reputation as a promising young officer were his by his own efforts. He could not despise his grandfather, or his own father for that matter. But he did not need them.

CHAPTER THIRTEEN

ARVID PULLED ON his gloves and nodded to Netta and Jostin, then pulled his hood forward and left the Dragon for the markets. Dattur had gone a turn of the glass before; that should be gap enough.

Low clouds hung over the city; though snow wasn't falling, Arvid thought it soon would. At some little distance from the inn, as he headed downslope to the city center, Arvid spotted two apprentice thieves shivering in what they thought was concealment, waiting for someone who might be easy prey, and an older man who, though wearing a brown cloak, not black, would be their senior. The man strolled out, not too close, and then walked on ahead, apparently unconcerned. Arvid did not look to see if the apprentices had emerged from their corners; he knew they would. He himself stumped along with the shorter stride he had adopted as Ser Burin, looking now and then into shop windows. When that street met a wider one, he turned into it and then into a cobbler's he favored, to be greeted there as Ser Burin.

"And your shoes is ready now, that broken heel all made new."

Arvid lingered in the shop; he could feel the interest outside . . . Something had caught their eye. Was it the hang of his cloak, all those pockets? He had hoped the green and brown plaid, the fur collar and hood ruff, would deter suspicion. Many merchants had pockets in their cloaks, after all.

The cobbler took his pay; Arvid thought of asking for the shoes to be sent to his inn but instead hired the cobbler's errand boy for the rest of the day. Thieves would be less likely to attack two; they might quit following him. Besides, he would need someone to carry the pots if he found them. He and the boy came out into the street, where he spotted the older thief and the two apprentices, now bunched together. His old master would never have allowed that. He stopped at the next baker's stall and bought a sweet bun for himself and one for the cobbler's lad and strolled on to the smiths' square.

The pots he wanted for Fox Company were made by almost every redsmith or tinker. Arvid compared prices without losing track of his followers. He knew when they melted away and others replaced them. This time it was a woman and a man, pretending to be a couple, and their sulky daughter. It didn't matter. He bought his pots, gave them to the boy, walked on to the next market area, where he greeted merchants he'd dealt with before. He bought more items he'd be able to sell for a small profit in another part of the city and two small stone jugs of mead for the inn. He put some small packages in his cloak pockets, making no attempt to conceal their existence.

A first snowflake fell in front of him, then others. He looked up. "Well, lad, I'd best start back. I need your help to my lodging, and then we need to get you back to your father."

Anyone the thieves talked to would know he lodged at the Dragon; that was a risk he had to take. But risk the boy, if he were attacked? No, he could not do that. In the cobbler's shop, he stood talking with the man as the snow came down more thickly.

"You want the lad to carry these for you, no doubt," the cobbler said, pointing to the basket.

"No," Arvid said. "I would make an extra trip then to see him safely home, and the snow's coming down. I'd rather just have my dinner."

"You'll never carry all this yourself!"

"I've carried more," Arvid said. He twirled the cloak off his shoulders expertly, the cobbler getting only a glimpse of pockets stuffed with parcels of various sizes.

"You could have given those to the boy," the cobbler said.

"Yes, but he had plenty," Arvid said, nodding to the basket. He pulled out his purse and paid the man for the lad's services, then fished out another bun and handed it to the boy. "Thanks for your help. And as it's getting dark, I'll just put these things in my tunic and tighten the belt. It will serve for the short way I have to go." As he spoke, he loosened the tunic's ties and tightened his belt. The flat copper frying pans he slid to the back, over his kidneys; the pewter plates fit reasonably comfortably along his sides. He laced up the tunic after disposing the rest of the items where they might do the most good. Then he replaced his cloak and picked up the sack, still containing the stone jars of mead. He slung it back over his shoulder, and bade the cobbler good even.

Outside, though it was not snowing heavily, snow did cut visibility. The slatternly girl ahead of him—now with a gray scarf on her head instead of the blue she'd worn back in the market square—moved out of an alley no wider than she and walked slowly, shoulders hunched against the snow, angling across the street toward him. He did not look back. He knew, as if he could see behind him, where the pair would be. The turn to the narrower, steeper street to the Dragon was just there—he would have to come nearer to her to turn.

Instead, he walked on. The girl turned, as if hearing his steps, when he did not swerve across her path to turn into the lane where they'd first found him. Arvid grinned to himself. He was sure they did not suspect who he really was. They had watched a small-goods merchant dealing as they themselves sometimes dealt, cheap goods for small profits. And they had seen him go to the mercenaries' winter quarters and return. He had not concealed that the mercenaries he'd met had given him a small commission. So now the thieves would want their slice of the pie they smelled.

A slice he was quite willing to give, but not of the pie they expected.

"HO! Look out! Thieves—!" A shout from behind, just as the girl moved closer; a yank to the sack over his shoulder would have pulled him over backward had he not expected it. He ducked that shoulder but kept hold of the sack; the thief had already let go, and he felt a blow in the back. Arvid whirled all the way around, the sack swinging wide with the weight of the jars in it. The man and woman behind him jumped back in time, but the slatternly girl, darting in with a wickedly long knife, took a solid hit and fell, snarling curses.

Arvid backed past her before she could clamber up, still whirling the sack to hold off the others. She grabbed for his leg; he evaded her easily and aimed another swipe, this time hitting her head. The impact made a hollow thunk, and she fell flat, unmoving. Back down the street, he saw a knot of people coming—not thieves, for the Guild would not waste so many to rob one minor merchant. As they neared, he recognized uniforms he had seen in the Dragon's common room. The thief couple had seen them, too, and were snarling at each other in thieves' cant, as understandable to Arvid as the clearest court speech.

"Simyits take the luck, *soldiers*! Get that sack, at least, as we pass. Show blade; he'll look at you; I'll get him behind."

"Cherin?"

"Leave the bitch; they'll catch us."

They both ran toward him; Arvid already had his sword out and put his back to the nearest wall as they closed in. This close, he could tell that the "woman" was a man in disguise; both had knives. Arvid flipped the sack around his left arm so the pots were on the outside.

"Thief!" he yelled at the advancing soldiers. "Help!" Shutters across the street banged open, and a man thrust his head out.

"HO!" he yelled, then ducked back inside.

The two men turned and ran up the street, the "woman" holding her skirts well up to reveal a pair of lean, muscled legs; the girl on the ground lay still. Arvid lowered his sword as the soldiers came up.

"Thank you," he said to them. Three stopped; the rest ran on after the thieves. Across the street a door opened; the man he'd seen in the window came out, armed with a club.

"Need help?" he asked.

"Not now," Arvid said. "But thank you. I would have been hard set against three—even two—"

"What've you got in the sack?" asked one of the soldiers. "Sounded like a rock when it hit that one's head." He nodded to the motionless figure in the snow.

"Two stone jars of mead," Arvid said. "I told the host at the Dragon I'd pick some up if I found any in the market."

"Ah—I've seen you at the Dragon," said another soldier.

"Yes, I'm staying there. My name is Ser Burin. Came south looking for trade and didn't realize how soon the pass would close."

"Fools some every year," the first soldier said.

"Could I beg the favor of an escort to the Dragon?" Arvid said. "And will you do me the honor of taking one of these jugs of mead?"

"Dragon won't let us bring in our own drink, ser," the soldier said.

"Then I will gladly buy a round for you all when I've handed it over to the host," Arvid said.

The pursuing soldiers straggled back now. "No luck. They got up a wall and over."

"Ser Burin here's offered to buy us a round at the Dragon," the soldier said. They all grinned at him.

They retraced their steps to the side lane that led to the inn, where the host greeted Arvid familiarly and took the two jugs of mead.

"I'm buying a round for these—" Arvid counted. "—these nine; I must leave the rest of my purchases in my room."

"Very well, Ser Burin," the host said. "And will you be eating in tonight? There's your favorite."

"Yes," Arvid said. "It's snowing again."

In the room, Dattur watched with interest as Arvid unloaded his cloak pockets and then his tunic. "Why did you put them there?"

"Look." Arvid held out one of the shallow pans, pointing to the mark on its bottom. "That was intended to go in just under the ribs." He stacked the pans and plates for the Phelani on his bed, handed Dattur the lump of beeswax and a cone of heavy thread he'd asked for, and piled the rest of his purchases at the foot of his bed. "I'm buying ale for the soldiers whose timely appearance kept me from enjoying a bit of swordplay. There would be three dead thieves instead of just one if they hadn't shown up, but as they did, I drew steel only long enough for them to catch up." He told the story briefly.

"You could be killed."

"I know," Arvid said with a grimace. "But I was not taken

unaware." He took off his sword belt and hung it on a peg. "I must go—I'm having supper in the common room. Shall I have something sent to you?"

"No need. I ate before I came back."

Back in the common room, the soldiers lifted their mugs to him; one of the maids showed him to his favorite table. He hoped to see Harnik again, but the man did not appear, nor did the freckle-faced man who had been at the next table. While he was eating, one of the Phelani captains came in with four of the soldiers. One of them was the scar-faced man. Arvid placed a small bet with himself that they had come to talk to him and counted it won when the captain, having scanned the room, nodded to his men and came directly to his table.

"May I, Ser Burin? Captain Selfer."

"Certainly, Captain," Arvid said. "I was able to find the pots and pans you asked for; they're in my room. Is there some urgency?"

"Not about those. Harnik's body was found today under the Drunkard's Bridge. Did you know?"

"No," Arvid said. "I've been out much of the day—I heard no gossip of it."

"Did you see him last night or this morning?"

"No to both. Last night I dined early; the common room was quiet, and I talked to the host to see if he had errands around town I might do for him, since I was shopping for you already. As he did; hence the mead I brought back and a few other things. I went early to bed. But it wouldn't surprise me if Harnik was drunk again; he was drunk the night before."

"I will be asking the host when he left and with whom. It was clearly murder, not accident, from the marks on the body."

"How so?" Arvid asked.

"Cuts and burns," Selfer said. "Very deliberate. Clart Company has very generously offered to split the funeral costs with us."

"A bad business," Arvid said. "That might explain my adventures today." He saw Tilin bringing a tray; she winked at him. "A moment—they're bringing my supper. Will you join me?"

"No, I should get back."

"Please. A short time only."

"Very well." Selfer turned slightly in his chair and caught the eye of one of his soldiers; the man came over at once. "I'll be sitting with Ser Burin for a while," he told the man. "Anything he should watch for?" he said to Arvid.

"Freckle-faced man, was wearing blue the last time I saw him," Arvid said. "Not a soldier; looks like a laborer."

Tilin arrived and began off-loading dishes to the table. "And for you, Captain?"

"A pot of sib and a couple of those cheese rolls," Selfer said. "And a dozen for my troops." The servant nodded and left with the tray.

Arvid unrolled the napkin and laid out the eating utensils in it, then arranged his side of the table carefully. "It serves my image as a slightly fussy merchant," he said. "And it lets my hot-pot cool just enough . . . and here is your sib, Captain, and your cheese rolls."

Selfer paid for his food, and Tilin left them alone. Arvid broke the pastry crust of the hot-pot, sniffed appreciatively, and then poured himself a glass of wine.

"That's Andressat wine," Selfer said.

"So the host told me, with some pride. It is a region? Or an estate?"

"A region," Selfer said. "Governed by the Count of Andressat, a famously fussy old man who has great scorn for the north—of course he's probably never been out of his own land."

Arvid looked at Selfer, a spoonful of vegetables and gravy halfway to his mouth. "Indeed," he said.

"There have been rumors that he traveled earlier this year, but I assure you . . . those were not . . . true." Selfer's lips twitched.

"I see," Arvid said. "Well, I have heard no rumors and know nothing but the name the host told me."

"So," Selfer said, breaking open a cheese roll and spooning jam onto it. "Tell me about your adventure, if you will."

Arvid gave a full account, from morning through afternoon. "They changed teams," he said. "When I returned the boy to the cobbler's place, I took the precaution of disposing of your pots and pans where they would do the most good before I went back out into the snow."

"You expected an attack?"

"I thought then it was my being a solitary, someone with money enough to buy goods—some of them modestly valuable, and all could be resold. But after what you tell me of Harnik's death, I think it may be that I talked to Harnik and then to you."

"But could you not have hired an escort? One against three—that's not good odds."

Arvid took a sip of wine and smiled. "I had taken their measure early. These were not the best in the city. I was even looking forward to it." He ate another two bites of hot-pot, then told Selfer how the game had played out. "I had only to hold them off until the troops came up, trusting my unconventional armor to protect me in back." He took another sip of wine. "Merchants often carry swords but are not expected to be expert with them."

"And you are," Selfer said, brows raised. Not quite a question.

"I killed that former soldier of your Company who would have killed Paksenarrion," Arvid said softly, breaking the rest of the pastry crust into the hot-pot. "Did you ever see that black-haired woman use a sword, Captain?"

Selfer blinked. "Yes." He poured himself a mug of sib. "Yes, I did."

"Then you know how good I am," Arvid said.

"Valdaire has become dangerous for us," Selfer said. "More dangerous for the Company, I mean."

"Yes. But you must be here, because your winter quarters are here, and I choose to be here, in this inn where I am known to be respectable. If Harnik was killed, as I surmise, because of what he blabbed the other night in his cups, then it must have to do with what he mentioned, that story of the hole in the mountain."

"And possibly that item."

"And possibly that item, yes. You were wise, Captain, to bring an escort."

"None of my people will be wandering Valdaire alone," Selfer said. He downed half the mug of sib at one swallow.

"Nor will I," Arvid said. "With your commission, I will say, I can afford a hiresword as escort—"

"If you will, Ser Burin, I can find you a reliable person, an experienced soldier."

"That is very kind," Arvid said.

"And now I must speak to the host—I do not know if he knows yet about Harnik."

"And when you are finished with that," Arvid said, "perhaps you would like your pots and pans?"

"Certainly."

Arvid watched as the young captain spoke to the host. He could read Jostin's reaction. No, none had come to tell him . . . the man was not worried, and that in itself was a mystery. He himself was worried, more worried than he wanted to show. If he had been targeted because he had talked to Harnik and the Phelani—because he had interfered with the spy listening to the Phelani soldiers—his disguise of harmless merchant had frayed past usefulness, his careful nurturing of that image was effort and time wasted. The two thieves who'd escaped earlier . . . What were they telling the Guildmaster?

He finished the hot-pot and the plum-jam tart with cream for dessert. The soldiers who'd rescued him hadn't stopped with the round he bought them; they occupied three tables nearest the bar and seemed to be interested only in dicing and ogling the serving girls. Selfer's escort, one woman and three men, did not drink, though they chatted easily with the others.

Selfer came back to his table. "The host says Harnik left long before breakfast, taking his things from his room but leaving a tip. Took his horse from the stable; the stable night guard had him sign out. Said he had a journey to go."

"A short one," Arvid said. "Well, let's get your purchases to you." He stood and led the way to his room. He knocked on the door in case Dattur was taking his nightly bucket bath—gnomes bathed more often than anyone needed, he was sure—and Dattur opened the door. "Captain Selfer," Arvid said. "He has come for the pots and things I bought for the Phelani."

"Is good," Dattur said. "You need talk?"

"Not much," Arvid said. "Stay."

Dattur sat cross-legged on his bed and picked up the work he'd been doing, sewing pockets into some garment, while Arvid showed Selfer the pans, including the mark on the one, and the receipts from the merchants who'd sold them. "These are said to be new—these two I bought used, because they seemed in good condition."

"Fine," Selfer said. "And you got them for less than my soldiers could. What's your price?"

"What would you have paid?" Arvid asked. Selfer's answer matched what he would have asked. Selfer paid over the coins, and Arvid put the pots in the sack he'd used for the jars of mead.

Selfer watched Dattur sewing for a long moment. "Does he ever make gloves?"

"Make gloves," Dattur said. "Is that you want gloves?" He leaned over and pulled a sack from under his bed. "Make these gloves." He spilled several pairs of gloves from the sack. "Already sold, these gloves. Take tomorrow."

"May I?" Selfer asked, reaching toward the gloves. Dattur handed him one.

"Make good. Gnomes never make bad."

"Would he—would you, pardon me—have time to make gloves for soldiers?"

Dattur looked at Arvid. "My lord?"

"As you wish, Dattur."

"Must finish work paid and work promised. Then make gloves. Need hands."

"Hands?"

"Measure. Not all hands same." Dattur spread his own. "My glove my hand. Ser's glove ser's hand."

Dattur, Arvid noticed, had a much thicker accent with Selfer than he now used with Arvid. Nonetheless, he and Selfer came to an agreement on the price of gloves if Dattur provided the leather or if the Company did.

After Selfer left, Arvid talked to the innkeeper.

"You're right," Justin said. "If they think you know what Harnik knew—what they killed him for—they'll be after you next."

"Already, I think," Arvid said, describing how he'd been shadowed and then attacked. "And it's deep winter, and I don't know where else to go. Yet I bring danger on your house by being here."

"Not that much," Jostin said. "And you're friends with the Foxes. They will not let much go wrong here, though I notice they're not coming down as much as they used to."

Arvid forbore to explain that he was one of the reasons.

"You can stay here, for all of me," the host said. "But you won't be able to go about and trade, will you?"

"No . . . I do have payment—"

"I'm not worried about that," Jostin said. "But how to explain that a man who's been in and out for tens of days never shows his face?"

"And just when I was thinking the Fox Company commissions would give me a start on the coming year," Arvid said.

"I don't like the feel of the city this past year," Jostin said. "The mercenaries are all right—they're rough folk, but mostly honest enough—the ones who come here, anyway. But there's been more trouble, more blood, more nasty talk . . . You've heard about the counterfeiting, I suppose, being a merchant?"

"To beware of false coins, yes. I came down here thinking Guild League coinage was safer than northern—"

"And so it was, once. But I'm telling you, I have to keep the scales and test-jar up front now. Not only for my people, but there's those complain about every coin they get in change. And some of 'em *are* bad, including what I get from my banker, though he always makes good any shortage." He shook his head. "And thieves is bolder. I've found thief-marks on the stable walls—don't know what they mean, but thieves made 'em is clear enough."

"Do you paint them out?" Arvid asked.

"Over and over," Jostin said. "But they come back."

"How long has that gone on?" Arvid suspected it had started when the rumors of the gnome road showed up.

"Last summer . . . around Midsummer. Can't remember if it was before or after, but around then. I used to know the thieves who worked this part of town—they knew me and knew they'd better pick no pockets nor start no fights in my bar. But now—I get that feeling, you know, that sort of prickle, that there's trouble about, but it's not faces I know. The ones I knew haven't been in since—oh, a little after the Autumn Evener." A knock came at the door, and a voice Arvid recognized as the cook asked for the host. "Just a moment," he said loudly, and then, softly, to Arvid, "Was I you, I'd take to my bed for a ten-day or so, and I'll say you're sick and like to die. Think of something in the meantime."

"Thank you," Arvid said. He had begun to think of something like that himself, but having the host on his side was an unexpected bonus.

When Dattur went up to Fox Company's winter quarters, he carried a note to Captain Selfer—Arvid explained his situation and suggested that Dattur might also be at risk.

Confinement to his room palled, but everywhere in the inn were staff who might chatter and customers who might not be what they seemed. Finally he begged the host to let him take the job of night watch in the inn stables. In the dark, he would not be recognized, he was sure.

"I suppose you can use that sword you've been wearing?"

"Yes," Arvid said. "I may come from a merchant family, but my father knew I would travel and thus would likely need to defend myself."

"Well, you can work alongside old Mardan if you want. He's wearing down, he tells me. If you catch someone coming over the wall, kill them if you can—you have killed?"

"Yes," Arvid said, careful to use a tone of disgust. "I did not enjoy it."

"No good man does," Jostin said. "But it is less trouble with the city watch if they're dead—t'watch know I don't go hunting, and they are glad enough to have no explanations to make. You'll need a different cloak, all dark; you can use my old bad-weather one."

"Thank you," Arvid said.

It was after closing when he ventured out, wrapped in Jostin's dark cloak, hat pulled low. No one was about but Jostin, just locking up the back door. "Here's a meat roll for your turn of night," Jostin said. "Mardan knows you're coming; he's in the stable."

Thin snow fell; the lantern burning at the inn's back door picked out one flake and then two. Across the stableyard, two more lanterns burned: one at the stable entrance, one by the back gate. Arvid made his way to the stable. Mardan was checking the horses in their stalls.

"Takin' my job, are ye?" He sounded half-sulky, half-relieved.

"Master Jostin said you could use the help."

"Well, then, ye walk the bounds for me. Up there, the cat-walk. Call if ye need me."

Arvid climbed the stairs. Down in the courtyard, three dim circles of light; over the stable wall, the lane that ran past it was solid dark. It reminded him of his early days as a thief apprentice, up on a roof in the dark and cold. Be a shadow, his trainer had said. And yet Mardan usually walked back and forth . . . He walked up to the corner of the inn itself; it rose another story higher than the stable roof. No windows out of which a guest could escape without paying, not on this side. He turned and walked back. From below, he might be visible in this light snow, a shadow moving through twirling flakes, no more. No one could see his face.

Back and forth once, twice, thrice . . . then down the stairs and across the court to the stairs on the north side. Mardan peered out to watch him start up the stairs, then ducked back into the warm stable. On this side, the catwalk circled the entire roof—over the cowbyre and adjoining storage open to the stableyard as well as a row of rooms that opened onto the street beyond. One, he knew, was a dormitory for the inn staff. Three adjoining housed prostitutes. Arvid faced into the biting north breeze and made the full circuit back to the roof of the north side of the stable and then back down and across.

The easy way in would be that—only a single story to climb and the catwalk to lead an intruder to the stableyard. But that street, wider, had more traffic even late at night; the women hung lamps outside their doors. Though men often clustered there, that in itself would make it harder for a thief to climb unobserved, though a night like this was a little safer. Still, the north wall, whitewashed, had neither nearby trees nor vines to aid a climb. Thief-assassins, Arvid thought, would be more likely to come out of the dark lane on the south side, where they might have placed climbing hooks and concealed them with thief-marks.

He made only two circuits of the larger catwalk and then moved back down and across to the south side and climbed up again. He wished he could risk going out to check the outside walls, but he knew the stable postern groaned on its hinges. He started off along the catwalk, feeling the grit of the snow underfoot, moving slowly but steadily as old Mardan would. One circuit. Two. On the third, instead of going back down the catwalk stairs, he simply sank down on his haunches slowly, as if descending. Drew his sword. And waited.

Snow fell silently out of the dark sky. Below, in the court-yard, Mardan paced across the stableyard, barely visible in the dim light of the gate lantern, and disappeared into the cow-byre. It would be warm in there, and Arvid hoped he would take his rest. The old man would not fare well in the fight Arvid expected.

Time passed. Arvid shifted his weight carefully, moving as slowly as a shadow might move, to ease one knee and then another. He thought of the meat roll in his pocket but decided against eating it.

Then he heard the first noise, a faint crunch from the lane . . . boots on snow. He looked across the lane. One possibility would send a partner up on that roof with a crossbow to shoot the watchman. That building had snow outlining every rough-ness; he should be able to see a shadow moving across it. But the next noise came from below, more vibration than noise . . . one then another. Someone tapping climbing hooks into the crevices of the wall with a padded hammer. *Ting-chink* . . . a hook slipped, hit a stone of the wall.

Silence again. Arvid easily imagined the thief below, listen-ing for any sound, hoping all were asleep or out of hearing.

Then the softened thuds of the climbing hooks being ham-mered in returned . . . paused . . . resumed again, nearer. Arvid slid his dagger out of his boot. While climbing a wall, it was almost impossible to hear someone on the other side of it;

one's attention fixed on the task itself, on balance and the stability of handholds and footholds.

Arvid had positioned himself in the corner, just beyond the stairs; the way he'd been trained, climbing the corner was considered bad technique. Sure enough, the shadow that rose above the catwalk and eased over to the roof, visible only by its disturbance of the falling snow, did so well away from the corner. Arvid waited. Another shadow joined the first; the two moved closer; he heard the rasp of drawn blades.

Though they would not see a motionless shadow, they might see an indistinct shape where snow had fallen on him. Would they believe some rubbish piled in the corner? Or would they attack? Arvid watched as they came nearer—they clearly knew where they were going—and turned at the head of the stairs. As he had hoped.

He had the best chance to kill them both as they went down those narrow, steep stairs, with the least disturbance to warn whatever thieves were left on watch in the lane. He took one last look along the catwalk before standing to take them in the rear—and froze. Another came over the edge of the roof, this time faster, with less care, and, as it moved toward the stairs, pulled something over its shoulder. By the dim suggestions of movement, Arvid knew it was not a blade he faced but a crossbow.

The shadow stopped in front of him, at the top of the stairs, and bent to span the bow. Arvid stood and lunged in the same moment, his sword driving through the thief's cloak and clothing, catching a moment on a rib. Arvid twisted the blade, and it slid on. The thief staggered and fell . . . but the bow was spanned, and the thief writhed, bringing it around. Arvid knocked the crossbow prod askew with his dagger; though the bowstring hummed, the bolt flew wide. Then he buried the dagger in the thief's throat and freed his sword.

Below, one thief had turned on the stairs and was almost on him; Arvid turned to meet the attack. He had height, but his back was to the outer wall, a sheer drop twice his height and only a low parapet. He parried, thrust, parried again, thrust again, using every advantage to drive the thief down the stairs, but the man was also skillful. And thief-cunning; a thrown

knife caught in the innkeeper's heavy winter cloak before
Arvid had seen it coming. It would not be the only one, he
knew, and they would all be tipped with poison.

And what was the thief now below doing?

"Ha! What's this!" Old Mardan came out of the cowbyre,
drawn by the clash of blades. Arvid didn't look. He had to
get past the one nearest before he could help Mardan. Mardan's call was just enough to distract the thief on the stairs as
Arvid thrust again; the thief made a weak parry, and Arvid
redoubled before the thief got his blade back in position. The
thief shifted his feet, and slipped on the trodden snow of the
steps. Arvid thrust again, closing; he felt his blade meet resistance and pushed harder. The thief slipped again, and then he
was tumbling backward, grunting. Arvid came down as fast as
he could without slipping.

As he reached the foot of the stairs, the lantern light glittering on the snow-covered stableyard was enough to see by.
Over by the postern someone stood hunched—was that Mardan or the first thief? The man who had fallen pushed himself
up and made a grab for Arvid's legs. Arvid kicked out, jumped
past him, then whirled and thrust hard into the man's body
even as he felt a breath of air on his cheek from another thrown
knife. He thrust again, this time at the angle of neck and shoulder; blood spurted out, dark against the bright snow, and the
man went limp.

When he turned, Mardan had advanced cautiously toward
the man at the postern, his club held before him. But already
the gate was moving; the hinges groaned, and someone outside pulled it wide. The noise it made should have waked half
the city. The man turned, and before Arvid could reach him, he
had dodged Mardan's clumsy swipe with the club and slashed
the old man across the throat. Mardan fell; two more men
came in, and Arvid faced three, all with blades out.

Well. Simyits was not with him tonight, that was certain.
You might ask me. His knees almost gave way. "Fine, then," he
muttered. "I ask you." *Say my name.* Arvid's mouth went dry.
Through his mind ran the names of saints and gods he had
never called on but to curse. *One is enough.* Gird. It had to be
Gird. He worked his tongue around in his mouth as the men

advanced, spreading out in a wide arc. The one on the right end had his blade in his left hand. "Gird," he managed in a sort of grunt. "Help."

Then they rushed him.

ARVID SHRUGGED AND charged, aiming at the one who was moving to his right. If he could get them into a spiral, getting in one another's way, maybe—but they knew better. He hesitated, luring them closer, and then once more charged at the left-handed man, sidestepped, and tried a backhanded draw cut as he strode past. The fellow yelped—against thieves' discipline, that—and then cursed, but Arvid was safe in his chosen corner, back to the staircase that led up over the cowbyre.

He could retreat up it; they could come at him only one by one then, but one of them, he could see now, had another crossbow slung to his back. And backing up a snow-slippery stair with a cloak he might step on and trip himself would be stupid. Still, in the corner, they couldn't all get at him, and in this corner in particular, he could dive to his heart-hand and roll around the frame of the cowbyre.

He glanced for an instant at the back of the inn, solid and silent . . . but . . . that lantern by the back door now showed a dark opening, and a dark figure—no, two—no, three—moved out onto the snowy courtyard. Arvid hoped very much these were not more thieves.

"Who are you?" one of the thieves asked softly in thieves' cant.

Arvid did not answer but parried the attack of the one on the right with his dagger and the one in the center with his sword. He huffed like a man out of breath. Indeed, he felt a tightness in his chest.

"Are you new in town?" asked another, this time in Common. "A hiresword? You've made a mistake, angering the Guild."

Two lunged, making the mistake of doing so in parallel; Arvid swept both blades aside with his, but they were quick and recovered before he could take advantage. The third had thrust at Arvid's cloak and now dragged at it, hoping to throw him off balance. Arvid slashed the cloak ties with his dagger, ducked his shoulder, and the cloak dropped off him, leaving him less encumbered than before.

He did not look beyond the three, though he was aware of moving figures coming across the yard. He was fairly sure now this was the innkeeper and two of his men from the common room. If he could keep the thieves' attention on him, the others would have a better chance.

From near the postern, he heard someone call, "What's this? What's to do?"

"Help! Thieves!" shouted the innkeeper, now running at the thieves, stave in hand.

"Get out of the way!" one of the thieves snarled at Arvid.

"No," he said. They pressed forward, clearly desperate to get to the stairway and escape over the roof; all he had to do was hold them. Easier thought than accomplished, as they were his equal in skill. They had worked together before—he was beset with blades from above, below, and straight at his head and barely escaped death.

Then one turned to face the threat behind. Arvid parried a thrust with his dagger and lunged, taking that thief behind the knee. He fell, and Arvid barely parried the thrusts of the other two . . . but Jostin and his door-ward Netta were close enough now, and both thieves fell to blows to the head. Arvid turned back to the wounded thief just in time to see Larin, the second door-ward, slam a club into the thief's head.

The night watch with his lantern on a pole was still by the postern; Arvid heard boots crunching through the snow outside.

"Why didn't you yell for help?" Jostin asked.

"Not enough breath," Arvid said, stooping to pick up the cloak. He did in fact have a stitch in his side. "Too much good food."

"Mardan's dead," Larin said. He looked at Arvid. "Did you see what happened?"

"He confronted that one—" Arvid pointed with his boot, then bent and wiped his blade on the thief's cloak, feeling all the familiar pockets and tools. He wanted a cloak like that again, the familiar black. "I was fighting the one over there—" He pointed to the body on the other side of the yard. "And there was another one, up on the roof there, head of the stairs. Mardan heard something and came out—I couldn't get past the two of them fast enough."

Six men in the city militia's uniform came in the postern, their short swords in hand. "What's this?"

"They're all dead," Jostin said. "No thanks to you. One of mine's dead, old Mardan. If it hadn't been for one of my guests who's good with a sword, we could all have been murdered in our beds. Five thieves—and the postern makes noise, you know that. Why did it take you so long?"

Arvid had retreated to the shadows of the cowbyre and listened to the discussion without taking part. The innkeeper wanted the thieves' clothes and possessions to sell "to give old Mardan a decent passing." The night watch claimed their traditional right.

"If you'd been the ones who killed them, yes," Jostin said. "But you didn't show up until it was over."

"The lantern man was here."

"And did nothing."

After some wrangling during which Arvid finished cleaning his sword, wiping it with snow and a clean cloth, Jostin won. While Jostin's men began the grisly business of stripping the bodies, he made his way through the cowbyre, past the inn's own cart and cart horses, and then into the inn to fetch a sheet from his bed for Mardan's body. Dattur, snoring, did not stir.

Well?

Arvid stopped short, sheet in hand. "Thank you," he said. He didn't mind saying that—he was alive, after all—but it still felt odd to be saying it to that one.

A chuckle ran through his awareness. *You will learn.*

"Why are you . . ." "Bothering me" would be rude. "Saving me" would be frightening to contemplate.

A different voice this time. *You are capable of more good than you know.* Arvid had no idea who that was but was sure he didn't want to know what "more capable" might demand of him.

The first voice came again, the one he was increasingly sure was Gird. *You do not know what you are. Neither did I.*

Arvid shivered and took the sheet out to the stableyard. Jostin or his door-wards had lit more lanterns. The night watch had gone back out to the street. The door-wards were dragging the bodies out the postern for the dead-cart to pick up in the morning. Jostin, kneeling beside Mardan's body, looked up at him. "Thank you for that. Where did you find it?"

"On my bed. Will it do?"

"Yes, indeed. Poor old Mardan . . . so brave to go up against a man with a sword, and with only his club."

"I'm sorry I couldn't—it was that third one up there, with the crossbow. Then the second came back up the stairs—and then—" Arvid was surprised to feel real sadness.

"It's not your fault," Jostin said as he stood up and patted him on the shoulder. "You'd have saved him if you could, I know that. It's amazing to me you lived—five of them—"

"I give thanks to the gods," Arvid said, surprising himself again.

"Of course," Jostin said. "Well, a crossbow—swords, all these knives—those will fetch good money in the right market. Their clothes—I don't know. I'll have them washed and mended . . ."

"If you're selling them, permit me to buy one of the cloaks," Arvid said. "It will contribute to Mardan's funeral fund, and I would have a dark cloak to wear instead of borrowing yours."

"I couldn't charge you," the innkeeper said. "Take what you want; you've more than earned it. Though I expect you'll have no use for the weapons."

"None at all," Arvid said truthfully. He had the same tools already neatly disposed in the pockets of his plaid cloak. "One sword and one dagger are enough for any honest man."

CHAPTER FOURTEEN

Tsaia: North Marches

JANDELIR ARCOLIN RODE east from the stronghold, bitter north wind bringing tears that froze on his cheeks. Behind him, the stronghold held only staff and the recruits, and he had to decide whether to let the troops now quartered near the Pargunese border come back to the stronghold for Midwinter Feast.

Kieri's earlier warning of possible unrest in Pargun had been followed—almost two tendays in transit—by a sharper one given to King Mikeli in Vérella and sent on to Arcolin. The Pargunese king and his brother were competing for the throne; civil war was imminent unless the Pargunese attacked outside. Both Lyonya and Tsaia were at risk, Kieri warned.

The count to Arcolin's south had only four hands of troops to add to the border guard; King Mikeli had sent Royal Guards north to bolster the lands nearest the Honnorgat, but he—with two hundred twelve trained soldiers spread thin along the border—was expected to hold the northeast. Nothing had happened so far—not a sign that the Pargunese were moving to the west—but they had done so before.

He wished he'd let Selfer and his troops come north, though they'd made a good escort for Andressat, he had to admit. But they were no use to him in the south.

Ahead, the wrinkles in the hills were marked with snow; he squinted to be sure he was headed the right way.

The camp, when he reached it, was laid out properly just as he'd expected: the ditch, the barricade, the jacks rows, the cooking tent. Cracolnya had the troops all lined up when he rode in. Arcolin dismounted and did a quick inspection. Kieri would have missed nothing; he must miss nothing. But they were all perfect, and Cracolnya knew it. Versin, Cracolnya's junior, wasn't there.

"He's taken a patrol south along the border to the next camp, sir," Cracolnya said when Arcolin asked.

Arcolin dismissed the cohort and followed Cracolnya into the mess tent. Cracolnya's own tent, half the size of other officers' tents, had always been a Company jest.

"Anything new from the Pargunese?"

"Not directly," Cracolnya said. "What I do have to report, though, is startling enough. One of my patrols ran into a party of gnomes."

"Gnomes! There aren't any gnome princedoms up here. They're all down south, along the flanks of the Dwarfmounts."

"That's what I thought, too," Cracolnya said. "But it's not what the gnomes think. Apparently this was once theirs—the hills of northern Pargun and some of the hills Kieri thought were his."

"I haven't seen a gnome north of Vérella in my whole career," Arcolin said. "And those were traders."

"My patrol rode back with eight: they said they were speaking for their prince."

"Where are they?"

Cracolnya nodded to the west. "They won't stay in our tents; they burrowed into that hillside, near as I can tell. Disappeared into the rocks, the way they do. They want to talk to you."

"Tonight?" Arcolin thought of the icy wind and the darkness.

Cracolnya shrugged. "I doubt they'll mind waiting until morning, and if they do, they'll come wake us up. I told them I expected you."

"If they're claiming any Tsaian lands, I'll have to tell the king," Arcolin said. "I don't know what he'll do."

"He'll yield them," Cracolnya said. "Gird's own word binds him—and us."

"Makes it easier for the Pargunese to flank us," Arcolin said. "They aren't bound by Gird's word."

Cracolnya grinned. "If what the gnomes said is true—and they're not liars—we won't have to worry about the Pargunese.

They had some kind of civil war amongst themselves, the gnomes said. Then they attacked Lyonya, but that failed, and they've been thrown out of those hills for breaking some rule."

"Now I'm curious," Arcolin said. "But also cold, hungry, and tired."

"We can fix that," Cracolnya said.

The next morning, the wind had dropped, though it was no warmer. Arcolin watched the troops as they came through the breakfast line, and Cracolnya watched him. "Any good news about Stammel?" Cracolnya finally asked in a low voice.

"He's still blind," Arcolin said. "He can sense light a little, he says. Turn his face to the sun or a lamp. But he can't see anything clearly."

"They're asking," Cracolnya said, nodding at the troops.

"I wish I had better word," Arcolin said. "He's—well, you know him. He does not complain, but he is losing hope."

"The gods should heal him," Cracolnya said. "After all he's done—and killing that demon-thing—"

"We've prayed," Arcolin said. "The Marshals in Cortes Vonja, the Marshal here, all of us who are Girdish and probably most of those who aren't. If I were a god—or a paladin—"

"Thought of sending for Paks?"

Arcolin shook his head. "She's not mine to command now. If she came, it would be because the gods sent her, and then it might do some good, but if she came on her own . . . I don't think so." He looked at his boots and then at Cracolnya. "I don't know what to do . . . He's said himself he can't function as a senior cohort sergeant, but I'm afraid he'll . . . waste away somehow, just die in a year, if I don't find the right job for him. He was useful that last few tendays in Aarenis."

"The Blind Archer," Cracolnya said, nodding.

"That and other things. He still knows more about the Company, about soldiering, than even Devlin, and he's . . . well . . . Stammel."

"Recruit training?"

"He says if he can't see them, how can he hold inspections? And outside he needs a leader to get around. That girl—Suli— they called her Stammel's Eyes, but she's in Valdaire this winter with the rest. Wasn't fair to use her for his guide, he said. And I agreed."

"Good soldier?"

"Suli? Good enough. Survived a rough campaign year." Too many hadn't.

"Did anyone ever ask Suli what she wanted? If she's set on fighting, that's one thing—though bodyguarding Stammel would give the opportunity, I've no doubt—but if she isn't, then being Stammel's guide isn't so bad, and you'd have the benefit of his experience."

"Here come the gnomes," Arcolin said, glad for a change of topic.

Eight gnomes—their lucky number, as he knew—paused to announce themselves to the camp sentries and came directly to the mess tent. He did not recognize their uniform—neither Gnarrinfulk nor Aldonfulk, these had a darker gray braid trim down the front of the jackets and on the wristbands.

The leader gave a stiff nod to both Cracolnya and him. "It is this one is your duke?"

"I am Count Arcolin," Arcolin said. "It is a new title, granted at Autumn Court. How may I address this one with due courtesy?"

The leader nodded more deeply. "Count. This one is title Karginfulk estvin: one speaks to strangers in name of prince."

"Estvin," Arcolin said. He had heard that title before but had never spoken to a gnome ambassador. "Be welcome. Would you enter, out of the wind?"

"It incurs obligation," the estvin said. Arcolin realized the gnomes would stand in the freezing wind until they turned to the gray stone they resembled if he did not find a way to convince them to enter. Hospitality to outsiders was not a gnome virtue. His ears and fingers ached with cold.

"My gods impose on me the obligation of a host," he said. "It is against law as we understand it to have visitors stand in a cold wind when shelter exists; I must ask you in."

For a long moment, the estvin stared at him without expression, then he nodded. "It is your law; it is not our Law. But it is not against our Law. Do you then admit we owe you nothing if we enter?"

"I admit it," Arcolin said.

Inside the tent, Arcolin ushered the gnomes to one of the tables; the benches troops used were too tall for them, but when he offered to prepare seats for them, the leader refused. "Your law may require shelter to be offered, but not comfort. We will stand. You may sit."

Arcolin sensed Cracolnya's annoyance at being allowed to sit in their own tent. "If you would bring sib," he said to Cracolnya. "There's still plenty hot." To the estvin he said, "I would offer a hot drink at no obligation, neither asking nor wanting any exchange."

Another long silence, then the now-familiar stiff nod. Arcolin sat, facing across the table a row of dour gray gnomish faces. They said nothing, nor did he, until Cracolnya and one of the cooks brought a tray with a pitcher and nine mugs.

"If you don't need me, my lord Count, I can get on with the day's work," Cracolnya said.

"Occupy the troops in camp until the estvin and I have finished talking," Arcolin said.

"Yes, my lord," Cracolnya said. Arcolin hoped the gnomes did not recognize the bite of sarcasm in his tone.

"The man who held this land," the estvin said without more preamble, "he fought against Pargun."

"Duke Phelan, yes. Pargun and Tsaia—"

"Enemies." The estvin put up his hand, and Arcolin fell silent. "It is not blame to that man; he did not know. And the prince forbade . . ." The estvin paused, sipped at the sib, then set down the mug. "It is Law that however wrong comes—by intent, by chance—wrong makes debt. Intent makes blame, but no-intent can make debt. Is clear?"

"In the Code of Gird intent to harm makes a crime—a wrong—worse. Without intent—no-intent—can still require a payment but not punishment." Arcolin paused. The estvin regarded him with no more expression than before, then spoke.

"Gird was—" The estvin shook his head. "Cannot say in Common." He stood even straighter than before. "But is time short, before must be done. You go."

"Go?"

"Go. This land not for you. Not for Pargun."

"I don't understand," Arcolin said. "This land has been Tsaian—and in this domain, now mine—since—"

"Since that duke fought Pargunese and pushed back. Not far enough. It is not land for humans."

"For gnomes?"

Now the blank face finally showed expression: grief. "It is not land for rockfolk. It is not land for Law. It is land for—" He uttered a long word Arcolin could not begin to pronounce.

"What is that?" Arcolin was thoroughly confused.

"Elder," the estvin said.

Gnomes were Elders, like dwarves and elves. "Elves?" he asked. What other Elders were there?

"Pargun attack Lyonya," the estvin said, as if that explained anything; he went on. "Pargun delve forbidden hill. Blackbone hill. Should not be. The—the sfizn rocks there, they break. Must not be." Now that stolid face glistened as if sweaty, and the dry, emotionless voice trembled. "Karginfulk fail. Karginfulk must go."

Arcolin felt his brows rise. Gnomes leaving their native rock? And what was sfizn rock? He knew dross and nedross, dwarf terms for the sound and the unsound rock, but sfizn?

"I don't understand," he said. "What has this to do with us—with my realm?"

The estvin turned to one of the other gnomes, who produced a thick wad of cloth from under his jacket and unfolded it on the table. Arcolin stared at the most beautiful map he had ever seen. The Honnorgat—every bend and crook of its path, every tributary. Hills, every one shaded so it seemed to stand up from the cloth. In fact, he realized as he concentrated on their location, the map was not static—it enlarged what he stared at, brought up details impossible to see before.

"When shipfulk—sea-fulk—came to here—" The estvin pointed at the distant eastern shoreline. "And upriver to here—" He ran a stubby gray finger up the line of the Honnorgat to the great falls. "They ask land-right of the prince, who then had rock-right here—" He spread his hand north-south from the falls and a handspan wide, more downriver than up. "Our prince saw they had order, though not Law, and granted surface land-right only, for we have no use for wet dirt or trees. Our prince set limits." He ran his finger in a broad arc that Arcolin saw encompassed where now lay both Pargun and Kostandan. "Not past rock-water, where ships cannot go. So those sea-fulk made pledge."

"And broke it," Arcolin said, "if they became Pargun, for Pargun claims this—" He pointed but did not touch the map.

"That is so," the estvin said. "The Webmistress said to them, *Go higher and be safe.* The Karginfulk prince said no. Then daskdraudigs—you know this?"

"Rock-serpent," Arcolin said.

"Yes. Bad. Years it grew under stone, then fell and crushed prince and most Karginfulk. And Webmistress threatened more. Then new prince bade us obey the Law and withdraw to the deeps, and there we lived, but with difficulty. For She sent orcs to harass us and her servants, the little webspinners, as spies and talebringers, liars in the dark to spread fear and mistrust. We dwindled but stayed faithful to our task—"

"Task?" Arcolin asked.

"One such webspinner bit our prince despite our care, and he died," the estvin said without answering Arcolin's question. "By then were few with the knowledge of Law that a prince needs, for so we had been pressed by trouble. The new prince knew less. We sent for aid from other princedoms, but none came—perhaps our messengers did not survive the journey. By Law they should have come and helped us."

The estvin looked down now; Arcolin glanced along the line of gnomes and saw that their black eyes glistened like wet pebbles. "They came not," the estvin said. "Our new prince— our prince was taken."

"Taken?"

"By secret treachery; it could not have been his intent." That had the tone of wish rather than certainty. Arcolin imagined a line of increasingly weaker princes. "And the Pargunese—the Pargunese came to see the hill forbidden to all."

"A holy hill?" Arcolin hazarded.

"Holy!" The estvin glared at Arcolin. "*Not* holy. Cursed. More perilous than daskdraudigs. And—" His head lowered again. "Our task. To protect—to warn away—any who might come there."

A cold tendril of wind blew under the tent wall and chilled Arcolin's legs; he shivered. "What is the curse, then?"

"Is not to say." Now the estvin looked squarely at Arcolin again. Then he shook his head. "Yet must. Humans must always know what and why or they do not obey." He leaned over the bench on his side of the table, putting both hands flat on the map. "Dragonkin."

"Dragons? They disappeared ages ago—"

"Human fool." The estvin did not raise his voice. "Not two hands of days agone Drakka—Dragon himself—came to Lyonya and destroyed the scathefire burning the forests. Then to us he came, and sent us into banishment for failing our trust."

"He blames you for the Pargunese finding the hill? But if you were few in number and hard beset—"

"It is not that. It is that Dragon believes our prince—our prince betrayed the trust."

"And your prince—"

"Has not returned. May be dead. May not. We that remain . . . Dragon requires to warn you to leave this land as far as this stream." He pointed to a line that Arcolin recognized as a third of the way from the recognized border to the stronghold. "It is for the lives of those that still live. Then we must go, by Midwinter, out from under stone to find our way as we can, taking nothing but what we wear."

Arcolin could not comprehend all this; the concept of a dragon, a live dragon—now, in this time, a dragon giving orders to gnomes—was difficult enough. "It is not fair," he said, fixing his mind on the dragon's demands. "It is not your fault."

"It is not your fault that you must leave this," the estvin said. "It is by our weakness Dragon came and thus by our weakness you and your king lose land long held. Our debt. We cannot pay; we must go with nothing. We are all kteknik, for with no prince, no guardian of Law, we all fail in Law."

"Kteknik?"

The estvin nodded. "Banished from our prince, nameless and clanless. We must not wear these clothes after we leave, for these declare we are Karginfulk, and we will not be Karginfulk."

"It's winter," Arcolin said. "You can't walk away without clothes, without food . . ."

"It is that we have no choices left," the estvin said. "The Elder rules. We have obeyed in telling you where you must go. Dragon . . ." The estvin paused. "Dragon is not safe," the estvin said then. "But Dragon is just."

"Where will you go?" Arcolin asked.

The estvin shrugged.

"How many of you? And . . . and women and children?" He imagined a string of small naked gray figures struggling through the icy wind, the blowing snow, going somewhere they did not know, and shuddered at the thought.

"It is—it was when we left seventy and eight. Fifteen children—" The estvin closed both eyes: Arcolin glanced along the row and saw that they all had closed their eyes. On each face a single tear ran down, then another.

"You must—" No, he could not say "must" to any of the elders. "Come to the stronghold—to *my* place," he said instead. "You can shelter there for a time, until spring at least, when it is warmer. There are hills west of us—perhaps they might suit you—"

"You do not understand!" For a moment, Arcolin thought the estvin was angry, then realized the gnome was shaking with grief, not anger. "It is . . . it is the judgment. We fail. We damage you with our failure. The debt—the debt is already greater than we can survive."

"It is in Gird's Code that we shelter fugitives unless they are criminals," Arcolin said. Fifteen little gnome children in the winter cold? *No.*

"Kteknik criminals. Elder—Drakka—Dragon said."

"Not by Gird's law," Arcolin said. "Gird's Code is *my* law— the law I must obey. Gird laid on us obeying the bounds kapristi set. I will have to tell the king—my king—but he will agree."

"Exchange," said one of the other gnomes. "No take without exchange."

The estvin looked hard at the other. "Dragon—" Arcolin felt the tension between them.

"It is not Drakka said no exchange."

The estvin looked at Arcolin. "Gird law not Law. For kteknik kapristi, must exchange make. Take service?"

Arcolin blinked. "Your service?"

"Service for debt owed. Kapristi service for shelter. Until balance level, service to Count. Yes?"

Holy Gird and Falk. He was acquiring seventy-eight gnomes as . . . as whatever they were good for. All the things he suddenly needed to do ran through his head. All eight gnomes stared at him; the map on the table seemed to squirm when he glanced at it.

"Yes," he said.

"Dragon may not like. Think before bindings."

A dragon he had never seen and wasn't entirely sure existed outside a gnome's round hard skull was nothing to his vision of those tiny gnome children.

"Yes," he said again. "I would make bargain with you, estvin, and your clan Karginfulk whether you be kteknik or not. I would trade shelter this winter, and food and other necessities, for service."

The estvin turned to the other gnomes and loosed a brief torrent of gnomish; they all answered one gnomish word Arcolin didn't know and couldn't pronounce. Then the entire troop came around the end of the table and prostrated themselves before him, and the estvin said, from his position, "Turn that I may kiss the feet of my master."

Across the tent, someone dropped a pan; Arcolin looked that way and realized that the cooks had been listening avidly. He turned on the bench; the estvin grasped his boot and kissed it, and behind him, each gnome kissed the boot heels of the gnome in front of him. Then the estvin stood, once more looking Arcolin in the face. "The master orders?"

"Have you eaten lately?" Arcolin asked.

"It is of no matter," the estvin said.

"It matters to me," Arcolin said. "Answer."

"Then, not since leaving Dragon and our home."

"Have you food there?"

"A little."

"You will eat here and carry what food you need back to your people and bring them. Understand?"

"Yes, master."

"And you will not remove your Karginfulk clothes until you reach the stronghold and are given others, that no harm comes to your people. Understand?"

"Yes, master."

"Are the Pargunese soldiers harrying you?"

"No, master, not since Dragon came."

"You will come here—and my men will escort you to the stronghold as we remove ourselves from this place. Will that suit?"

"Yes, master."

Arcolin looked over to the cooks. "Feed these eight gnomes with as much as they will eat and give them food to carry. They will be coming back with the rest of their clan, and I will give Cracolnya orders about that."

The gnomes worked their way through two bowls of porridge each, accepted a bag of oats, and left, bowing deeply to Arcolin. He called Cracolnya back in.

"What was that about, and why are you giving them oats?"

"Because that's all they'd take." Arcolin repeated what the gnomes had told him and what he'd done. "And you'll escort them to the stronghold when they come."

"You're inviting kapristi into the stronghold?"

"For the winter."

"But they're . . . they're *gnomes*. Did they ask?"

"No, I offered. They finally accepted." Arcolin shook his head at Cracolnya's expression. "It's not for nothing. They're exchanging service . . ."

"But if the dragon doesn't like it—"

"If there is a dragon," Arcolin said. "I wasn't going to argue; those gnomes were near the end of their strength."

THE GNOMES ARRIVED with Cracolnya's troops three days before Midwinter. Seventy-seven—one had died before the gnomes Arcolin had met reached their home again. He could not judge the age of the elders; the women, huddled in a group in the midst of the men, clearly did not want to be seen. He did not let his gaze linger on them.

To the estvin he gave welcome and then asked, "Would your

people be more comfortable under stone? We have cellars
here, enough for all."

"It is not comfort is important," the estvin said. From the
midst of the group—from a gnome female, Arcolin thought—
came a shrill rapid chitter of sound. The estvin looked at the
ground and then up at Arcolin. "As the master says, cellars."

Arcolin led the way through the main courtyard, into the
smaller private one, and then to the stairs down to the cellars.
The gnomes followed. He had a lantern and showed them the
storerooms he'd had cleared for them.

"Can bring water?"

"From the well in the courtyard," Arcolin said.

Faster than he would have believed, the gnomes settled into
the cellars of the stronghold. When they insisted they could
not wear their clan uniforms, Arcolin gave them furls of the
maroon and brown wools the Phelani uniforms used, the cloth
he had. Soon the gnome males appeared above stairs every
morning, wearing maroon shirts and brown trousers. They
began their service without asking, bringing up supplies to the
kitchen staff in the officers' court first and then taking over
other menial chores.

CHAPTER FIFTEEN

Lyonya

THE BRIEF WAR ended; the taig, aided by elves, flushed the last Pargunese stragglers—hungry, exhausted, and scared—out of the forest into the hands of Kieri's forces. Most were alone, a few in small groups. Kieri put them under guard in one of the abandoned steadings and waited for word from Pargun's king.

Before it came, he, Arian, and Aliam Halveric went north to the ruins of Riverwash to attend a ceremony for those who had died and to reestablish a presence there. Though none had escaped from the town itself, those who lived nearby and were not burnt out came, a small group of farmers and fisherfolk compared to the crowd at his last visit.

Kieri looked out over the Honnorgat. A skim of ice reached almost shore to shore. Across the river, a raw scar in the trees looked to him like scathefire damage. He wondered where Torfinn was. Then he and Aliam and Arian laid the sacred boughs on those bitter ashes. Under a clear sky, the sun cruelly bright on the ice and snow, the little group of farmers, the Halverics in their neat array, and the royal party sang the mourning songs Kieri had so recently learned.

A hail from the river alerted the Halverics; Kieri squinted against the glare and saw a boat being shoved through the ice, men leaning out to break the ice with their oars. One figure stood upright, wrapped in a long cape, with the sun glittering on his head . . . his crown. Pargun's king, from whom he had heard nothing.

Torfinn clambered up the bank, limping heavily and bracing himself with a pole in his left hand. He had, Kieri saw, lost his right arm above the elbow. When he reached the level, he bent his knee to Kieri. "Lord king," he said.

"Rise," Kieri said. "I am glad to see you alive."

"Was near thing," Torfinn said, using the pole to lever himself up. "Is Elis—?"

"She is not here," Kieri said. "She is safe and well but has duties at Falk's Hall for Midwinter." He paused, but when Torfinn said nothing, he asked, "Iolin?"

"He lives," Torfinn said. "His elder brothers—not."

"I'm sorry," Kieri said.

"Was not you starting it," Torfinn said. "My fault, not seeing Einar for what he was. Not seeing Her, either."

"Was that the dragon or the dragonkin?" Kieri asked, pointing across the river.

"Dragon," Torfinn said. "Lord king, can we sit? My leg weakens."

"Of course," Kieri said, and led him to the royal tent. He could not help contrasting the tent, its sides bulging and rippling in the wind, with the comfortable inn where they had rested and eaten before. Instead of the sturdy leather-padded chairs, simple folding chairs; instead of a feast laid out by servants in a room with a roaring fire, marching rations on a couple of planks with a basin of cold water for washing at one end. His Squires brought them both hot sib and placed a brazier nearby for warmth.

Torfinn sat awkwardly, almost falling into the chair, grunting with pain. Kieri saw the bulge of bandages under his trousers and caught a whiff of a wound gone bad.

"You should not have spent yourself coming here," Kieri said. "I hoped for a messenger."

"I have few to send," Torfinn said. "And it is your land my people harmed. I must come myself to beg your mercy and save what little I can from this disaster. So the dragon said."

"Lord king," Kieri said, "I have no reason to attack you or your people if you do not attack us. We have enough to do trying to repair what has been lost."

"What is lost . . ." Torfinn sighed. "My *kingdom* is lost, as you should know. The dragon . . . demanded back all lands above the falls and now seeks out its young. Einar's army, anyone who did not make it across the river to your lands, is dead. I do not know if any of those who invaded you survived."

"Some," Kieri said. "They are under guard now; if they swear allegiance to you, I will release them to you."

Torfinn scowled. "They are traitors. How could I trust them?"

"They are defeated; most were bespelled. And they have no leader to follow but you," Kieri said. "Would you have me kill them? Have they no families in Pargun?"

"Some do," Torfinn said. He shifted in his seat, wincing. "I . . . I do not know how to go on. My sons, all but Iolin, dead. My brother a traitor; his sons dead. So much lost—what kind of man am I that so many would turn against me?" Tears glittered in his eyes.

"You were betrayed," Kieri said, "but not because you were a bad man. Indeed, had you been bad, you would have been lauded, I believe. Until the dragon came, at least." He poured himself another mug of sib. He had planned to start back that afternoon, but with Pargun's king at hand, he might achieve more here. "Let us think what can benefit both our lands."

"Mine . . . nothing," Torfinn said. He was slumped in his chair now, his face sagging. "You saved me once; it would have been better if I had died."

Kieri reached over and grabbed Torfinn's left wrist. "It would *not* have been better! It is because of you alive that any of your people live. It must be your wounds talking, because I never thought to see a Pargunese give up like this."

"My leg doesn't heal; I have no right arm. How can I rule if I cannot stand up and wield a sword?"

"Is it always sword-right that rules?"

"Yes, although some kings have grown old and retained the crown because of wisdom. But the people decide."

"And have they rejected you? Are you come here as a beggar?"

"No—not yet. But—"

"Then, Torfinn, show them you are a king indeed, with a king's wisdom, if not a right arm. And what do your physicians say about your leg?"

Torfinn shrugged with slightly more energy than he had shown. "My palace burned; I have no physicians now."

"We do," Kieri said, and turned to the Squires at the tent's entrance. "Find the Halveric surgeon and bid him come here; the king of Pargun needs assistance."

ᛏORꟻINN'S WOUND WAS hugely swollen and leaking stinking pus. "There's still a chance," the surgeon said. "But I must work now. Drink this," he said, pouring from a stone jar into Torfinn's mug. "It will strengthen your blood."

Torfinn grimaced at the taste, but swallowed it all. "Tastes like medicine," he said afterward, nodding. "Should be bitter to work." He did not make a sound or flinch as the surgeon cleaned the wound and packed it with an herbal poultice, then wrapped it in clean bandages and propped it on a stool.

"You can't go back tonight or tomorrow," the surgeon said. "You'll have to keep that leg up—no standing but to get to the jacks—for two days at least. Who's expecting you, over there?"

"My son."

"Well, send your boatman back. I wouldn't risk you on the river again, and I can't leave." He turned to Kieri. "If you have any kind of bedding, he needs to lie flat with his leg propped up." Kieri beckoned to the Squires, and they found a low camp bed and helped Torfinn move onto it.

After the boatman left, Torfinn slept for a glass or so, which the surgeon said was normal. "Got enough pus out of his leg to relieve the pain—man's tough, I'll say that for him."

"But he'll live for a certainty?"

"Yes, and he'll have use of that leg if you give me another few days. If he has an appetite when he wakes up, give him whatever he wants to eat. And another draft of this—or call me."

"I'll call you," Kieri said. Now, watching the Pargunese king sleep, he thought what the man had faced and still faced as a king who had lost control of his kingdom . . . faced treachery and a civil war, feared enemies to both south and west, and then the dragon. All those people dead . . . a city destroyed . . . his sons, his wife, his other daughters . . . the fires . . .

"He was not wise," said a familiar voice from the door of

the tent. Kieri roused from that reverie and stared at the man in dark leathers who now stood inside the tent. The dragon again.

"*You,*" Kieri said. "You enjoy startling people, don't you?"

A flash of teeth and a flare in the yellow eyes. "We have few amusements," the man said. "That may be one of them." He came nearer; the tent warmed, and the forge smell emanated from him. "You are caring for him?"

"He is hurt, and though you say he is not wise, I do not think him a bad man."

"Fools cause as much harm as bad men. Yet your wisdom, Sorrow-King, is correct in pursuing no vengeance. What was done is done. What I have done . . . is done. That land—"

"Pargun," Kieri said.

"The land you call Pargun, then . . . that land is no threat to any and will not be for ages to come. Tell me, what do you think of the new lord of the north, where you once ruled?"

"That is Jandelir Arcolin," Kieri said. "He was a captain under me."

"Some land humans may not inhabit," the man said. "As I told you before, land where dragon eggs are is not safe. He must keep away."

"You want Arcolin to give up land? To whom?" That wasn't going to make Tsaia's king happy.

"To me."

"He will have to have his king's permission. Have you met the king of Tsaia?"

"No." A huff of hot air filled the tent.

"They govern by the Code of Gird in Tsaia," Kieri said. "You said gnomes guarded your eggs. Gnomes and Gird had a pact. Have gnomes tell him to release the land."

"I had a pact with gnomes. Gnomes failed me."

"Why?"

"It matters not why. It matters that they failed."

Kieri opened his mouth to say that for a creature supposedly interested in wisdom and justice, this sounded more like haste and vengeance, but it was, after all, a dragon in man's shape. Instead he said, "Give them a task within their ability—have them tell Arcolin."

"I have done so already." The man looked again at Torfinn. "If he were awake, I would offer him my tongue. Do you think he would accept?"

"He is a brave man," Kieri said. "I think he would."

"He is wounded?"

"Gravely. He lost his right arm and has a deep wound in his leg. Our surgeon cleaned it."

"Show me."

Kieri folded the blanket back; the man touched the bandage on Torfinn's leg with one hand and laid the other on Torfinn's forehead. For a long moment, the tent warmed even more, then the man withdrew both hands. "He will live, and his leg will heal in time," the man said. "By your word and deed, Sorrow-King, you have saved his life. Tell him the dragon has no quarrel with him so long as he does not intrude into the dragon's land. It will be clearly marked. Will you do so?"

"Yes," Kieri said. "I will."

When Torfinn woke, he had better color and an appetite. They ate together, and Kieri told him about the dragon's visit. Torfinn shuddered at the mention of touching his tongue to the dragon's but nodded.

"A king must do what a king must do," he said.

Kieri went on then and laid out what he hoped for—an agreement about the end of the war and the peace to come. "It is not the peace I wanted," Kieri said, "but it is the peace we have. Both lands wounded, but both lands alive."

"I do not know how long," Torfinn said.

"Nor I," Kieri said. "And I am not wounded, as you are, so it is easier for me. But I swear I mean you no harm, and you have no reason to harm me. Your men who came were many of them bespelled, and all misled. Show them you will govern well, and they will follow you, I truly believe. Are your women safe?"

"More of them than men," Torfinn said. "But some—my wife among them—died, and so did some children."

"And some lived, and you are the only king they have or know." Kieri was not sure why he was so eager to have Torfinn survive and lead . . . just that it felt right. And he did not want to be Pargun's king as well as Lyonya's. Elven blood did not belong there. "Let me have them brought here—you should not travel for days yet, until the surgeon says you may—and let them swear fealty, if they will."

"As you will," Torfinn said.

"I will send for them, and I will send a message to Elis that you live." Kieri went out, sent Arian with another Squire to carry the news back to Chaya, and told Aliam to have his people build shelters rather than fortifications. By nightfall, they had put up a log shelter large enough for the two kings, and Torfinn lay on Kieri's camp bed, his injured leg carefully padded. Already the surgeon saw improvement; he had cleaned the wound out twice. Kieri did not tell the surgeon about the dragon's visit.

The Pargunese prisoners, when they arrived, also looked better than they had when captured. Kieri knew that quite a few spoke some Common; some had been to Aarenis, sailing around the Eastbight to trade at the Immer River ports and even west to Confaer. He forbade his people to mention the possibility of a Lyonyan port but gathered all he could learn of the sea trade.

After several days of rest and the surgeon's care, Torfinn's leg was healing cleanly. "I must meet them on my feet," he said. "Whatever it costs."

"Then do so," the surgeon said. "But do not walk far or stand longer than you must. And you must take a full jar of this medicine back with you when you go and drain a mug of it twice daily. It is too long until the green comes again in spring—you must drink a tea of spruce needles meanwhile."

Torfinn limped, but he could now walk without the support of a stick. Aliam had suggested he belt a sword so he could draw it left-handed, and Aliam's captain lent him one.

Torfinn nodded and let the man put it on him. "But alas that I must be armed by my enemies," he said. "It is bitter indeed—"

"We are not enemies now," Kieri said. "And it is not so bitter as death."

Torfinn grimaced. "What you say is true, and I owe you life twice, and thanks, and yet—"

"And yet it is hard," Kieri said. "But you are a man of courage for whom hard things are only a test, is it not so?"

"It is so," Torfinn said. He looked down at the sword at his side. "Will you permit me to draw it?"

"Of course."

"Sometimes I think you are mad, king of Lyonya." Torfinn drew the sword, a little awkwardly, with his left hand, but his grip was firm. Turning from Kieri, he made a few passes with it; Kieri could tell that he was used to having a dagger in that hand. Resheathing it was difficult without a hand to steady the scabbard, but he managed. "And now I will see my forsworn and perhaps redeem something from this disaster."

The prisoners waited outside the log shelter; when Torfinn emerged, Kieri saw in their faces the shock they felt at Torfinn's missing arm. They stared; Torfinn stared back, impassive. Kieri gestured; one of the Halverics ducked into the shelter and brought out two folding camp chairs and set them up. Torfinn glanced at the chairs but did not sit. Instead he limped along the line of prisoners as a farmer might walk along a row of milk cows. At the end of the row, he turned back to Kieri and came to stand beside him.

"King of Lyonya," he said. "Are these all you found?"

"Yes," Kieri said. "And I believe all who remain alive."

"Then let us sit, and I will hear their pleas." Torfinn remained standing as Kieri sat and drew his borrowed sword. Some of the Pargunese prisoners gasped loud enough to be heard over the wind. "You swore oaths to me once," Torfinn said to the prisoners in Pargunese. "And you broke them. A broken pot will always leak. Lyonya's king tells me you were bespelled. He tells me I should trust you. Think well, before you beg my mercy. You will lay your necks beneath this blade and kiss my boot, and you will abide my whim, whether it be life or death."

Kieri saw dawning respect on the prisoners' faces. The front row said nothing; behind them, well back, murmurs he could not quite catch ran through the group. A few shifted their places.

"Who among you are the commanders?" Torfinn said.

Arms went up; each group, as with the ones Kieri had taken

to Chaya, had chosen a leader. Now the leaders stood in the front row, along with their seconds.

"You come first." Torfinn pointed the sword at the sword-side end of the row, then sat down in the other chair. His arm, Kieri noted, had been steady as oak.

The first man knelt and bared his neck to Torfinn, hands and arms spread wide. Torfinn laid the edge of the blade on the man's neck. Kieri's stomach tightened.

"My king, I failed you; my life is yours."

"Your life is mine," Torfinn said. "What do you swear?"

The oath contained some Pargunese words Kieri did not know, but he understood enough. The man leaned over and kissed Torfinn's boot. Torfinn lifted the sword.

"You live by my word and by my sword," Torfinn said. "Use your life well." The man backed away on his knees, then stood; another came to replace him. Eventually, all had done so but one. Kieri had noticed him shuffling first to the back row and then to the tail of the line. The man stood hunch-shouldered, clearly hesitant. Torfinn glowered. "What of you?"

"I fear, lord king." The man's gaze shifted from side to side. "I—I would stay here—" He looked at Kieri then, pleading.

"King of Lyonya, do you want this man?"

After the mercy shown to others, Kieri could think of no good reason for this man to be so afraid. "He is not my subject, but yours," he said to Torfinn.

"*Please,* my lord!" the man cried, and rushed toward Kieri. The Halveric commander grabbed for his own sword—but it was in Torfinn's hand, and Torfinn struck the man down before Kieri could draw his own.

Torfinn grinned at Kieri. "Life for life," he said, then thrust the sword into the man's neck and finished him quickly. "Let this be the last Pargunese blood shed here, and the last blood between us."

"May it be so," Kieri said.

Torfinn wiped the blood from the blade on the dead man's clothes and looked at his soldiers. "Now you see your king has strength in his arm, and you have sworn. Make signal over the river for a boat to come."

They obeyed; Kieri walked about with the Halveric commander, discussing what would be done after he himself returned to Chaya.

"Do you think their king's speaking truth?" the commander asked.

"Yes. He is not like us, but he is not a liar," Kieri said. "You may not have heard, but I have spoken with him before." By the time he came back to the shelter, a boat was halfway across the river, and Torfinn spoke to the captain who had lent the sword.

"By your mercy, would you grant me use of this sword until I come to my own again? I swear not to use it to your hurt and to send it back, but I must not return weaponless."

Before Kieri answered, the commander bowed. "Certainly, lord king."

"Thank you, Captain," Kieri said.

When the boat arrived, the king and four hands of men embarked, the king with the jug of medicine the surgeon insisted on. Then the men laid to the oars, two to each, and the boat moved away.

"Fare well, Torfinn of Pargun," Kieri called.

"Fare well, Kieri of Lyonya," Torfinn called back. That was the first time he had used Kieri's name.

The borrowed sword and belt came back with the third boat trip; Kieri clapped the Halveric commander on the shoulder. "I must go now; I have been longer away than I meant; I must be in Chaya for Midwinter Feast."

"Yes, sir king. These will not give us trouble and will all be across the river soon enough."

Kieri's tent had been sent south already; he and the Halveric and two Squires rode with the wind behind them at a good pace. He was back in Chaya two days before Midwinter.

CHAPTER SIXTEEN

Chaya, Lyonya

On the night of Midwinter Feast, with all fires extinguished, Kieri went alone into the royal ossuary. Unlike his subjects, who could eat and drink all night to keep themselves awake and share songs and stories, the king must be with his ancestors, alone and fasting.

The Seneschal met him outside shortly before sundown and led him inside with a small candle.

"I will be within call, sir king, but it is our tradition on this night that the door be closed to ensure that the king is not interrupted in his converse with the honored dead."

"That's different," Kieri said. Now that he thought of it, he remembered Aliam, when they were in Lyonya, disappearing into the attic on Midwinter night. It must have been freezing up there with no fire; he had come down at midnight, Kieri remembered, and joined the festivities.

"It is," the Seneschal said. "It is the night of all nights that the ancestors speak. You have had guidance already; you may expect more." He handed Kieri the candle as he opened the door for him to go in. Kieri glanced up; to his surprise, no green lay above the door. The Seneschal, following his gaze, nodded. "One night in the year they have no green. Tonight all dies, and all wander the void together. What you learn tonight, sir king, is like to be dark, at the roots of what they know, and it is from roots that sprouts return to the light."

"I welcome their wisdom," Kieri said.

"It is well." The Seneschal took the candle again; Kieri walked in and stood—no stool or chair to sit on this time in the wide central aisle—and the Seneschal shut the door.

The darkness pressed on him. Midwinter enforced no silence, so Kieri spoke to the bones as he usually did.

"I am here. I listen."

The darkness returned his attention; he felt the hairs rise on his arms. Nothing new in this. Briefly, quietly, he told them of events since Midsummer. As if the chamber had light, he could feel their reactions, as individual as they had been in life. When he was done, he felt that some of them withdrew a little while others pressed nearer.

His father's presence, stronger than he'd felt it before, warm and steady on his sword-side, conveyed approval of his report. His sister's, on his heart-side, breathed joy about Arian and a settled distrust still of the Lady and other elves. They seemed to fade, and others made themselves known. He felt the need to move, to walk here and there, hands before him, feeling the edge of the platforms as he moved, touching the bones lightly. Those with a message came clearer in his mind.

One by one, they led him deeper into the ossuary. He had been shown these vaults, but he had not lingered in the other aisles, in the far corners; he had thought those bones too old, those spirits too distant, to have messages for him. He had been wrong.

Without light, without the records that would remind him who lay where, and how far back this bone had been king or queen, he did not know whether what he heard was ancient or merely old—and the bones had no interest in a history lesson. What they wanted him to know—what they pressed into his mind in great urgency—were the secrets of their own realms and the problems they had not solved and had not felt solved since.

His sister had not been the first to have dark suspicions of the elves . . . not the first to suspect treachery . . .

The taig was ours as much as theirs . . . from a king in the second aisle.

Long ago, before they came . . . from a skull in the farthest corner from the door—or so Kieri thought, because he was no longer sure where in the ossuary his body moved.

For years—for half my life—they disappeared—and my

people prospered . . . a queen in the third aisle on the women's side.

Kieri tried not to frame questions, to let them speak all they would first, but he could not help it and finally asked aloud, "Are they evil?"

Silence as thick as the darkness. Then, steadily growing, awareness of their uncertainty and their unwillingness to accuse without evidence. Wrongness, yes. Treachery somewhere, yes. Unfair advantage over humans, misuse of their ability to enchant, yes. But . . . evil?

Here, below ground, Kieri had no sense of time flowing, whether the night had turned or not, and gave up wondering, attending only to the bones and their revelations. He struggled to make sense of it all, but without sequence—without knowing who said what or how far back—he could not make a coherent pattern, anything to give him what he felt he needed.

Then, feeling along a wall, his hands dipped into a niche rougher-finished than the rest. He ran fingers lightly along the top of it, deeper and deeper—arm-deep—and touched a skull. No other bones, only the skull.

They forbade this.

What? Kieri wondered. His being here, underground, with the bones? And why?

They fear the long memory of bones.

Kieri drew the skull nearer and felt over its surface. Where had its bones been laid? he wondered.

They are not so old, or we so young, as they wish.

"You speak of elves?" Kieri asked softly.

Singers of songs and dreamers who make seeming. Touch my head with yours, child.

Kieri thought of the dragon and touched the skull's arched forehead to his own. As if from his own imagination, little bright pictures formed—a ring of trees and a ring of little houses, men and women and children in strange clothes all holding hands and dancing around a roofed framework over stacks of bones. It changed: more houses and a line of people coming from outside the ring of trees, following a man and a woman dressed in white.

Inside the hill. Power.

Inside what hill? Then . . . the arrangement of trees suddenly made sense. The King's Grove . . . without the mound. Once there had been a village there? A bone-house?

Yes. Place of power.

It was still a place of power . . . but he had assumed an elven place of power, the place where human and elven powers were joined. The skull offered no more; Kieri held it a moment longer, stroked the bony arch, and then kissed it and put it back in its niche. A niche, now he came to think of it, that he had never been shown, or noticed, on previous visits.

He was cold, he realized, his bare feet standing not on the stone floor that had warmed him before, but on cold soil. He smelled not the clean dry freshness of the ossuary but the rich, earthy dampness of forest soil. Yet the entire floor of the ossuary was stone-flagged; he had seen it. Stone walls plastered and white, stone floor. He knelt and touched the soil, felt its texture . . . There was something's root; some tiny creature scuttled across his fingers. He jerked his hand back, stifling a cry. Ancient fear entered his mind: cold, dark, silent, the weight of the earth pressing down, lost and alone in the grave.

As they were, you will be. Dead. Rotting in the ground. Though your bones be raised, you will remain, neglected and forgotten, as years pass.

Something larger crawled onto his foot; he shook it off. The niche, when he felt for it, had vanished along with the wall he had touched before; under his hands was a surface of crumbling earth; a clod came loose. He was afraid to move, for he had no idea how to return.

Death ends all. Silence ends all. Cold ends all. All is unmade, and all names lost.

Kieri felt deadly cold rising from the soil he stood on; he shuddered violently and stamped his feet. How was he to find his way out, back to the ossuary, back to daylight when it came, back to . . . back to Arian?

"I am the king," he said aloud. "And I will die. I will come to a grave, and if my people will, my bones will rise and be painted with my life. If the gods grant it, my children will come where I have come and know what I know, but this is not my time."

It is always death's time.

"It is always *life's* time, and the death of one year is the birth of the next," Kieri said. "I choose life and light, for my kingdom and for me." He turned about and strode into the dark, choosing—whenever he bumped into a stone, an earthen wall, a tangle of roots—the way that felt most like life.

THE FINAL BARRIER was stone. Not the rough native stone he'd fallen over and into several times, but dressed stone, a smooth wall. He laid both hands on it. On the other side, he was sure, was the ossuary. He could feel his sister's bones there and his father's. He could feel something else as well, a thread of life, not bones, calling him. He leaned on the stone, pressing his forehead into it.

"Let me in! My place is there, not yet here."

Something with too many legs fell on his neck and scrabbled its way down his back inside his clothes. He did not move. If it stung, it stung, but he was going to open this rock if there was any way to do it. Whatever the thing was went on down the back of his heart-hand leg and disappeared. *Life,* he thought with all his strength. *Arian.*

THE SENESCHAL LIT a candle from the King's Squire's new-lit torch and carried it down the steps to the outer chamber, fixed it in a holder, and opened the door.

"Sir king! The sun returns, life wakes again, and spring . . ." His voice faltered. Where he expected to see the king . . . where in other years the ossuary's own magical light had risen . . . nothing. Darkness, emptiness, cold.

"Sir king!"

No answer but the sharpened attention of the bones. A stale smell, unlike any he had smelled before in this place. Not true corruption, but . . . His throat closed as he considered what might have happened. He entered the ossuary, candle held high, and stopped abruptly. He could not go farther; the bones forbade it.

"He is our king," the Seneschal said. "Our hope. And his bride awaits. You cannot have him!"

No answer. The soft voices of the bones that he had heard ever since his first visit to the ossuary were silent.

"Alyanya . . ." the Seneschal said, struggling to get the word out. But this was Midwinter, and no live green remained in this place; he had himself removed the branches, the leaves on eyeholes and earholes. He started to turn, thinking to fetch something—but how, if he came out without the king?—and could not take even a single step. "Alyanya!" This time louder, more desperate. What evil magic had taken the king, and such a king? What could he do? He mumbled every potent name he could think of: Alyanya, Adyan the Namer, all the gods, all the saints, and finally the lineage of the human rulers of Lyonya in case the bones would help.

He heard voices behind him in the outer chamber, calling him, calling Kieri. He could not turn; he could not answer but went on with his litany, ending with the oldest he knew.

From far in the darkness, from the distant corner of the os-suary, came the grinding of stone moving on stone. His candle flickered wildly. Was it a daskdraudigs? Was that the evil that had taken the king? But the bones, which surely would have reacted in horror to that, gave no warning. Another sound now; his heart leapt. For this was breathing—harsh, uneven, but the sound of someone alive, not dead.

"Sir king!" he called into the darkness.

A hoarse sound answered him, not true speech, and fear filled him again. Had something reft the king's mind? He had judged the king to be strong in himself, in no danger from a night alone. Whoever it was coughed, deep racking coughs, then the familiar voice came from the darkness, asking the ritual question: "Is the long night over, Seneschal?"

"The sun returns, life wakes again, and spring will surely come, sir king."

Light bloomed in the ossuary, drowning the light of his can-dle. Out from between the platforms came Lyonya's king, his clothes, his hands and face, all stained and streaked with dirt, his bare feet caked with mud. The Seneschal had one horrified thought that the king looked like a corpse raised too soon after burial, but then the king grinned at him. "Lord Seneschal, I need a bath. And breakfast would not come amiss. Am I late?"

CHAPTER SEVENTEEN

THE REST OF the morning passed in a blur as Kieri hurried to bathe, eat something, and dress in the clothes appropriate for the ceremony scheduled for midday. No time for explanations, no time for a private conversation with Arian. No time even to wonder what his people thought.

The Knight-Commander of Falk and the Captain-General of Falk both came to his chambers as he was dressing.

"I brought your ruby, sir king," the Knight-Commander said. "Accept it now, and Falk's blessing with it."

Kieri paused. "As the king, I cannot be Falk's alone."

"We understand," the Captain-General said. "Yet you are Falk's, in all honor. Will you accept it now, or shall I make a public presentation?"

"Now," Kieri said. "My Squires can witness . . . and Arian, if she has time."

"For you, always," Arian said from the doorway. She wore a gown Kieri had not seen before, though he knew it was taken from the former queen's wardrobe: gold and crimson brocade.

Kieri knelt, and the Knight-Commander repeated the formal words of commissioning a Knight of Falk. "Receive this ruby as a sign of Falk's Oath. In mind and heart, be as Falk: speak only truth, keep all promises, and shed blood only in the protection of those who cannot protect themselves." The Captain-General touched his head and throat with the tip of his sword.

At last, clean and fed and dressed in robe and crown, Falk's ruby on his collar, Kieri came down and stood on the palace steps in the thin winter sun. The green of his robe, the gold and red of Arian's, blazed in that light, a promise of life and health. He and Arian made their vows in sight of all. Midwinter vows, that could not be unsaid or unmade short of death itself. And death, Kieri thought to himself, had already lost even that power. They were, from this moment, essentially man and wife, the wedding ceremony being only the final stage of the process.

A party of elves attended, including the Lady; they smiled and bowed, and Kieri tried not to think what might lie behind those smiles and bows. He would have to talk to his grandmother about what had happened to him, what he now knew about the King's Grove, but not today. Aliam and Estil Halveric headed the line of friends, both healthy and clearly joyful. Estil said, "I told you, Kieri, right after the coronation."

"I didn't understand," Kieri said. "My mind was on the horses, not the riders."

"Clearly," Estil said, with a grin to take the sting out of it. She took Arian's hands in hers. "May you have the joy that I have had, both of you."

Midwinter Feast had been laid in the courtyard, table end to table end piled with hot foods and cold, savory and sweet. Kieri and Arian sampled tastes, but outside the palace walls the rest of Chaya waited to see their future queen, and winter days were short. After hearing what others had said about his parents, he'd decided that they should ride matched horses, fire-colored to celebrate the sun's return. So out they rode, on a pair of red chestnuts with green and gold braided into their manes and tails, and an escort of King's Squires to clear the way and throw sweetmeats into the crowd for the children.

All along the way, people threw knots of ribbons or yarn, candied fruit, and little spiced cakes and offered blessings. Back at the palace, in the waning light of a winter afternoon, the celebration had moved indoors. Kieri ate more, but he was tired; his eyelids sagged. Arian poked him in the side. "My lord, you need sleep, and these friends will lose no joy by your being in your bed."

"Especially," Aliam said, leaning close on the other side, "if you are not *alone* in your bed."

"Aliam!" Estil thumped his shoulder. "It is their choice."

"True, but the wise choice—all right, all right, I will give over." But Aliam's smirk said all the rest of it.

Kieri took his leave rather than fall asleep at the table, very glad that he had not indulged in the wines and ale when he found himself a little unsteady with weariness alone. Feasting would continue through this second night, and he hoped a short sleep would let him take part.

"I could wish it was our wedding night but that I'm so tired," Kieri said when they were upstairs.

"In Lyonyan custom, it could be," Arian said. "But you need sleep before anything else." She turned back the great bed and slid the warming pan with its coals under the covers. "Is there reason to expect bad dreams? Would you like a posset?"

"No . . . no posset, at least. I think I met the source of all bad dreams last night, and yet survived. If more come, I will still survive." Kieri struggled with the elaborate frogs of his formal dress. "Where's Fedrin? I'm being clumsy with these, and I don't want to rip something."

"I told him I would care for you tonight," Arian said. "We have had no chance to speak together this day, but for making our vows. If you prefer, I can send for him."

"No . . . no. But I can't get this one undone." He pointed to the highest, at his neck.

"Let me." As if her fingers held magic, the fastening opened, and the one below; then she stood behind to help him free of the long tunic and hung it up while he pulled off his shirt. Arian said nothing about his scars, those or the others, and before he had time to worry about that, he was in a warm bed, sinking into the pillows, and asleep in that instant.

When he woke, the fire still burned brightly, and Arian had fallen asleep in a chair beside the bed. He had not seen her asleep before. He wondered what she would do if he woke her with a kiss.

The fire popped loudly, and a shower of sparks shot up the chimney. Arian woke at once and, when she saw him looking, grinned. "So—you are not sleeping the night through?"

"I just woke," Kieri said.

"Are you hungry? They're still feasting downstairs."

"I could eat a whole roast sheep," Kieri said. He stretched. "Though I confess I'm not eager to get dressed again."

"No need." Her grin widened. "I asked for something I

could keep warm for you by the fire. Unless you want to go down to the others . . . there's enough food for three or four."

This time, the shared meal had a different flavor; it was as if he and Arian had shared such meals for years.

"I was frightened when I heard the Seneschal calling and you did not answer," Arian said. "And when I looked past him and saw nothing . . ."

"I do not know what happened," Kieri said. "It was not what I expected or what the Seneschal had told me about . . . I need to talk with him. I would rather not talk about it tonight."

"Of course," Arian said. "But my joy, sir—Kieri—when you appeared, *that* you need to know about."

"I felt you," Kieri said. "You are how I found my way back." In spite of what he'd said, he began the tale in the middle, the moment he realized he was not on the ossuary's warm stone floor but lost somewhere underground. "I was afraid—I have not been that afraid since I was a slave in Sekkady's domain— but I was not going to despair, not with my kingdom, not with you, waiting for me. And I felt . . . I felt a pull, as if someone held the other end of a rope I touched." He looked up at her. "I felt your presence in it."

She nodded but said nothing as she spread butter and then jam on a roll and handed it to him. He took a bite, swallowed it, then another. Finally he went on.

"It seemed a very long time—of course, in the dark, it's hard to tell—"

"Before dawn," Arian said, "we Squires were together, shoulder to shoulder, and we all shuddered at once. The elves had brought snow-sprites for the first time in years; we had watched them dance, but then they vanished. We went to the salle, but the elf-light did not rise, and then we went to wait outside the ossuary. I wanted to be the first to bring you light."

"It was life you brought me," Kieri said. "At the last—" He told of the wall that he was sure had been the outer wall of the ossuary, of how he fell through at last, with a mouthful of soil nearly choking him.

"I wonder where you were," Arian said. "The dirt on your clothes was real enough."

"The King's Grove," Kieri said. "And the mound. Under it."

Arian stared at him, eyes wide. "Yes, I'm sure," he went on. "It is something about the secrets elves keep. Under the mound is a sacred place for humans—old humans—and in that place is a skull they missed when they cleared it away."

Arian frowned. "I thought the elves were here first," she said. "They granted humans the use-right. Do you suppose they came later, after humans had lived here?"

Kieri tore a leg of the roast chicken. "I don't know," he said. "I think they are Elders, created before humans, but they do not live everywhere and perhaps never did. So they might move to a place where humans were—"

"And easily take over," Arian said. She carved the rest of the chicken and slid several slices onto his plate and some onto her own.

Kieri finished that chicken leg and the rest of the chicken before him before speaking again, then wiped his fingers on a napkin. "We know the Lady has made errors. We know she moved the elfane taig under stone. She could have made errors before that. Or after." He shook his head. "I do not want to quarrel with elves or start trouble with them. But we must know what really happened, and when, to make the best path forward for this kingdom. For humans, yes, but also for elves. I do not think they prosper as it is."

"Not with the rockfolk so angry with them," Arian said. "I always knew—everyone knew—that rockfolk and elvenkind were not close friends, but I thought they had respect for each other as Elders."

"So did I," Kieri said. "And I wonder about other elven kingdoms. Are they all connected by custom or by birth? Do they travel back and forth? An elf I met in Fin Panir spoke of an elven kingdom in the mountains of the far west . . . why so distant?"

"Why none in Aarenis except travelers?" Arian asked. "And Tsaia is larger than Lyonya: why no elven homeland there?"

"I am beginning to think I know nothing of the world despite my fifty odd years and my travels," Kieri said. He grinned at her. "But I do know one thing, Arian: I love you, and I am no longer hungry for food or sleep . . ."

She grinned back. "Are you not? Are you certain you should not return to bed until daylight comes?"

"Not to sleep," Kieri said. He held out his hand to her.

"Not to sleep," Arian agreed, taking his hand.

KIERI WOKE SLOWLY, at first aware only of unusual lassitude. He had not felt so at ease in a long time; the dim light of predawn outlined the gap in the curtains but showed nothing of the room. He stretched, a bone-cracking stretch . . . and brushed against something else in the bed. Something warm. Breathing. Memory returned in a rush, just as the something warm became obviously Arian—and he heard her yawn.

Well. All the doubts, all the misery of their separation, all his fear for her when he found the arrows—all that had vanished in the night. More than Midwinter vows now made them one.

"Morning joy," she said, warm against him, shoulder to hip.

"And to you," he said. "I suppose we should get up and dressed before the whole company of Squires comes in to witness." He slid out of the covers. Cold. Still too dark in the room to see her. The temptation to slide back in was strong, but he heard just a little noise in the passage outside: others were up, would soon intrude, and he and Arian would have more nights. He pulled on his robe and went to the hearth.

He stirred the fire, lit the candles, opened the curtains to the soft silvery light of a snow-dawn, the flakes coming down lazily. When he looked back at the bed, Arian had propped herself up on the pillows, watching him. It was all he could do to turn away, open the panel to his closet, and bring her a robe.

"We shall have to open the queen's chambers for you," he said.

"As long as the king's bed is open to me, I am content," Arian said, wrapping the robe around her. "And we have weapons practice, do we not?"

"We do," Kieri said.

More quickly than he wanted, they were both dressed. Outside the door, Kieri found Garris . . . Garris alone.

"That was tactful," he said.

"Some of them were thinking things up," Garris said. "I cleared them out. You'll find them in the salle."

Drill in the salle followed its usual routine; the armsmasters kept everyone too busy for comment on the king's new situation, for which Kieri was grateful. Everyone was breathless by the time the glass had turned again, and Kieri went up to bathe and dress for a day he hoped would be equally routine. Breakfast included leftovers from the previous day's feast.

"Did all this come from our kitchen?" he asked the steward when yet another tray came in. Sweet and savory stuffed pastries, candied fruits, little round spice cakes.

"No, sir king. Guests brought some already made to save our cooks the work."

Kieri took a handful of honey-flavored pastries and toasted nuts along to his office. Garris met him there with the first of the day's chores, the schedule for testing the new applicants for King's Squires. Then he had meetings with his Council and a review of the damages of the war with a group of merchants, headed by Geraint Chalvers, who wondered if the scathefire path might become a useful road to the river port they wanted to build. He needed to write dispatches to Tsaia, Pargun, Prealíth, Kostandan, as well as to his own troops. He had no time to talk—really talk—to Arian or to the Halverics, to tell the Seneschal all that had happened in the ossuary, or to ask the elves what really lay under the mound in the King's Grove. He jotted down some of the things he felt he must do—questions he must ask, issues he must solve—but other issues stood before him as live persons, demanding immediate attention.

The next day was the same—urgent matters, all made more urgent by the recent war, by the season, by the short time (so claimed those involved) in which to plan the state wedding. Kieri wanted to resettle those whose steadings had been destroyed by scathefire, but that required negotiation with the elves, new grants of land to replace the old, and so did the proposed river port.

And the elves had vanished again.

A HAND OF days later, a royal courier from Tsaia arrived. The man wore a Serrostin knot on his heart-shoulder—a

nigan, then, nephew or cousin of Duke Serrostin, not one of
his sons, as the colors were reversed—and the insignia of a
Knight of the Bells.

"Sir king, an urgent message from King Mikeli on a matter
of great import." He bowed.

"I receive it, Sir nigan-Serrostin," Kieri said formally as he
took the velvet pouch embroidered with the Tsaian royal crest.
"Be welcome here. Have a seat near the fire." Two servants
came in with trays: one with a tall pot of sib and mugs, the
other with an array of pastries. They set these on a table near
the fire and pulled two chairs into position. Kieri sat in one,
then the man sat; the servants poured sib for both of them and
then, at Kieri's nod, left the room.

Kieri took the message tube out of the pouch, untied the
rose and silver ribbons, and slid out the rolled message. "Do
you know what this is about?"

"Yes, sir . . . or partly. I have not read it, of course."

"No, of course not." Kieri unrolled the message and began
reading. Beyond the flowery formal greetings, thanks for
Kieri's timely messages about the situation with Pargun, and
wishes for Kieri's good health, the first sentence took his
breath:

*We are concerned that Our choice of Dorrin Duke Verrakai
as Constable was an error, due to the serious harm done two
of her squires while under her care, including Our cousin
Beclan Mahieran, fourth in succession.*

"Harm to squires? Do you know about this?"

"Indeed yes, sir king. And King Mikeli bade me tell you
what I know." The courier launched into a tale that made
Kieri's neck hairs rise.

He saw at once how a squire's capture and maiming by Verrakaien renegades would be taken by the king and other peers
in Tsaia. Injury—even death—in war was one thing, any hint
of magery quite another. And a Verrakaien attack on another
squire—especially a member of the royal family—would
complete the ruin of Dorrin's reputation, even though it was
clearly not her fault.

"She had been made Constable, is that not right?" Kieri asked. "So once she knew of war, she would have to leave home to take command."

"Yes, but she didn't protect her squires. Sending the Marrakai girl off alone—and then Daryan's capture. She said she tried to heal him, but—"

"Do you doubt she tried?"

"Sir king . . . I don't know. She's a magelord. How can we know if she really tried or merely said so?" The courier's doubt showed clearly. "And then—letting a Kuakgan heal him. I see by your ruby you're Falkian, but our family's been Girdish for generations. Kuakkgani are . . . strange. Uncanny. Maybe not evil—"

"Not evil at all," Kieri said. "Unless you count trees evil."

"Of course not. But—but they deal with the green blood, mingle it with theirs . . . Did you know that?"

"Yes," Kieri said. "Although I do not understand how it could work."

"So now," the courier went on, "Daryan has a—a twig where his sword-thumb was. I've seen it myself. It has what looks like bark, but Daryan can move it. It's . . . disgusting."

"Only one thumb?"

"Only one thumb now. There's a chance another may . . . may bud, the Kuakgan told Daryan."

"That's good news, isn't it? He's not crippled now?"

"No, but . . . he has the green blood in him, you see. It's not . . . not natural. And he's defied his father the Duke. He says he's not crippled, can still do his duties, and there's no reason for him to go home like a naughty child. He won't see that it's the Duke's fault."

"I don't see that either," Kieri said. "If I had been there and an enemy was between me and a young squire, I'd have sent the squire away for his safety. It wasn't her fault—"

"She should have anticipated more of them, not just one."

"Perhaps. No one knows all. I could have assumed that the message from a former soldier was false . . . but I didn't, and because of that I was captured and the paladin Paksenarrion suffered five days and nights of torment. Was that all my fault, or would you blame those who tortured her, the Liartians?"

"Liart, of course . . . but . . ." His brow furrowed. "I suppose she *could* have intended no harm."

"She was trying to do her duty to her king and to her youngest squire," Kieri said. "And he is alive by her effort to find and save him. If she proved unable to heal wounds most consider beyond healing, and if healing came from a Kuakgan, what matter?" He glanced down at the letter. "And as for Beclan—"

"That's even worse," Serrostin said. "She did not wait for him to come back from patrol before she left."

"How far out was he?"

"He was not expected back for six or seven days, weather depending."

Kieri snorted. "Of course she could not wait that long before taking up her responsibilities as Constable," Kieri said. "Duty required her to leave. No one knew, those first days, what the Pargunese intended—they'd invaded Tsaia before."

"Yes, but—" Serrostin went on to detail what he had been told. Kieri noticed that he seemed honest, unaware of the interpretation he put on things. At the end he looked at Kieri as if expecting him to agree that Dorrin had done something wrong.

Kieri tried again. "From what you tell me, Duke Verrakai made the best decisions she could: she had to respond to the news of war by the king's own order. Delay could have cost Tsaia dearly had the Pargunese invaded."

"Yes, sir king, but—"

Kieri ignored the interruption and went on, ticking off his points on his fingers. "That Verrakaien renegades existed, she knew and had warned the king about—and also me, because our borders adjoin. She sent a troop of Royal Guard cavalry to find and protect Beclan. They would have been in time to do so had Beclan himself not disobeyed her orders and put himself and his escort in danger. She could not have known about the Kuakgan's trap."

Serrostin squirmed a bit in his chair. He stared into the fire, lips clamped tight, the very picture of someone who does not intend to be swayed from his opinion. And yet . . . Dorrin deserved the attempt to persuade the man, even if it didn't work.

"I say this not because she was one of my captains," Kieri said. "I would say the same of anyone."

"I understand, sir king," Serrostin said, in the tone of one who did not. He didn't argue, at least; Kieri had to be content with that.

Kieri read the rest of the letter to the accompaniment of silence from the other chair, a silence radiating disagreement. He ignored it. Mikeli, obviously, had not ignored similar sentiments. He was concerned, as any king must be, about threats to his realm, and despite all that Dorrin had done since the previous spring, he was concerned about her.

"Well," Kieri said, setting the letter aside on the table. "This demands an answer, and quickly."

"I am ready at your command," Serrostin said.

"Tomorrow, then. I cannot have an answer ready before dark. The steward will show you to guest quarters. If you are not too fatigued, join us at dinner."

"Thank you, sir king."

Kieri called Arian in to read the letter and asked her what Dorrin's squires were like, how she thought Dorrin was doing with the domain, anything she had observed.

"I met only one squire," Arian said. "A girl—Gwenno Marrakai. Black hair, green eyes, lively and intelligent. I met her on the last day of her patrol and rode with her and her escort back to the Verrakai house."

"Her father is a friend of mine," Kieri said. "A long story, but the Marrakaien were the first nobles of Tsaia to accept me. I remember meeting her as a child—bright and lively, but all the Marrakai children are. I gather she rode with you to Harway?"

"Yes. And we had no trouble. When we left, she said she would follow as soon as the youngest squire returned—he was due to arrive that day or the next. She had them on some kind of rotation. She was concerned about the king's cousin, the eldest, both because he was in the succession and because he was brash, as young men that age are. But he had the largest of the escorts, under the most experienced sergeant."

"I know the other two dukes well," Kieri said. "Sonder Mahieran is the king's uncle. Very aware of being in the royal family, a man of high temper, but I found him fair enough, as long as he received what he considered due deference. Serrostin's quieter, slower to judge, but again, I've found his judgment sound before. We did not always agree—any two of us—but I respected them and felt they respected me. We were united in our distrust of Verrakai and proved justified in that distrust last spring."

"But their sons were injured," Arian said. "They would react to that."

"Indeed yes. I understand their anger and concern. Still, Dorrin did nothing wrong. To blame her makes no sense." He remembered his own rage after his wife and children were killed, his struggle not to blame the soldiers at the stronghold—how he had not blamed the man really responsible, not seeing for decades the truth of that ambush.

"Verrakai has long had a bad name, has it not?" Arian asked, breaking into his memories.

"Yes . . . for generations, at least, with the other dukes."

"Then perhaps it is hard for those who did not know her to accept that Dorrin Verrakai is truly different. Perhaps every time they say 'Duke Verrakai,' it brings up memories of the former dukes, including the one who tried to kill the king. If she had taken another name—"

"Another name?"

"Elves do, you know."

"They—no, I didn't know. Why?"

"They live so long—I think they get tired of being who they were, so they take another name and live into it. That's what I've been told, anyway. Even you, Kieri. You were named Falkieri at birth, and called Falki first; then you became Kieri and lived into that name—"

"And changed its meaning," Kieri said. He did not realize how his voice had hardened until her expression changed to alarm. "I'm sorry," he said. "But the Kieri who suffered those years had to change or could not have lived, and I changed again with Aliam Halveric, and once again when I moved out on my own."

"And you did not change your name, but yourself. I do understand. It's just—other people do change their names and their lives."

"Usually for a bad reason," Kieri said. "At least in my experience."

"I do not know all the reasons of elves," Arian said. "Perhaps they are bad reasons. But when I try to imagine living a thousand years . . . I think I would not be the same person throughout."

"Um. But the reality is that Dorrin did not take another name, though she did not use the Verrakai name openly. I think you may be right, though: the Verrakai reputation has affected hers. I had not thought of that; I cannot really think of her and the former duke as related."

"Do you think any of it's because she's a woman?" Arian asked.

"In Tsaia? Why? They're Girdish; the Marshal-General's a woman. It's true that most titles are held by men, but with her background, she's clearly qualified to hold a domain in her own right."

"But do they think so?"

"From what I heard, the king and the other dukes did, and they're the ones who count." Even as he said it, he had a moment's doubt. More counts than dukes, more barons than counts—and all of them peers.

"Except that now . . . it's the dukes' sons who were hurt."

"Yes. I know. I know that makes a difference." He wished it didn't. He wished Tsaian peers had more experience in war—then they might understand.

"What are you going to tell Tsaia's king?"

"What I told him before. She's honest, she's loyal, and this is not her fault." He sighed. "And I don't know if it will do the least bit of good. I wonder if I wrote the dukes myself, in addition to the king—"

"I had hoped to have her at our wedding," Arian said. "But if she's under suspicion there—"

"We must invite her. And the king. Perhaps on neutral ground, here, it will work out." Kieri shook his head. He hoped Mikeli wouldn't do anything rash or remove Dorrin as Constable. The Pargunese threat might have ended, but it wasn't the only one, not with Alured in the South. Tsaia would need Dorrin if Alured came north; none of the other peers but Arcolin had recent military experience. Some now holding titles had been children in that last Pargunese incursion.

Kieri thought about Arcolin: could he function as Constable if the king removed Dorrin? Solid, reliable, loyal, honest . . . but Dorrin had always been the better tactician of the pair. Arcolin was competent enough; Dorrin was brilliant. And Arcolin was, at this time, only a count, not a duke. Would dukes obey him? At the moment, perhaps, angry as they were with Dorrin, but when it counted, in a future invasion? He tried to imagine Arcolin chivvying all those household troops into one coherent army in a time of crisis, choosing the best strategy.

He wrote his letter to Mikeli, laying out his reasons for considering Dorrin to have done the best she could and reminding him that he, Kieri, had lost squires to death in combat in Aarenis, a risk that parents knew they took when they sent their boys to him.

I myself lost children to violent death; I know how it wrings a parent's mind and heart to have any harm come to their son or daughter. I know the temptation to blame anyone who can possibly be held responsible. But from what you wrote and Sir nigan-Serrostin said, I do not see that Duke Verrakai was negligent with her squires.

He rolled it, sealed it, and put it back in the message tube, tied now with ribbons in Lyonya's colors. A final drop of wax sealed the ties. Into the velvet pouch, and it was ready for Serrostin when he came to dinner. The next morning, Serrostin rode away.

CHAPTER EIGHTEEN

Tsaia: North Marches Stronghold

At Midwinter, the gnomes declined to come up and celebrate with the others; Arcolin felt bad about that but not bad enough to make it an order. For himself, that Midwinter Feast completed the process of becoming comfortable with his new role. The newest recruit cohort, smaller than usual, included youngsters who had never known any other commander or the stronghold without a Marshal near. Having a Marshal to light the fire of Sunreturn made him as happy as having the title himself. Or almost.

Immediately after Midwinter, he sent a courier south to Vérella, informing the king of the gnomes' arrival and what they had said. He had no idea what the king would do. The secondhand report of a dragon might seem—would seem, Arcolin was sure—highly suspect, though the arrival of visible, recognizable gnomes would certainly carry weight. Though he himself was convinced the gnomes were telling the truth— the truth as they knew it—no king, he thought, would want to give up territory on the word of beings he had never met.

Yet the gnomes refused to go to Vérella unless he himself did, and he was reluctant to give them hard orders, they were so obviously distraught.

A few nights after Midwinter, Arcolin sat busy with the year's account rolls, considering what he should budget for equipment replacement in the coming year, when one of the gnomes—the estvin, he thought, though they still looked all alike to him—came to his door.

"Master, Dragon comes."

"Dragon? Here? Why?" In the lamplight and firelight, the estvin seemed to waver; Arcolin realized the gnome was trembling so hard he could barely stand.

"It is—it is not to know. It is—it might—to burn us—"

"No."

With no warning, a dark-clothed stranger stood in the doorway to the passage, eyes reflecting the yellow firelight. And there had been no alarm—there should have been—

"It is not to burn kapristi or human that I am come," the man said. He looked like a man, but the room seemed warmer, with a faint tang of hot iron, and as he came nearer, into the light, his dark skin showed a pattern of fine lines. "The kapristi should withdraw, as he is frightened."

"Go on," Arcolin said gently to the gnome, who made a wide circle around the stranger and disappeared down the passage. Then to the stranger he said, "I am the Count, if that is whom you seek; my name is Jandelir Arcolin. May I have yours?"

The man smiled. "Bold you are, Jandelir Arcolin, but so I expected from one who had been captain under the new king of Lyonya. Who fares well, though lately having some difficulty."

"Pargunese," Arcolin said. Except for the bright eyes, whose yellow gleam seemed brighter than reflected fire would account for, and the tracery of lines on his skin, the man seemed completely human. A spy, perhaps? But certainly not—his mind blanked as the stranger opened his mouth and a tongue red and hot as iron in the forge-fire slid out farther than any human tongue, little flames writhing from its surface. The air wavered with heat; Arcolin felt sweat break out on his body.

"My name does not concern you," the stranger said, after that tongue withdrew once more into the semblance of a human face. "My nature does. Kapristi told you truth, as kapristi usually do. Tell me, man of war, are you wise?"

For a long moment, Arcolin could say nothing, could scarcely bring his mind to understand those words at all. Then he gathered his thoughts. "You are . . . a dragon."

The stranger nodded gravely. "But are you wise?"

"Not . . . very," Arcolin said. "As you said, I am a man of

war, and war is not often wise." He nodded to the chair across the desk from him. "You might as well sit, if you will."

The man sat; Arcolin felt no diminution of menace or power. "If war be not wise, why, then, do you pursue it?"

All the answers Arcolin could think of were too little or too much, and a shrug of the shoulders would be rude. "Choices," he said finally. "Choices made when I was a lad that made this road the likeliest to follow."

The stranger leaned back in the chair and tented hands that had ordinary fingernails. Arcolin had half expected talons. Surely dragons had talons . . . in the old legends they had talons.

"Only in my true shape," the stranger said, as if Arcolin had asked aloud. "They would be inconvenient here." He smiled again. "You claim no wisdom, and yet you are correct in your understanding of why you became a man of war. All have choices; choices both create new choices and close off old ones. I think you may be at least somewhat wise. For a human."

Arcolin wanted to ask what dealings the dragon had with Kieri, what news from Lyonya, but more urgent, he knew, was the dragon's purpose in coming here.

"I would not come to Vérella if it can be avoided," the dragon said. "Cities . . . are inconvenient for my kind, tempting to rash action. But your king must understand that some land is forfeit, and why, and that it is beyond my power to restore it."

"Our law requires us to accede to gnomish—kapristi— claims of territory," Arcolin said. "The kapristi told my captain, who told me, and I have sent word already to the king."

"It is not of kapristi," the stranger said. "It is of my kind and our history. The kapristi were but stewards of our trust and failed. In their failure lay the seeds of much evil, including that enmity between Pargun and Tsaia. My children—our children—are jealous and most unwise in their youth."

"Your . . . children . . . ?" Arcolin could not follow this.

"As it falls on you to lose land you thought you owned, and on you to explain this loss to your king, I will speak plain, though . . . plain is not always wise."

Arcolin's mind drifted to the refreshments on his desk: the

jug of golden southern wine, the glasses, the plate of leftover Midwinter pastries. "Will you share a glass?" he asked.

The stranger chuckled. "I judge you meant to impose no host-right, but no—I drink nothing but wind and eat what you cannot eat. It was, however, a courteous impulse, and I consider it well done." He glanced at the door; it swung closed silently, and Arcolin could just hear the faint snick of the lock. He thought he should be afraid, but he wasn't.

"Here is the short tale, clear-spoken," the stranger said. "In times ancient to you, dragons lived here, having come from lands you cannot imagine. But always we had too many children . . . and our children, as I said, are rash and wild and dangerous. They are fire's spirit and burn all. The Sinyi, who have few children, begged us to limit our growth for the sake of the taig, and so we did, burying the eggs deep in stone, cold stone, away from any that might disturb them and bring them to life. Then came the Severance."

"Severance?" Arcolin had not meant to speak.

"In time, humans had been born, and one came near the Sinyi in love for the One Tree. He sang to the Tree; the Tree sang back . . . and that was the first Kuakgan. You have heard that story?"

"Something of it, yes. It angered some elves."

"Indeed. Some reproached the tree; all reproached the man. The Sinyi severed in twain—those who left took vengeance on those who stayed, on humans, on the very land itself." The stranger closed those golden eyes for a long moment, then opened them again, looking past Arcolin into the fire on the hearth, which crackled under that gaze. "We are all Elders. Sinyi of both kinds, rockfolk, and dragons, each created for a purpose in this world by those more powerful, who juggle worlds as you might toss pebbles. As Elders, we too have choices, and the consequences of our choices affect all the lateborn, for we can shape—to some degree—even the fabric of this world. Wisdom meddles little. The iynisin, those elves cursed in the Severance, are not wise. They . . . meddle. They stole our hidden eggs and loosed scathefire on the world once more." The stranger looked down at linked hands. "Or it may be that there was no theft, that one of our own turned traitor."

"How did any survive?" Arcolin asked.

"That is an even longer tale," the stranger said. "A tale of great loss, great courage, great changes in the world. A night and a day are not long enough to tell it, and we both, man of war, have much to do."

Arcolin said nothing, though curiosity burned in him.

"These kapristi you shelter had care of one clutch of dragons' eggs. Mine, in fact. I do not blame the kapristi for the trouble that befell them from Achrya, but they did not send for aid, and in the end their prince gave in to her and told where to find the eggs and how to wake them. For that great unwisdom many have suffered already and yet more will suffer. Wine spilled from a broken jar cannot be gathered back into it, nor can the shards of a dragon's egg be fitted back together and made whole . . ." Again the stranger's eyes closed for a long moment. "What they loosed," he said, still with shut eyes, "must be destroyed, and yet . . . they are my children."

"Is there—?" Arcolin began; the stranger lifted a finger and he fell silent.

"No other way? No. Two of them only, streaming scathefire, rent great holes in the Lyonyan forest taig, tracks it will take more than a human life to bring back to healthy forest."

"You stopped them," Arcolin said.

The stranger smiled, a slightly wistful smile. "Not alone. I met a half-Sinyi woman on my way to find the Lyonyan king. Braver than any human woman I had ever met; she helped me."

"Paks?" Arcolin asked. He could not think of any other woman it might be, though he wondered that someone would think her part-elven.

"That is not her name: she is Half-Song to me, and Arian to her lover, the king." The stranger shook his head as if to clear it. "But that is not to the point. You, man of war, must be wiser than you believe yourself to be. The place where the eggs were—where these kapristi lived—is near the border between your land and that of the Pargunese. That is why I told the kapristi to tell you it must be barred to all lateborn. I must find all the eggs, transport those not shattered, find all pieces of those that are . . . and any that escape will loose scathefire."

"If Achrya began this evil, will she not attack you? Prevent you?"

The golden eyes opened wide. "Achrya has been given a lesson; she will soon be . . . nothing again."

"But she's a goddess," Arcolin said.

"No." The stranger shook his head. "She is not even Elder. She was created of fear and loathing, stealing power from greater powers. You must tell your king why the land is barred and long will be. I can assure you that the Pargunese will take no advantage."

"The Pargunese are indeed my concern," Arcolin said. "For my king bids me defend the eastern border and stand ready to help other lords between here and the Honnorgat."

"The Pargunese have more pressing concerns," the stranger said. "Including me." He yawned; the inside of his mouth glowed like a bed of coals, and once more heat rolled out. "You said you sent a courier. Did you tell your king of a dragon?"

"Not . . . precisely," Arcolin said. "I told him of gnomes, which our law covers, and what the gnomes told me, but I thought the gnomes—I thought they were mistaken. So tired, so ill, perhaps, that they had mistaken some bane of Achrya's—"

"And now?"

"I understand they were not mistaken." What else could he say with those fiery eyes looking at him, that heat and forge smell all around him?

"Good." The stranger stood. "We must go outside to seal this agreement. There is not room here for the change."

"The . . . change?"

The stranger smiled. "You would not want to miss seeing my true form, would you?"

Arcolin shook his head, unable to speak. The door to his office opened before they reached it; they passed through the halls and down the stairs and out into the inner court with no one to see them. The night air struck bitter cold, but warmth and a dim light came off the stranger, less than the light of the oil lamps that burned in their niches either side of the entrance.

"Stand there," the stranger said, pointing to the well in the center. Arcolin obeyed. Across the court, he could see the orange glow of another lamp in the arch between this courtyard and the larger outer one, where a soldier should have stood guard, but he did not see the soldier. Had the stranger—the dragon—taken his guard away? "I did no one here harm," the stranger said. Then he shimmered, as if he were made of water on which sunlight glittered, and grew until the space around the well was full of scaled dragon: head and neck and body and tail. Talons rasped the stones; near Arcolin the dragon's snout blew a jet of forge-smelling steam that warmed him, and above and to his right the dragon's golden eye peered down at him.

"I named your commander and Lyonya's king Sorrow-King," the dragon said. "You I will name . . . Kindly-Death."

Arcolin shivered; he felt that naming had a terrible power. "May I ask why?"

"You kill, but you are kind of heart," the dragon said, as if it were obvious. "Do you not know your own nature?"

"Not . . . entirely," Arcolin said. "No human does, I think."

"Indeed, man of war, you have some wisdom. But we must seal our bargain, that you leave the land that I must take, and allow none to wander there, lest they take hurt." The dragon opened its mouth and extended its tongue, red-hot and smoking in the cold air. "Come, now: touch your tongue to mine."

Arcolin stared a long moment. He had not really imagined a dragon at all, and being asked—commanded—to touch tongues . . . He wanted to ask if Kieri had done so, but thinking of Kieri gave him courage. Of course Kieri would have. He knelt on the cold stone flags and with great difficulty forced himself to open his mouth and extend his tongue into the heat that rose from the dragon's tongue.

That tongue felt dry and hot, stinging a little, but no hotter than a roll from the oven. It left a taste like bread-crust in his mouth.

"Well done, man of war," the dragon said. Arcolin sat back on his heels, then stood. "Your courage commends you. Though I take from you lands you were granted and give you a task you may find difficult, convincing your king, and am no kapristi who cannot give or take without exchange, yet I would gift you in return, as you asked no return. Is there aught that dragonfire can do for you or your realm?"

"I do not know what dragonfire can do," Arcolin said, but as he spoke, one face came unbidden to his mind. Stammel. "Unless it can cure blindness."

"Blindness of mind or eye?" the dragon asked. "You are not blind either way, I perceive."

"My sergeant," Arcolin said. "He was blinded when a magelord tried to steal his body; he fought it off through days of fever, but—"

Scales clattered like dropped armor, echoing off the walls around the court. "What magelord?" the dragon asked. Now Arcolin faced both eyes, the dragon having rearranged itself.

"I do not know the full name," Arcolin said. "He first appeared in the body of someone who had been a recruit here, but he had apparently yielded his body willingly. Duke Verrakai believes it was a Verrakai who had such powers."

"So it comes again," the dragon said.

"What?"

"Mageborn evil," the dragon said. "Tell me more of your sergeant."

Arcolin did his best to describe what Stammel had done in that office in Vonja, but the dragon asked more and more questions about Stammel's life. "He was a paladin's sergeant," he said finally. "Paksenarrion's—"

Steam rushed over him. "He nurtured *that* paladin?"

Arcolin would not have called a sergeant's untender care "nurturing" but said Stammel had been her recruit sergeant and her cohort sergeant later.

"Would she not heal his sight?" the dragon asked.

"She heals as Gird commands," Arcolin said. "Stammel is not Girdish, but Tirian. I think he is drawn somewhat to Gird and if not blinded, might have sworn to Gird soon, but being blinded, he thinks it unfair to do so seeking a cure."

The dragon blinked. "A man of high honor and courage. I do not know, man of war, if dragonfire can cure what magefire ruined . . . humans are fragile to Elders. Speak to your sergeant. If he will risk, I will try. Now I must go, lest harm come to all."

The dragon rose into the air, still in the coil that had circled the courtyard, scales clattering as it then uncurled wings Arcolin had not noticed, black against the stars. It glided away, that dark shape; he shivered and turned to go back inside. By the entrance stood the guards he had not seen before, looking at him with surprise.

"Sir! I—how'd you get past us?"

"No matter," Arcolin said. He took the route to the cellar stairs; the estvin waited there.

"The dragon's gone," he said.

The estvin nodded. "It is felt. Does—does dragon demand we go?"

Arcolin felt his brows going up. "Why would it?"

"For that we did not hold to bargain."

"No," Arcolin said. "The dragon said you had failed but no more than that about you. The dragon's command for me was to tell my king about the lands lost, which I had already done by courier, and prevent my people wandering there. That is all."

The estvin just stared at him.

"Did you think I would break faith with you?" Arcolin asked.

"Your law is not our Law," the estvin said. "But I am relieved to see trust justified."

THE NEXT MORNING, Arcolin went to see Stammel, who had settled into the barracks as usual. He found him in the main courtyard, sparring with the new armsmaster, the two of them rolling around on the cold stone as if it were summer.

"Sir!" the guard at the archway said. The two disentangled and stood, panting puffs of steam in the cold air that looked nothing like the dragon's.

"Sergeant Stammel," Arcolin said. "I need to talk to you— barracks empty?"

"Squads still scrubbing out," Stammel said. "Bit of a problem last night."

"Ah." Arcolin didn't ask; if he needed to know, the recruit

sergeant would tell him. "We'll go to my office, then." He moved closer; Stammel touched his shoulder, and they started off.

As they came into the inner court, Stammel said, "If it's about my sight, sir, it's no better. Just that bit of light blur, is all. And sir—much as I want to be with the Company, I'm not what you need. Like I said before."

"It's not just about you," Arcolin said. "And it will take some explaining."

Once in his office, with the door closed and Stammel sitting across from him, where light from the window revealed the cloudiness in his eyes, Stammel looked, but for that, the fit, healthy sergeant of middle age he had seemed before. But how many campaign seasons could anyone sustain? Most sergeants retired with the first bad wound. Why, Arcolin asked himself, was he so sure Stammel should not? If the man himself had been willing . . .

"You remember what the gnomes told me," Arcolin said. "About the dragon."

"Yes, sir. And you weren't sure of it, you said, but don't tease them."

"Right. I thought they were frightened, hungry, confused— anything but a dragon, which, Gird and the High Lord know— hasn't one been seen in Tsaia in generations. Since before Gird's day, anyway."

Stammel did not ask anything, just sat, composed and steady as usual.

"Last night," Arcolin said, "a dragon came here."

Stammel jerked as if he'd been pricked. "Sir?"

"A dragon. I—I can't begin to describe it, except that it was here, in this room, in the guise of a man, but for the markings on its skin, its yellow eyes, and its tongue—such a tongue you never saw."

"A tongue . . ." Stammel sounded half mazed.

"In the shape of a man who could put out a sword's length of tongue—*my* sword's length—and the tongue like red-hot iron and giving off heat."

Arcolin related the tale of the Pargunese stealing a dragon's egg, of the scathefire, of the dragon-man changing shape in the courtyard into the dragon of legend, and of touching the dragon's tongue with his. Stammel's hands, he saw, were now clenched on the chair arms; his body rigid and sweat trickling down his face. Arcolin knew what that was: the memory of those days Stammel had burned inside with the spirit that had tried to consume him.

"You—touched fire, sir?"

"I had to," Arcolin said. "Kieri would have. I'm sure Kieri did, though the dragon didn't tell me that."

"And yet—you live and are not . . . consumed?"

"No. It seemed burning until I touched it, and then it was warm, no hotter than fresh bread. And that brings me to you, Stammel." It felt indecent that he could see Stammel's distress and Stammel could not see him, but there was no help for it. Yet. Maybe never. "At the end, for sealing the bargain so and because I asked nothing in return for the lands I and this realm must lose, the dragon chose to grant me a favor."

Stammel did not move, though his eyelids flickered.

"I thought of you," Arcolin said. "I asked if dragonfire could heal blindness, and it asked if I meant blindness of the mind or of the eyes."

Stammel's breath came short; his voice sounded different when he asked, "And . . . you told it of me?"

"Yes." Arcolin sighed. Perhaps this had been a very bad idea. "It told me to ask you—to see if you were willing to attempt it—but it offered no guarantee. Humankind are fragile to Elders, it said. I don't know what it will ask of you if you are willing. I do know it was upset at the mention of magelords who can change bodies—"

"Not as upset as I am, sir," Stammel said. He grinned, the grin of a man facing danger.

"It wants to see you, I gather. It might heal you or might not, but—I must know, what is your wish?"

Stammel said nothing a long moment, then turned his face to the light from the window. "I had given up hoping for sight," he said. "Despite the glow that tells me where the sun is. I wanted to stay here, among people and places I knew. But to have the chance of real sight—this—a dragon—but fire—"

His hands opened and clenched again. "Do you think I will have to . . . to be burned again?"

Arcolin watched Stammel struggle with his fear. "Did Paks ever tell you the whole story of her becoming paladin?" Arcolin asked. He went on without waiting for an answer. "The Kuakgan raised a magical fire, and she had to reach into it. But it did not burn her. Just as my tongue felt heat, as from hot food, but no worse. Yet if you choose not to, Stammel, no one would call you coward. You have endured more fire than anyone I know, more than we thought you could survive."

"How could fire heal my eyes, when fire burned out my sight?"

"I don't know if it can. But the thought of you would not have come to me, standing there with the dragon, if a god had not put it in my head. It may be something beyond your eyes: the dragon seemed interested that a magelord had invaded you. It's been so long since dragons were here—perhaps they know things about the magelords and Old Aare. And with the regalia Dorrin told me about and the trouble in the South, there may be more than one reason for dragons to return."

"More than one dragon?"

"I don't know," Arcolin said, raking his fingers through his hair. "All I know is the dragon offered a favor, and your face came before me, and . . . here we are. Think about it, is all I ask."

Stammel frowned. "I should have gone Girdish back then, when Paks was here and saved us. I just . . . it felt too easy."

"I understand," Arcolin said, thinking of his own years of fading faith, now renewed. "I think she made us all more what we were rather than changing us to something else."

"I suppose," Stammel said slowly. "I—I'd rather ask Paks for a healing than a dragon, truth to say, sir. If I was Girdish."

"I understand," Arcolin said again. "So would I, if I had that choice. Just . . . think, will you?"

"Of course, sir. Any idea when the dragon's coming back?"

"None at all," Arcolin said. He sighed. "And now I must write another report to King Mikeli . . . He's likely to think I'm winter-crazed."

"Should you go yourself, sir?"

"No—I think not, with the gnomes still unsettled and the move of the border. It's not that I doubt the dragon—or for that matter the gnomes—but as Count, I should be here, ready to do whatever needs doing. It's not as settled a situation as when Kieri governed here."

Stammel nodded. "Makes sense, sir. And you don't have experienced captains, other than Cracolnya. Though Captain Versin and Captain Arneson are both well respected."

"I hope Selfer's found a good one in the south," Arcolin said. "But that's not your problem. I'll be taking Cracolnya and Versin south with me; I think Arneson's ideal for recruits. If the Pargunese are truly settled, then I'll need only one captain up here. Especially with the gnomes in the west hills—they'll know if any orcs threaten."

"They aren't very many to fight off orcs, sir," Stammel said.

"No, they couldn't drive them off alone, but they'd know where the orcs were when we go after them. And it'd give our young troops some experience, as well." He shook his head. "Well. Let's go down."

Captain Arneson had the recruits paraded in the large courtyard and was delivering as professional a reaming out as Arcolin had seen. Four recruits, it seemed, had taken extra Midwinter sweet tarts and tried to hide them in the barracks for later consumption at a private celebration. As clean as the stronghold was, any place that stored grain and other foodstuffs attracted rats and mice, and when the recruit corporal made his mid-third-shift round through the barracks, he'd seen a couple of rats—undeniable rats—scuttering along the wall behind the bunks.

That led to the discovery of the illicit food—no food was ever allowed in the barracks—and to the guilty parties—and to two other stashes—and thence to the morning spent scrubbing the barracks twice over as punishment. Plus no breakfast.

"My lord Count," Arneson said when his recruit sergeant announced Arcolin's arrival. "Your pardon, my lord."

Arcolin looked at the recruits as if they were darkling beetles. "Captain, they're your recruits. But if they were my recruits—"

"My lord?"

"I'd hope my commander gave me another turn of the glass alone with them. When you're quite done, I'd like to see you about another matter, entirely unrelated."

"Yes, my lord."

"I'll see you later, Sergeant," Arcolin said to Stammel, and went back to his office, stopping at his scribe's cubbyhole to warn him that he'd need to be on hand in the afternoon. He allowed himself a few moments to contrast today's Captain Arneson—healthy, fit, with only a neat patch over his missing eye—with the starved-wolf-looking man hired last summer in Valdaire. He'd become a superb recruit commander, approved by both Valichi and Stammel, and on top of that a companion-able officer to share a dinner with.

Arcolin sighed and forced himself to start writing. Drafting a report to King Mikeli was as difficult as he'd expected. "A dragon came to me last night . . ." What would the king make of that? What proof did he have other than the gnomes in the cellars? And yet . . . the tip of his tongue tingled with the re-membered heat and flavor of the dragon's tongue. The dragon was real. If he'd imagined the taste of a dragon's tongue, it would have been something exotic, spices from Aarenis or a flavor he'd never tasted before. Fresh-baked hot bread-crust . . . that was real.

"A dragon came to me last night in the guise of a man." But that wasn't the beginning. The beginning was the gnomes.

"While inspecting Captain Cracolyna's dispositions on the Pargunese border"—that was better—"gnomes arrived with a report." "Demand" was more like it, but "report" sounded better.

"My lord, you asked me to come?"

Arcolin looked up with a start. "Captain—yes, I'm sorry, I'm trying to write a letter to the king, and I'm having trouble. Please, sit down."

"I apologize for my cohort, my lord. By now they should be more disciplined."

"Think nothing of it. Every recruit cohort does something stupid at Midwinter. Then they get back to business. What I wanted to ask you was this: I need a trusted messenger to carry this letter to the king in Vérella."

Before he could say more, Arneson spoke up. "Why not Sergeant Stammel, my lord? He's well known as a senior veteran, trusted by all. I could go myself, of course, but there's much to do with the recruits before you march them south."

"He can't travel alone," Arcolin said. He did not want to mention the possibility that the dragon might return and heal Stammel.

"Of course, my lord. But with one of Captain Cracolnya's veterans, perhaps?"

Stammel would be better, Arcolin realized. Arneson had never been at court; he was not known and might not be believed. "Let me tell you what the king must know," Arcolin said. "Since you will be staying here while I am in the South, you also need to know it."

It was as hard to say as it was to write. "Last night a dragon came here." At Arneson's startled look, Arcolin nodded. "Yes, an actual dragon. You know the gnomes mentioned one, but I did not believe it." Arneson nodded and listened without asking questions; Arcolin went on, finishing with the dragon's demand that he touch tongues with it to seal their agreement.

"What did it taste like?" Arneson asked then.

Arcolin felt his brows rise. "Taste like? Like hot breadcrust, fresh from the oven. And the smell, as well, which had been all hot iron before."

"I wonder if it tastes the same to all," Arneson said. Once more Arcolin was surprised. "I mean," Arneson went on, "it is a magical creature, and it can appear in two shapes. Does everyone who sees it see the same thing? Or is its appearance— even its taste—a form of enchantment? Or drawn partly from the person who sees it?"

Arcolin shook his head. "I have no idea," he said. "It never occurred to me to ask . . . If you had seen it, Talvis, I doubt you would have asked anything either."

"You're right," Arneson said with a chuckle. "But the morning after, and in its absence, questions come to me."

Arcolin went to the map cabinet and spread the map of the domain on his desk. He had already marked the line the gnomes had told him about, using their map as a reference. His preliminary dispositions still looked adequate to him, but what would the king say about them? At the south end of the newly cropped domain, the border angled east abruptly before meeting the old Tsaian-Pargunese line.

"Where is the new Pargunese boundary?" Arneson asked.

"Here," Arcolin said. He had marked it lightly—two days' ride from their new one. "I don't know how one dragon can patrol all that, but it should at least help keep them out."

"That corner's going to be the problem," Arneson said. "Whatever the Pargunese are now, if they cause trouble again, we'll need a permanent fort in there—right here, I'd say." He pointed at the angle itself. Then he looked at Arcolin. "I wish I'd seen the dragon."

"So do I," Arcolin said. "Then I'd have a witness to send to Vérella."

CHAPTER NINETEEN

STAMMEL WAS ENJOYING a pot of sib with the recruit sergeant, Naris, when Naris said, "Sir Count!" and his chair scraped on the floor. Stammel set his mug on the table and stood, only a little slower.

"Sergeant Stammel, I need you," Arcolin said. "Get your cloak." Arcolin sounded tense.

Stammel wondered what it was. He kept one finger on the battered old table around a corner, then took two steps to the wall with its pegs for cloaks, knowing that his was on the end.

"We'll be awhile," Arcolin said to Naris. "Any more excitement in barracks?"

"No, sir," Naris said. "They were glad enough to be back to schedule today, all quiet."

Stammel had his cloak on when he sensed Arcolin near and put out his hand; Arcolin took it and put it on his shoulder. They went out into the cold wind, out the postern with a word for the watch, and then some distance from the gate but still in the wind shadow of the stronghold when Stammel felt a vague warmth ahead and smelled hot iron. They had gone the wrong direction for the stronghold forge.

"Captain?" He hated the quaver in his voice; he knew what it had to be.

"The dragon I told you of wants to meet you," Arcolin said.

Stammel felt the prickle of sweat breaking out; his stomach churned. "Where is it?" he asked, but he was already turning toward the warmth and smell.

Densely packed into the shape of a man, fire outlined the parts of an obvious dragon. Snout, neck, sinuous body, legs, tail curled up around the whole . . . Were dragons so little? Curiosity nudged against his fear.

"Is this your sergeant?" The voice sounded human, a deep man's voice.

"Yes," Arcolin said. "This is Sergeant Stammel."

The shape in his mind jerked nearer, close enough that he could feel the heat on his skin. Stammel fought the urge to step back.

"I would speak with him alone," the man said. "If that is acceptable to you, Sergeant Stammel."

Stammel struggled to get any words out. The heat, the unnatural sight of fire shaped like a man and a dragon in one brought back the terror of the invasion he had suffered. "It . . . is," he managed at last; his voice sounded to him as harsh as a breaking stick.

"I will not go far, Sergeant," Arcolin said.

"You may return to your work," the man said. "I will bring him to you, and I will not hurt him," the man went on, but Stammel saw the flickering of flames. How could fire not harm him? Yet . . . Arcolin said he had touched the dragon's tongue, in its own form, with his own tongue and had not perished.

Stammel heard Arcolin's boots on the frozen ground, going away, out of hearing. The dragon in man's shape was near enough to warm him, and despite the midwinter cold, he did not shiver. Not from cold, at least.

"Tell me," the man's voice said. "What do you see?"

"Usually nothing," Stammel said. "Though latterly, a faint blur of light sometimes at midday. Nothing clear enough to tell shape or distance. And what my mind sees now is not from my eyes."

"Tell me," the man said again.

"A man's outline filled with fire shapes that I imagine are . . . parts of a dragon," Stammel said. He shuddered despite himself. "I was filled with fire once . . ."

"Your captain said you were attacked by the spirit of an evil man who tried to take your body . . . but you say fire?"

"It felt like fire," Stammel said. His throat closed tight again; the memory choked him.

"That was not my fire," the man said.

Stammel said nothing.

"Tell me, are you wise?" the man asked.

"Wise? I do not know what wise is," Stammel said.

"How, then, do you judge what is right to do? Your captain tells me you are good with recruits—what do you think he means by that?"

"I teach them what will most likely keep them alive in war," Stammel said. "I decide which will make good soldiers and which will not."

"Judgment," said the man. "A task impossible without wisdom." He walked around behind Stammel, the warmth moving with him, and Stammel forced himself to stand still. He could see, with the not-sight of his mind, the fire-shape moving there. "What are you most proud of, Sergeant Stammel, in all your years of training recruits?"

That one was easy. "That I trained a paladin, Paksenarrion. That I saved her from an unjust punishment."

"And your greatest shame?"

"That I did not see the deeper evil in two other recruits that year."

"What happened?"

"One of them later did Paksenarrion a great injury; the other was the one who invaded me."

The man was back in front of him now. "And it is from that invasion you lost your sight?"

"Yes."

"But your captain said you fought later—shooting a crossbow—how did you do that without sight?"

"I could hear where they were—and there was a kind of . . . of . . . not exactly sight, but a bright place."

"You called yourself the Blind Archer, he told me."

"Yes. It came to me—I had heard the legend, but in the battle it seemed the right thing to say."

A sound like steam from a spout, a hiss. "What do you want to be, Sergeant Stammel?"

To be? What did that mean? "I am a soldier," he said.

"Yes . . . did you always want that?"

"Yes, from boyhood." The man-outline, fire-filled, stood in front of him again. Man . . . dragon . . . he did not know how to name it.

"You are a brave man," the voice said after a pause several breaths long. "To endure the mind's eye seeing a man-shape full of flame when you have been a man full of flame, or so it felt—that alone shows your courage. But I sense more courage: you have not killed yourself by grief, as some might have done. You do not ask for a quick death. You do not beg . . . and yet, you have no thoughts—this long after your blinding—for what else you might be. You have no plans for being a blind man."

"I . . . cannot."

"May I touch your face?"

"Yes."

Warm dry hands against his cheeks from chin to brow, thumbs light on his eyelids, warm as summer sun, pushing them gently up. In his mind, eyes stared into his, eyes unlike any he had ever seen. Huge, golden, light flickering in them. A tongue reached out—a wiggling tongue of flame—and he felt himself tremble. It touched his forehead . . . but did not burn him. Then it withdrew, and the hands lifted away. He felt himself blink.

"Sometimes," the man said, "what fire has burned can be healed by another fire. And sometimes not. My fire will not heal you, Sergeant, and I am sorry for it. If there is healing for your sight, it is not mine to give, and I do not know where it might be, other than the world-maker."

The hope Stammel had not let himself admit died, and in spite of himself he groaned.

"You are all of a piece, true soldier, as iron is iron," the man said. "You are not wise as men are wise but wise as iron is wise, by being of one kind and one mind only. I do not know how to help you but in one way."

Stammel waited.

"I have need of an archer."

That was not what he had expected to hear, if he could have expected anything.

"An . . . archer?"

"Yes. Dragonspawn freed by the men of Pargun threaten that land and this, and no common weapon will kill them. If you are willing, you can do so as the Blind Archer. It is dangerous; you may well die."

"It would protect this land?"

"Indeed. I believe if you see me, even in man-shape, you will see dragonspawn . . . and you are courageous and skilled in war. I can give you the right weapons, arrows that will kill them. But there is danger for you and for me. You must come into me, as the queen in Lyonya did—"

"The elf?"

"No." That came with a wave of stronger heat. "No, Half-Song, the king's betrothed and perhaps by now his wife."

"The Duke—the king—is married?" Stammel felt a wave of joy that Kieri, so long alone and grieving, might have found another love.

"She came to me without fear," the man said. "And when I changed to my own form and asked her to touch her tongue to mine, she did so. And then walked into my mouth, courage bright as my own fire, and helped me slay two of the dragonlets that burned Lyonya's forests." A pause, then, "With a bow and arrows tipped with dragonfire, she slew them, and it is that task I would ask of you, since she must stay with the king now and heal that land of its wounds."

Stammel felt a rising excitement. Could he really—he had shot those southern brigands, but dragonspawn? "I have sworn fealty to Lord Arcolin," he said. "He holds my oath, and my duty is first to him."

"Would you come with me if he released you? I must tell you that you are not like to return."

Would he? Could he leave the Company, which had been his life since he left home all those years ago . . . leave Arcolin, leave Devlin, leave all the people he knew . . . leave Kolya Ministiera, who had offered him a home? He struggled to bring those faces to mind, but they had faded in the time he had not seen them. He could leave them if by leaving them he could save them.

"I will," Stammel said. "If he releases me from my oath."

"And will you ask him?"

"Yes."

"It is our way to seal acquaintance by taste, tongue to

tongue," the man said. "And for that I must be in my own shape, and you must touch your tongue to mine. Stand there, and I will change."

The dark outline of a man vanished, and in its place what seemed a huge dragon-shaped heap of burning coals and embers flickering in all the colors of fire grew larger and larger. Finally one line of red ran out toward him. "Kneel down" the dragon said, a voice that rang in his head more than his ears. "And taste my essence."

Heat beat against Stammel's face, heat that brought tears to his sightless eyes, sweat to his face, his neck, even his back. Fear shook him as a dog shakes a rat, but he knelt and opened his mouth and put out his tongue.

It was not hot; it was not cold. It tasted of salt and iron, of blood, in fact. Then the heat withdrew, and he stood up again. The shape of fire shifted, contracted, and once more had the shape of a man, but now Stammel could think of it as nothing but dragon.

"I will guide you to your commander," the dragon said. "Put out your hand."

Stammel did so and touched a shoulder, the cloth familiar to his fingers. Together they walked back to the stronghold; together they came through the gate. Stammel heard nothing in the forecourt but the sound of their four feet on the stones—no challenge of sentries, no voices, no pots banging in the kitchens, no sound from the horses. Silence like this, even past the turn of a winter's night, was unknown, and yet it was silent.

"Your commander is in his office," the dragon said. Their own footfalls on the stones of the courtyard made no sound; Stammel knew their way by the faint whiff of horses here, wash water there, an inexplicable sense of constriction that must be the archway between the outer and inner courts, and then the indoor smells and warmth that meant they were inside, and he could hear their footsteps on the stairs, along the upper hall, the snick of the door lock and the faint squeak of a hinge that needed oiling.

"Stammel," Arcolin said. Stammel recognized relief in his voice, and hope.

"Sir," Stammel said. He took a breath. "Sir, I want to leave the Company."

"Stammel—"

"I cannot be what I was," he said. "We both know that. This dragon tried but cannot restore my sight. I can't—"

"But we still need you."

"No, sir. You need a senior sergeant with eyes as well as ears. Dev's good; promote him. It's only come sooner than I thought, years back—everyone retires someday."

"You'll stay near—in Duke's East, perhaps?"

"No, sir, not if you release me from my oath. I'll go with this dragon, sir."

"With the dragon!" Arcolin sounded angry. "Did you come here to steal my sergeant, then, instead of heal him?"

The room warmed noticeably; Stammel saw the fires stir inside the man's shape. "No. I came to heal him if I could, but I cannot. You yourself told me about his talents, and I have need of an archer to help me with the dragonspawn. With his help, it may be I can prevent more damage to this land and the others."

"But—but he can't see."

"He can see dragonfire," the dragon said.

"Is this true, Stammel?" Arcolin asked.

"Yes. I see the shape of a man full of fire where he stands, and I saw his shape in fire when he changed."

"And you truly wish to go?"

Stammel sighed. "If life was all wishes, sir, I'd have my real sight back and be the man I was. I'd have known Korryn for what he was and never signed him on, or never let him live, or struck him down, there in Vonja, before he could kill those guards or invade me. None of the bad would've happened. But that's wishing, and it did happen. I can't—I can't be anything but what I am, sir, and that's a soldier, and yet blind as I am now, I can't be a soldier here. Eyes all around is what sergeants need, sir. The dragon's offered me a way to do what I can do that doesn't put risk on you and my—your—recruits." Stammel swallowed, then went on. "Please, sir—my lord—this is best."

"You could die."

"All men die; we both know that."

"I won't take the protection of my name from you," Arcolin said. "But I will send you, as on a secret mission, under command of this dragon, if you truly wish it. Will that do?"

The dragon stirred; Stammel perceived the man-shape extruding a long tongue, longer than human. The tongue curled back inside, and the voice came. "You are merely lending me your sergeant?"

"If your mission prospers and Stammel survives, will you then take responsibility for the rest of his life?" Arcolin asked.

"*I* will do so. He has a home here, with friends, whenever he chooses it, and as my sworn man, anyone might help him find it should he go astray."

"So it is care for him and not mistrust of me?"

"Yes."

"Will that content you, Sergeant?" the dragon asked.

"Yes," Stammel said. "Captain—my lord Arcolin—I thank you for your care, for your letting me go and your offer of shelter when I return. And you—I don't know your name and 'Dragon' seems rude—"

"It is what I am," the dragon said.

"I thank you for a task I can do."

"Will you say goodbye to the others?" Arcolin asked.

"Better not," the dragon said. "Explanations are tedious."

"They must have some explanations," Arcolin said. "They're his friends; they need to know something . . ."

"Tell them you sent me to Vérella," Stammel said, "to tell the king about the change in the border and possible danger. I am known there; I was at your investiture. It is a reason you might send me."

"It is a good thought," the dragon said, "as I must, in courtesy, meet your king, of whom I know nothing other than he is king. I mislike cities, but with this man I am less likely to provoke violence."

"He is young," Arcolin said. "Scarcely more than a youth, though he has survived threats and attacks. You will find him intelligent and courteous but wary."

"Wise?"

"No wiser than any man of his years and not less, I would

judge. Now, with turmoil in Pargun and the attack on Lyonya you tell me of, he will be more wary and perhaps quicker to judge."

"Write your letter to your king, and I will take your sergeant with me there, before our other mission."

Stammel heard the scratching of Arcolin's pen, the crisp sound of the paper edges scraping as Arcolin rolled them tightly. He smelled the hot wax, heard it drip on the roll, heard Arcolin's seal ring pressing down, the faint huff of the message tube opening, the paper sliding in. And yet he heard without thinking of them, for his mind could think of nothing but the man-shaped flame beside him. What would it be like to be the man—the creature—for whom being filled with flame was natural? How could the dragon hold the shape of a man without the pain of burning?

"Did I look like that?" he asked when the chair scraped back and Arcolin, he knew, stood up.

"Like what?" Arcolin said.

"I don't know what he—the dragon—looks like in man-shape," Stammel said. "What my mind sees is a dark outline filled with flames. Did I look like that when I was burning?"

"No," Arcolin said. "Not like that and not like the man I see here now—dark skin faintly patterned, golden eyes that seem to be reflecting flames. You were red, as if sunburned, the whites of your eyes red, the pupils red-clouded as with blood."

"It is not the same fire," the dragon said. "Mine is the fire of making; that was the fire of unmaking."

"Unmaking?"

"Death, then, if you will. But we should depart."

As if he had normal vision, Stammel could see in his mind Arcolin's expression, that familiar mix of determination and uncertainty. He would never be what the Duke had been; somewhere in that steady, competent mind was a soft place, a weakness, that he'd never felt in Kieri Phelan. Yet Arcolin had never failed the Duke or his people.

"It'll be fine, sir," he said, as he'd said many times before, and knew that Arcolin would relax just that little bit. "It's the right thing now."

"Go well, Sergeant," Arcolin said. "Here's the letter."

Stammel reached out; Arcolin put the message tube into his hand. Stammel tucked it into his belt pouch and saluted. The dragon's arm nudged his; he laid his hand on it, and the dragon led him away downstairs, out into the chill, through it, out where he heard only the wind blowing across open ground. "I am changing," the dragon said. Then the dragon's tongue touched his legs, a warm, living presence.

"Stand on it," the dragon said.

Stammel stepped up. The tongue now felt solid as a plank. He was aware of movement without knowing how. To his surprise, his heart lifted. He still had adventure in his life—who else had been inside a dragon's mouth? He staggered suddenly and felt himself rolling down a slope on something warm and soft; he landed at last in what felt like a pile of warm cushions.

"Sleep," said the dragon. "I must fly."

WHEN THE DRAGON spat him out, a surprisingly dry and comfortable process, Stammel stepped off the dragon's tongue onto snow.

"We must walk as men the rest of the way," the dragon said. "We must appear as your count's messengers to the king."

Stammel said nothing. He could smell resinous pines and cedars in the wood around them, but he had no sense of direction, and if it was day, it was too cloudy to give him any hint of the sun's direction.

"I could have flown to the palace roofs," the dragon said, "but that might have caused some concerns."

Stammel snorted. "Some concerns indeed. Don't you have a name I can use? Or a title?"

The dragon hissed a little. "Should I take a human name, do you think?"

"If you cannot share yours."

"Indeed I will not. Call me . . . call me Sir Camwyn then." The dragon chuckled. "It is fitting that a dragon should be its own master."

"What time is it?" Stammel asked.

"Are you hungry?" the dragon asked.

"No . . . but I would like to know if it is day or night."

"Night, but soon dawn above thick clouds. We are walking south on a road toward Vérella."

Day had come, though Stammel could not see it, when they were stopped by men on the road. Stammel assumed they were militia or city guards.

"Who are you, and what is your business?" one asked.

"Sergeant Stammel, come from the north with a letter for the king from Count Arcolin," Stammel said.

"But you're blind," another one said.

"Indeed I am," Stammel said. "And that is why the count sent this guide with me, Sir Camwyn."

"He's not wearing marks of rank," the first one said. "How do we know—"

"He is known to Count Arcolin," Stammel said.

"Have you been to Vérella before, sir?" the man asked the dragon.

"No," the dragon said. "I came to Tsaia another way."

"Well . . ." the guard said to Stammel. "If you vouch for him . . . We know about you."

"I'm not sure I can find the palace entrance," Stammel said. "When I went through with troops, we marched along the back walls. And Sir Camwyn, as he said, doesn't know the way, either. Should I ask the guards at the gate or someone in the city?"

"At the gate. They'll give you an escort. I can't detach any of my unit, but the road's clear enough from here in."

It was a short walk to the gates; the guard officer there provided an escort, and shortly Stammel was speaking to the first of several palace officials—he had no idea what their titles meant—who were all reluctant to let the pair see the king. Stammel did not shift from his insistence that he himself must put Arcolin's message into the king's hand. He had worn no sword; they took his dagger and his saveblade and finally decided he was harmless enough. The dragon they would not permit.

"It is all right, Sergeant," the dragon said. "I have brought you where your count wished, and I can wait."

Stammel put his hand on the shoulder of someone who was wearing weapons—he could hear the sword's scabbard brushing against the man's breeches with every stride and feel under his fingers the edges of the baldric that held it. No doubt there was a dagger or two on his belt; no doubt the man walking behind them had weapons. He himself did not feel as naked as he'd feared.

"Bow when I do," his leader said. "In normal case, you would bow a knee, but since you are blind—"

"Blind but not crippled," Stammel said. "I can take a knee as well as anyone."

"Then do so," the man said. He stopped. "Here is the door; we will go in three steps or four; you will feel my shoulder dipping as I bow. Make your courtesy then."

The door creaked just a little as it opened; warmer air spilled out to meet them, rich with the scent of cooked food. "Sergeant Stammel, sir king, with a message to hand from Count Arcolin." Stammel's leader stepped forward. Stammel could hear several people breathing in the room and a gulp as someone hurried to swallow. Someone else bit into something that sounded like apple, and the smell of apple touched his nose.

When the man beside him bowed, Stammel dropped to one knee, bowed deeper, and said, "My lord and king."

Then he raised his head, pulled the message tube from his belt-pouch, and held it out. A hand brushed his in taking the tube. "Rise, Sergeant. Show him a seat, if you will." Stammel had heard that voice once before; it was indeed the king. "You are welcome here; we had hoped to see your sight restored."

Stammel bumped a little into the chair and sat. "I am still of use, lord king."

"So you are. I wonder the Count sent you on such a long errand in winter, though."

"I had a guide: Sir Camwyn."

"We do not know enough of him, sir king," said his leader. "He seems strange. Sergeant Stammel said he came from the south, but from the man himself no details."

"Count Arcolin knows him?" the king said to Stammel.

"Yes, lord king. He bade me come with him and introduce him to you."

"I see. Bring us this Sir Camwyn," the king said.

"Sir king, what if—"

"I will read this in the meantime. And we will need more refreshments. Camwyn, move that other chair over here."

For a moment Stammel was confused, but then remembered that the king's younger brother, now crown prince, was also named Camwyn. The prince said nothing, but Stammel heard the scrape of a chair being moved, then things being moved on a table. Had the brothers been having a private meal?

The king said nothing; Stammel assumed he was reading. Suddenly, he said, "Dragon!" and then "*Dragon?* Surely not!"

"Lord king, there *is* a dragon," Stammel said.

"A real dragon?" the prince asked. Stammel could hear eagerness in his voice. That wouldn't last, he thought. "Mikeli—sir king—remember the rumors from the east—"

"Rumors," the king said. "Nothing more. Until I hear certainties from those whose perceptions I trust . . . And why send me a blind man to assert the reality of a fantasy?"

"He did not send only a blind man," Stammel said. "Sir Camwyn is sighted."

"And did he see a dragon—not just a bolt of lightning in a cloud or some wizard's apparition or some other phenomenon that could fool the gullible?" the king asked.

"Yes," Stammel said. "And so did Count Arcolin."

"Don't worry, Mikeli—sir king," the prince said. "If there is a dragon, Camwyn Dragonmaster will protect us."

"We're Girdish, Cam." The king's voice sounded as if he were trying not to laugh.

"And the man's name is Camwyn. Maybe he *is* Camwyn Dragonmaster."

"Your name is Camwyn, and you're not . . . Cam, of all the great saints, we know the least about Camwyn. Gird we know lived, and he is our patron. Falk we are fairly sure of. But Camwyn—"

"Our father named me Camwyn for a reason," the prince said. Stammel could easily imagine the impetuous young prince; rumors had said for years that he was wilder than Mikeli had ever been. He heard Mikeli sigh.

"Sergeant, the Count says that you know about the gnomes that came to him as refugees and their claim that this dragon drove them from their land and insisted on changing the boundary with Pargun."

"Yes, lord king. The gnomes are living underneath the stronghold now. When the dragon came to Count Arcolin, the dragon told the same story the gnomes had."

"And he told you all about it?" A tone between doubt and disapproval.

"Not all, but much of it, lord king," Stammel said. "We're up there to defend the border; captains and sergeants and all needed to know."

"Are you—" The king cleared his throat. "Are you staying in the Company, Sergeant?"

"Now that I'm blind, you mean? Not as a regular sergeant, no, lord king. But the Count sent me on this mission and, I've no doubt, will send me on others. I've been in the Company long enough people recognize me as part of it, not someone who might've stolen the uniform."

Several people came in; he could smell more food now. The king said, "Cam, are you still hungry?"

"I'm always hungry," the prince said from a slight distance. "Especially if those are ham pies."

"Yes, lord prince," a woman's voice answered. "And custard tarts with farron." Stammel's mouth watered. Farron, the most expensive of spices, very rare in the north and uncommon in Aarenis. He'd tasted it only once in his life and remembered it still.

"Guests first, Cam," the king said as the servants laid out the food, with gentle thunks and clinks on the table. Then they left, and a moment later the man who had brought Stammel said, "Sir Camwyn, sir king, as you requested."

Stammel saw the fire-filled man-shape move to his side. The man bowed slightly, and the fire swirled within. "Sir king," the man said.

"You are Sir Camwyn, known to Count Arcolin. I am Mikeli, the king; this is my brother, Prince Camwyn. Will you sit and take refreshment?"

"I will sit, but I am not, at this moment, hungry," the dragon said. "Grant me leave to let others eat in my stead."

"As you will. Sergeant?"

"Thank you, lord king."

He knew the foods put on his plate only by the sound they made and the smells. Ham pie . . . redroots . . . a custard tart with the heady aroma of farron. He fumbled a little at the table and found eating utensils, including a dagger-sharp knife. In the mess hall, a ham pie—a rare treat—would be picked up and eaten in hand, but he heard the clink and scrape of knife and fork from the king and prince and hesitated.

"I eat ham pie out of hand," the prince said. "Except at formal dinners, when a third of it's lost to the plate." The sound of the crust crunching; the prince chewing, swallowing. "Though there's no way to eat redroots in honey sauce with your fingers without getting sticky."

Stammel picked up the ham pie and bit into it. Ham, mushrooms, onions, other tastes he didn't recognize. A tangy sauce. With his last bite, he heard the soft sound of another being slid onto his plate.

"As I am not eating," said the dragon, "there is no need to let food go to waste."

Stammel had never imagined himself eating in the palace, let alone in a private room with the king and prince. And of course a dragon. He had not felt this kind of excitement for a long time. He loved the Company; he had enjoyed everything about his life there. But it had, he now realized, become so familiar that the joy was all in the familiar. He had forgotten the joy of the new. He had forgotten the joy of not knowing what was coming next.

"Count Arcolin said there was a dragon," the prince said.

"Cam!"

"Sorry, Mik—sir king."

"I would have waited until you had eaten, Sir Camwyn," the king said. Stammel picked up the second ham pie. "But since you are not eating, and that was the essence of Count Arcolin's message, I'm curious . . . I had thought dragons were gone from this world long ago. Then came a rumor out of Lyonya and then this—"

"Dragons exist, sir king," the dragon said. The flames Stammel saw shivered inside, as if chuckling. Perhaps they were.

"And you have seen one yourself?"

"Yes," the dragon said.

"I wish I could," said the prince. "A great flying monster breathing flame . . . You must know, with your name, about Camwyn Dragonmaster taming the dragons forever . . ."

The flames fell and leapt high; to Stammel's nostrils came the hot-iron smell for a moment, and then it vanished.

"That is not . . . quite . . . how it happened," said the dragon.

"I thought so," said the prince.

"Cam—" The king's voice held warning.

"But he *does* know," the prince said. "I'm sure of it! Please, sir, tell us—you are Camwyn Dragonmaster yourself, aren't you? Come to capture or kill that dragon? You've ridden on a dragon's back, you've put a bit in its mouth—"

"No." The word came out with the tongue—to Stammel's eyes a long curling flame; he wondered what it looked like to the others—and something breakable shattered on the floor.

"You—!" That was the king; Stammel heard the sssh of a drawn sword.

"My pardon, sir king. I would not have caused you this distress. But I am, in fact, a dragon, taking a man's shape to move among men, and only because of great need. If you lay steel to me or cause it to be laid, I must defend myself, and that will bring more damage than one broken goblet."

"You're . . . a *dragon*?" The prince, his voice more full of awe than fear.

"I am. And named myself Camwyn as a jest, for a dragon should be master of himself ere he venture into lands humans know, lest he cause such harm as cannot be mended."

From the king came a sort of grunt, then the sound of the sword sliding back, the quillons snicking against the scabbard. "So . . . you are a dragon who can take a man's shape, and you bring word that I must yield territory to you—"

"Only because of the danger," the dragon said. Stammel noticed, and was sure the king noticed, the lack of honorific. In the moment's tense silence, Stammel found and bit into the custard tart. King, dragon, and now sweet fragrant farron-flavored custard . . .

CHAPTER TWENTY

"I am not best pleased with Count Arcolin," the king said after a long pause. "Telling me he was sending proof of the dragon's existence is not the same as telling me he was sending a dragon itself."

"He did not *send* me, king," the dragon said. "A dragon does no man's bidding. I knew I must meet you, lest more harm come, and thought you would not willingly meet a dragon. Few men would."

"You . . . influenced him?" the king said.

"A dragon does commonly influence humans who encounter him," the dragon said. "But yes, in addition to that, I was in his office as he wrote you, and I helped choose his words. Tell me, O king, are you wise?"

"Wise? That is something no man should claim for himself," the king said.

"Prudence is not all of wisdom," the dragon said. "I am not a courtier, king, or fond of false modesty. Are you wise?"

"I spoke not lightly," the king said. "So I was taught, that men should not claim wisdom for themselves but, as judgment is the duty of a king, seek to judge rightly as they can."

"And what are the elements of right judgment?"

"To judge rightly, one must know what came before, as much of the issue as men can know of facts and character and all circumstances, and then think ahead to the consequences. Elves, we were taught, by living long see long behind and before alike, but we humans cannot remember all or see so far ahead. Still, we must try. It is easier to judge rightly material things—craftsmanship, artistry, the quality of a fruit or an animal—than issues of conflict or love."

"And you—have you made difficult judgments yet, in your time of kingship?"

"Yes," the king said. "Before my reign began, when I was yet a prince, a peer of the realm tried to assassinate me, and later attacked my brother here, and me again on the day of my coronation. And since—it has not been an easy year."

"Difficult situations, and as you are still alive and king, you must have made sound judgments. Tell me what you consider the most difficult."

"When I attainted the Verrakai family, all but one, for their conspiracy to kill me and my brother . . . and when I let that one live, after she committed a crime punishable by death."

Stammel knew who that had been: Captain Dorrin. "Because she saved you," he said, surprising himself.

"Yes," the king said. "And because she did not defend herself. She asked no mercy; she spoke of the law with respect; she would have accepted death as a just punishment. For all that I pardoned her."

Stammel heard in the king's voice some doubt that this had been a wise decision and wondered what had changed his mind. He took another bite of the custard tart to keep himself from speaking in Dorrin's defense. The dragon spoke instead.

"And yet you doubt that was a wise decision. Why?"

"I cannot tell you," the king said. "I have reasons . . . not to believe she is harboring treason, but to think she is a danger nonetheless."

"But so far you have not taken action against her?"

"It would not be fair," the king said. "When she had done us such service."

"So you are withholding judgment until you know more?"

"Yes."

"Then I account you wise in part, at least. And you, young prince?"

"Me? I am not wise, I am told often. I am hasty and rash and excitable." The prince's voice sounded resentful.

"Hasty, rash, and excitable is, indeed, not wise. But I was not asking for wisdom from a boy, prince, but what you thought of this person your brother pardoned."

"Duke Verrakai? She's wonderful! She was one of Phelan's

captains, and now she's a duke, and she's fought in real wars, and—"

"Cam!"

"Well, I like her, Mikeli! And so does Duke Marrakai. I know what you think about Beclan, but Gwenno Marrakai said Beclan was already being less full of himself when it happened—"

"Cam! Where do you hear such things?"

"Aris. Gwenno writes him letters, you know, things she wouldn't say to Juris or her father . . ." The prince's voice trailed away. Stammel swallowed a grin along with that bite of tart. Some of Kieri's squires had been like the prince, rattle-mouths who realized only afterward what they should not have said. "Gwenno likes Duke Verrakai," the prince went on more quietly. "But is it about the—?"

"Cam! No more."

"That you have secrets is certain," the dragon said. Stammel could sense amusement. "But your very concern for secrecy reveals wherein your secrets lie; they flare in your mind like torches in the dark. Your brother speaks of someone . . . this Duke Verrakai? Do you think this person seeks a crown?"

The king's sigh was that of defeat. "No. She brought me a crown that her family had concealed. But I think that the crown seeks her. And if it is her fate to be crowned, I do not want it to be here, to bring division and war to my kingdom, to my people."

"You would seek peace?"

"If it is possible, but it may not be. Pargun invaded Lyonya before Midwinter—that had not happened in living memory. I hear of trouble in Aarenis, over the mountains; I have been warned of a war-leader there who wants to rule all. If invasion comes, then I must meet it. But if I can prevent division *here,* civil war *here,* then that is what I want."

"Indeed, you have more wisdom than I hoped. And your brother prince, I think, may have heart-wisdom, which the young often do before they develop adult judgment."

"What do you want of me?" the king asked.

The dragon sighed. Stammel fished around on his plate with the fork and found something; he stabbed it. A redroot in sticky sweet sauce. "You are in haste, I perceive. Well, then, I came to apologize that I must take some of your land for the safety of all, but mostly your realm. It is like to be perilous for the rest of your life and perhaps more, but I swear to return it to your heirs once that is possible."

"You are a dragon . . . you have powers I cannot imagine . . . and you apologize?"

"Discourtesy is not wisdom. Come, king, I would have agreement with you."

"Agreement that you can take what you have already taken? That I will not mount an army to take it back? Fine—I agree."

"More than that. For your courtesy and wisdom, for your yielding of this land for a time, I will grant you a boon each hundred years—"

"Hundred years!" said the prince. "We'll be dead in a hundred years!"

"But someone will be king. Or queen. I do not know how long the land must be forbidden you. I have seen mountains rise and fall, the sea withdraw and return; I will not forget what I owe."

"Very well," the king said. "Then I agree that I relinquish claim on that land as long as you say it must be. And my heirs shall collect what boon you grant. Shall I call scribes to write the agreement?"

"No," the dragon said. "Dragons seal agreements differently. We must touch, life to life, essence to essence. Let us go down to your palace courtyard."

The king said nothing more but rose and went with the dragon, the prince offering Stammel an arm as he followed. Once more there was silence.

In the palace courtyard, nothing stirred. "I must change," said the dragon. "Stand there." Stammel saw again the strange expansion of the flames as the man-shape vanished and the shape he thought of as dragon curled around them. "For our bargain to be sealed," the dragon said, "you must touch your tongue to mine, king." A line of red stretched out; Stammel could feel the heat along his right side; the king stood to his left.

"With my tongue," the king said, as if bemused. He did not

sound at all frightened. Stammel heard the rustle of the king's clothes as he moved two steps forward and knelt, heard the prince's indrawn breath beside him. He could imagine how the waves of heat felt on the king's face, remember his own terror. The dragon would speak in the king's mind, he knew. Then the line of fire retracted; the king, he could hear, stood.

"Let me!" the prince said. "Please!"

"Camwyn!" the king said.

"You would go where Camwyn Dragonmaster went?" the dragon asked.

"I—yes, if I could. I know you said the stories aren't right, but—but he did fly with dragons, didn't he?"

In Stammel's mind, the dragon's fire-shape brightened almost to white. "In a way, but not in the way you think. What would you have, prince? Think well before you speak."

For longer than Stammel expected from such a boy, the prince was silent; the king also said nothing. Then the prince said, "My brother needs me, or I would ask to go with you. I have wished dragons still lived since first I heard of them and saw pictures . . . I was named for the Camwyn in the stories and dreamed of being like him, a hero who drove away peril and rode a dragon. Now I see that you are not that kind of dragon—if that kind of dragon ever existed—and so I will not again dream of killing dragons or taming dragons, but still— I still want to be where dragons are. To fly, if it is possible. Only Mikeli is my brother and my liege, and I am his heir. I cannot go. Only—if it is possible—could I ride on your back and maybe you could fly just a little way? As high as the palace wall?"

"Dragons are not birds, prince, and we do not fly as birds fly, but by powers given us at the world's beginning. Feel my scales."

Stammel heard the prince step forward.

"They're—slippery—but not wet or greasy—it's like glass over them—"

"What you touch is not really my scales but the space in which I fly, prince. If you would fly with me, it must be in my mouth."

"You mean you will—? You'll let me?"

"If you touch your tongue to mine, as your king did."

"Cam!" the king said. "Don't—"

"Please, Mikeli! Don't forbid me! It didn't burn you, did it? And Sergeant, isn't this how you flew with him?"

"It is, lord prince," Stammel said.

"Then *please,* Mikeli!"

"I need him back," the king said to the dragon. "And he is my brother, whom I love." And to Cam, "If the dragon agrees, you have my leave."

"I have no time for a long flight," the dragon said.

Stammel heard the boy's clothes rustle as he knelt. "It didn't burn!" the prince said a moment later. "Now how do I—"

"Sergeant," the dragon said. "Come onto my tongue. When I have returned the prince, we must away at once."

"I'll help," the prince said, grabbing Stammel's arm. Unnecessary; Stammel could see the fiery shape of the tongue for himself, but he let the boy lead him; he stepped first onto the firm surface, and they were drawn inside. He heard the king gasp.

"Put your hand on his arm," the dragon said in Stammel's mind. "He is over-young and excited." Stammel gripped the prince as if he himself were frightened. Sure enough, after a moment the prince tried to take a step forward, but Stammel held him back. Cool air blew in; Stammel guessed the dragon had kept its mouth open to let the prince see out. He did not feel them rise, but he felt the prince's excitement.

"It's beautiful!" the prince said. "I never imagined it would look like this—I can see almost to the—oh." That last in disappointment; they must be descending again. With a little bump, they were on the ground; Stammel let go of the prince and patted him firmly on the back. "Thank you, sir dragon," the prince said. "And you, Sergeant." He moved away; Stammel had just time to hear him say to the king, "Mikeli, it was wonderful! I could see everything!" and then he was sliding once more into the soft nest where he'd been before.

Once more he had no sense of time passing and slept until the dragon woke him.

"If you cannot perceive my offspring," the dragon said, "it is no shame—tell me and I will find another archer. You are now near the outside, but my mouth is closed. You must put your arrows point down in my tongue."

Stammel realized then that he had a crossbow in one hand and a quiver in the other, yet he had no memory of them. He hooked the crossbow under his arm and knelt, sticking the bolts into the dragon's tongue; they stood upright, and when he regained his feet and reached down for one, it was at his fingertips.

Cool air rushed in. At once he saw, at some distance he could not estimate, small shapes of white flame. Suddenly a gust of air brought smoke—woodsmoke—and he coughed.

"What did you see?" the dragon asked.

"Small fiery shapes, white," Stammel said between coughs.

"You did not see the mortal fire, the forest burning?"

"No. Was that the smoke?"

"Indeed. They are burning the forest—not in Lyonya but in Pargun. I cannot put you down close to them, for the mortal fire would burn you."

"Can you tell me how far they are?" Stammel asked. "I need to know—the bolts do not fly as straight as sight." Would a dragon understand that? He spanned the bow and set a bolt in the groove. The bolt did not feel hot when he took it from the dragon's tongue, but he did not touch the point.

"Yes," the dragon said. "That and the direction and strength of wind. I see one on the edge of the fire . . . That one I can get you near. But there is smoke."

Stammel wrapped his woolen scarf around his head against the smoke and put the bolts into the quiver he felt hanging at his side. The dragon set him down on ground that felt cushioned; he scuffed a foot and felt forest duff.

"We are beside a stream," the dragon said. "The spawn is coming upstream, turning the water to steam for amusement; there is no impediment to your arrow's flight." Stammel saw a white shape emerge from apparent nothing. But how far away was it? How fast was it coming? He could not tell.

"Distance!"

"Now," the dragon said, rather than giving one.

Stammel aimed at the center of the white and closed his fingers on the trigger. A tiny speck of white flew through the space between—the point of his bolt that had been in the dragon's tongue—and as it touched the white shape, a purple bruise-like shape formed, spread, and the white vanished.

"Well done," the dragon said. "Come onto my tongue again and we will seek more."

STAMMEL HAD IMAGINED, in that time within the dragon, that they would quickly clear the dragonspawn. After his first success, he was sure of it. But the next hunt proved him wrong. In the back of his mind—as he choked on bitter smoke and ash—he recognized this as another kind of war and, like all wars, longer and more difficult than expected by those who started them.

Despite the scarf, he often could not get his breath; heat from the mortal fires the dragonspawn started scorched his boots; the tangle of burning trees and the fierce winds of the fires ruined his aim. The dragon, he found, had no notion of calculating the movement of hot air and at first reported the bolts as being magically shifted aside from the dragonspawn. Stammel tried to explain, between hacking coughs.

"I do not understand," the dragon said. "Your arrows are not like birds that indeed are shifted by the winds as we dragons are not—"

"All that flies in the air is moved," Stammel said. "Light things more; the stones thrown by catapults will not shift for a gust that will move an arrow." He coughed again, then went on. "A sighted archer will judge the wind and aim a little upwind, according to its strength, but an unexpected gust will still foil his aim."

"Half-Song aimed straight into the wind," the dragon said.

"And so the wind would not shift such an arrow aside," Stammel said. "But in a wildfire, the wind twirls and shifts unpredictably."

His bolts had struck only one other before he ran out of them. The dragon could not make bolts, nor could Stammel. By then he was exhausted and shaky, anyway. "I need to breathe clean air," Stammel said. "And eat something—how long has it been?"

"Since we left your king's palace? Or since you began shooting at the dragonspawn?"

"Either. Both." Stammel sat down on the dragon's tongue. "Since the king's palace, in regard to food."

"Two risings of the sun and two nights between. It is near sunrising again. We have been hunting all this past night."

"Humans usually eat at least once between the rising and setting sun," Stammel said. Knowing he'd fasted that long made him feel even weaker.

"My error," the dragon said. "I did not realize my substance would not sustain you. I will find you food."

Stammel felt movement under him and then the slight roll as he was deposited back in the cranny where he'd slept. He dozed off, ignoring his stomach's demand for food, and woke only when an icy breeze brushed his face.

"We are near a town with a market open," the dragon said. "Can you stand?"

Stammel rose, breathing in clean cold air. He felt lightheaded from hunger but steadier than he'd expected. As soon as he stepped off the dragon's tongue, the dragon changed into human shape; he could see it as clearly as the other. He tipped his head up; as before, he could just make out a dim light overhead, but nothing more.

"You need other clothes," the dragon said. "We are summerwards of your lord's domain, where more towns are, and you still wear that uniform."

It was all he wanted to wear, but he knew appearing alone among civilians in that uniform would cause comment.

"And it is discolored by smoke," the dragon said. "By your leave, I will go to buy clothes and food for you."

"Thank you," Stammel said. He felt shaky and would have been glad to sit down but did not want to show weakness to the dragon. "And a water bottle, if you could." His feet crunched on snow; he could melt snow for water if he had a way to carry it.

"I will not be long," the dragon said.

Stammel found a tree by walking into a snow-covered branch—by the smell, a fir. He licked off a little snow to ease his parched mouth, then felt his way into the center, acquiring an icy lump of snow down the back of his neck as well as snow on his face, some of which he ate to ease his thirst. At the center, as he'd expected, he found a clear area where his boots did not crunch on snow and he could stand upright. It was even dry enough to sit on the soft layer of needles with his back against the trunk. Here the breeze did not penetrate; he felt slightly warmer. He rubbed his hands in the duff to dry them—they still smelled of smoke.

He heard the dragon returning, then caught a glimpse of the fire-shape, but did not try to fight his way out of the snowy branches. "Stammel?"

"Here," he said, pushing himself to his feet.

"Wait," the dragon said. "I will come in. I have what you need, and news."

Branches creaked and snow fell from them in a rush as the dragon came into the sheltered interior of the tree. Stammel kept one hand on the tree trunk.

"Ale," the dragon said, nudging Stammel's free hand with something; Stammel took it and found a leather-wrapped jug. "They charge strangers more for water from their wells than for ale, and the stream is frozen."

Stammel unstoppered the jug and took a sip. Not the best ale, but liquid and refreshing. He stopped after one swallow, pushed in the stopper and put the strap over his shoulder.

"And this is bread," the dragon said. "Stuffed with meat and cheese, they said." Again Stammel felt something bump his hand, and he took it. A good-sized stuffed roll . . . He bit into it. Fried ham, onions, and some spice . . . He gulped down a couple of bites, then paused.

"Thank you," he said. "This is very good." Already he could feel his strength returning; he finished the loaf and drank another few swallows of ale.

"I told them in the market that I had a blind friend who had become fatigued and was unable to come so far without food and drink," the dragon said. "I said we would both come later, when my friend had recovered. It would perhaps be as well for you to spend this day and a night in a human dwelling. There is an inn."

Stammel imagined an inn—a bathhouse, jacks, a bed less

comfortable but more familiar than a dragon's gullet. "But I have little money," he said. "I did not bring my savings when we left the stronghold."

"It is no matter," the dragon said. "You are with me; it is my responsibility. Now: I bought clothes for you—yours are dirty—and you will need more, for I understand now that if we fly through smoke, you will become stained. Change."

Stammel stripped off his uniform, all but his socks, and put on the long trousers, shirt, and overtunic the dragon had brought. The dragon described them: gray trousers, blue shirt, brown overtunic, a brown cloak. Stammel put his uniform into the sack the dragon had used for the new clothes. When he had finished the food and felt stronger, the dragon led him to the town.

The town was larger than either Duke's East or Duke's West but not as clean, as Stammel could tell by the sounds and smells as the dragon led him through the outer buildings, the market square and into the inn. On this winter market day, he heard people haggling over the price of merchandise in familiar north-Tsaian accents, but in a friendly way.

The inn's common room, stone-floored, smelled of the same inferior ale, with overtones of onion, garlic, hot bread, wine, wet wool, leather, dogs . . . drovers, Stammel assumed. The dragon led him on, along a stone-flagged passage.

"In case you want a bath or a place to exhale filth," the dragon said. "We are facing a courtyard—the filth place is across it; baths to the heart-hand."

"We call it a jacks," Stammel said, taking a step forward.

"I will lead," the dragon said. "I should appear to use it as well."

"You don't . . . do that?"

"I don't eat your food; I do not need to exhale it."

Stammel could smell the jacks from twenty paces away; his nose wrinkled. No cohort would be so lax . . . but this was a civilian town and not under the Duke's—or Count Arcolin's—control. Obviously. The dragon guided him to one of the places and, by the sound of it, perched on one beside him. When he was done, the dragon led him across the courtyard to the baths and paid the attendant for a hot tub for "my blind friend."

Stammel was glad to get the smoke smell off his skin and out of his hair; now the clothes felt even better.

"We have a room on the ground floor," the dragon said. "For your convenience, I told them. Food can be sent there, or you can eat in the common room."

"My uniform must be smoke-stained," Stammel said. "I need to wash it."

"It will bring questions," the dragon said. "And questions we may not wish to answer here. Food and sleep first, I think."

At the mention of food or the smell of it wafting from the kitchen to the passage, Stammel's stomach growled. The rolls had been enough to get him to town, but now he felt shaky again.

"The room," the dragon said. Stammel heard the creak of a door and sensed a narrower, stale-smelling space. Heat touched him from the heart-side. "A brazier," the dragon said. "And a warming pan with the handle left where a blind man might bump it." A scrape of metal on metal. "Now it is safer. Here is your bed against the wall." Stammel put out a hand and found a rather hairy wool blanket under it. "And a table and chair here—" The dragon turned him about, and Stammel felt the back of a wooden chair, the edge of a table. "Sit there, and I will bring food and drink."

Stammel sat and after a moment put the bundle with his uniform on the floor. To his surprise he felt happier than he had since the attack that blinded him. Here he was alone with a dragon-man, in a town where he knew no one and had never been before, wearing civilian clothes such as he had not worn since he was a lad, without the coin to pay his bill, and yet . . . and yet he had been to a palace and met a king and a prince, eaten with them, and killed two dragonlets while riding in a dragon's mouth. Whatever came next, whether he ever regained sight, he had done things unthinkable in his old life.

"Here, sir." A young woman by the sound of her voice. "Your friend said you'd eat in here. Let me just put this down . . ." A slight thump as of a heavy tray, and other thumps that must be individual dishes. Whatever it was smelled delicious. "Do you need help, sir?"

"No, thank you," Stammel said.

"Well, then. The jug's to your heart-side, and the plate right in front of you. I'll be back to pick up the dishes."

When she left, closing the door, Stammel felt along the table, located the jug, sniffed it—water, not ale—then the mug, and poured himself some. All those days and tendays of practice . . . he could almost, he thought, have passed for a sighted man eating. When he was done, he wiped his mouth and chin and made his way to the bed, pulling off his boots. The bedding smelled fresher than the room had, and the brazier was warming it. He felt sleepy, but stayed awake until the girl came to take away the dishes.

The dragon returned some time after that. "I brought you more clothes," he said. "And a pack to put them in. And a stick—you lost your stick in the snow, I explained. The towns-folk are giving me great credit for not leaving a blind man to die in the snow . . . Several have come to ask me what god I serve who commands such expense for a stranger."

"I thought you'd said I was your friend."

"Indeed. But they did not believe it. So I told them what is true, that one man is as much my friend as another."

Stammel thought about that for a moment. "I would think that meant no man is your friend. Do dragons have friends?"

"I do not know what humans mean by 'friend,' but from what I see . . . no. We do not eat or drink as you do, and much that friends do seems to involve eating and drinking together."

"Do you understand 'friend' as opposed to 'enemy'?"

"The opposite of enemy is ally," the dragon said.

"And what do you consider me?"

"An ally," the dragon said promptly. "It is unusual for a dragon to have any ally but a dragon, but when I met Half-Song on the night of the first attack and saw her bow, I knew at once she could be my ally if she would." After a brief pause, the dragon said, "Does it worry you that I do not call you friend?"

"No," Stammel said. "I do not ask that allies be friends, though it is more . . . more pleasant if they are. But I was correct, then, in my understanding of your statement?"

"Yes, completely. The others, however, seemed to think it was a god's command that I consider them all my friends. That would be unwise. In any group of beings, some are hostile and some are not."

"The humans I have lived with consider allies as those fighting against their enemies, and friends as those who care for them—who wish them well, who help them," Stammel said. "You have cared for me; you have carried me safely through peril, and now you have clothed me, fed me, provided this room for me. I would call that the act of a friend."

"Did not your commander do the same? Would a commander not care for his troops, see them fed and clothed and housed?"

"Indeed, but . . ."

"You are a hiresword; I hired you. It is true I offered no payment, but my agreement with your commander was that I would care for you. I would care for any I hired or any who offered alliance."

"Well," Stammel said, forcing aside a desire to laugh aloud. "I am glad we understand one another."

CHAPTER TWENTY-ONE

Tsaia: North Marches Stronghold

ARCOLIN RECEIVED THE king's response to his report about the dragon's demands sooner than he expected. He made sure the courier was cared for and then took the message pouch upstairs to his office. Working the ribbons free of their elaborate knots, pulling out the stiff curl of paper, sliding his thumbnail under the seal, he was conscious only of concern that the king might not have believed him, might have thought the dragon a mere fantasy of his own winter-twisted mind.

What he read convinced him that whatever wisdom the dragon had, it also had a sense of humor. Sir Camwyn indeed! The king had certainly been convinced of the dragon's reality and now made no complaint about the loss of territory. He granted Arcolin permission to settle the refugee gnomes in the hills west of the stronghold.

For we consulted with the Marshal-Judicar, and hold that Gird's alliance with the kapristi requires that they be granted stone-right where they will. Your offer was well-made, and we agree to alienate those lands to their use. As for your plans to campaign next season, we must confer. Though the dragon assured me the Pargunese lack both will and power to attack across our eastern borders, I am not as certain, for if a dragon can come, so also can it go. There are other urgent matters as well, on which we would value your opinion. Settle your gnomes as quickly as you may, and come to Vérella.

What else did he have to do? He had taken all the recruits' oaths already; he had held Count's Court in three locations; he had met with the entire population of every village and town. They knew him already from his years as Kieri's senior captain; they were, he thought, all content to have him as their lord, since Kieri was irretrievably lost to them. He had dealt with the crisis of the gnomes' arrival and the dragon's demands.

So—how soon could he leave? He had no contract yet, though it was a little early to expect offers for this year. Would anyone hire him after last summer? The Vonjans, he was sure, would talk only of his failures. Well . . . he could find that out more easily in Vérella, where some Guild League cities had permanent embassies, or in Valdaire than up here, a long way from any news.

He started downstairs to find the estvin and met him on the way instead.

"My lord," the estvin said.

"I have news from my king," Arcolin said. "Some of it concerns you. Will you come to my office?"

"Yes, my lord."

"The king has granted me permission to settle you in the hills there to the west," Arcolin said when he had closed the door. "Gird's agreement with your people covers this, he said, and allows me to grant you stone-right if the land suits your needs." He read out the relevant part of the king's letter.

The estvin bowed. "My lord, we are your people. Your favor gave us life; your word renews us."

"I do not know if you will feel safe enough, so few of you," Arcolin said. He felt uncomfortable with the estvin's words and hurried on to something more practical. "And at one time, orcs laired in some of those hills, as I said before. I would not have you harried again."

The estvin bowed again. "By your leave, may we go and see these hills?"

"Of course. But in this weather, you will ride, surely—"

"No, my lord. Stone gives strength to the legs."

While the estvin gathered a group of gnomes, Arcolin sent a messenger to Cracolnya, asking him to bring Versin to the stronghold for a captains' meeting by nightfall of the next day. Valichi would not make it from their southern border, but he did not need Valichi, who had kept insisting he must retire by the Spring Evener. Then he went down to the forecourt, where he found the gnome men waiting, mounted his roan ambler, and led the way west.

THE HILLS PRESENTED a confusing mass of snow-covered lumps. Arcolin had had no chance to explore this part of his domain, and the maps Kieri had left suggested that no one had bothered with the steep, rocky terrain except to follow a few watercourses. Arcolin could tell little about the underlying bones of them from the few rocks that rose above the snow.

"Nedross above, dross below," the estvin said, sniffing one of the boulders fallen from the first hill. "Is this the hill, my lord?"

"Surely you need more than one," Arcolin said. "I thought you might take all these hills, where the slopes are too steep for farming."

"Is too many for now," the estvin said. "But I think another than this serves better." He pointed through the gap between the two nearest to a hill that seemed taller, with a blockier outline. "Rough rocks between—snow covers. Horse maybe not safe."

Arcolin contemplated slogging through the snow over rough rocks on foot. Gnomes might derive strength from the rocks under the snow, but he wouldn't. "It is farther away from us if you should need our aid with orcs. We used to hunt them into these hills, so I know they have lairs here."

The estvin nodded and said something in their language that brought the rest to his side. They all laid hands on the same boulder the estvin had sniffed. They muttered in gnomish, faster and faster. Arcolin's horse threw up its head, ears pinned. Then he could feel, through the horse's body, the ground trembling; the horse squealed, whirled, and tried to bolt as the shaking grew. Arcolin wrenched it back around. Then a loud noise, deeper and louder than any drum, rolled out of the hills. Clouds of snow and dirt flew up from several hills, including the two nearest, and hung there a long moment before slowly settling again. The gnomes stepped back from the boulder, dusting their hands. The estvin looked up at Arcolin. "No more," the estvin said.

"No more?"

"Orcs. Lairs. Gone."

Arcolin stared at the shaken hills. Were they lower? The tops were certainly not the pure white of the others. "How did you—"

"It is not to speak. Not in human tongue. You would say magery, but your magery does not do."

A form of rockmagic? By repute all the rockfolk could shape rock to their will. Arcolin said nothing more about that, stroking the lathered neck of his still-trembling horse. He was very glad it had not been the more excitable chestnut. "Will this do, then?"

"Very well, my lord. We will make as small a hall as we can and then move from your fort. Very soon."

Back at the stronghold, Arcolin met Captain Arneson just riding in from Duke's East. "How are the gnomes getting along?" Arneson asked. "And what was that noise?"

"They're about to move out to the hills," Arcolin said. "The noise—be glad you weren't closer. They say they've dealt with the orc lairs there. They made the hills jump." Arneson stared. "I'm holding a captains' meeting in my office when Cracolnya and Versin arrive; the king's summoned me to Vérella."

When Cracolnya, Arneson, and Versin gathered in his office, Arcolin read them the king's letter. "I don't know what he wants to confer about," he said after that. "With a dragon— and Stammel—between us and the Pargunese, that border should be safe enough. He said nothing about recruiting, but we must continue—even expand recruiting as before. With the danger rising in Aarenis, we need three full cohorts there. And we need archers, Cracolnya."

Cracolnya nodded. "Though if you take all mine, sir, and replacements, that doesn't leave even a full cohort up here."

"True. And I don't know what the king will say about that. What's your estimate of recruits we might get from this domain? Anyone?"

"Not enough," Cracolnya said. "Population's too low, too scattered, and the settlements not old enough. At most five to ten from Duke's East and West and maybe another five from Burningmeed. But we'll need a recruit staff, and for the first year or so it'll be taken from our actives."

"That was my thought, too," Arcolin said. "Valichi is determined to retire this spring, so we need a recruit captain to command them and the stronghold's other troops, however many or few." His were not the only eyes to look at Arneson, he was glad to see. "Captain Arneson, you've done well this year and you've regained full health—how do you feel about taking over as permanent recruit captain and seneschal?"

"I—but I'm—new—"

"And very effective," Arcolin said.

"I agree," Cracolnya said. "I had my doubts at first, when you came riding up thin as a lathe and with that missing eye, but what I've seen all this past year, you're perfect for the job. Kieri would've—" He glanced at Arcolin and then said, "Sorry. It's not what Kieri would or wouldn't do; it's your domain now, and I'm happy about that. Just habit."

"I know. Mine, too, sometimes. But I'm glad you agree Talvis is right for this task. Versin?"

"Certainly," Versin said. "I must admit I'm relieved; I was afraid you'd ask me to take it on, and I'm happier with more experienced troops."

"And he's got a tactical sense for mixed weapons," Cracolnya said. "I want him for my second, if that suits you, sir."

"Well, then—Arneson, what say you?"

"I—my lord, I would be honored." Arneson's voice caught for a moment, then steadied. "Thank you."

"That's settled," Arcolin said. His eyes stung, and he thanked the gods for the chance to rescue such a man from so bad a situation. "I'll name you my seneschal to the king and send permission for your recruiting effort when I receive it." He went on to detail the way they had set up their recruiting before, with Cracolnya adding details he'd missed here and there and Arneson taking notes.

"Are you going to hire a more experienced captain for Selfer's cohort? Keep him as junior?" Cracolnya asked when Arcolin finished.

"I'm not sure. It's true he's young, but he had that experience with us in Siniava's War and then up here as junior captain. Maybe he's ready to move up. I'll find out when I get down there. I sent him permission to hire on a short-term contract."

Cracolnya nodded, apparently satisfied.

"So," Arcolin said, "I need all your reports to carry to the king. I'll pick up Valichi's on the way down."

Two days later, Arcolin was ready to leave for Vérella. Arcolin took only a small escort—a clerk, a couple of soldiers—and they made good time on the road. At Burningmeed, he told Valichi he'd be free to retire at the Spring Evener.

"You're keeping that one-eyed fellow? I was sure he'd catch fever and die over the winter."

"No—he's perfectly healthy now but for missing the eye. Young, strong, and I've watched him with the younger troops up there. You aren't having second thoughts, are you, Val?"

Valichi shook his head. "Not really. I don't mind living in the stronghold, but I'm getting old, Arcolin, that's the truth of it. Managing recruits is too much. I'll settle in Duke's West, in my daughter's house. If the lad wants my help, he can call on me, though."

"You can tell him that when you go back north," Arcolin said. "There'll be gnomes in the hills west of the stronghold by then, where we had orc troubles." He explained all that had happened there. Valichi looked shocked and then worried.

"The gnomes are . . . honest, you think? I mean, if they were cast out . . ."

"Cast out by a dragon, Val, not their prince. They're honest, I'm sure of it. And everything's in good order. I'm not sure what the king wants to confer about, other than to be sure the north is secure—"

Valichi scowled. "Dorrin," he said. "That's what."

"Dorrin! What about Dorrin? Everything was fine with her at Autumn Court."

"You won't have heard the scandal," Valichi said. "You know she had dukes' younglings as squires—"

"Yes, I met them at Autumn Court. A Marrakai girl and two boys—Mahieran and Serrostin. Quite a handful, I thought."

"Indeed. Well, the Serrostin boy, the youngest, was captured by renegade Verrakai—" Valichi went on to tell all the details he'd gathered from the visiting count—the capture, the injuries, the healing by a Kuakgan. "Now the lad is walking again," Valichi finished. "He has one thumb. A *Kuakgan* thumb." Valichi gave him a look that meant something; it took Arcolin a moment to figure it out. Then he remembered Kolya's tales of the Kuakkgani.

"Not—" He glanced at a nearby cedar.

"From a twig, yes. Green blood mixed with red. In a family that's been Girdish since the Girdish wars."

"Gird protect him," Arcolin murmured. "And Dorrin."

"Nor is that all," Valichi said. "The Mahieran boy got mixed up with another group of renegades, or maybe the same—he's alive, but his father took him home in a cloud of rumors. That count southeast of you, he or one of his sons goes down to Vérella fairly often and stops by here on his way back north. Love to talk; they all do. So what I hear is that the boy lost his mind and killed his own sergeant and they've spirited him away somewhere. The count's son told me he heard that from someone who knows someone in the Royal Guard contingent that found him."

"Gossip," Arcolin said with distaste.

"Gossip people are listening to," Valichi said. "And in addition, he says the counts not on the Council think the king shouldn't have named her Constable. She's not Girdish, and she wasn't Kieri's senior captain."

"What does that have to do with it?"

"They'd rather have had you," Valichi said without more explanation.

"But I'm not a duke—and I wasn't here for the coronation."

"No, but you were Kieri's second in command, and many of them had met you at court. They never met her. And—you know Dorrin. Give her a task and she goes for it full speed. Which means she's been pushing all the lords to fit up their troops, drill them, and coordinate with the Marshals and grange drills."

"Makes sense," Arcolin said. "We talked about that back in the autumn, when I came to court. She's just doing what the king commanded."

"Yes, but—" Valichi changed his voice, clearly mimicking someone. "'She's a woman—hasn't been a woman duke in more than a generation, except a widow as regent for her son.'" He relaxed to his normal tone. "Let alone a woman like Dorrin. And now she's telling them what to do." Valichi shook his head. "Most of 'em never liked the Verrakaien, and they'd be suspicious of her for that alone. Her being a woman, and especially her being Constable—just more to dislike."

"Do they all feel that way?"

"I can't tell. I'm getting this from just the one family. The Count said if it weren't for the fact that she charmed—his term—the king and the other dukes, they'd have her thrown off the Council. She should have died at the coronation, is what he said."

"But the Marshal-General doesn't think she's evil," Arcolin said.

"Yes, but—it's bad, Arcolin, is my feeling. *We* know her. Most of the others don't. All they've seen is her nagging at them or her killing by magery in public at the coronation. They never saw her as the decent, efficient cohort commander we knew."

"Mmm," Arcolin said. "I see what you mean."

"Thing is, now that two squires have been in peril under her guardianship, she may lose the support of their fathers. If it's true that many counts oppose her, she can't afford to have two dukes against her. She might lose the other one, too. I can't see a girl's father leaving his daughter with someone suspected of conniving at the injury of the others."

"No one could think that," Arcolin said.

"People can think anything," Valichi said. "Especially if it suits their aims. By the tale I heard, she'd been having the squires lead out small groups of Verrakai militia to the various vills on the domain. Poor protection if they were attacked."

"We talked about that on my visit," Arcolin said. "I thought it was a good idea. Give them some command experience. I know she's got some Phelani veterans who wanted to stay with her."

"All of *us* think like soldiers. Of course it's a good idea if you're training young officer material. But if you've got the children of the highest-ranking lords in the kingdom, one of them the king's cousin, fourth in succession?"

"So . . . what do you think I'll meet? A torrent of questions about Dorrin?"

"I'm not sure. But you needed to know she has enemies. Aside from the oldest lords, who fought in the Prince's War with Kieri, you and Dorrin are the only two with combat experience. She was the obvious choice, as a duke, resident in the kingdom, to be made Constable. But you're better liked. If it comes to a competition—"

"I can't stay here in campaign season," Arcolin said. "I can't support the Company—or the domain, for that matter— without that income. And anyway—you said it—she's more like Kieri than I am. She would be better—"

"She would be better if they'd follow her. But will they?"

"I'm not competing with her," Arcolin said. "I won't. She's my friend as well as a higher rank—"

"For now," Valichi said. His voice hardened. "I must speak plain, my lord." He dipped his head, the first real deference he'd shown. "I'm older than you, and I've heard Kieri talk court intrigue even more than you have. You cannot afford to place Dorrin's friendship above your duty to the king. You swore that oath to *him: he* is your liege, not Dorrin."

"I know, but—" Arcolin bit his lip. His mind ranged back over the years to that first day Dorrin had appeared near the stronghold. He had seen Kieri's first reaction to her in the stiffness of his stance; he himself had thought her a likely prospect—a Knight of Falk, after all—but it had not been his to decide. Then she had slid into that muddy ditch and put her weight on the pole they were using to lever the axle up . . . had come out at last all sweat and mud and looked at Kieri without hope. *Hire her,* he had wanted to say, but he was too junior himself to intervene. Kieri had glanced at him; he had given a short nod, and then, when Kieri smiled, when he said yes, she was one of them. All those years, first as his junior captain, then with a cohort of her own, always the same.

"I hope it won't come to that," Valichi said. "I hope something will change opinions. But you needed to know before you walked into the hornet's nest."

"Indeed. But it's like when Stammel was blinded . . . I blamed myself for that, but it was not my fault, really. Nor yours. You could not have known that Korryn would collude with a renegade Verrakai or that fate would bring him in contact with Stammel again, or with such consequences."

"Indeed, I've wished time and again I'd had him killed," Valichi said. "But only the gods know all. What I do know is that you're the king's vassal . . . and for the sake of your domain, we would prefer that you not alienate him."

"I will do my best," Arcolin said.

VALICHI'S WARNING PROVED sound; as soon as Arcolin announced himself to the Royal Guard officer at the gates, he was given an escort to the palace and ushered into the king's presence.

King Mikeli had matured, Arcolin had noticed last fall at Autumn Court, from the crown prince just past an assassination attempt. But now the king seemed not just older but more strained.

"We have much to discuss," the king said. "I know you have just arrived, and I will not long delay your rest, but I must know one thing at once: have you had private communication with Duke Verrakai?"

"With Dorrin? She sent word that she had released the cohort Selfer commanded, as she had promised at Autumn Court, and gave the names of those who had chosen to stay with her."

"Ah. And how many was that?"

"Fifteen, sir king. Older veterans who had no obligation to remain—it had long been Kieri Phelan's policy that all with more than five years' service might withdraw between campaign seasons, without their death benefits, and those who served four hands of years might withdraw at any time, taking their benefits."

"Had they pledged fealty to you? Did you formally release them?"

"No, sir king. I have not seen them since they came south a year ago with Kieri Phelan; he left them at the south border of his land when he came to court. He released them from their oath to him after he arrived in Lyonya. Dorrin—Duke Verrakai—brought them back to Tsaia and hired them to help her carry out your commands."

"And they pledged to her as their liege?" The king looked down at a paper on his desk.

"No," Arcolin said again. Surely the king knew this already. "She considered them still part of Phelan's estate, to be transferred to his successor. She contracted with Selfer, formerly her junior captain, on the same terms as any other employer, for their service. She and I discussed this at the Autumn Evener; I told her I would need that cohort this coming campaign season. She said she would send them on when she got back from Autumn Court; I went on north to confirm my new rank." Arcolin paused there. Should he go on? Explain every decision that had taken Selfer and the cohort south instead of north for the winter?

"So . . . they had not given their oaths to you or to me." The king sounded disapproving. Arcolin understood: the chain of fealty had a gap, and oathless soldiers were considered virtual outlaws, suspect at best.

"No, sir king, but Selfer is reliable, and I have no doubt that when I get to Valdaire they will."

The king nodded but was still frowning at the paper in front of him. "Do you know whether any of those who stayed with Duke Verrakai were born Verrakai, bastard or other?"

"Not without reviewing the Company rolls, sir king. We have records of what each one swore when recruited, but those rolls are in the north. Should I send for them?"

The king stroked his beard. "I . . . am not sure. That is the problem. I am not sure, and my advisors and other lords are not sure. We trusted too much before; we must not trust too much again. There is something uncanny about Duke Verrakai."

Remembering Dorrin with Stammel last autumn, Arcolin could not argue that. "What is it you fear, sir king?"

The king moved restlessly. "I don't quite know. She saved my life, that I do know. And I saved hers in return. She is a Knight of Falk, which should mean a person of honor . . . but how do I know what it really means? A Knight of Gird would be guided by Marshals, who would recognize if . . . if one turned from Gird's way to . . . to something evil. Who has authority over a Knight of Falk? Does that ruby they wear turn to a dull pebble if the Knight goes astray?"

"She said the Marshal-General had visited her and seemed content. And Paks."

"Yes. In the summer." The king shifted again in his chair. "I think . . . I wonder . . . if the Marshal-General can be . . . can be so surprised by any virtue in a Verrakai that she would overlook . . . could be fooled."

"Paks wouldn't," Arcolin said. "What she sees is real; she has the gods' own light to see it by."

"I would like to believe Duke Verrakai as honest and loyal as you tell me she is," the king said, meeting Arcolin's gaze. "But you must know that some of the other nobles do not trust anyone of that family and do not trust someone who uses magery, as she does. Even the other dukes, who all supported her at my coronation."

"But they sent their children as squires—"

"Squires, yes. And spies," the king said. He shifted a little in his chair. "At least Beclan Mahieran was. His father, my uncle, suggested it to me. I agreed, and both his father and I gave the lad his assignment. Keep watch, take note of any use of magery and the circumstances of it. Any sign of honoring evil deities—we didn't actually think she *was* Liartian, but in that environment, isolated on Verrakai domain, could some other evil influence her? Take note as well of the population, the way they behaved. The number of sound men: she claimed that most had been killed or injured in that battle with the Royal Guard and her cohort, but . . ."

Arcolin could not keep surprise out of his voice. "But you made her your Constable, to oversee Tsaia's military readiness, to command in the field. If you didn't trust her—"

"I did . . . to a point. And she was the only war-trained person of rank in the kingdom at the time; she had convinced me—and others—that we might face danger from Aarenis as well as from Pargun. You, you recall, were over the mountains, out of contact with us." The king paused for a moment; Arcolin could think of nothing to say. "And the other thing is, she's . . . a woman. A woman as duke . . . as war-leader . . ."

"But you're Girdish," Arcolin said. "The Marshal-General is a woman. Many Marshals are women." That burst out before he could stop it, and no "sir king" to soften it.

"Yes. And the Marshal-General, when I mentioned one cause of a general distrust of Dorrin Verrakai, was displeased with what she called our intransigent aristocratic attitudes. But Gird himself allowed Tsaia to retain its monarchy and its aristocracy so long as we obeyed the Code. Which we do. It is only that her being Verrakai, and female, and using magery . . . that is a lot to swallow."

"So you set a mere boy to spy on her and hoped that she would slip?"

"And hoped she would prove herself," the king said. He sighed. "You cannot understand, Count Arcolin, all the pressures on a king. At any rate, at Autumn Court, Beclan reported to me. Reported nothing suspicious or dangerous, except . . . You yourself saw her perform magery, did you not?"

"Yes—my sergeant had been blinded and invaded by someone we now know was a Verrakai; he had not died, nor let the other take over, but had it still deep in his soul. She cast it out, destroyed it."

"What did you think at the time?"

"I had not known he still had the demon or monster inside him; I was shocked when she called it out, relieved that Stammel survived, and saddened that this did not restore his sight."

"And then came the Pargunese invasion of Lyonya. King Kieri and I established a courier service early in his reign, so I was aware of his concern about the Pargunese. He actually met the Pargunese king before the invasion—did you know that?"

"No, sir king."

"Their king came to assassinate him because of some ridiculous notion he had about women soldiers and his daughter. However, they parted peacefully—it is a long story, and I do not yet have all of it because of the war. Very shortly after, a Lyonyan courier brought word that the Pargunese had crossed the river. Duke Verrakai's first dispatch came a few

days later—understandable, as she was then at home, two days
from Harway. I trusted she would move at once to muster what
Verrakai troops she could and proceed there to take command."

"Did she not?" Arcolin said.

"Indeed. What I did not expect is that in those first chaotic
days a royal courier would die on Verrakai lands, killed—she
claims—by renegade Verrakaien she had not yet captured. Or
that two of her squires would be attacked by more renegade
Verrakaien. The youngest suffered crippling injuries and was
healed by a Kuakgan, not a Marshal of Gird. There's a twig
where his thumb was, and it moves. His family's appalled, of
course. Now he's refusing to obey his father and come home."
The king paused and pushed the papers on his desk around for
a moment.

"My own cousin Beclan, fourth in succession," the king
continued, "patrolling *her* domain by *her* orders with an escort
of *her* former soldiers and Verrakai militia, was caught in a
Kuakkgani trap along with those Verrakaien renegades." The
king's voice had risen; his hands closed into tight fists. "All
died but him; he killed them because the Verrakaien took control of them and they would have killed him. Three Verrakaien
men, a veteran sergeant of Phelan's Company, and four Verrakai militia, killed them all. So he says—and there are no
witnesses to gainsay him. But can a stripling, a squire, strike
down so many by his own strength and skill?" Arcolin was
speechless with shock. This was no rumor hatched by envious
counts; the king would have searched out the facts as best he
could.

"Holy Gird," Arcolin murmured at last.

"You see how it looks," the king said.

"Indeed." He did not dare say what he was sure the king had
thought: a boy Beclan's age, no matter how talented with the
sword, should not have been able to kill that many grown men,
not without forbidden magery. And if magery—in the presence of Verrakaien renegades—then the likely explanation
was that he had been invaded—against his will or with his
cooperation. He was only a boy; he could not have withstood
such an attack as that aimed at Stammel. He pushed aside the

horror of a member of the royal family harboring a Verrakai magelord and brought up the next topic that came to mind. "Sir king, I had intended to ask the hospitality of Verrakai House; I know she told her house-wards I might stay any time I was in the city—"

"No," the king said. "I will not risk you in that house, not now. If you trust her, you may house your escort and servants there, but you will stay in the palace."

He would not be harmed in Dorrin's house; he knew that. And yet . . . the king's words were so very damning.

"We want another analysis of our military situation," the king said. "You will need to present your ideas about our military situation to those of the Council who are present now. Can you be ready by the day after tomorrow, our next meeting?"

"Yes," Arcolin said, "if someone has the current figures from the various domains."

"I've had them sent to your chambers. We'll meet again at dinner."

Arcolin bowed; a servant led him to a pleasant apartment. A fire crackled on the hearth. He wrote a note to his escort and another to Dorrin's house-wards.

BEFORE DINNER, HE met Duke Serrostin and Duke Mahieran. "The king has told you about our concerns," Mahieran said. "You should know that we had, initially, a favorable impression of Duke Verrakai. You told the king that she had had no contact with her family for years—"

"She had not, my lord," Arcolin said.

"It was a delicate matter, granting her the title and the domain," Mahieran went on. "We did not have time, after that assassination attempt, to ask Kieri Phelan about her character. The Council did, of course, send word to him, as well as to her, but we could not wait for the answer. None of us had ever met her. The king relied heavily on your advice."

"I spoke the truth, my lord," Arcolin said. "And I'm sure King Kieri said much the same when you did have word from him."

"That's so," Mahieran said. "And so I believed when we did meet her. A very unusual woman, to be sure, with her experi-

ence. A bit . . . intimidating, perhaps, to some of the nobility.
Yet frank and open with us, and I very willingly assented to
the king's pardon of her after she killed that Verrakaien who
had invaded a groom."

"I liked her," Duke Serrostin said. "No question about that.
And I did not think it a charm—though I am not sure of my
judgment there. My wife, as well. Said she was odd but felt
sound. M'wife's a fine judge of horseflesh and hounds."

What that had to do with judging people, Arcolin did not
know.

"And the Marshal-General: I relied on her judgment,"
Mahieran said. "Surely, as head of the whole Fellowship of
Gird, she would sniff out any taint of evil."

"And you think she did not?" Arcolin asked. "That Dorrin—
Duke Verrakai—was so tainted?"

"No," Mahieran said. "But I think she was wrong without
being evil. A life spent as a soldier, with no experience at
court . . . It was unfair; there were things she could not know."

"And a Falkian," Serrostin said. "I've heard they're closer to
Kuakkgani than the Girdish are." He looked away for a moment, then back at Arcolin. "You know about my son?"

"Yes, I heard."

"He would have been crippled—lame and thumbless—but
now has two legs and one . . . *twig.* Was a twig, at least, though
it now looks somewhat more like flesh. His heel-strings were
mended with *spruce needles* and singing, Duke Verrakai said.
She said, and my son confirmed, that the local Marshal, the
Captain of Falk, and she herself all tried healing and were unsuccessful."

"The witnesses agree," Mahieran said.

"I asked if they tried healing while she was not there," Serrostin said. "And they told me yes. She had a surgeon in as
well, but he would do no more than dress the wounds."

"It troubles you that a Kuakgan healed him?"

Serrostin scowled. "It troubles me that a Girdish Marshal
could not, when our family has been Girdish for generations.
The Marshal said only that the gods did not give the healing . . . but then they did give it to a Kuakgan. If it was the
gods."

"And it contaminates the boy with green blood," Mahieran said. "Tell him the worst."

"I talked to the Kuakgan myself," Serrostin said. "He said he had not the strength to heal the other thumb at once, but that if the graft took, then the green blood might perceive the correct pattern for Daryan's body and . . . and bud another thumb on his other hand. *Bud!*" He strode the length of the chamber and back. "I would not wish my son a cripple, of course. I am grateful, beyond words, to the gods for allowing his healing. But this—"

Arcolin could think of nothing to say, neither comforting nor useful. When the silence lengthened, he finally said, "Do you then blame Duke Verrakai for the Kuakgan's healing?"

"Not . . . exactly. But how he was taken—" He went on with the same story Arcolin had heard from Valichi and the king. Before he could answer, Mahieran began.

"And she had been sending them out—all the squires—in command of small squads, to patrol her domain, take census of the vills, and so on. That is how my son was taken," Mahieran said. "He was farthest away when the invasion began; she chose to go directly to Harway rather than await his return."

"You know that was the king's orders," Serrostin muttered. He was staring out the window.

"Yes, but—yes, I know. And she sent word for him to return directly and bade him bring what troops he could raise."

"What happened?" Arcolin asked.

"I don't know exactly. I know what he's said, but it seems . . . hard to believe. I'm sure the king told you as much as I know." With that, Mahieran launched into a much longer account. Arcolin thought of the tall, handsome, confident squire he'd met the previous fall in Verrakai House. He could easily imagine that boy being excited at the onset of war, eager to prove himself, insisting on changing routes, insisting on splitting his force, pushing his authority as far as he could. Dorrin, he was sure, would have given Vossik guidelines that allowed her squires some independence—that was how squires learned. He hadn't been surprised Vossik stayed with her or that she'd assigned him to Beclan. Vossik had been to her what Stammel was—had been—to him: utterly reliable in any crisis. He believed the boy's version, that Vossik had killed himself rather than be taken over. Stammel would have done the same.

"Vossik was a nineteen-year veteran," Arcolin said, nodding to show he had been listening. "Good man. I'm sure he did everything he could—"

"But he's dead. And no witnesses to back up Beclan's story."

"He's your son. Do you not believe him?" He could not keep the surprise out of his voice.

"*Is* he my son? That's the question, Count Arcolin. We know now—we saw at Mikeli's coronation—that evil magelords can take over others' bodies or force them to obey. What I know for certain is that Beclan's body came alive out of that cursed place. Whether it was his spirit . . . Was it really your sergeant with that—that evil spirit inside him?"

"Yes," Arcolin said. "I have no doubt of that. How he acted after that—every detail—was the man himself, a man I've known for years. I would not have detected that evil inside."

"But Duke Verrakai did."

"Yes. She said only a man of his strength could have withstood it, forced it into hiding so long."

"But she insisted it be expelled?"

"Yes, of course." He saw from Mahieran's expression that it was not "of course" to him. "My lord, no one would want such a thing inside—something that might, over long time, find a way to attack again, seek control again. Stammel—my sergeant—had suffered enough. He was glad to have it out."

"Are you sure there was something to come out?"

"Oh, yes." Arcolin described what he'd seen that day and Stammel's own description afterward, the sense of lightness, the end of bad dreams. "Have you had Duke Verrakai examine your son, my lord?"

"No." Finality in that.

"Anyone? Marshals of Gird?"

"No. It is too dangerous to bring him here—even to our household. He is . . . in a safe place."

Arcolin doubted that. "My lords, it is not my place, but if you will hear me, I have a suggestion."

"Go ahead."

"You surely know there are rumors abroad about both your

sons. Nothing had reached me in the far north, but on the way here one of my captains reported gossip he'd heard from another count. About your son, Duke Serrostin, it was your displeasure with the means of his healing and his refusal to come home. But"—Arcolin turned to Duke Mahieran—"things are being said about yours that could bring evil upon him if he is not invaded, or loose more evil if he is. Both renegade Verrakaien and Bloodlord priests might seek him out. You must find out what his true condition is. I suggest a Marshal with a potent relic of Gird could be sent to test the truth of his tale. A Marshal might be fooled, but not one of the true relics."

"Sonder, he's right! Why didn't we think of that? A Marshal—two, perhaps, a High Marshal, even the Marshal-General—relics—" Serrostin paced back and forth. "If we sent now, even in winter, the Marshal-General could be here in—"

"We can't risk it, Parlan. If he is—if he took over a Marshal—Gird forbid the Marshal-General—think, man! It could be worse—we can't let him contact anyone—"

"My lord, you can't do nothing!" Arcolin started to say more, but Mahieran forestalled him.

"I know you're Duke Verrakai's friend—"

"This is not about Duke Verrakai," Arcolin said. "It's about your son. If you don't find out, you put more than him at risk."

"But risking a Marshal—"

"Gird risks us all," Arcolin said. "Marshals, yeomen, paladins . . ." He felt a sudden burst of compassion for Mahieran—the man had lost a brother this past year to assassination, had nearly lost his nephew the king and his son—and had never, so far as Arcolin knew, faced the kinds of risks he and Kieri and Dorrin had faced year after year as mercenaries. "Trust Gird," he said more quietly. "Gird and Falk and the High Lord will surely help you find the truth."

The two dukes looked at him as if he had sprouted wings and then at each other.

"We can at least ask High Marshal Seklis what he thinks, Sonder," Serrostin said.

Tears glittered in Mahieran's eyes; he blinked them away.

"We can," he said. To Arcolin he said, "Count, I am reproved by your faith."

"You say you have him in a safe place," Arcolin said. "Well guarded, I assume."

"Yes, by Royal Guardsmen. He cannot escape—no one can get in. He is forbidden speech with any, on pain of death—"

"Death!"

"As you yourself recognized, Count Arcolin, if he is invaded, he is a danger to the king. We cannot allow him a chance to invade anyone else or weapons to attack his guards."

And so they had locked up a boy who had just survived an attack by evil, who had made his first kills, with no one to talk to, no way to defend himself if the guards were overcome. How better to ensure that he would cooperate with any who came to free him, no matter who they were?

"Test him," Arcolin said. He had no appetite now, his imagination picturing the boy sinking into a potent stew of grief, rage, hopelessness that he remembered all too clearly.

Through the rest of his visit, he could not get Beclan Mahieran out of his mind. He laid out his suggestions for the realm's military to the Council and, as he expected, found they differed little from Dorrin's.

"It is not because we are friends," he said firmly. "We are both experienced field commanders—we both have twenty years and more of military experience. You, my lords, have not . . . and that is no insult to you, for in the same way I do not have twenty years' experience as a count, nor has she as a duke."

Someone said, too audibly, "That's certain!" Someone else snickered.

Arcolin held his peace and let the last murmur die away. When they were all attentive again, he said, "My lords, whether you like me or Duke Verrakai or not—whether you think we do not dress to your liking or not—we are both soldiers with experience in the field. What you want in a commander is the experience we have. If it were my choice, I would choose her as Constable, because she is that small margin better than I am at handling mixed forces. A small margin wins battles, my lords."

"Would Kieri Phelan say the same?" came a voice from the far end of the room. Arcolin wasn't sure which count it was.

"Indeed he would," Arcolin said. "He did, in fact."

"But you were senior, weren't you?"

"Yes. I joined him earlier. I've no doubt that if Duke Verrakai had been hired first, she would have been senior. For one thing, she was also a Knight of Falk, trained in Falk's Hall: I came to Kieri from Aliam Halveric's company. I was a sergeant until he made me captain."

That silenced them for a while, and they accepted his agreement with Dorrin's plans and suggestions without further argument. After the Council meeting, he had another with the king.

"Duke Mahieran tells me you suggested having his son tested by Gird's relic," the king said, as soon as they were alone. "We have spoken to High Marshal Seklis; he agrees this is a good idea and is considering which of the relics here in Vérella might be most suitable. I thank you, as does he, for the idea."

Arcolin bowed. "You are most welcome, sir king."

"You must not speak of it to anyone," the king said. "I know the rumors . . . Let them be wide of the mark, if they will; the lad's location is secret, and any contact with him must be secret as well."

Arcolin barely stopped himself from pointing out that a location, however remote, with a circle of Royal Guards around it and the necessary supplies arriving would not be secret, but he had trespassed enough on higher ranks. "I will say nothing, sir king, of course."

"Especially not to Duke Verrakai."

"Certainly not, sir king." Better to tell Duke Verrakai than some peasant driving a cart full of food for the guards, but it was too late for real secrecy, anyway.

"You asked about taking your troops south . . . you have my permission to do so. Having met the dragon, I have no concerns about our eastern border for the time being, and your troops in the south are likely to do us a service by learning if danger really threatens there. And if an invasion is attempted, you will be best placed to intervene."

"Thank you, sir king."

"For the time being, I am leaving Duke Verrakai as she has been, as Constable. Who are you leaving in command in your domain?"

"Captain Arneson, sir king. He has taken over from Captain Valichi—Kieri Phelan's recruit captain, now retiring—and I have found him honest and reliable. He is from Aarenis but of northern parentage. The village mayors are the same as before."

"Very well. I will want to know your employer, when you have a contract. Do you plan to make contract here or in the south?"

"Here, if I can; with your permission, I will visit their embassies in the next day or so."

The king nodded. "Do so, then."

A few days later, Arcolin settled with the Foss Council representative, a full-season contract for three cohorts. "We worried last year, when you couldn't deliver more than one cohort—understandable, but we need a larger force."

"I'm glad to be able to put the Company back together again," Arcolin said.

When he came to the palace to present a copy of the contract for the king's approval, the king's senior clerk took it instead. "He's taken a few days for hunting," the clerk said. "But I know he'll approve a Foss Council contract. Will you be staying or heading back north?"

"North," Arcolin said. "There's always something more to do to get troops ready to march."

"I'm surprised he didn't ask you to take over as Constable," the clerk said, marking the contract with the date of delivery. "I suppose you've heard about Duke Verrakai."

"Many things," Arcolin said. "Most of them untrue."

"They can't all be," the clerk muttered.

Arcolin thought of Dorrin and her squires all the way back to the stronghold. Then he was faced with all the decisions that must be made and work that must be done before he could march two full cohorts south in order to reach the pass almost as soon as it opened.

CHAPTER TWENTY-TWO

Lyonya: Chaya

NEAR THE HALF-EVENER, Arian woke one morning feeling a difference in herself. Something had come where nothing had been. Kieri, uncharacteristically, was still asleep. She eased out of the bed and went into the queen's chambers by the private passage. There she looked at herself in the long mirror. Nothing to be seen yet, and the feeling was so faint she could not be sure.

But neither could she ignore it, nor hide it from Kieri. She went back to the king's chamber and found him awake and stretching. "What is it, love?"

"I'm not sure," Arian said. "Do you . . . sense anything new?"

"New? Trouble?" Then his expression shifted. "You—do you think—?"

"I don't know. I'm not sure. I never had a child before."

"Come nearer," he said. "I remember some of the signs." He touched her hair, sniffed at it a little, felt her pulse. Then he sat back, and abruptly his eyes widened. "There's definitely something—the taig's noticed."

Arian felt that, a surge in the taig that rolled up through her body and heart. "Oh—" she said. "And a boy!"

Kieri grinned. "You are amazing . . . and wonderful . . ."

"I didn't do this alone," Arian said. She felt filled with light, with joy. Spring was on its way, and a baby—their baby—would come into the world.

"We should tell someone." Kieri looked thoughtful.

"Already?"

"I don't even know who the best midwives are . . . and the Council . . . and the Seneschal . . ."

"Do we have to tell them this moment?"

"Don't you want to?"

"Yes . . . and no. What if something happens?"

Kieri reached for her, pulled her close. "What's going to happen is that we're going to have a son. I won't tell them now if you don't want me to, but the way the taig's reacting and the way we're both happy, everyone with taig-sense is going to know it, anyway. Then they'll wonder why we're hiding it."

"All right, then." She laid her cheek against his for a moment.

"And the Council members can quit staring at your midsection wondering . . . They'll know."

Arian laughed. She had noticed those not-casual-enough glances herself.

All had been sorted out by midday: the Council knew, the household knew. Arian had enjoyed a brisk weapons practice with Siger during which she made two touches on him and earned one of his rare compliments. He at least had not treated her as if she'd turned into a crystal goblet. Nor had Kieri, despite his obvious joy at the news. He did insist that she have two King's Squires with her at all times.

"I suppose I can get used to someone following me about everywhere—well, almost everywhere," she said. "But I have things to do—I can't stay in one place."

"Indeed," Kieri said. "Because I'm going to need your help on something delicate." He took a mouthful of the hot soup they were having for lunch. "Remember what I told you that night after our betrothal? About the . . . um . . . problem?"

Arian glanced around the room. Two servants, three Squires. "Yes."

"It's time we got on with that. We—" He stopped; Arian felt the same faint pressure that had alerted him. The Lady was coming.

And then she was there.

"I rejoice for you, Grandson, and for your betrothed," she said. She was as beautiful as ever, Arian thought, and yet . . . a little less. Was that glamour, to conceal her power, or had she actually faded a little?

"Will you join us?" Kieri asked. "We just began lunch."

"I am not hungry now," the Lady said. "I but came to congratulate you and assure you of my joy in this new life you carry."

"Thank you," Arian said. She glanced at Kieri and recognized a guarded expression, though he seemed quite at ease.

"The taig rejoices in an heir to the house," the Lady said. "It rejoiced so at your birth, Grandson, and at your sister's."

Why, Arian wondered, was the Lady making such obvious, almost formal statements?

"And you, Arian: you are well, as anyone can see. Once more I cry sorry for my past mistrust of you."

"It is no matter," Arian said.

"And now," the Lady said, smiling brightly at both of them, "you must come to the mound, when you have eaten, to present the child there for blessing—"

"No." Kieri's tone brooked no contradiction; Arian looked at him with concern.

"No?" The Lady's delicate eyebrows went up; Arian felt the first tremble of the taig in response to the Lady's anger.

"No. We go to the ossuary to pay respects and introduce our child to my ancestors."

"*Half* your ancestors," the Lady said.

"You are here," Kieri pointed out. "So you have already met him."

The Lady glanced at Arian; Arian felt a wave of power wash over her, pushing her away as the Lady had pushed her away before. Fear for the taig rose . . . she felt once more that *she* was the problem, *she* was the one who erred. But this was not then; *this* time she would not be pushed out, leaving Kieri alone. She stood; the Lady nodded, as if expecting Arian to leave the room. Instead, she moved up the table to Kieri's side; he reached for her hand. In their clasped hands, she found the taig, her connection to it unhindered.

"I must talk to my grandson," the Lady said.

"My betrothed, the mother of my son and the light of my heart, stays here," Kieri said. "You cannot separate us."

"I am not trying to separate you," the Lady said. "I am trying to introduce your child to elvenkind as early as possible to protect him. That is more important than visiting piles of old bones, surely."

"Do you know what is under the mound in the King's Grove?" Kieri asked; his hand in Arian's tightened.

The Lady said nothing for a long moment, her face unreadable. Then she said, "Nothing. Nothing at all."

"You are wrong, Grandmother," Kieri said. "If you truly do not know, I am sorry—there has been a traitor among you who lied to you long ago. If you know . . . you are lying to me, the king of this land."

"There is nothing," the Lady insisted. "There had been, I was told, a few huts, long untenanted, but they were no more than rotting heaps."

"Then you were misinformed," Kieri said. "And we may discuss this later. For the moment, Arian and I will finish our lunch—you may sit with us, if you choose, or go—and then Arian and I visit the ossuary together." The Lady nodded, then turned and left the room without speaking.

"She's angry," Arian said.

"Most people are, when their desires are not met," Kieri said. To one of the servants, he said, "Bring Arian's things here; there's no reason for us to have a long table between us when we've no guests."

The ossuary, after the Lady's visit, seemed almost comforting: warm stone under bare feet, bright colors, the stories graved on one skeleton after another. Arian had grown up thinking that the taig was an elven thing, that it was her elven blood that gave her taig-sense. But here she felt a connection to the taig as old, as strong, as that the elves claimed, a purely human connection to all that lived.

She held Kieri's hand; as before, light rose around them and then withdrew. He had a listening look; she understood that his family's bones were speaking to him, but she could not hear. Then she herself felt . . . *something* . . . something between the feeling she got if someone stared at her back and an actual touch. She shivered as the sensation ran over her body and lingered there, where the tiny engendered spark lay in safety.

Not safe enough.

Whether a thought of hers or a voice from without she could not have said, but she felt the hairs rise up on her arms, her neck.

Beware.

Kieri's grip on her hand tightened. Was he, too, hearing warnings of some danger? Arian tried to ask—who was this? what did they mean?—but only cryptic phrases filled her mind.

Treachery . . . beware . . . beware . . .

"Kieri?" she murmured. He put his arm around her shoulders, pulling her close.

"My sister," he murmured. "I don't understand . . . I don't know if she knows all . . ."

At the door, the Seneschal tapped. "Sir king, my apologies, but there's need—"

"Coming," Kieri said. He pulled Arian to face him; his expression was grim. "What you heard—what I heard—I still don't fully understand. But that there is treachery somewhere, I do not doubt. Please, love, do not resent my care for you and for our child."

"I will not," Arian said. "And I will not be fooled by elves' glamour again."

"So I saw," he said with a quick grin. "Arian the brave—bless you for that."

They went out hand in hand. The Seneschal was ready with their boots. "Sir king, the Squires tell me of two things—a winter storm has come upon us in the last hour, and a courier found a body. Your elven tutor, Orlith."

"Orlith!" Kieri stood and stamped down into his boots. "Orlith dead?"

"And not from cold," the Seneschal said. "They say it's murder."

Arian stood, murmured thanks to the Seneschal, and looked past Kieri to the ossuary stairs. The Squires waited with fur-lined cloaks; she could feel a swirl of colder air.

Outside, snow flew sideways in a strong wind; across the courtyard, the mews was only a blurred dim bulk. Kieri, to her surprise, laughed. "The half-Evener storms," he said. "We had them in northern Tsaia; I wondered if you had them as well.

Always that hand or two of days clear-skied with snow going soft on the south side of the stronghold, tempting us to ride back and forth to Duke's East and take the recruits out for a long march. Then this would come."

By the main entrance, with the palace blocking the worst of the wind, spiral flurries of snow rose and fell; there a horse stood, a snow-caked heap on its back and a courier beside it. Servants had brought him a cloak; he was shivering even so. "My lord king! I found him on the way from Riverwash—I didn't know what to do—"

Kieri moved to the horse and brushed snow off the bundle there and peeled back the wrappings. The courier had rolled the body into his own cloak. Orlith's face, gray and pinched in death, showed only by the bones his elven grace.

"Where can we lay the body?" Kieri asked.

"An elf should be laid in the forest," Arian said. "But we must know . . . must find out . . . how . . ."

"Indeed." Kieri looked at the courier, a ranger serving as courier since the Pargunese war. "How long ago did you find him, Deriya?"

"Day before yesterday, sir king. Heard wolves in the woods, not far from the fire's road. There've been more, you know, since the war—more for them to feed on, too. I'd made good time; I thought I'd try for a wolfskin. So I rode into the trees a way and found a pack on the carcass of a horse—a gray. I might not have seen it, mostly snow-covered as it was, if they hadn't broken it open and the blood—"

"Orlith," Kieri said. "Where was he?"

"When I drove the beasts off, sir king—I put arrows into three of them—I looked for the rider, and there he was, propped against a tree. He'd been cut down. Arrows and sword both; someone made sure of him. Who would kill an elf?"

"And who *could* kill an elf?" Kieri asked. "We must find out."

"I thought Pargunese, sir king. If some were still running wild in the woods—"

"No," Kieri said. "Not Pargunese. They'd have taken the horse; they're great horse breeders and riders." He turned to Arian. "Take Deriya inside, to my office, and let no one else talk to him until I come back. I'll see Orlith's body laid in honor and safety in the salle. I must find out what his wounds tell me, and then—"

"You must tell the elves," Arian said. "He may have relatives—friends—"

"First I must know more," Kieri said. "And why do they not know already? Do they not sense where each other are? Would this not have disturbed the taig? Why didn't the Lady know? She was just here."

Arian felt chilled by more than the storm. All around swirled dangers she had not imagined; she looked at Kieri. In that storm-dimmed afternoon, he almost blazed, it seemed—his hair, his anger at Orlith's murder, his stark determination. The cold receded in her heart as well as her body. "Come," she said to Deriya. "The king will take care of Orlith, and we will take care of you."

Within the palace, light and warmth ruled. The steward had servants waiting with fur-lined slippers. Arian felt the warmth, the comfort, as she had not before, as a home welcoming her, caring for her—she had been so concentrated on Kieri, or before on her duties as Squire, that she had only begun to relax into her new role. Even at that moment—and wondering that she could feel it at such a time—she looked at the carpets, the wall hangings, the hall itself, as she led the courier through it to Kieri's office. *It is real,* she thought. *And I belong here. It is mine as well as his, and it will be our son's.*

The presence of her own Squires beside her no longer fretted her spirit.

CHAPTER TWENTY-THREE

KIERI FOLLOWED THE servants who carried Orlith's body into the salle. Siger and Carlion were training a group of palace guards in the middle range; they stopped and stared.

"It's Orlith," Kieri said. "Murdered. I needed a place to lay him."

"What happened?"

"I don't know, but I intend to find out," Kieri said. "A courier found the body two days ago—his horse was dead nearby."

"Sir king, should I call for Captain Lornyan?" one of the guards asked.

Kieri remembered that this was the city militia officer who dealt with the occasional crimes in Chaya. "I would say yes but for this storm."

"I know where he lives," the guard said. He was young, full of eagerness. "And I could go to that inn the elves favor—"

"Not that," Kieri said. "Not yet. But Captain Lornyan, yes, if you think you and he can make it back. Two of you go."

When they had left, he had Orlith's body laid on the stone floor and unwrapped the cloak. Orlith's familiar gray winter tunic, piped in green, was marked not only with rents the weapons had made but with his blood. Kieri had wondered before if elven blood still held silver in death, and now he saw it did—a faint sparkle on the stains as he moved the body a little to see better. Kieri touched his finger to one of the stains and sniffed.

It smelled like human blood, or near enough that he could not distinguish it. "Siger, come and look."

Carlion and Siger both knelt beside him. Siger grunted as he looked at the wounds. "These are from arrows—and the shafts pulled free." Together he and Kieri rolled Orlith's body on its side.

"Longbow arrows?" Kieri asked. "There's no penetration to the back—could they have been crossbows?"

"Not one of our blackwood bows," Carlion said. "So certainly not a ranger or Royal Archer. Nor crossbow bolts—the Pargunese bolts make a different wound. But the elves—" He swallowed and went on slowly. "The elves, lord king, use a smaller bow sometimes, and slenderer shafts. The wood— they won't say what it is."

"And these wounds are from a blade," Siger went on, pointing to the slashes in the tunic. "Someone wanted him dead for certain."

"And the taig didn't warn him," Kieri said. "Wouldn't it? He had taig-sense enough."

"I don't know if it would," Siger said. "The taig has its own ways."

"If it was elves," Carlion said. "This looks . . . this looks like rage to me. Some quarrel among the elvenkind."

Kieri thought immediately of Arian's father and the Lady's quarrel with him. But she had assigned Orlith to him; she had no quarrel with Orlith. That he knew about, at least. "The courier thought it might have been Pargunese stragglers, but the horse—that would not have been the Pargunese. And I can't imagine Pargunese soldiers delivering enough injuries to kill him twice over . . ."

"Unless they thought elves were hard to kill," Siger said. "You know how our novices were in their first battles. Wasted extra blows on a man already dying out of battle fever."

"So you think it was humans?"

"I don't know. With Verrakai renegades just over the border, how do we know they didn't make it into our woods during the confusion of the war?" Kieri shook his head.

"True, sir—sir king, we don't know. Verrakaien—they'd use crossbows, wouldn't they? But stragglers, out in the woods— they might have to contrive a bow . . . but why attack Orlith if not to take the horse?"

"The horse for meat? But the wolves drove them away?" Carlion said.

"I suppose." Kieri unfastened Orlith's blood-soaked tunic, struggling with the frozen laces. Beneath it, the shirt showed the same rents, the same blood. On his neck, an abraded line showed dark against the pale skin. "Was he strangled as well? This makes no sense!"

"Not strangled," Siger said. "I've seen this on the battlefield, and so have you, sir king. He wore a chain or thong—possibly a jewel or other pendant on it—and it was ripped off."

"Robbers, then," Carlion said. "Tsaian scum, no doubt—"

"No," Kieri said. "Look, there's his belt-purse, still fat with coins. A robber would find it easier to use coins than an elven pendant to buy himself meat and drink." He stood. "I must go hear what the courier has to say in detail. Stay with Orlith until Captain Lornyan comes; be sure no one takes his body away, and that includes the Lady. Send to me at once if elves come and when the Captain comes."

"Yes, sir king," Siger said, and Carlion echoed him.

Back in the palace, Deriya had finally warmed and was halfway through a meal; he came to his feet as Kieri entered. "Finish eating," Kieri said, and moved to his own desk, where Arian sat with pen in hand. She had covered two sheets with what he'd said. Kieri read it over her shoulder, then pulled a chair nearer the courier and sat down with his feet to the fire. The storm raged outside; the wind's howl was audible even in here. "I will have many questions for you," he said to the man. "Arian will keep a record."

"Yes, sir king," Deriya said, wiping his mouth.

"But first you need my thanks—you have done well, coming through such a storm and bringing his body as well . . . It could not have been easy."

Over the next turn of the glass, Kieri led the man through finding Orlith's body, his examination of the site—"Bootprints, yes, sir king, but I couldn't tell whose"—what else he might have noticed, and how long it had taken him to reach Chaya. "I was lucky the wind was behind me," the man said at the end. "It pushed me this way."

"Did you recognize the body at once as an elf's?"

"No, sir king; only when I got close, I could tell—those

cheekbones, that shape—but when I first rode up on it and shot the wolves, I thought it was a man."

"And after, did you realize who it was?"

"No, sir king. I never met this Orlith."

"But you brought the body here, to the palace . . ."

"Tell the truth, sir, in the storm I was glad to get to a wall and turn in the first gate I could find. Someone here would know what to do, I thought."

"Right enough," Kieri said. He sighed. Too much in one day, as usual. Arian pregnant with their child—a great joy. His grandmother elf's claim to be ignorant of what lay under the mount in the King's Grove—a great puzzle and worry. Those warnings in the ossuary—a great mystery and possible threat. And now Orlith's death. For all that he had resented Orlith in the beginning, he had come to respect the elf, even like him. Such a vicious murder—so brutal, so blatant—argued for something more dire than simple assassination. And yet something was wrong with the elves, something deeper than he had yet discovered.

"Sir king, Carlion said you asked to know when the Captain arrived. He's looking at Orlith's body now." This time it was one of the palace guard.

Kieri took the inside route to the salle, with only a short dash across the little entrance court exposed to the weather. He found the Chaya militia captain crouched beside Orlith's body.

"You knew him?" Lornyan said.

"Yes. He was my tutor in elven magery," Kieri said. Anticipating the next questions, he went on. "I had not seen him but two or three times since just before Midwinter. He had not given me formal lessons since the Pargunese invasion, and I understood him to be busy with the other elves, healing the scathefire damage."

"So his being away a tenday or two did not concern you?"

"No. Besides that, I myself have been busy and distracted since Midwinter and my betrothal."

The man smiled and nodded. "Understandable, sir king. And you say someone found this body two days ago?"

"Yes, and can probably find the place again when the storm's over, though I'm sure all sign will have been erased." Kieri told him what he now knew of the courier's movements and findings. "I'm sure the armsmasters have told you about our speculations earlier: whether this could be a Verrakai stray from Tsaia, or a Pargunese, or . . . or who else would kill like this, so messily?"

"Was he bound to the tree where he was found?"

"The courier didn't mention that—I'm sure he would have. You will want to ask him yourself, perhaps."

"Indeed," the man said. "I'm sure you, sir king, have seen more dead men than I, in your years at war. We have few acts of violence here; the elves, as you know, abhor conflict, let alone violence."

"And yet the Lady brought them to my need, before I arrived, and they fought then." Kieri scowled, trying to remember. He had seen that line of elven warriors coming down on the foe . . . but he could not remember how they had fought. Odd. He hadn't thought of it in all this time . . . the length and shape of their blades—or did they have blades?—the kind of bows—or did they have bows? He remembered the elf-light, the splendor of the Lady on her silvery horse . . . tumult . . . and then kneeling before her . . .

"I have never seen them fight," the man said. "But they carry blades much like any other person who bears arms."

"Orlith didn't," Kieri said. "He had a dagger . . ." He looked at the body. No dagger, just an empty sheath.

"With your permission, sir king, I will unclothe him now."

"Certainly." Kieri watched as the man, with the armsmaster's help, removed Orlith's shirt. Three arrow wounds, he thought, and at least five slashes and stabs with a blade. One of the thrusts had transfixed Orlith's body. "No marks on his trousers," Kieri commented. "He was wounded only on the upper body."

"There's blood." Carlion pointed to a stain.

"But no rent in the cloth. It's from these wounds."

"I don't understand it at all," the captain said, rocking back onto his heels. "The arrows would have killed him—not instantly, but soon enough, especially when drawn out. Why then hack at him, stab him? He could not have been able to fight."

"How are you sure the arrows came first?" Kieri asked.

"I'm not, but it makes sense. Arrows—he falls off his horse—wait—was the horse shot?"

"The courier didn't mention that. You can ask him."

"It may have stopped—but something killed it. But if he was shot and he fell off his horse, he'd be helpless."

"Duke Verrakai found one of her squires bound to a tree, crippled and left in the cold. Could that have been the plan?"

"But then why the bladework?"

"I don't know," Kieri said. "If this were a battlefield—" He hoped with all his heart that it would not become one ever again. "If it were," he said again, "I would think this an act of frenzy . . . vengeance against an enemy, anger, hatred, something like that."

"And the elves—they will want him laid in the woods," Lornyan said.

"Yes. But I remind you that his death—and such a death as this—should have disturbed the taig when it befell him. And yet the Lady herself visited this morning and said nothing of it."

"Did you ask her?"

"I didn't know yet."

"Did she say why she had come?"

"Yes. Arian is with child, and she had felt that in the taig, she said."

Lornyan's face lit up. "Oh, my lord—sir king—what joy!"

"Yes, it is," Kieri said, grinning. "But surely she would have—should have—known of Orlith's death."

"Perhaps she didn't mention it at such a happy time, not to disturb you."

"Perhaps." Kieri sighed. "I wonder that I myself didn't feel something. Orlith helped me develop my taig-sense . . . though I never had been able to feel him through it, come to think of it." He looked down at Orlith's body. "We can at least clean that up and wrap him decently before the elves see him."

DESPITE THE STORM and Orlith's death, the mood that night at dinner was joyful. No one had been able to leave the palace, so the table was filled—Council members, Squires, the courier, Captain Lornyan—when Kieri and Arian came in. A cheer went up; Kieri grinned. The steward had spread dried rose petals on the tablecloth; the room smelled of roses and fresh herbs before the food came in.

He had not expected such a feast, but clearly his staff felt the announcement of an heir deserved celebration. Dish after dish appeared—clear soups and cream soups, roast fowl, haunch of venison, ham, winter vegetables in every combination of spice and sauce.

Kieri could not help thinking where he had been the year before. In a palace, yes, but in Vérella's glittering pink and gray granite edifice, under suspicion in the Regency Council, thanks to the Verrakaien influence. As Duke Kieri Phelan, he had expected to spend the rest of his life in Tsaia when not campaigning in the south . . . a widower who would never, he had decided that winter, remarry . . . a peer with no heir of the body.

Was it this day, or the day before or after, that Paks had arrived to tell him that the sword he had given Tammarion was in fact a relic of the Lyonyan royal house—the sword made for him by elves at his mother's behest, found by Aliam Halveric, who had not known its history. He had paid little attention to half-Eveners then; he had held himself aloof from the common celebrations of the year. And yet that day had brought him to the second great change of his life . . . from a life as a man with no family, no past, to the inheritance he now held.

For the first time in a season, he thought of his former domain: the hills, the streams, the little towns he had founded, the stronghold itself . . . the people. Would he ever see them again? What would he feel if he did? He pushed that away—his place was here, now, with these people. No king could ask for better . . . and what had he brought them but war, invasion, after all those lifetimes of peace?

"Kieri?" The touch of Arian's hand on his brought him out of that bittersweet reverie.

"I'm fine," he said. "But trying to remember if it was this day or one very near it last year when Paks arrived in Vérella with the sword."

"And your life changed," Arian said. "A very busy year for you, whichever day it was."

"Indeed. And a change I could not have imagined. Including you. Including our son." He addressed himself to his food then and finished a serving of roast goose with brambleberry sauce. The feast went on; he had eaten almost all he could before the dessert came in, custard tarts topped with sugared fruits. By then it was dark, and the snow continued pummeling the windows.

"It has to stop sometime," Sier Halveric said. He had been one of the Council members trapped in the palace by the storm. "Perhaps by morning?"

"Half-Evener storm," Sier Davonin said. "Remember last year? The king was dead, that paladin had gone off with the sword—been gone a long time, it seemed—and we all sat here wondering if the storm was an ill omen. Blew three days, it did, and then we'd hardly got the snow all cleared away, seemed like, when the air softened, and next we knew here came the king riding in with spring all around him."

"A big change," Sier Halveric said. To Kieri he said, "I'm sorry, sir king, you never got to meet him—he was not a bad king, just not strong, and without taig-sense."

"I'd like to have known them all," Kieri said. "But now that dinner's over, I'd like to meet with those of you on the Council—and you, Captain. A turn of the glass, and we'll use the small dining room."

He went to the kitchens next to thank the cooks for the feast and then went to his office. Arian was there, waiting for him. "Do you want to come to the meeting, love, or would you rather rest?"

"I was thinking I might go see Orlith's body," Arian said. "It bothers me that neither of us felt any disturbance when he was killed. If he had just died peacefully—not that elves do die that way—it would not surprise me. We are not of his family, after all. But for such violence to go on—I should have felt something."

"And the Lady?"

"Of course. And my father." She paused, brow furrowed, then went on. "Though . . . it was close to the scathefire track, was it not? The taig is still wounded there; I can feel that. It's possible that overwhelmed the other . . . as one does not notice a scratch when hit by a sword stroke."

"A good thought," Kieri said.

"And I think I should come with you to the meeting after I've seen Orlith's body. I should know what you know . . . and they should know that I know."

"As long as you're not too tired."

Arian laughed. "Not now, Kieri. Later, I'm sure I shall tire more easily, but right now I feel wide awake and fit for anything."

He had not meant to think of Tammarion again, but that was almost exactly what Tamar had said at the start of her first pregnancy. "Good," he said to Arian. "I will expect you then." As she turned to go, he added, "With this murder . . . take no chances, Arian. Wear mail always."

"Indeed I will," Arian said. "And listen to my Squires. Whatever has sought to harm this realm is still there and still active."

With that she was gone with a wave; he watched her Squires follow.

The five members of his Council who were in the palace that night reacted to his news about Orlith's murder with varying degrees of concern. Sier Davonin voiced the most obvious fear: "I hope they won't find a way to blame us." Others nodded, but Sier Tolmaric, whose steading had been burned by the Pargunese, glowered. He was still waiting to learn if the elves would grant him land to replace that ruined by scathefire.

"Blame *us*? It's us should blame them for not being there when the Pargunese came, to help us."

"They couldn't," Kieri said. "They were trapped under stone—an old quarrel with the rockfolk."

"Elders have no business making quarrels," Tolmaric said. "They're supposed to show us better, aren't they?"

Kieri secretly agreed with him but said, "We're not the high gods to know what duties they gave the Elders. Ours is clear enough and hard enough for us."

"You'd excuse them?" Tolmaric said. "Seems I remember you being annoyed with 'em back then—"

"And I was," Kieri said. "I didn't understand why they didn't come, and I'm not sure I understand all of it now. But anyone can make mistakes, and any people can have some who aren't what they should be. As king, it's my responsibility to seek understanding before I leap to judgment."

"And you find them blameless?"

"I find them fallible, as we are," Kieri said. "Sier Tolmaric, I know your grief for your losses—but I do not think the Pargunese invaded because of the elves' mistakes. My mistakes, perhaps, but perhaps also because they had been misled by the webspinner into evil."

"But will you stand up for us humans if they try to lay Orlith's death on us?" Tolmaric asked.

"We don't know who killed him," Kieri said. "I can't ignore the possibility that he was killed by humans. Verrakai stragglers from over the border, maybe, or some of our own people who blamed elves for the invasion."

Tolmaric flushed. "I didn't—"

"I'm not accusing you or any of your people," Kieri said. "But someone from Riverwash, say, who had been burned out and whose family died, might in grief and rage slay anyone he blamed. The wounds—more than needed to kill him—suggest a frenzy of some kind."

"But it could have been another elf," Tolmaric said.

"It could have been anyone with a bow and a sword," Kieri said. "Or more than one. We do not know. We do not know why—was someone intent on killing Orlith specifically, or was it more that anyone where he was would have been killed?"

Sier Halveric leaned forward. "You and Orlith had become close—he was the only elf here for the first days of the invasion. Many knew that—so I would not expect even a grief-stricken refugee to kill him."

"If they recognized him," Sier Davonin said.

"True, but he was fairly well known," Halveric said. "But did you not say, then, that he had consented to your trying to contact a Kuakgan?"

"Yes. Very reluctantly, but yes."

"And we all know how elves feel about Kuakkgani in general. So maybe an elf who knew about that considered him a traitor."

"But we didn't call a Kuakgan," Kieri said.

"But that might not be known. Or, as you say, it could be someone from over the border. We've had skulkers in there before, Verrakaien and others."

"So we don't know who did it or why . . . but we have to tell the elves something or they will blame us. Sir king, you have to realize that."

"Have they blamed humans before when an elf was found dead?" Kieri asked.

Silence; the Council members glanced back and forth.

"It's rare," Sier Galvary said. "You know—they keep themselves secure in the Lady's realm. But your mother—the elves said humans killed her. And you, since we didn't know you'd been stolen away. Brigands, they said, or some Sier's armed men. And it was clear they suspected one of us had given the attackers the information. They questioned all who lived on the borders of the elvenhome—and not gently."

"I did not know this," Kieri said.

"No, sir king. How could you? And you so eager to bring understanding between the peoples, which I agree is important . . . I was not going to tell you."

"Sier Tolmaric, do you think they blamed you?"

"Me? I was a child then. My grandfather, yes; they blamed him. He and my father were both taken away for a tenday; my mother was terrified. And I swear, they had done nothing. They came back pale and shaking, not the same, ever after."

"It's no wonder you have some resentment of elvenkind," Kieri said. "That, and now the damage to your steading."

"My father, too," Sier Belvarin said. "And my uncle. And Sier Galvary's." He glanced at Sier Galvary, who nodded.

"It wasn't fair," Sier Galvary said. "We were as shocked and horrified by the queen's death—and yours, as we thought—as elves could be. No one wanted to kill either of you; she was beloved among humans from the moment your father introduced her as his betrothed."

"Nobody's equally loved by everybody," Kieri said. "And someone did kill her."

"None of us," Sier Belvarin said. "Nor our families. Brigands—well, they'll kill anyone and sell any likely child into slavery. But not us."

"I understand," Kieri said. His sister's warnings echoed in his mind. Someone had wanted his mother dead; someone had wanted him gone, ruined; someone had wanted the joint realm to fail. He must find out who, and why, or he and Arian and their child were like to suffer the same fate. And he must reassure his human subjects that he would not let them be punished for someone else's crimes.

Тне nехt mоrninɢ, the storm still raged. Elves had not come; no one had ventured back out into the city. The palace steward reported that guide ropes had been strung between all the buildings of the palace complex. Orlith's body, wrapped in clean cloths, had been moved to the outer chamber of the ossuary.

The day passed without word or sign of any elves, and it was not until the next day, when the storm finally died down, that one of the King's Squires could look for elves in the city. He came back within a turn of the glass, trailed by four elves. Kieri met them in the forecourt. He did not recognize any of them.

"A courier found one of yours dead in the forest," he said to them. "Orlith, who was my tutor. He was murdered."

They looked at him and then at one another. "Where is he now?"

"In the outer chamber of the ossuary," Kieri said.

The elves exchanged glances again. "The Lady must come," one said. "She will not be pleased."

"I have no doubt," Kieri said. "I am not pleased at any murder. But she has not come, though I tried to call."

Again those glances back and forth. Kieri felt his patience fraying away.

"She has many concerns," another of the elves said. "It is not carelessness, sir king." He bowed. The others bowed then, though less deeply.

Within a glass, the Lady appeared with an escort: the same

four elves who had come before. She moved over the drifted snow without leaving footprints.

"Who did this?" the Lady asked when Kieri came out to greet her.

"I don't know," Kieri said. "He was found a few days before the half-Evener, and the man who found him brought his body here."

"It should not have been moved," the Lady said.

"You would have it lie unprotected, at the mercy of wind and wild animals?" Kieri said.

"I would have had it reported sooner," she said.

"How? Were you on call so I might let you know? I had seen no elves about for hands of days."

The Lady moved restlessly, her robes swirling around her. "I was not hiding from you, Grandson," she said. "We have much to do to repair damage to the taig and to make a better peace with the rockfolk, who are still angry about the elfane under stone."

"I am glad you were not hiding," Kieri said. "Will you now look at Orlith's body?"

She shivered. "When we die, we die. I will take it into the elvenhome, and there it will be laid to rest."

"You need to see," Kieri said. "We must know who did this—man or elf or something else—"

"It is done, it is over. Have it brought out here; I cannot go into that place." She shivered again, looking at the ossuary entrance.

"Lady—Grandmother—"

Her eyes seemed to blaze for a moment. "Sir king, I tell you I *cannot*. And so long after the spirit flies, what can the husk tell?"

"That the wounds were not made by crossbow bolts," Kieri said. "Not by the arrows our rangers use or the Royal Archers. My people fear that you will blame them, as you blamed them before when my mother was killed. Did you then turn away from her body, as you are refusing to see Orlith's? She was your daughter; he was your servant and becoming my friend—"

"We do not look at ugliness," the Lady said. "It weakens . . . it infects us as disease infects you."

"No one likes looking at ugliness, but it must be done to find out why and prevent more," Kieri said.

"Humans can see and live," she said. She seemed to shrink a little, as she had when she knelt to him on the scathefire track. He distrusted that, as he had distrusted her seeming humility then. She went on. "We have been healing the forest's wounds, but—but such ugliness is a blow to the heart of Sinyi."

Was this an excuse or an insight into her nature, the nature of all elves? Were they really so fragile—and how could an immortal be fragile and still immortal? He was still struggling with these thoughts when she waved her escort forward.

"We will convey it," one of them said. "Have it brought forth, sir king."

The Lady started to turn away.

"Wait," Kieri said. "Lady, tell me, do you believe me that this was not of human doing?"

She turned back, and he saw tears like crystal sliding down her perfect face. "Grandson . . . I grieve. I cannot see, but I grieve. And I offer no blame. Let me go . . ." And she was gone into a silver mist that faded in an instant.

After that, Kieri could do nothing but have his Squires bring out Orlith's body on the low bed where it had lain. The elves did not touch it, but from their fingers light wove a net between the body and the bed. Then they lifted the net, and, turning their faces away from the body, they too moved into a mist and vanished.

CHAPTER TWENTY-FOUR

BECLAN MAHIERAN, isolated in a cottage at the far end of the family estates, paced the length of the largest room again and again. Outside, on every side of the cottage, Royal Guard soldiers stood watch a half-bowshot away with orders to kill anyone who crossed the line of flags stuck in the snow. A single servant, an elderly female, prepared his meals in the cottage kitchen and pushed them through a hatch in the door; she would not come closer or speak to him. He had a fireplace for warmth and a room upstairs with a bed. Every third day a squad dragged in more wood, during which he was required to stand at the upstairs window, where he could be seen—and shot—if anything went wrong downstairs.

And it was all completely unfair and unnecessary because he knew he had not been invaded by any evil Verrakaien. True, he and his escort had been caught in a Verrakai trap. True, his escort had died, leaving no proof that he was still just Beclan Mahieran: a sobered Beclan Mahieran, who had seen his first violent death, faced his own folly and its consequences, and made his own first kill. He was not the boy Beclan anymore, but a man, a man who knew he had far to go to be the man he wanted to be. The last moments of Sergeant Vossik, when that grizzled old veteran had killed himself on Beclan's sword to give him a chance to escape . . . Beclan had seen then, in the raw, what it meant to be courageous and honorable, traits he'd seen in his father and the other dukes in more cultured form.

He understood now why Dorrin Duke Verrakai had not been impressed with his royal lineage, his evident—or so he'd thought—superiority to the other squires. Night after night he lived it again, woke crying or screaming, soaked in sweat. Hadrin's horse rolling down the slope; Hadrin's death . . . the

Kuakkgani trap closing in on them . . . Vossik trying to warn him . . . Vossik's face as he pulled Beclan's sword into his body . . . the stiff, awkward movements of those men in his escort he'd had to kill . . . their terrified expressions . . . that horrible, tempting, insinuating voice in his head. All his own arrogance, all his mistakes and failures, repeated over and over and over.

And no one, no one at all, to talk to, to ask if his increasing misery and fear meant he was going crazy or had been invaded, after all. They were all afraid of him; they all thought he'd become a monster. Who could possibly understand what he felt? Did anyone care? Would he ever have the chance to talk to anyone ever again, to hear his name spoken without fear, without loathing? He still had his Girdish medallion; he held it hour after hour, begging Gird for help. But none had come.

He had pens and paper; he could write—had written—his father, giving his account of what happened and taking blame for what he knew was his fault. Every hand of days, a royal courier came to deliver and collect messages, and at that time he had to stay upstairs, by the window, from the horn call announcing the courier's arrival to the one announcing him safely back outside the Royal Guard perimeter.

He knew nothing of what was going on outside. When the Kuakgan opened the spiral trap, the commander of the Royal Guard troop, Sir Flanits, answered no questions. Beclan had argued, tried to explain . . . but he had been forced to drink some potion that put him to sleep, and when he woke, he'd been in bed here, upstairs, alone. A letter from his father, in one of the royal courier's bags, had laid out the conditions of his life "until we know for certain what occurred."

No one now would tell him anything, because no one was allowed to be in the same room with him or converse with him. He imagined Duke Verrakai leading troops into battle, Gwenno Marrakai and Daryan Serrostin with her, winning glory or falling nobly . . . and here he was, trapped. His father answered no questions about them, about the war, about anything. Only, over and over, warnings to obey the rules, to wait. He felt so helpless. So miserable. This sort of thing happened to people in bards' songs: to the misunderstood, misidentified young hero brought up in poverty and hardship but destined for greatness, not to young men of good family.

Midwinter was the worst. His entire life, every Midwinter had been the same: the family gathered with all their house servants, huddled together in the dark and cold, singing and telling stories. Mahierans preserved some of the oldest customs; he had been coached into the role of "youngest boy" when he was just able to lisp the words; he had given up that role two years later to the cook's youngest. He enjoyed the circle dance in the dark, when bumping into the others was not only allowed but intended. He loved to shout the Sunreturn greeting with the men at dawn and throw on the new fire the symbols of the new year he hoped for. And the food. Always the food. And the laughter and songs and family close around him.

Here . . . it had been nothing. He'd been ordered upstairs, and when he came down the hearth was bare, all candles removed, and his Midwinter dinner barely visible in the dim light coming through the window. A lump of honeycomb stood for all the delicacies; the rest of the food already chilling to sodden lumps, like the one he felt in his stomach. After a long, cold, dark night . . . a night in which everything and everyone he had loved in his childhood tormented him in visions . . . the horn blew again at daybreak, and once more he had to stand by the window while the soldiers dragged in wood and replaced candles. No one so much as called a Sunreturn greeting up the stairs.

The rules of his captivity allowed him to take exercise outside in daylight, walking a track around the cottage, but knowing that archers were focused on his every step made that less attractive, especially on a day like this, when a cold fog lay over the little valley and the archers moved in closer. And inside, he fretted . . . pacing back and forth, over and over, up the stairs, the length of the upper room, back down.

The rules did not permit him weapons, not even a knife to cut his own food. For eating he had a fork and spoon; the cook cut his food into what she thought of as bite-sized pieces, and they probably were, for a small child. He felt naked without a sword, reduced to the status of a child in every way. He would gladly have traded his warm bed, his clean dry clothes, the predictable meals, for the cold, filthy floor of the old sheepfold that had so disgusted him in the snowstorm. To have the men alive once more whom his willfulness had killed would be better than the comfort he now enjoyed in royal solitude.

Tomorrow, if he'd counted aright, another courier would come. With that thought, he sat down at the desk, put a few drops of water in the bowl, and rubbed the ink stick in it. What could he say that he had not said before? That would persuade his father to mitigate the conditions of his imprisonment?

He picked up his pen.

Father, greetings. I understand that I must stay immured here until you are sure I have no taint of ancient Verrakai magery, and that you cannot trust my sworn word. I understand why you do not grant me weapons or tools of any kind. But consider, sir, that I have nothing to do day after day. I have no tasks taking more than a turn of the glass—to keep my rooms neat is no effort, since I can do nothing to disarrange them. I have read what little is here to read—a few pages someone stuffed in a hollow of the bedroom fireplace is all—and I am like to go mad with no one to talk to and nothing to do. Please send me something—old accounts of grain harvests even—or any other thing you think I should study. If I were inhabited by an evil Verrakai, I would know such things already, so you would risk nothing in that way. I do not ask for those things which formerly interested me, but for anything at all to occupy my mind and time in some way that will profit me later.

He had just finished writing this much when a horn call sounded. Had he lost track of days? Or was the messenger coming early, and if so, what did it mean? He sealed the letter quickly, burning his finger on the spill that melted the wax and then placed it on the table where the courier would find it. Then he ran up the stairs to the window. Out of the fog came a rider . . . two . . . more riders. The rose and white Mahieran standard flapped listlessly as the rider carrying it spurred his

horse to a plunging attempt at a canter. Then a Girdish standard . . . So at least one Marshal had come. Beclan's hopes
rose: surely a Marshal could tell that he had not been invaded.
The group stopped at a little distance, the standard-bearer
alone ahead of them.

After some time, five rode forward toward the house: one in
Royal Guard uniform, one Marshal in Gird's blue, one Knight
of Gird, the standard-bearer, and a man Beclan recognized
from halfway across the field as his father. He wanted to run
downstairs, fling himself at his father. Instead he stood where
he'd been told to stand. Archers moved still closer to the cottage, where the fog would not obscure their aim.

He lost sight of the five when they came too close and rode
to the other side of the house. He heard the distant sound of
someone pounding on a door—the kitchen door, he supposed.
It seemed a long time before he heard voices in the main room
below, low voices in serious discussion, too low to hear clearly.
Then he heard the front door open, shut, open and shut again.

Finally his father's voice from below: "Beclan! Come down."

Heart hammering, Beclan went down the narrow stairs and
found himself facing a ring of drawn swords. Including his
father's. His mouth went dry. Had he been condemned? Was
he to die here in this remote place without seeing the rest of
his family again? Had this morning's porridge been his last
meal? He had not, he realized, believed he would be killed, not
as long as he did what he was told. Those drawn swords told a
different tale.

"Sit on that stool," his father said. Beclan sat on the stool by
the fireplace; he was glad of the heat. "Bind him," his father
said. The Marshal laid his sword on the desk where Beclan
had written his letter. The seal was broken, the paper unfolded,
so at least one of them had read it. Firmly, but without unnecessary roughness, the Marshal bound Beclan's arms behind
him, and then knelt and bound his ankles as well.

"Bring candles," Duke Mahieran said. "We must see his
face, his eyes, at all times."

The Royal Guard commander put down his sword as the
Marshal took up his own, and opened the door to the kitchen.
For the first time, Beclan saw the face of the woman who pre-

pared his food and washed his shirts: wispy white hair, faded blue eyes, a mass of wrinkles that suggested she was used to smiling. He did not think he had ever seen her before. Behind her, the kitchen looked a far more interesting place than his side of the cottage, mostly because it was full of things to do—a small loom in one corner on which she—or someone—was weaving, all those kitchen tools, and the enticing smell of something roasting over the kitchen fire. The Royal Guard commander came back with a four-branched candleholder and placed it on the table.

"Now, Beclan," said his father. "You will answer our questions fully, and you will not speak except to do so. Is that clear?"

"Yes, Father," Beclan said. "But—"

"No. Nothing but answers to the questions you will be asked. I can tell you this much. We can wait no longer to find out if you are invaded. I must know; the king must know. It is our hope that your letters have been truthful—but if you were invaded, you would say the same. We cannot trust you or Duke Verrakai."

"I—"

"Silence," the Marshal said. He, too, was one Beclan had not met before. "I am High Marshal Seklis, approved by the Marshal-General to test your truthfulness with a relic of Gird himself. We would have brought a paladin if we could, for they are known to detect any evil, but none was available."

"We will go over the points of your story as related first to the Royal Guard who found you and then in your letters to me," his father said. "I must warn you that if you do not answer truthfully and in detail, I have the king's warrant to execute you here and now. Though you are my son, I will not hesitate to give that order."

His father's face, Beclan realized as he was finally over the first shock, held as much misery as he himself felt. The Duke was holding himself to a hard duty, as the sergeant had, and once more Beclan was faced with the reality of the responsibility—not the privilege—of rank.

"Do you understand?"

"Yes, Father."

The High Marshal sheathed his sword and opened a sack Beclan had not noticed beside the table. It held several items wrapped in blue cloth. One was a gnarled length of wood such as old men used for canes, polished to a gleam by long use.

"This was Gird's, as he aged, and was also used by Cob, one of his marshals in the war. It is a potent relic and has detected lies and evil before. I will lay it alongside your head, and if it detects anything, that will be the last thing you feel."

Beclan said nothing, for that was not a question. The knob end of the stick, resting against his jaw, did not hurt, but he could not ignore it. The questions began simply, about his life as Duke Verrakai's squire. What had his duties been, how had he felt about the other squires, what had he seen Duke Verrakai do? Beclan made no attempt to hide his errors; he could not, as they stood out in his memory like blazing torches.

"Do you feel she was unfair to you, a member of the royal family?"

"At first," Beclan said. "I did not know how arrogant I had become; Rothlin had tried to tell me, but I thought he was but playing the elder brother. So I thought Duke Verrakai favored Gwennothlin Marrakai most and was determined to set me down. But then she gave me the longer patrols, because I was the eldest and because, she said, she thought the people would respond to me as the king's cousin."

"And what escort did she provide?"

"Four hands, one hand of them the most experienced of her former troops. By then I had begun to understand what she had meant earlier, though I still—I still made mistakes. When I argued with Sergeant—"

"We will come to that," his father said. "But now think: when you left on that last patrol, was any stranger at the Verrakai household?"

"No, sir."

"No one from Lyonya?"

"No, sir. Gwenno—Gwennothlin Marrakai—was on patrol in the east, due back in a day or two. If anyone had come that way, she should have picked them up. Daryan was on patrol but due back several days later—because of winter weather, we had more leeway, you see."

"So when you left, had Duke Verrakai spoken to you of the likelihood of war?"

"She was concerned always about the possibility of the Pargunese coming, as they did last winter, but she said she was more worried about that man in Aarenis."

"Now to your patrol." Duke Marrakai took a sheaf of papers from under his tunic. "You told the Royal Guard that it was routine until the blizzard."

"Yes, sir." Had he told the Royal Guard commander every detail? He couldn't remember; he had better tell it all now. "I tried to push on to the next village, though Sergeant Vossik thought we should stop, and we ended up having to stay in a filthy herders' shelter with a leaky roof that night. It was my fault; I wanted to make the schedule in spite of the weather."

"And was it the next day you met the Duke's messenger?"

"Yes . . . in the next village. He brought word that the Pargunese had invaded Lyonya and might invade Tsaia and orders from the Duke to collect her militia from each village on the way back."

"And what happened then?"

"We started back. The Duke's messenger had told each village he came to what his errand was, so some men on the muster rolls were missing. I thought the villages along the track north would not have heard, and it might be easier to muster them."

Guided by questions, Beclan went on to tell of the more successful muster on this northern track and then his decision to send the main mass of them eastward to link with the improved road north, while he and a handful of the better trained militia went on north to a few more villages.

"That's when I heard a call for help."

Telling yet again how his horse had plunged off the ridge and could not climb back up, how the others had come down, how Hadrin had died and he'd forgotten names and all the other mistakes of that miserable day, Beclan saw once more just how stupid he had been.

"I didn't understand why my sergeant insisted we not go help whoever was calling—I mean, I was taught to help those who asked it—" Silence from the men around him; the wood knob against his cheek did not quiver, but he felt that even it condemned him. The rest came more quickly . . . realizing that they were not making a straight line, that the dense pines and firs were forcing them into a contracting spiral and they could not turn back.

"Did you realize then what you faced?"

"No," Beclan said. "Nor did my sergeant, though he expected trouble. By the time he realized it was a Kuakkgani trap, it was too late. We couldn't go back. We didn't know a Kuakgan was anywhere around. Neither did Duke Verrakai; I asked her once, after the first Marshals came last summer, if any of her people were kuakgannir, and she said she didn't think so, that the Kuakkgani had always been hostile to Verrakai."

"She never said anything to suggest that she might be in league with one?"

"In league?"

"Setting a trap for you, Beclan. She could have had the Kuakgan set the trap for you and caught the others by accident—or by design, if she placed them there."

"But the Kuakgan said—you heard him, sir," Beclan said, looking at the Royal Guard commander.

"I heard him, but I have no reason to trust him," the commander said. "Kuakkgani are uncanny. I follow Gird, where right and wrong are clear."

"Beclan." Beclan looked back at his father, reading the tension in his forehead and jaw. "Pay attention. Answer questions; do not argue."

"Yes, sir." He knew mortal danger hovered over him; he thought of Gird and tried to take heart, but he did not feel brave, just scared. He wanted to be home—his real home, not here—safe in his own rooms in his father's house. He felt cold to the bone: would he ever be safe again?

"Tell me exactly what happened when you came to the opening in the trees."

Beclan told of the three apparent vagabonds, trapped like them, one wounded. "They asked our help. The sergeant said wait . . ." And he had waited. He had been obedient in that at least, hand on the hilt of the sword he no longer had. Step by step he told the tale as he recalled it. A sense of pressure, similar—he had thought the same—to the pressure in the Kuakkgani trap. Vossik's attempt to charge—his jerky movements—his strained voice.

"He said 'Run,'" Beclan said. "And I had promised to run if he told me to, but I couldn't—if he was helpless like Sergeant Stammel, I couldn't leave him." He squeezed his eyes shut; his voice shook, and he couldn't keep it steady. "I had my sword out—I couldn't—I didn't know what would help him—"

"What were the others doing?" the Marshal asked.

"I don't know—they were behind us. His eyes were bloodshot—it's what Count Arcolin said about Sergeant Stammel. He said 'Run' again, and I couldn't move." In his memory, it was still perfectly, horribly clear. Those last minutes and seconds of Vossik's life as the sergeant tried to fight free of the magery and save the boy, his own disbelief that it was real, that this could happen, his terror. He blinked against the tears that ran down his face, trying his best to tell it all, every detail. "I was still holding my sword out, and he said, 'Now! Like this!' and reached out with both hands and pulled, and the blade went in and he died."

"You did not thrust?"

"No . . . I mean, maybe I should have, but I didn't. I couldn't move . . . and then when he had finished . . . died . . . I could move again."

"And then," his father prompted.

"The one who'd first spoken said they still had three bodies. I looked, and the others were walking forward, like—like those dolls on strings at the fairs." He told the rest of it, how he'd killed his own escort, because they were meant to capture him, bind him, so the injured Verrakai could transfer into his body.

Against his cheek, the wood felt warmer now but not hot, and the Marshal said nothing. It had been true—it had been Beclan's truth at the time, and he still hoped very hard that there had not been any alternative that anyone could have thought of, not just that *he* had not thought of.

"Sergeant Vossik was right," Beclan said. "It would have been better to die if that had been possible, but they weren't going to let me die. I remembered what people said about the attack on the king last winter, how even the Marshal-Judicar and my uncle could not move, how one magelord could hold four people motionless, and . . . and I was only one. I was scared." He felt the fear again, the sick tightness in his belly, the weakness of his knees . . . a fear worse than what he'd felt this day, he realized. Here, if he died, he would be killed by honorable men for an honorable reason, and he could trust that his body would not be used to hurt those he loved.

"Of death?" asked the Marshal.

"No," Beclan said. "Or . . . not mostly. I was afraid of being what they wanted me to be. A traitor. An agent of Liart. Any of that." He looked at his father. "They wanted me to do blood magery with Sergeant Vossik's blood and become one of them. They promised me . . . everything. Even the crown—two crowns, in fact. In my body, they would have killed you, sir, and contrived the deaths of the king, Rothlin, and Camwyn . . . but Father, I was saved by Gird."

"Gird." The Marshal's voice carried disbelief. "And just what makes you think that?"

"I prayed," Beclan said. "Their magery had forced me toward Vossik's blood—but then I saw his Girdish medallion. I touched it. It came away in my hand, and my mind cleared. I could stand up. Then their voices in my head were silent. They knew . . . somehow . . . and came at me with swords. They said . . . things. I fought; I was sure I would die."

"And you, a mere stripling boy, fought and killed two grown men, no doubt experienced swordsmen, as well as those in your escort?" Still that tone of disbelief.

"Gird helped me," Beclan said.

"Hmmph," the Marshal said. "*Something* gave you the power to kill so many and live unscathed. I am not convinced it was Gird, though the relic does not give you the lie. At least *you* think it was Gird."

"Were you tempted, Beclan, when they offered you the crown?" his father asked.

"I saw what they wanted me to see," Beclan said. He would die for this, he was now sure. "Visions—dreams—all bowing before me. 'You are strong,' the voice said. 'They are weak.'

But I . . . but you're my father, Rothlin's my brother, Mikeli is my cousin, as well as king."

"The king," said the Marshal. "To whom you feel yourself oathbound?"

"Yes," Beclan said. "I have not made my formal oath yet; I am not of age. But my father taught me from childhood that we owe the king our fealty, and I would not betray that oath."

"Um." That from the Knight of Gird.

"Would you swear that oath if your age were not at issue?" his father asked.

"Yes, sir. I would swear it before you and the High Marshal or before the king himself. But I know you do not wish to risk him."

"High Marshal?" His father looked past him.

"He has told the truth as far as he perceives it, or Gird's relic has lost its power. I sense no evil in him, but I wish we had a paladin's word on that. Can you recite the Ten Fingers, boy?"

"Yes, High Marshal." Beclan had learned the Ten Fingers as a boy in the family grange, and he rattled them off quickly.

"I would advise it," the High Marshal said. Beclan's father nodded, as did the other men.

"Leave him bound," the Knight of Gird said. "I don't want any surprises just in case that relic isn't accurate."

"Fine," Mahieran said. He looked past Beclan. "My lord . . ."

Beclan hardly had time to consider which lord this might be when his cousin the king walked past him and turned to face him. "Sir king," the High Marshal said, "Gird's relic reports him telling the truth."

"Beclan," the king said. His expression was grim.

"Sir king," Beclan said. His mouth went dry. He had not seen Mikeli since his brief report to him at the Autumn Evener; Rothlin had told him that Mikeli had changed after the assassination attempt; facing Beclan now was no boyish king but a full-grown man.

"You are below legal age for the full oath of fealty," the king said. "You would not normally be allowed to swear, and you cannot be required to. But hard decisions have been forced on me, and I cannot let my realm be jeopardized by evil I can prevent. The High Marshal declares that you are telling the truth and are not harboring a renegade Verrakai in your body. But until I personally take your oath, you must stay confined away from me and any other peers. I understand you find this confinement onerous—"

"Yes, sir king," Beclan said. "But I understand the reasons for it."

"Well, then." Mikeli's smile was more challenging than encouraging. "Do you wish to make your full oath? You will be held to it, I caution you, as if you were of age. Should you breach it, you will be guilty of treason, and will face the same fate as other traitors."

Beclan wanted to ask if this meant he could go home, back to that familiar, safe place, with his family, but he knew he must not ask, only answer. "I will swear," he said.

"Free him," the king said to the others.

"Sir king—" The knight got his protest out first.

"The full oath requires that he kneel and that his hands be free," the king said. "In a roomful of us, alert and aware, I choose to trust Gird and the High Lord will aid you should anything happen."

The High Marshal unbound his hands; Beclan's father unbound his ankles and helped him stand. The Royal Guard commander and the Knight of Gird stood either side of Mikeli while Beclan's father cleared space with one of the chairs set near the fireplace at the far end of the room; Mikeli sat there.

Beclan took a few awkward steps to get the stiffness out while the men lined up on either side of the open space, as if it were the great hall in Vérella. Mikeli nodded, and Beclan walked forward and knelt, placing his hands in the king's. Once more Gird's relic touched his cheek, and a sword tip as well. He did not know whose; he did not look around.

Mikeli led him through the oath phrase by phrase; it was not the time to brag that he knew the whole thing. Mikeli's hands holding his were more callused than he expected, and he scolded himself for that errant thought. Finally it was done, and he himself, in his own name and person, had pledged hand and heart to the king's person, to live and die by the king's command. Beclan was not sure what he felt. "Rise, Beclan Mahieran, cousin and dear to me as a brother," the king said, standing as he said it. Beclan clambered to his feet. Mikeli pulled him into an embrace and pounded his back. "We can't afford to lose any of us, cousin. But I have one final test."

"Yes, sir king," Beclan said.

"Suppose I bid you stay here, as you were."

Beclan bit back the protest he would have made a quarter-year ago with little effort. "I would say I am yours to command, sir king."

"Good. Gentlemen, let us sit down and have a meal. I need to discuss those matters we spoke of with Beclan."

As the men rearranged chairs, the Royal Guard commander went into the kitchen, leaving the door open behind him. Duke Mahieran took Beclan aside. Beclan saw tears in his father's eyes. "I was afraid I'd lose you, boy. I still can't figure out how you survived as yourself, but—" Mahieran shook his head, saying nothing more as the Royal Guard commander and the cook carried in food and plates and utensils.

They sat down to a hearty meal; Beclan realized that they must have brought some of the food with them. He had a knife at his place now.

"We want to use you as bait," Mikeli said. "Word that you might have been invaded by a Verrakai has spread . . . and if there are other Verrakai still loose—as there may well be—they will want to find you, free you from confinement, and thus we may capture them. The schedule of communication would be the same. In case they attack a courier—which so far they have not done—your messages should be much as they have been, pleading for news, for release. Are you willing?"

Kept here as bait was far better than kept here as a suspected Verrakai traitor. He would have something important to do. "Yes, sir king."

His father said, "We could not risk a smaller party, yet we cannot conceal this visit entirely. However, the king came to Mahieran estates to commiserate with me about your situation; he rode in Royal Guard guise from the house to here. The old woman knows he's here; the guards outside do not."

"You want me to just wait here?"

"Not entirely as you were," Mikeli said. "You have an assignment now—and you will have weapons. You should not display them, certainly not wear them outside, but you will have them. And you won't have to let someone else cut up your food." Now Mikeli's grin was mischievous; Beclan grinned in response.

"You will stay the night, sir king?"

"No. We must go back to the estate house after the unsuccessful hunt I insisted on." Mikeli paused, then went on. "Beclan, most of what I know about you, I heard from your brother Rothlin. You should know that Roth stood up for you from the first. But the changes that come to a young man your age are such that they could be mistaken for something else. I'm sorry we had to be so hard on you. You cannot know how glad I am you are safe."

Beclan said, "Thank you, my lord."

"There have been indications of some searching for this place," his father said. "Strangers seen about the place, on the roads. But they faded into the woods. So I think there will be someone coming. We do not intend to expose you to the same danger again. We have more Royal Guard, all Girdish, all bearing relics. There will be a High Marshal on guard day and night. It will look as if they're keeping you under guard and hidden, but it should be possible to contain them, the High Marshal thinks."

"They are strong," Beclan said. He could not describe what he meant in words they would understand, he saw by their expressions. "They . . . say things," he said. He pushed his fear aside. His father—his father and the king—trusted him; he must be the man they thought he was.

FROM THEN ON, though the old woman still cooked his meals, she now invited Beclan into the kitchen and treated him as she might a grandson. "Just call me Granna Surn," she said. "Or Granna . . . doesn't matter." She was a little deaf; he had to speak loudly to make himself heard. He hoped that meant she'd not heard his cries when he dreamed.

Beclan had not hung about the kitchens or chatted with women servants since he was a small boy, so her stories and sayings were all new to him. She seemed to have a connection to the past very different from the formal histories and family traditions of his own family and those of other peers.

"And I says to Colm, that's my sister's youngest, you know, if you want to be liked, you have to like others, but he's proud as a young lord, beggin' your pardon, my lord, I don't mean you, and it doesn't do for him, bein' as he is only a forester's son on a lord's estate. So he says there's more than one way to like others, and next thing you know there's a girl expectin' her first and he's the one made the dance with her and now there's no more of his nonsense." She pushed a platter toward him. "You have another one of those stuffed rolls, my lord, you're too thin for a lad your age."

She was as different from Farin Cook at Dorrin's house as could be, but they shared an earthy practicality. Now that he was allowed in the kitchen, she insisted on teaching him how to wash his own socks and clucked with annoyance when he admitted he'd never learned to darn a sock, knit a scarf, or so much as sew on a button or mend a rip. Cackling with glee, she pushed the implements at him: the darning egg, the knitting needles, the sewing needle—which she threaded for him only once.

He stabbed his thumb repeatedly, sewing a button on for the first time. Granna Surn shook her head, put a dab of something black and gooey on it, and the pain vanished. She didn't answer when he asked what it was. His first try at plain knitting produced a lumpy mess. She made him pull it out again. He had never imagined the skill that went into knitting even a scarf, let alone a sock, but not many days after that, he was knitting a tube on four needles, amazing himself. Still, he was glad his brother and the other young men—and the king— didn't know what he was doing. He was sure they'd never knitted anything.

And yet he had seen Dorrin's troops busy with the same tools. Sergeant Vossik had explained that soldiers must be able to maintain equipment and uniforms; he'd given Beclan a sharp glance that Beclan had ignored. Those tasks were for common soldiers, he'd told himself; now, in his shame, he did his best to learn what the old woman taught him.

Then one night he woke in the dark, touched by the same

pressure he had felt before. Fear chilled him. They were near—and no alarm had been given outside. Were all the Royal Guard dead or spelled into sleep? He pulled on his clothes without lighting a candle, choosing the soft-soled low boots he wore inside the house. It was only two strides—he'd practiced this—to the peg where his sword belt hung. He wrapped it around, snugged it, and loosened the sword in its scabbard.

All those times, pacing through the rooms, up and down the stairs . . . he knew the distance to wall, window, cupboard, stairs. He eased across to the opening and then down, knowing which treads creaked, which didn't. But where was best? If no one remained to help him, where should he wait? Surprise, Dorrin Verrakai had told the squires, was a sovereign military virtue. *Be where the enemy does not expect you,* she had said.

Where would they expect him? If himself, and not one of them in his body, they would expect him in bed. If one of them, they would expect him to know they were coming . . . and he did know. For an instant, he went cold all over. He knew—as they would have known. Did this mean he harbored evil even though the Marshal had said he did not? Was he contaminated, after all, at some level a Marshal could not detect? But though he felt the touch of their magery, he felt revulsion, not attraction. Would they know that?

And could he stand against them? He had done so once, but—this felt subtly different.

CHAPTER TWENTY-FIVE

Tsaia: River Road

DORRIN VERRAKAI, SUMMONED to Vérella at the king's command, met Duke Mahieran riding east with a contingent of Mahieran troops. Her first thought was for Beclan—she had heard nothing but that he had been returned to his family. Exactly what had happened, she did not know, except that Beclan had been found alive and all with him were dead. With Daryan and his father at odds over his healing by a Kuakgan, she hoped that Beclan's continued absence did not mean anything dire. She also hoped Mahieran did not blame her for whatever had happened to Beclan.

"Well, Duke Verrakai," he said, halting as he came near. "So you are on your way to meet the king." It was a cold day with a biting wind, but his voice was colder.

"At his command," Dorrin said. "How is Beclan faring? Was he wounded? I have heard nothing definite."

Mahieran's mouth tightened, then he said, "He appears well. Do you truly know nothing?"

"Nothing but that he alone survived some kind of attack. Sir Flanits—the Royal Guard commander—sent only a brief note. I had asked him to find Beclan and escort him safely to Harway, and apparently Beclan wasn't where I thought he would be. The commander was quite annoyed."

"Why did you leave him alone?"

That stung. "He wasn't 'alone.' He had an escort of twenty militia, five of them experienced soldiers, headed by a sergeant with years of experience in Phelan's Company."

"Only six were found with him, all dead—"

"And he alive and unwounded—so it seems to me they protected him well."

"Perhaps." Mahieran sighed and waved his troops back, out of earshot. "Let me tell you his story as briefly as I can—we would have asked you, when you got to Vérella, what you thought, but perhaps it is better here, with fewer listening ears."

What he related seemed incredible to Dorrin. The first part, Beclan's decision to deviate from the assigned route, she could well believe. And the Kuakgan had told her of trapping some wandering Verrakaien in a treehold. Certainly she could believe those Verrakaien would try to take over Beclan's body; that was exactly what she'd feared, why she'd sent the Royal Guard to find and guard him. But the rest, from Beclan's resistance to his current situation, set up as bait to lure other Verrakaien—

She stared at Duke Mahieran; she could not believe he'd been so stupid. "You did *what*?!"

Mahieran lifted his chin. "I doubled the number of guards, and he's perfectly safe—"

"He is *not*," Dorrin said. "You've had him in the same remote place for near a quarter-year—since before Midwinter, and it's now past half-Evener. Easy to find anyone in that time. And as for guards—it would be no harder to immobilize or put to sleep fifty than one. Did you learn *nothing* from that attempt on the king's life?"

"Duke Verrakai!"

"He is your son," Dorrin said, ignoring his anger as her own rose, "and if you want him dead, then I cannot stop you. But I tell you that he is not safe no matter how many ordinary guards you have around him. It is not merely my relatives who may come but Bloodlord priests . . . Had you even thought of that?"

"No. But we killed them—"

"You killed those you found in Vérella. Do you think that is all in the whole of Tsaia? Or that they might not come over the mountains from the south? Do you know their powers? We fought some of them in Aarenis, Kieri and I; it took a paladin to hold one at bay."

"So . . . what do you suggest, since you know so much about this evil?" From his tone, he still distrusted her.

"You need a paladin, not just a Marshal, and you need a magelord. Or more than one magelord."

"You are the only one we know of," Mahieran said. "And we are not sure of you."

Dorrin stared him in the face. "Do you still think I connived to harm your son?"

"I don't—I don't know. You're—how can I know you're not charming me now? How could I tell if you lied?"

Dorrin controlled her voice with an effort. "Do you trust Kieri? The king? You did once . . ."

"Before I knew he was half-elf. I don't know what powers he has, save that I've heard they are great. And he's your friend; he has spoken in defense of you. The two of you together could overpower me."

"My lord . . . I am at a loss. You supported me when that attempt was made on the king's life—"

"And perhaps I was wrong to do so."

"Our king is alive," Dorrin said. "His brother is alive. Why do you doubt that my actions then saved them?"

Mahieran grimaced. "It could have been a ploy—"

"To do what? I don't want the throne. I have never wanted a throne."

"But there is a crown in Vérella you say talks to you. A crown and regalia. And the necklace went missing from Fin Panir—"

"If I was willing to give up the crown, why do you think I would hire someone to steal a necklace?"

"I don't—I don't know." Perspiration glistened on his brow in spite of the cold. "I don't understand you, and that's the truth. You're not . . . you're not like other dukes. You're not like other women. You've killed—"

"Yes," Dorrin said. "And I have saved. Including our king."

"Celbrin says"—Celbrin, Mahieran's wife, who had been no more than formally polite at the coronation and cooler yet at Autumn Court—"you are a man in a woman's body, quite possibly invaded as a child, and have no memory of it."

"If I had been so invaded," Dorrin said, "the invader would

know—and my life would have been very different. I would have been like the other Verrakaien."

"Unless it was a long-laid plan. Or she says perhaps you're sisli—"

Dorrin let out an incredulous noise before she could stop it. "Sorry, my lord Mahieran, but in the first place, no, and in the second place, what difference would that make?"

He was flushed with embarrassment now but plowing ahead. "She says it's unnatural, that you've had no lovers, no husband—"

"Uncommon, yes," Dorrin admitted. "But neither has Paksenarrion—does your wife despise her?"

His gaze shifted aside. "She doesn't want to meet her. She says she's not worthy to be in a paladin's presence."

That would be true, Dorrin thought, if indeed Mahieran's lady thought all women with swords were unnatural.

"And she says the other women feel the same." Mahieran stopped short at that, brow furrowed.

Frustration edged Dorrin's tone. "So—the noble ladies distrust me because I'm not like them, is that it? And use their pillow wiles to work against me?"

Mahieran glared at her. "It's more than that. We are not ruled by our wives, Duke Verrakai. We have our own concerns about you."

"Sufficient that you would risk your son's life—and possibly more than that—should he be successfully invaded?"

"He won't be. He withstood them before."

"He withstood one attack, yes. You have much to be proud of in that. Verrakaien renegades, one of them badly wounded, trapped and away from any other resource. No way to access blood magery. Even so, formidable for anyone to defeat. But what he may face could well be much greater than that. A planned attack by those knowing the disposition and nature of the guards you set—"

"How would they know?"

Dorrin wanted to shake him. "Does your wife know?"

"Yes, of course. But Celbrin would never—"

"Never tell a friend not to worry, because you had set plenty of guards? She talks to other women about me. How much

more likely it is she talks to other women about her children?"
His expression shifted from angry denial to thought. Dorrin
went on. "Somewhere, Duke Mahieran, there is more treason
to be found, and someone may have connections to your wife
you do not know. That she does not realize are dangerous."

"I suppose . . ." His voice trailed away. "But she would
never do anything to hurt Beclan."

"Not intentionally, no," Dorrin agreed, though to her mind
Celbrin Mahieran was as likely a traitor as anyone else. "But
you do not know what she said to whom, or what those other
women said to their other friends, even their servants." She
watched the expression on his face as it shifted and dared to go
further. "And if there is a traitor still in the nobility whom you
have not unmasked, what better way to gain information than
by sympathetic questions from wife to wife, friend to friend?
Verrakaien women, as well as men, were trained to evil; so no
doubt were some among their allies."

Duke Mahieran chewed his lower lip for a moment. "Do you
really think Beclan's in serious danger?"

"I do. They have had ample time to locate where you have
held him, ample time to make a plan and carry it out."

"I wish it were not you alone who could intervene," he said.
His gaze went past her to the wintry landscape and then came
back, a piercing look.

Dorrin shook her head. "I cannot do it alone, my lord. But I
can do what no one else but a paladin can do, and we have
seen no paladins of late. I would have thought, with Pargun
invading Lyonya, that Paks might come, but she did not."

He squeezed his eyes shut, as if that would help him think,
and then opened them again. "Well. I will try to fix my mind
on your better deeds and your better traits, Duke Verrakai, and
put out of thought your treacherous family and the concerns
others have had. But if Beclan dies—"

"If Beclan dies before we arrive, it is not my fault," Dorrin
said. "I will do my best if he is alive then, but I can promise no
more than that."

"I want to believe you," Mahieran said. "But it is hard . . .
Serrostin's son with green blood in his veins . . ."

"But not a cripple," Dorrin said. She was tired of apologiz-

ing for Daryan, when the lad himself was delighted to have
nimble legs and a usable thumb growing ever stronger. He'd
told her he hoped the other thumb would bud as well. His family would just have to accept it.

THE SHORTEST WAY across country would take too long,
Mahieran insisted. Dorrin was equally insistent that they not
approach by the direct route from the Mahieran country house.
They compromised, taking the River Road west, then a forest
track Mahieran knew that bypassed his home and led to another that approached the cottage from the east. They had with
them Mahieran's personal guard, ten of his household troops;
he had refused her suggestion of a Royal Guard contingent.
Dorrin hoped it would be enough.

On the second day, Mahieran would have stopped at dusk to
camp again. Dorrin insisted they ride on. They reached the
outer ring of guards at the turning of night. No one answered
the hail, and with only a little searching they found the first
bodies, garroted. "Holy Gird help us," Mahieran said.

Dorrin touched her ruby, calling on Falk. The ruby glowed.
"They're still here," she said. "In the cottage, and soon they
will know I am here. Speed and surprise is Beclan's only chance
now. They expect no visitors." She dismounted, pulled off her
spurs, and put them in the saddlebag. They tied the horses;
Dorrin tried a soothing spell on them; she was not sure it
would work. "My lord," she said, "this is now a military problem. I ask your leave to take command."

"Very well," he said, and nodded to his men.

The inner ring of guards also lay dead; the attackers had
made no attempt to hide the bodies. Dorrin murmured her orders and could only hope they'd be followed. They hurried on
and were almost at the cottage when the first scream wavered
through the night. The cottage, a dim shape in the snowy clearing, showed a dark gap where a door stood open. Around the
corner, light streaked the snow from another open door. Another shriek came from there.

"Granna Surn, the cook," Mahieran muttered.

"This door," Dorrin said quietly. She waved the tensquad
around to the other. Mahieran plunged forward; she caught

him by the sleeve. "Carefully," she said. "May be trapped."
Probably not, since the attackers expected no interference, but
if they'd sensed her before she realized it—she flattened herself against the wall on one side of the door and eased her
sword into the black gap. No reaction from inside.

She moved in and heard Mahieran's harsh breathing behind
her. When she felt the first touch of magery from another, she
immediately called her light. There in the main room of the
cottage two red-masked figures—priests of Liart—had hold of
Beclan's arms and were dragging him toward the door that led
into the kitchen. Beclan wasn't struggling, but she didn't think
he was dead. Dorrin tried to hold them still, but Duke Mahieran
pushed past her to attack. The priests dropped their grip on
Beclan; his head hit the floor with a hollow thunk. One of the
priests threw a spiked ball at her, then drew his barbed sword.
As fast, Dorrin caught the ball on her buckler. Mahieran, in a
blind rage or panic, had tried to stab the nearest red-masked
figure but instead took a swipe from the man's blade that
parted his clothes and drove his mail into his shield arm.

Dorrin parried Mahieran's attacker's blade just in time. She
moved close to the Duke, but he was already moving again.
Mahieran had never fought in formation; he had no idea how
to work with her, how to let her protect his injured side while
fending off attacks with his blade.

"And now we have all of you," one of the priests said. He
sounded confident. Perhaps he had not detected the tensquad.
"The boy will be ours . . . and the two of you as well."

"No," Dorrin said. "You cannot force Falk from my heart."

"Or Gird from mine," Mahieran said. Though he'd lost his
buckler, he now had a dagger in his heart-hand. Nonetheless,
his face streamed with sweat, and his hands trembled.

Dorrin could feel the waves of hatred coming off the two
priests, but they did not slow her. Protecting Duke Mahieran
did; he was clearly not immune to attacks of blood magery
that affected his body if not his spirit. She stamped, signaling
him to advance with her.

Just as they moved, a clamor broke out in the kitchen. One
of the priests glanced aside; Dorrin lunged, parrying the other's blade with her buckler. The jagged edge caught on the

buckler and jerked her arm aside, but her blade went home in the priest's knee. He staggered sideways, his blade flailing wide; the other one's dagger grazed her shoulder, raking the mail beneath her clothes.

She whirled, staying low and tried to free her buckler from the first's blade, but he was yanking at it, jerking her off balance. "Get that—" she said to Mahieran as the other priest's dagger thrust at her again. Then she dropped her buckler as her own opponent yanked and drew her dagger as he staggered back, both arms flailing. Her sword went home in his neck this time.

Before she could turn to help Mahieran with the other priest, the fight in the kitchen spilled into the main room—two more she recognized as Verrakaien backing away from Mahieran troops, all hampered by the kitchen and its furniture, the narrow door between rooms. She got one of the Verrakaien in the back; the other, turning to meet her attack, was caught in the side by one of the Mahieran troops. The troops moved immediately toward their duke; Dorrin focused on the remaining Verrakai in the kitchen, whose magery felled one of the troops as she watched.

When the melee was over, Mahieran clutched at his sword arm. Blood soaked his sleeve, dripped from his hand. Beclan lay, still unconscious, with blood beneath him. The two priests and both Verrakaien were dead—she hoped—but so was the old woman in the kitchen. She had been burned with the kitchen poker—the screams they'd heard—and killed during the fight by a sword stroke. Of the tensquad, eight were wounded, three seriously. Counting all the dead outside, the enemy had sold their lives dear.

Dorrin felt no triumph, only grim satisfaction. With the two unwounded men of the Mahieran squad helping, she bound Mahieran's wound and then tended the others. Duke Mahieran had lost a lot of blood; he closed his eyes as they laid him down and seemed to drift off. The pool of blood under Beclan proved to be from one of the Liartian priests, not his own, though he had a lump on the back of his head and now a darkening bruise where his head had hit the floor.

"Will he live?" one of the men asked her, nodding at Beclan.

"I don't know," Dorrin said. She stripped off her gloves and touched his head gently. Her hands tingled. Would she be given healing for him? "One of you—are the doors closed and secured? Someone posted to give warning?"

"But—but it's over—we're safe—"

"That's what the Royal Guard outside thought," Dorrin said. "This may not be all of them; we don't know. Close the doors—make up the fire—and one of you see if there's hot water in the kitchen—if not, put a kettle on. We need heat and light." She looked around. Those with minor wounds were sitting or leaning against the wall. One had only one bandage. She pointed. "You—we need to get Beclan out of these wet clothes and warm. Go upstairs and see if there are blankets or a straw tick we can use."

"Carry him up?"

"No. Too dangerous until I know all that's wrong with him." The man nodded and headed for the stairs.

Should she try to heal him now? With his father unconscious as well, with the suspicious eyes of those who did not trust her watching every move? She had helped the Marshal-General with Duke Marrakai's similar injury, but— Beclan groaned a little, and then his whole body stiffened. She knew what would come next.

"What are you doin' to him?" one of the soldiers asked her.

"Nothing but feeling the lumps on his head," she said. "But if I don't try a healing—" Beclan convulsed, something she'd seen before with head injuries. "This will kill him."

"Then make it stop," the man said, pulling out his dagger.

"If you kill me," Dorrin said, meeting his gaze, "he will certainly die. You cannot heal him." With that, she ignored him, letting the power flow out of her hands and praying—trusting—that Falk's goodwill guided it. Beclan went limp; Dorrin closed her eyes, wishing there'd been any period in that tumultuous year when she could have learned more about healing. How could she tell if—when—Beclan was healed unless he opened his eyes and sat up?

After a time she felt herself drifting into darkness, an empty husk blown along a forest floor. Then nothing.

When she next opened her eyes, daylight came through the cottage windows. She was on the floor of the main room, wrapped in a blanket, and she had scarcely strength to move a hand. "She's awake," she heard someone say. And then, "Can you sit up?"

"No." Someone behind her lifted her shoulders and pushed a support behind her; she felt dizzy for a moment, but that eased. She looked around. The bodies of the dead had been removed, the blood scoured from the floor. Duke Mahieran lay on blankets, as did Beclan. Both appeared to be sleeping; she saw them breathe.

"You fell over," one of the men said. "But they're alive."

"Paladins don't get weak when they heal," another said. "At least that's what the Marshal says."

"Want some sib?" asked yet another.

"Thank you." Dorrin wormed a hand out of the blanket to take the mug offered her. Sib—hot and thick, a soldier's brew—cleared her head, though not all of her memory. She could feel strength returning. She freed her other arm. "What was the housekeeper's name?"

"My lord?"

"The woman who died. Who was she?"

"I—I don't know—"

"Surn," said another. "She was nearly blind."

"Where is her body?"

"On the kitchen table, my lord, where they were hurting her."

Dorrin unwrapped the blanket and clambered to her feet, stiff and aching. She had not noticed her own minor wounds at the time, but the soldiers had bound them up after she fell. She'd taken worse in her years as a mercenary.

In the kitchen, the soldiers had laid a tablecloth over Surn after straightening her limbs. "The only thing is, my lord, you said build up the fire—it's so warm in here." It was hot, and it smelled like death. Dorrin's stomach churned.

"Is there a shed, some protected place in the cold we could lay her safe?"

"A woodshed only. But it's nearly empty." The man looked at her, hesitating, clearly waiting for orders.

"We'll use that. Find us a plank or a hurdle."

"Yes, my lord." He hurried out and returned in a few minutes with a plank. They moved Surn's body to the plank and carried the old woman's remains out to the woodshed.

Once Surn's body was out of the kitchen, Dorrin could see that the soldiers had done their best to clean it up. Considering only two of them were unwounded and they'd had the wounded to look after as well, she commended their work. "But we need to eat," she said. "All of us. Which of you is the best cook?"

Feet shuffled. "Um . . . my lord . . . don't none of us know how. Only sib."

Dorrin had not expected this. All the mercenaries learned at least some rough cooking. But from their expressions, these had not.

"I will, then." On the hob, Surn had set grain to soak overnight for breakfast porridge and beans for some later meal. Dorrin washed her hands in hot water (they had at least been able to boil water) and set to work. First the porridge pot onto the fire, then a check of the pantry. Surn must have baked the day before: there were three and a half round loaves on a shelf. That was a mercy, but it wasn't enough if they had to stay more than a day.

The sizzle and smell of frying bacon and sausage drove away the other smells and soon brought the less-wounded to the kitchen. Dorrin set one of the men to slicing bread and another to chopping onions and mushrooms; she put those in a frying pan and set them to the fire. A third she told to stir the porridge.

"He's waked up," someone called from the other room. Dorrin left the pan of mushrooms and onions, now beginning to sizzle, and looked through. Duke Mahieran and Beclan both had their eyes open; Beclan was speaking to his father.

"Breakfast soon," Dorrin said, and turned back to the cooking. Let them think what they would; they were alive. The shift from warrior to healer to cook suddenly seemed funny to her, and she chuckled.

"What, my lord?" asked one of her helpers.

"We're all alive," she said. "And we have food to eat and a fire to cook it on. Isn't that something to rejoice in?"

"I suppose . . ." He eyed her warily as he sliced into another loaf.

Porridge, sausage, bacon, bread, honey from the jar in the larder, dried fruit . . . Dorrin set it out on the table, and while the soldiers carried food to those in the other room, she took one of the raggedly cut slabs of bread, dipped honey onto it, and ate. Then she went to speak with Duke Mahieran.

Though pale from blood loss, he looked in no danger of dying, and he had an appetite . . . he was halfway through the bowl of porridge already. Dorrin made a pad of the blanket she'd been wrapped in and sat on the floor near him.

"A bloody business," he said. "Too many lives lost. But at least Beclan's alive and himself." He glanced at Beclan, who nodded at Dorrin, his mouth full of bread. "He is, isn't he?" Mahieran asked softly.

"He is indeed," Dorrin said; she had sensed nothing evil in him from the first. Nor would the enemy have nearly killed one of their own. "He was not invaded." As Mahieran's face relaxed, she said, "My lord, I'm afraid I must remind you that we are not safe yet."

"You think there are more?"

"There might be. The worst of this is that I do not know—no one knows but themselves—how many are left, of either Verrakaien or the Bloodlord's priests. We must get you and Beclan back to the safety of your home—however safe it may be— and more than that ensure the safety of the king. But eight of your soldiers left alive are wounded, and three cannot travel."

"One will have to go and take word that we need help," Mahieran said. Then he grimaced. "No . . . if they are waiting, they'd simply kill him."

"Exactly," Dorrin said. "We must travel together when we go, or stay together when we cannot travel."

"If we had carts—"

"They brought provisions in a cart," Beclan said. "And surely the outer guards have carts."

"The outer guards are all dead," Mahieran said. "At least— we believe so; the ones we found were dead."

"But the carts might still be there," Dorrin said. "Maybe

even animals to pull them. We'll look." She pushed herself up, wincing at the various pains.

"My lord, you should rest."

"There isn't time," Dorrin said. "Or you'll be suffering from my attempt at making bread, because Surn's won't last the day. My cook taught the Verrakai children to bake this year, but I was too busy. I can fry things or boil them, but not bake."

The two able-bodied soldiers went out with Dorrin to search. They found more bodies, a mutilated horse— "They used it for blood magic," Dorrin said—two hitch lines of horses, and five two-wheeled farm carts. Despite the need for haste, Dorrin paused beside each dead Royal Guard to say a prayer. As the soldiers gathered the horses and hitched some to the carts, Dorrin tried to think how to move the bodies, but there were too many. In the end, they dragged them into groups and covered them with branches for protection until a larger burial party could retrieve them.

Slowly—too slowly for Dorrin—horses, carts, and some provisions from the Royal Guards' camp arrived at the cottage. By then it was well after midday, and the beans and beef she'd started after breakfast were ready.

"No, we can't make the house by dark, not starting this late," Mahieran said. He had slept awhile; Beclan, whose only injuries had been to his head, was now up and around. He had brought down all the rest of the bedding and warm clothes from the upper story, and without being asked had taken on the job of cleaning up dishes and pots in the kitchen.

"Then we should leave tomorrow," Dorrin said. She went outside again; the bodies of the Verrakaien and the priests still lay in a heap. They should be burned, she knew from Paks, to dispel any lingering evil. When she put a torch to them, the flames leapt up as if she had poured oil on the bodies. Flame and smoke whirled, making dire shapes. Dorrin stood watching until the flames died down and the ash blew away on a clean north wind.

Nothing happened in the night; Dorrin slept soundly and woke at first light. She roused the others, then started breakfast in the kitchen. By full daylight, the more able-bodied were packing to leave. They had ample horses—the Royal Guard horses, except for the dead one, as well as those they'd brought. Provisions could be packed on the unridden horses; the carts would carry the wounded. Beclan insisted he could ride and helped with the packing. Dorrin didn't argue with him, but exchanged glances with his father, who shrugged.

Before midmorning, the little caravan started for Mahieran's country home. Surn's body rode alone in one cart. Duke Mahieran rode alone in another, swathed in blankets and cushioned on straw, and six of the injured soldiers rode in the other three.

They did not stop except to rest the horses and in the dusk met the first outer guards of the household. A messenger rode on to alert the household that the Duke was on the way.

When they reached the house, torchlight glittered on the snow outside and the house windows blazed with light. Servants came with a padded chair to carry the Duke inside; Beclan started to follow and then looked back at Dorrin. "My lord?" he said just as his mother, Celbrin, appeared, wrapped in a fur cape.

She grabbed Beclan and hugged him, then turned to Duke Mahieran. "If *that person* is out there in the dark, I will not have *that person* in my house! She nearly killed our son—and now you come home injured—"

"If by 'that person' you mean Duke Verrakai, she is welcome here as my guest," Mahieran said.

"You can't mean that! And I won't have it." She pushed past Beclan to scream at Dorrin. "You sent your own mother to her death; you killed your own father. You nearly killed my son and the Duke! You should have been killed with the rest of the Verrakai—better ones died and you still live!"

Before Dorrin could speak or move, Celbrin yanked a long curved knife from under her cape and thrust it at Dorrin. Only the years of training and war made it possible to flinch aside; the knife grazed her shoulder but did not penetrate her mail.

"I'll kill you!" Celbrin said, lunging again. But Beclan had moved, grabbing her arm and pulling her away. "Let me go!" she cried, flailing at him with her empty hand.

"No," Beclan said. He took hold of her other arm, and held her firmly.

"Then she's enchanted you—"

"She's saved my life," Beclan said. "And Father's. It was not her fault."

"Drop the knife, Celbrin," Mahieran said. He waved servants forward. "Take it, if she will not drop it."

"You will find out!" Celbrin said, her voice still high and shrill. "She is not what she pretends to be. She brings doom with her." She spat at Dorrin, but the gobbet fell short. Beclan turned her around, and servants moved in to take the knife and force her up the steps and into the house.

"You *are* welcome here," Mahieran said. "You saved Beclan and me, and whatever Celbrin feels—"

"I would not intrude," Dorrin said. "You have outbuildings. I have slept on hay many a night. I can stay there overnight and leave at dawn."

"No," Mahieran said. "We have much to discuss—what other dangers you foresee, how best to meet them. I will not lose the value of your experience and knowledge, or so ill repay what you have done for me and mine to satisfy her. And I need to know what set her on this road."

"Fear for her son. Fear for you."

"Not alone. As you suggested. Please, as my fellow peer, enter my house and take refreshment and rest."

Dorrin hesitated, but it would be an insult to Mahieran—to the royal house—if she refused. She was tired and in pain. A bath, a night's sleep . . . She bowed slightly and went up the stairs; the servants carried the Duke in his chair through the wide doorway and shut the great leaves of the doors behind them both.

Mahieran's house was larger than her own and far more luxuriously appointed. Mahieran ordered his servants to carry him into his study and another servant to summon his physician. Dorrin followed him, as he asked her to do, and found herself in a large room with a fireplace at one end.

More servants brought food and drink and at Mahieran's orders poured mugs of sib for them both.

"Father, I told her maid to give Mother a quieting draught," Beclan said as he came into the room. "I went with her to her chambers and tried to talk to her, but she burst into tears and would not answer me."

"Thank you," Mahieran said. "And now will you take care of ensuring that Duke Verrakai has a room far away from your mother and that it is prepared for her?"

"Yes, sir," Beclan said. He looked at Dorrin. "My lord, I will have your baggage taken there unless you wish it elsewhere."

"Thank you," Dorrin said.

"My lord Duke, I hear that you are injured." This was a physician by his gown. One shoulder bore the Mahieran crest, and his robe was belted with crimson. Behind him, servants carried his paraphernalia.

"We both are, Gans," Mahieran said. "Duke Verrakai sustained wounds in the same engagement."

"Yours are more serious, my lord," Dorrin said.

"We shall see," the physician said. He attended Mahieran first, however, tut-tutting over the most serious wound. He offered Mahieran numbwine before he started, but Mahieran refused with a quick glance at Dorrin. She hoped he wasn't making a competition out of bearing pain. Soon the sharp smell of herbs steeping in hot water replaced the fragrance of the food the servants brought. Mahieran ate one-handed while the surgeon worked on his arm.

"Not too much, my lord," Gans said. "It's been long enough with only a field dressing to bring up a touch of fever. You'll drink this—" He offered Mahieran a goblet of water mixed with an infusion of herbs; Mahieran grimaced but drank it down. "—to purify the blood. Anything else?"

"No," Mahieran said. "Barring a few scratches."

"Scratches can go bad," the surgeon said in the voice of one who had said that many times before. Dorrin repressed a grin; he sounded so like the surgeons of Phelan's Company.

Then it was her turn. In the interim, she had eaten soup and bread and cheese and was thinking of starting on the slices of roast, but the surgeon had the servants move her table away. "First we see how bad yours are, my lady—er, my lord—and then I'll advise you."

"Bruises under the mail, but no skin broken there," Dorrin said. "I've got some cuts . . ."

He sighed, then cleaned the gashes she'd taken and laid herbs in them before wrapping them again. "It will do you no harm to have a dose as well," he said. "One of those has puffed up a bit. Hurts the least, I daresay."

"True," Dorrin said.

"You'll do better for restful sleep," Gans said. "But I suppose you won't take numbwine either."

"No, thank you," Dorrin said. "It turns my stomach."

"Then take your bitter brew and keep it down," Gans said, the corner of his mouth quirking. "I advise you both to keep to your beds a day. I don't expect either of you will agree."

"Hardly," Duke Mahieran said. "Not with the safety of the realm at stake. But I thank you for your care, Gans. See if my lady needs anything."

"Her maid came to me for a dose of numbwine when I was on my way here—I haven't yet—"

"Give it to her, by all means. She was overwrought with concern for Beclan and for me."

"Do not sit up late tonight, my lord. The safety of the realm can last until daylight." With a swirl of his robe, the physican was off again, snapping his fingers for servants to bring his things along.

"My apologies," Mahieran said. "He's—"

"He's a surgeon," Dorrin said. "The ones Kieri hired were all like that. Are you going to tell him about Beclan's injuries?"

"No. Don't want him fussing or questioning what you did to heal him. Boy seems fine to me." He turned to one of the servants standing along the wall. "I need to send word to Vérella—send my scribe and ready a courier. The rest of you may go." He turned back to Dorrin. "And now you and I can discuss what is best to tell the king."

When the servants had gone, Dorrin said, "My lord, if you would rather have no one else aware of what is in your message, I write a tolerable hand."

"You do not trust my scribe?"

"I do not know your scribe. Nor do I know how important secrecy is."

"Mmm. Well, this is what I plan to say: Mikeli has lost forty

Royal Guards to this adventure, Beclan is alive and unstained, and once more Mahieran owes a debt to Verrakai."

"Who owes a far larger one to the crown and to Mahieran," Dorrin said. "For I count the king's mercy outweighs all my deeds in one."

"Gracious words, and I do not doubt you mean them. But yet, Dorrin, my son lives as himself—as my son—because of you. Had we not arrived in time—"

"It does not bear thinking of," Dorrin said.

Once she finally had a bath and a bedroom—large and luxurious, both of them—with no servants about, Dorrin placed a chair before the door, eased into the nightshirt laid out for her, and lay awake a long time thinking about the implications of everything she had heard and seen. Sonder Mahieran's wife hated her: she could understand that as concern for Beclan.

But the slow poison that contaminated her relationship with the other peers and with the king had not started with the squires' injuries or even with the war . . . it had started long before. Rumors of the crown had preceded her to Vérella . . . that must have begun as soon as the king announced her as the new duke. She had not anticipated—even after the coronation, even after proof that her relatives still had the power to invade others—that they would also be working against her this way, seeking to isolate her, destroy her relationship with the king.

She should have seen that. She should have done . . . what? What could she have done? They already had a network of spies and tattlers; she had never developed any such thing. Her contacts had been in Aarenis, and few enough there. Arcolin had been the one to gather information; he had always been easy in any company, less reserved than she.

What you could not do, waste no time regretting. Kieri had said that to one of his squires; she had found it unexpectedly helpful then, when as a young woman she had worried so often that she should have done something about her family. And now . . . She fell asleep and woke the next morning to a soft knock on the door.

"A moment," she said. She would gladly have rested in that warm soft bed another turn of the glass. With a quick stretch, she slid from under the covers, swept the robe laid on a chair around her, and padded barefoot to the door. Moving the chair took only a moment.

"It's Beclan, my lord. I know it's early, but if I could have a word—"

"In a moment. I'll dress." When she let Beclan in, he wore his Verrakai squire's tunic with the Mahieran knots on his shoulder.

"What's this?" she said.

"I'm still your squire," he said. "I'm not going to abandon you and break the contract, no matter what Mother says."

"Beclan—"

"Unless you send me away. Please don't. Please, my lord, there's a reason—"

"And reasons I should send you away, as you surely realize. Your mother's hostility is only one of them."

"Please, my lord. Please listen."

He sounded truly distressed. Dorrin nodded. "Have a seat, Beclan. You must know that I have not heard the full story of what happened."

"Yes, my lord. I was wrong, to start with. I didn't listen to Sergeant Vossik . . ." He went through it all—she could tell he'd told it before—not sparing himself, admitting his mistakes and the pride behind them. She asked questions only to keep the narrative moving, when he seemed blocked by memories too vivid to bear, near the end.

"I should have died—he showed me how—but I was afraid they'd take me over even if I did. The way we'd heard about, like that groom at the coronation. They wanted to. They said so."

"How did you fight off the attack, Beclan?" Dorrin asked. She hoped her voice did not reveal her sudden fear.

"It must have been Gird, I think," Beclan said. "But there was something else, too. They offered—you can imagine what, if I would yield of my own choice. Vile ideas . . . the throne, in the end. They were in my head; they seemed to know that I'd thought Camwyn a fool often enough . . . thought myself a better younger brother for the king, had things been different. And I've been angry with Roth, for treating me like a child. They worked on that, hinting how easily he could die." He gulped; tears marked his cheeks. "But kill my own brother? Connive at his death? Never!"

"You stood fast," Dorrin said, to give him time to recover himself. "You have great courage, Beclan, worthy of your family."

"I have great stupidity, too," Beclan said. "Time after time, if I'd done what Sergeant Vossik told me, none of this would have happened. They wouldn't have died. *He* wouldn't have died."

"But Gird and your own courage saved you," Dorrin said. Surely it had to be that.

He flushed. "And . . . maybe something else. My lord, before you regained your magery, did you ever . . . *feel* things?"

The hair on her arms rose before she had time to think what this might mean. "Feel things?" she managed to say calmly.

"Yes, my lord. I could feel them in my head, the pressure—and then—it was like ice breaking, when the water pours out over the skin of it." His voice trembled as he went on. "I'm afraid . . . I'm afraid, my lord, that . . . that even if they didn't invade me, they forced me into magery."

Dorrin's mouth was dry. She got up, poured water from the pitcher by the bedside, and offered him a glass. He shook his head; she drank. "What did you do, Beclan?"

"I . . . I pushed back against them. And it seemed to get stronger . . . I didn't mean to . . ."

Her own magery, when she touched him with it, found his—weaker than hers, at least for now, but undoubtedly of the same origin.

"Did you kill them with it?" she asked.

"No. Well . . . I'm not sure." At her questioning glance, he went on. "They did something to my other men, as I said. I had to kill them; they were coming at me with nothing at all in their eyes. But they weren't very good, and I killed them with the sword . . . too easily. And the Verrakaien were pushing and pushing at me. They wanted me alive and unharmed, to be their pony, they called it. So they didn't attack me until the others were dead. Only the two could fight—and since they didn't want to harm me, at least not badly, I had the advantage. I killed one. Then the other fought me harder, but his sword broke. It—twisted in the air and broke. And I killed him and the other one on the ground. And then I was sick, over and over."

"Twisted in the air?" Dorrin said.

Beclan's hands clenched and relaxed. "I—I wanted it to slow down, not hit me. I was trying to resist—and I pushed— and—it didn't look natural, my lord."

"It wasn't natural," Dorrin said. "It was magery. And did you tell your father about this, or the king?"

"No, my lord. I knew I had not been invaded, but I thought— I hoped—that if I had used their magery or they had put magery in me, it was gone. Then when they came to the cottage— they called, and I woke."

"They called—"

"I knew it was magery, and evil, my lord. I knew it before I heard anything with my ears. They—they were calling me to come to them; they thought I had been invaded, that I was one of them."

"What did you do?"

"I tried to think what you would do; I started down the stairs, sword in hand, and I tried to do whatever it was I had done before with the magery."

"And?"

"The next thing I knew I was on the floor and you were falling over."

No more useful information, then. The blow had come out of the dark—physical, not magical. A fifth man in the house, someone who climbed into that window? Or had Beclan come down farther than he thought, easily struck from behind by someone in the lower room?

"But I have to know—do I really have that? What you have?"

"Yes," Dorrin said. "And I'm sorry. You do realize what this means—"

"Am I part Verrakaien? Mother is Konhalt; Konhalten are— were—Verrakaien supporters."

There it was, the connection she had suspected. Konhalten had intermarried with Verrakaien; the talent for magery could well have been passed that way. "Perhaps," Dorrin said. "That

I do not know. But one thing I know is that Mahieran was chosen for the throne because they'd lost their magery long before Gird's time. A minor house, then, considered lesser for that reason. Acceptable to the Girdish because they were without magery. And it's in the Tsaian Code: no one with the taint of magery shall succeed to the throne or be considered in the line of succession."

"I don't care about that," Beclan said.

"Your father will," Dorrin said. "Your father will care very much about that, and so will your mother. So, very likely, will the king."

She ran her fingers through her hair. What a mess this was. And she could see how easily she herself might be blamed for it. Beclan had been living in the home of an active magelord for almost half a year—had contact with her awakened his buried magery? Surely not . . . but who would believe that? And what about his mother? What was her role in this? Had she known what she carried? Had someone else, using her without her knowledge?

"Can't you get rid of it?" Beclan asked. "I don't want it. What if I do something bad by accident? Can't you do something—make it so I can't use it or something?"

"I don't know how, Beclan. The Knight-Commander of Falk did it to me, as a girl." He looked so miserable that she wanted to comfort him, but she had no comfort to give. "I don't know how he did it, so I don't know how to do it to you. But I do know we must tell your father."

"Will they—will they imprison me again?"

"I don't know. I hope not. I will argue against it, for what good that does. Is your father up yet?"

"No. But the cooks are."

"I need to finish here," Dorrin said. "Wait outside for me, and we will go down together. Speak of this to no one until we've talked to your father."

Downstairs they met a line of servants carrying platters of food to a dining room. Beclan led her back to his father's study. Light came from the open door, and they saw Duke Mahieran at his desk, frowning at a scroll. He looked up.

"Come in, come in. Early like me. My arm's sore; it woke me up. Gans has looked at it, advised me to stay in bed, but if I can't sleep, why lie abed? Shall we go in to breakfast, then? They're almost ready, I'm sure."

"There's a matter we must discuss before breakfast, my lord," Dorrin said.

"Before sib? Is that wise?" He smiled, but his eyes were wary.

"My lord, I deem it necessary," Dorrin said. "Beclan?"

Beclan looked like a child caught stealing sweets. "Please, my lord. You tell it."

"It's your story, Beclan. Your father should hear it from your lips. I will make my comments at the end."

It came more easily this time, Dorrin thought, as Beclan went through the tale again, this time leaving out all his mistakes and feelings of guilt—he must, she realized, have told his father those things before. He went straight to the battle with the Verrakaien in the Kuakkgani trap, describing their attack on his mind, their offer to give him great powers and make him king, his own struggle to keep from being invaded or persuaded.

"You said nothing of this when we visited you," Mahieran said. He was white around the lips, whether with shock or anger Dorrin could not tell. "You lied when you gave your oath—"

"No, my lord, I did not," Beclan said. "I thought then I had been mistaken in my earlier feeling . . . that Gird had given me whatever I used to defeat the Verrakaien. I had felt nothing like it since. And you had bade me say nothing but to answer questions."

"But when you felt it again—"

"It was when they came to attack the cottage. It woke me . . . I could tell what they wanted—"

"Though even those with no magery can know that sometimes," Dorrin put in. "Sergeant Stammel, blinded by a similar attack in Aarenis—Beclan saw him, in Vérella, last Autumn Court; I'm sure you heard about him. He had fought the invader, confining it helpless in his mind, but felt something inside trying to get free."

"Like your crown," Mahieran said.

"No. For Stammel, it was agony to resist that voice, to remain himself, agony finally resolved when I called out and destroyed the one who had invaded him. The crown has never hurt me. Go on, Beclan, tell the rest."

Beclan told about his attempt to push the others' magery out of his mind, his creeping down the stair in the dark, sword in hand, hoping to find the attackers slowed or immobilized. "And then Surn screamed, and I was angry and tried to go to her, help her—and that's all I remember."

"They would have known by that, if they didn't before, that he had not been suborned or invaded," Dorrin said to Mahieran. "And I've no doubt the blood magery they raised with that horse was enough to cloud his perceptions . . . giving them a chance to knock him on the head shortly before we came through the door."

Mahieran shook his head. "It can't be helped, can it? Not now. Beclan, you gave your full oath to the king, and you concealed this from him . . . that's treason."

"My lord, I did not understand, or certainly know, at the time, and I gave my oath in good faith. I know that having magery cuts me from the succession—I don't care about that—"

"I do," Mahieran said.

"And I know it casts a shadow on our family, presumed free of the taint since before Gird's day. I went to Duke Verrakai this morning to ask her to examine me, to find out whether I had magery or if it was something else, some other sense—"

"And?" Mahieran said, with a piercing glance at Dorrin.

"He has some magery, my lord," Dorrin said. "He is not invaded; there is no Verrakaien or other spirit inhabiting him. But he does have magery. It is not very strong. It is untrained, of course. It is my thought that in the extremity of his need, there in the Kuakkgani trap, Gird may have unlocked what had been locked in your family so long, just enough to save him."

"Are you saying I have it, too? That the king does?"

Dorrin shook her head. "Not you, my lord, and not the king. None of you that I met in Vérella seemed to me to have magery. Nor did Beclan until recently. Nothing in the time he spent with me as squire even hinted at it. In that you have other witnesses, my other squires, should you wish to ask them."

"But where could he have—oh." From Mahieran's face some thought had come to him that might explain it. "Celbrin is Konhalt, and Konhalt has intermarried with Verrakai more than any other house."

"That's what I told Duke Verrakai just now," Beclan said.

"Indeed." He looked at Beclan. "If your mother carried the seed of magery in herself . . . if you were born with it, but with no training . . ." Now he looked at Dorrin. "If a child is born with it, how does it show, and when? Could it be hidden so long without the child's knowledge? Could she have had it and not known it?"

"I do not know that much," Dorrin said. "In my family, we of the pure blood were all thought to carry the ability, but in different amounts. Without training, it could remain dormant, even wither, though in the strongest it would continue to grow."

"I want to find you innocent," Mahieran said to Beclan. "I want to find you my son, my honorable son whose oath was given freely and honestly, with a whole heart. But I must tell you, Beclan, that I am cold to the bone with the fear of this— fear of magery itself, fear of what it means for you and all of us. It could knock Mikeli off the throne, plunge the realm into chaos—"

"But *why*?" Beclan said. "I'm the only one—*he's* not—"

"And the only reason we know he's not is because Duke Verrakai here—a known magelord—says he's not. I believe her, but how many others will? You don't know, Beclan, of the rumors spread about her since the coronation. As with Duke Phelan before . . . and that just occurred to me. But think, lad: Bloodlord priests and Verrakaien renegades killing Royal Guards on our land. Do you not see what could be made of that?"

"No one will believe it of Mikeli," Beclan said, his jaw set.

"I think we should not discuss this outside this room until we've decided what's best," Dorrin said.

"You're right about that," Mahieran said. "Certainly not with any in the household. But we cannot long delay telling the king and the Marshal-Judicar."

* * *

THEY ATE BREAKFAST in near silence. Duke Mahieran's wife
did not appear, nor any of his daughters resident in the house.
Dorrin, Beclan, and the Duke ate alone in the great dining
room, clustered at one end of the table. When they had done
eating, they returned to the Duke's study. He had sent a courier
to Vérella the night before, to inform the king of the attack and
that he and Beclan were both alive. Now he organized a party
to retrieve the bodies of the dead Royal Guards so they could
be buried with honor. He also gave orders that no one was to
leave the household but those he himself sent.

"But my lord," said his steward with a worried frown, "my
lady and your daughters rode away early this morning—did
you not know?"

"Rode whither?" Mahieran asked.

"She said something about visiting her family in Vérella,
my lord, and she took the north way."

Mahieran paled. "When did she leave?"

"Early, my lord. Is there a problem?"

"No," Mahieran said. "Not as long as the whole household
doesn't head for the city. Rothlin's there; the house will be open.
I'd planned to go myself, later today; she could have traveled
with me, but I suppose she thought my wound would keep me
here longer. I am surprised she took Naryan and Vilian."

"If you're leaving later, shall I have your mounts readied?
And will Duke Verrakai be traveling with you?"

"Yes," Mahieran said with a glance at Dorrin. "We'll all be
going: Duke Verrakai, Beclan, and I. And an escort, but only a
small one."

"And the retrieval of the bodies, my lord?"

"Will go on—to be brought here, and I expect a burial party
from the Royal Guards will arrive before I get back."

"I must change," Dorrin said, aware that she was still wearing the royal family's colors. That would not do. Mahieran
nodded, excusing her from the room.

THEY RODE AWAY within a turn of the glass, Dorrin mounted
on one of Mahieran's horses, spares led by the following escort. Both before and behind, the escort kept out of earshot.

"I can't believe it of her," Mahieran said. No doubt which "her" he meant.

"Whatever you surmise may not be so," Dorrin said. "She was angry last night; she may go only to make complaint of me."

"She should not go at all, not without telling me," Mahieran said. "At least she cannot know the news about Beclan."

"She knows he survived the attack," Dorrin said. "And she knows I would know if he were invaded . . . so she knows he's not."

"She could not want her own son to be invaded, surely!"

Dorrin shook her head. Duke Mahieran's wife had borne his children and been, to all appearances, exactly what she should be these many years. Rothlin and Beclan, the two of them third and fourth from the throne. An eldest daughter recently married. Two younger ones. Dorrin had met her at the coronation and again at Autumn Court; she had been coolly polite, apparently concerned only with the honor due herself as part of the royal family. But Dorrin had not then known of the Konhalt connection. What did that mean? Or did it mean nothing?

Had she missed magery in Celbrin? She had not noticed anything in Beclan, either. Undeveloped magery . . . she had been intent only on detecting those who had been invaded. She'd never tried to find out if other nobles had magery; she'd accepted the convention that they did not.

What if more did? Rothlin, Beclan's older brother, the king's friend, cousin, and potential heir . . . or even Duke Mahieran himself, unknowingly carrying the seed of magery, passing it to his children? What if the king himself did?

She glanced at Mahieran, his face pinched with cold and pain. Was he thinking the same thing? What would happen to Tsaia and its relation to Fintha, to the Fellowship of Gird, if it were known that magery still existed not only in the Verrakaien but in others . . . in all?

"How fast is she likely to travel?" Dorrin asked after they had slowed the horses for a breather.

"If it were not for the girls, very fast indeed. Celbrin rides well, but I've never known her to push the pace. But angry as she was last night—and with whatever intent she has today—I don't know. And she has a long lead on us."

"Are we sure she's going to Vérella?" Beclan asked.

"We are not sure of anything," Mahieran said, "except that all has changed, not only for you and our family but for all."

"Where else might she go?" Dorrin asked.

"Her parents' home," Mahieran said. "Western Konhalt. It's close to your border. Not far from where Beclan was patrolling."

Dorrin thought back to the maps in her office. She had known Konhalt land was south of hers and that not all Konhalts had been attainted; once those who were had been captured and taken to Vérella, she'd ignored Konhalt domains. Had his mother's relatives planned the attack?

The rest of the way to the city, the party said little. Traffic between Vérella and the Mahieran estate continued through the winter, with couriers back and forth almost daily, so the hoofprints heading north might be—or might not be—those of Celbrin and the Mahieran daughters.

Dorrin paused at Verrakai House to let her house-wards know she was in the city, then rode on to the palace with Mahieran and Beclan. Mahieran sent one of their escort to Mahieran House.

The guards at the palace gates let them in. "Did my lady come earlier?" Mahieran asked.

"No, my lord. Did you expect her?"

"I thought she might have. She's in town," Mahieran said. He dismounted with difficulty, grimacing; Dorrin knew his arm must be giving him great pain. They handed their horses off to stable staff and at the entrance met one of the palace staff hurrying to meet them.

"My lords! We did not expect you today."

"I know," Mahieran said. "But circumstances brought me here—and Duke Verrakai and my son Beclan as well. Please inform the king that I beg an audience as soon as may be."

"Trouble?" the man asked.

"A matter of concern," Mahieran said.

"I will tell him," the man said. He bowed and withdrew.

Servants had appeared by then and led them to a room with a fireplace; others came with hot sib and pastries.

"Are you all right, Father?" Beclan asked.

"My arm hurts, I'm cold, I'm stiff, and I'm hungry," Mahieran said. "I'm also worried. Aside from that, I'm all right."

They had been waiting only a short time—still not through with the large pot of sib—when Rothlin Mahieran opened the door.

"Father—Beclan—my lord Verrakai—I was told you were here. What's amiss?"

"I must speak to Mikeli first, Roth," Mahieran said.

Rothlin plucked a pastry from the tray and sat down in one of the empty chairs. "Did you send Mother ahead of you?"

"No," Mahieran said.

"Well, past noontide, Mother sent me a note from our house here. She wanted me to arrange an audience with the king but did not say why. I sent it in, but Mikeli's been busy with other matters. He'll see you before he sees her, he says."

"That's good," Mahieran said. "I was hoping for that."

"Can you tell me what it's about?"

"No, Roth, I can't. Not until I've talked to the king and the Marshal-Judicar."

"Beclan's not . . . invaded . . . ?"

"No," Dorrin said. "He is not."

"Then—you'll tell me later, won't you?"

"Yes. My word on it."

"If I'd done what Duke Verrakai told me, none of this would have happened," Beclan said. The Marshal-Judicar, who had asked for the tale "from the beginning," harrumphed.

"What did she tell you to do, Beclan?" Mikeli asked. The king's gaze did not waver.

"Gather up troops from the villages along the way back to the main house and then follow directly to Harway. But that's not what I did. I thought I could gather more troops going a different way."

"Why?"

Beclan flushed. "To show off, sir king. I—I wanted to bring in more than she expected."

"I see." Mikeli glanced at Dorrin, then at Duke Mahieran. "Were you alone when you made this decision?"

"No, sir king. My escort—two tensquads—was with me, and Sergeant Vossik said I shouldn't."

"Sergeant Vossik was . . ."

"A veteran of Phelan's Company, sir king. He died to save me." Beclan's voice wavered. "I told that before."

"I have the Royal Guard commander's report on this," Mikeli said. "And the reports your father has sent, as well as the letters you wrote him. And there is an oath between us, Beclan Mahieran, an oath I think must be in doubt, since you and your father and Duke Verrakai come asking immediate audience with me and the Marshal-Judicar." He leaned forward a little, his face stern. "I warned you, Beclan Mahieran, that the oath you swore was binding as if you were of age. That false swearing was treason. Did I not?"

"Yes, sir king."

"So tell me now, Beclan: did you swear falsely? Do you come to beg mercy for being faithless, with all these additional deaths to your name? Every one of those men now lying dead, men sent to guard you, was known to me personally. Every one had a father, a mother; some were fathers themselves. They are dead because of you, Beclan, and I tell you I will not forgive you if you are guilty of designing their deaths."

Dorrin glanced at Beclan. Tears ran down his face, but his voice was clear as he said, "Sir king, when I gave you my oath, I swore truly, as far as I knew. I thought Gird himself had given me the strength to resist those men, their attempt to invade me."

"And now?"

"And now . . . I think . . . Duke Verrakai has confirmed . . . that something—maybe their attack, maybe Gird, maybe both—awakened some talent of my own, some innate magery I did not know I possessed. The night they attacked the cottage, I woke aware of danger. I heard a noise; I felt the same pressure I'd felt before. A sort of . . . of call. I took my sword and tried to sneak down the stairs, but something hit my head, and when I woke up again, it was all over."

"That was the night the cottage was attacked, sir king,"

Mahieran said. "I had met Duke Verrakai on the River Road, on her way to Vérella, and when I told her about Beclan's situation, she insisted the precautions against attack were not enough. She convinced me. We rode for the cottage and arrived to find the attack in progress."

"As you wrote in the report I received this morning."

"Yes, sir king."

"But you did not mention this . . . possibility."

"No, sir king; I did not know of it until Beclan came to me this morning and told me. That courier went off last night. I was wounded in the attack, as were many of my soldiers, and Beclan had no chance to talk to me privately."

"And *her* part in this?" The king's glance at Dorrin was cold.

"She saved my life and Beclan's," Mahieran said. "If she had not insisted we go to the cottage, he might very well be invaded or dead. He was knocked unconscious, went into convulsions—and she healed him."

"I could wish she had not been so hasty," the king said.

"Mikeli—! Sir king—" Mahieran's face paled.

"I do not hate Beclan, Uncle," the king said. "But he has complicated my life, and yours, and that of the realm. If he had died of injuries inflicted by rogue Verrakaien, he would have been a tragic and heroic figure, deeply and honestly mourned. Think how many people have died on his behalf, trying to save a Mahieran from evil . . . and yet he is tainted, and yet he is alive. Is that fair?"

"It is not fair to blame Beclan for the deaths of those who guarded the cottage," the Marshal-Judicar said slowly. "They were ordered there by you, sir king. You and Duke Mahieran chose to make the lad bait—you knew trouble might come. The lad is not responsible for that."

The king and Marshal-Judicar exchanged stares. "Well, then," the king said finally. "Not those, perhaps, but the men he had with him—"

"His disobeying Duke Verrakai is his fault," the Marshal-Judicar said. "He should have listened to his sergeant, yes. In my view, since he admits his fault, their deaths are sufficient punishment for that. He will carry that burden the rest of his life. As for whether he gave his oath in good faith, I know he was tested, at the time of his oath, and found to be truthful in his account of what happened. As he had never shown signs of magery before, it seems reasonable to me that he might think Gird had given him the power to resist evil. It is what we all pray for, after all."

"And yet he has magery *now,* and that is against the Code of Gird and the laws of Tsaia. His magery taints the whole house, including me."

"Not without a Bill of Attainder, sir king," the Marshal-Judicar said. "And your Judicar-General would say the same. Gird himself did not approve of attainder; it's preserved here as a concession. There is no such thing in Fintha. Beclan's magery—assuming it's magery and not in fact Gird's power lent him—is his responsibility. Certainly he cannot succeed to the throne and must be removed from the list. And whether he can succeed to his father's title, should something happen to Rothlin—"

"I don't want it," Beclan said. "Um . . . sir king. Sir."

"Don't be ridiculous, Beclan," Mahieran said. "This is not about what you want, but about what's best for the crown and the realm."

"Duke Verrakai," the king said, looking at Dorrin with slightly less hostility than before. "You believe his magery is innate and not implanted by those rogue Verrakaien?"

"I do," Dorrin said.

"Do you detect any such in me or Duke Mahieran?"

"I do not, sir king, but I detected none in Beclan before. I wasn't really looking for it, though, and a very small power might not be noticed."

"What do you think awakened it?"

"Sir king, he prayed to Gird in his shock and grief and fear—I think it likely Gird used what innate powers he had and strengthened them at need."

"But Gird hated magery. He would not use it—"

"That's not quite true, sir king," the Marshal-Judicar said. "The oldest writings we have—some discovered in the far west only a year or two ago—show that Gird hoped magelords and non-mage could live together in peace. Gird was a practical man; I can believe Gird might waken Beclan's powers."

"And you agree," the king said, looking at Dorrin. "But you are not Girdish."

"No, sir king. Yet I have lived most of my life here, in this realm, and honor Gird as another of the great saints, as Falkians do."

The king sighed. "You must know, Duke Verrakai, that many distrust and dislike you both for your family background and your use of magery."

"I know that, yes, sir king."

"It has made me question my decision to make you Constable—even to create you a duke. It seemed best at the time, but—now—with what happened to the Serrostin lad and Beclan—"

"It's not her fault," Beclan said. "It was mine."

"Is this what she taught you, to interrupt your king?"

"No, sir king, but—"

"In other circumstances, your squires' defense of you would bear more weight," the king said, ignoring Beclan. "Now it seems it might be some effect of magery."

"I cannot prove it is not," Dorrin said. "But if you want to test my word with a relic—"

"You would submit to that? You are Falkian!"

"Yes, but Falk and Gird agree on honesty," Dorrin said. "And I know there is a Field of Falk here. If you want certainty, get a Captain and a Marshal."

"Do you Falkians test truth with relics?"

"No," Dorrin said. "The ruby can be used, though." She touched hers. "However, you might consider its light under mage control, and you will not so consider a relic of Gird's day."

The king looked at Mahieran. "Find us a Captain of Falk, Uncle. And you, Marshal-Judicar—will the relic in the palace grange be sufficient?"

"Yes, of course."

"Then we will put them both to the test."

Though Dorrin understood the reasoning, she still found it annoying to be tested in front of all the peers then in Vérella, as well as the king and the Marshal-Judicar. Her three fellow dukes, a handful of counts, one baron . . . most of them looking decidedly unfriendly. The Captain of Falk, whom she had not met before, greeted her warmly.

The test itself went as she had expected: the Girdish relic and Falk's ruby both indicated she was telling the truth about everything she was asked. The king, prompted by the peers observing, asked if she had put any geas on the squires; the Marshal-Judicar was more interested in her adherence to the law.

When the test was over, Mikeli sat back and heaved a very dramatic sigh and tented his fingers. "Well," he said to the assembled peers. "Beclan's situation is a problem, but it is not, by all the tests, Duke Verrakai's fault. From now on, I expect you all to speak the truth of that, whatever your opinions of her otherwise and whatever gossip you may hear. You may go; I need to speak with Duke Verrakai privately."

They shuffled out. Mahieran said, "Do you want me to leave?"

"No. This is family business as well as crown business. I want Marshal-Judicar Oktar to stay as well, as there are legalities involving both the Code of Gird and Tsaian law." He looked at Beclan. "Beclan—cousin—you know you cannot remain in the succession. Your very presence in the Mahieran family compromises your brother Rothlin's place in the succession as well—even your father's. Yes, we all think your magery came through your mother, and your mother is now confined to the city house until her active magery can be proven or disproven. But you, as a Mahieran, imperil the realm."

Beclan looked at his father, at the Marshal-Judicar, and then back at Mikeli. "Sir king, I—I don't want to harm you or the realm."

"I believe you," Mikeli said.

"I agree," Oktar said. "On both, sir king: that his being a Mahieran, more than his having mage power, imperils the realm and that he had no such intention."

"Intention or no, the results—the dangers—are the same. You must be cast out, Beclan," Mikeli said. "I'm sorry—it is not fair, if your heart is true as I think it is, but so it must be."

"But what will I do?" Beclan asked. "How can I live—I don't know—"

"Please, sir king," Mahieran began, but was silenced by Mikeli's gesture.

"I do not intend to beggar him or drive him naked from the gates, Uncle. He is my cousin and your son; we share blood—but that is the problem. He must not be Mahieran anymore, and he must not attend court anymore."

"Keep him in my household? As a . . ."

"No, Uncle. He must not be associated with Mahieran. But he is already associated with another family—and a family with known magery." Mikeli looked at Dorrin. "You, Dorrin Duke Verrakai, must adopt this former Mahieran: give him your name and—unless some accident befalls him—make him your heir." Before she could speak, shocked as she was, he went on. "I know you have another heir, a cousin with no magery, who was judged innocent of treason and who now serves in the Royal Guard. But he had not, until last spring, any notion of being an heir to Verrakai; I doubt he will be much put out. Whether he is or not, that is my command, and he as well as you must abide it. Beclan, as your kirgan, would be under your command and would be your responsibility—and all our magelords would be in one basket, so to speak. He will eventually have rank—be a duke in his own right—and by then perhaps opinions will have changed. If I am still king and he has proven himself honorable, he can then come to court as a Verrakaien."

"I—" Dorrin tried to think what she could say that might convince the king to let Beclan remain in his own family and realized nothing would work. In strategy, the king was right. This—or outright exile to another land. "Sir king, I would be honored to adopt Beclan and name him my kirgan, with the consent of his father."

"Uncle," Mikeli said, "you must see this is the only way."

Mahieran bowed, jaw clenched. Finally he said, "I want to speak to my son before—alone—"

"Yes, of course."

Mahieran took Beclan aside; Mikeli gave Dorrin a rueful look. "I'm sorry," he said. "This is the only way I could think of, and it must be done quickly. It will be hard for both of you. But if we face war with the south, I must have Girdish support, and that means dealing with my own family as the law requires."

"He may someday be a valuable peer in your realm," Dorrin said. "And you hold his oath now: I ask that you take care for him as you would for any other who has pledged you fealty."

"I will do my best," Mikeli said. "And I think this—what I do now—is my best. For this time, at least."

Beclan and his father came back to the others, both pale but calm. Beclan moved to stand near Dorrin; Mahieran glanced at the Marshal-Judicar. "Will you be writing up the decree?"

"As the king wishes," Oktar said.

"Let it be done," Mikeli said.

In a turn of the glass, Dorrin and Beclan left the palace. The horses they had ridden in were waiting, freshly groomed, saddled again. They mounted in silence, rode in silence to Verrakai House. Dorrin's house-wards had raised the Duke's pennon on its staff by the door, and the house-ward opened to them, smiling.

"A fire in the small parlor, my lord, and a meal within a glass—will my lord be staying long?"

"A few days," Dorrin said. Though the adoption had been signed, other legalities remained, and Beclan would have to have new clothes with Verrakai colors and no hint of a relationship to Mahieran. She hoped they would not need to stay longer in Vérella; the sooner she got Beclan away from here, with all its Mahieran associations, the better. "A pot of sib, perhaps, with honey."

"At once, my lord."

In the small parlor, a fire crackled cheerfully enough and two chairs were pulled near it. "Sit down, Beclan," Dorrin said, and settled into one of the chairs. She glanced at his face: pale, stiff, miserable. "You have lost everything, you think," she said. "You have lost your whole family . . . and believe it or not, I do understand. I was not much younger than you when I lost mine—cast out, though by my own will."

"I c-can't believe I'll never . . . never see them again . . .

never see my home . . . and I've *always* been a Mahieran!"
Tears stood in his eyes.

"I had always been a Verrakai—and now I am again. I know
it's hard, Beclan, but you're young, you have a place to go, and
you've come through worse."

"I don't want—" He shook his head abruptly and turned
away from her; his shoulders shook. "It's not what I want," he
said thickly. "It doesn't matter what I want. I know that, it's
just—I love them. My brother—my father—my sisters—"
And in a lower voice, "My mother."

"And that makes it harder than it was for me. Yes. But
however you feel now, your life is not over. You have shown
courage, Beclan, and honor. You have grown much since you
became my squire, and though I was surprised—even shocked—
by the king's command, I think you can become a worthy heir
of Verrakai. I think you can help me change Verrakai's reputation, make it into the family it should have been."

The sib arrived; Dorrin poured for both of them. Beclan finally turned around and took a cup, gulped, nearly choked, and
then sipped more quietly.

"My lord, a messenger in Mahieran livery." Her house-ward
handed over a message tube.

Dorrin read the message silently, then spoke to Beclan.
"Your father is sending things you might want, he says, and
two additional horses, as well as a sum of gold, which I am to
put in trust for you until you come of age." She did not mention the money Mahieran had sent to her for the expenses of
Beclan's new clothes or that he had already spoken to the family's tailor, who had Beclan's measurements.

"Why?"

"Why? Because he cares for you. Even your cousin the king
cares for you. And—this is surprising—he grants us both
leave to attend Kieri Phelan's wedding in Lyonya if he does
not. Have you ever been in Lyonya?"

"No, my lord."

"Even if we don't go for the wedding, I'm sure we'll visit
Lyonya on other occasions." Dorrin glanced at him. Beclan's
shoulders were slumped, his head down, a perfect image of
misery. "It will be an adventure, Beclan. Last summer you told

me you wanted adventure—well, you've had a taste, and there's more to come. Now—sit up properly. You have a backbone for a reason. As both squire and kirgan, you have new responsibilities."

Beclan's head rose. "You're serious . . . my lord."

"I'm serious. Moping and moaning won't help—and I won't tolerate it. You've got more breeding than that—on both sides. You know—and I just thought of this—if your mother's Konhalt relatives intermarried with Verrakai, as many did, you and I may be related, after all."

"I can't think of you as my *mother*—"

"Holy Falk and Gird, no! Of course not. Distant cousin at most. But as your duke—as the head of the household—and yourself as heir—*that* you can manage, I daresay. You probably learned from your father and brother what is expected of a duke's kirgan."

"Will I—will my magery grow?"

"I have no idea," Dorrin said. "But implicit in your adoption is the king's awareness that it might, and it should be trained by someone who knows magery—just as a talent for anything else." She stood up; Beclan stood out of courtesy. "Come, now: we've had a hard day already, and we'll eat a meal and make our plans."

Two days later, Beclan came down to breakfast in his new clothes, the blue of Verrakai replacing the rose of Mahieran, and the formal knot of Kirgan Verrakai on his shoulder instead of the family colors squires wore. He looked glum again. The last of the legal ceremonies lay before him, in the grange-hall of the Bells, where he would never now be a knight-candidate. Dorrin knew it would be difficult. He had always assumed he'd be a Knight of the Bells someday, wear the silver insignia on his collar as his brother Rothlin and his father both did.

Instead, today the Knight-Commander and two High Marshals would accept the Marshal-Judicar's report of the adoption the king commanded. His father would once more renounce him; he would have to renounce his father; he would see his name blotted out in the family records.

"We're starting for the east as soon as the ceremony's done," Dorrin said. "So eat a hearty breakfast."

"Yes, my lord." He worked his way through half a bowl of porridge as she finished hers and began on the ham. "It's . . . it feels so odd to be wearing these clothes—these colors—everyone will know—"

Dorrin put her fork down. "Most people don't know you, Beclan. They didn't know you as Mahieran's younger son . . . and they don't know you as my kirgan. Most we pass will see 'a young Verrakaien' as they formerly saw 'a young Mahieran,' without seeing Beclan-the-person either way."

"I hope I don't see anyone I know, then," Beclan said.

They saw none but servants on their way through to the grange-hall where the Knights of the Bells trained and were tested. Early as it was, Duke Mahieran and Rothlin were there—and to Dorrin's surprise, the king and his younger brother, Camwyn, as well. The others—Knight-Commander of the Bells, Marshal-Judicar, and High Marshals—began at once, asking Mahieran for the family rolls, which he produced, a ribbon marking the place where Beclan's name had been recorded.

Dorrin knew that her own family had not bothered with a public ceremony when they blotted out her name; she had never attended any such before. What impressed her most was the care taken to be sure that the parties understood and gave consent. Agonizing as it must be for Beclan to hear his father cast him out three times and to be asked thrice if he himself renounced his allegiance to the family of his birth, if he fully accepted the authority of his adoptive family—impossible as it was for him to protest— the ceremony was still an attempt to be fair, to ensure no coercion. Yet coercion attended in the person of the king.

At the end, when a great blot of black ink covered his name in the Mahieran rolls, when Dorrin had formally acknowledged him her heir and sworn to have a Marshal witness her writing him into the Verrakai rolls, the ceremony ended with acknowledgment of Beclan's new status. His father, his brother, and the king each embraced him, gave the ritual kisses on each cheek, and greeted him as "Beclan Kirgan Verrakai."

The king's younger brother stood by, looking slightly alarmed and bewildered.

As they rode east toward Verrakai lands later that day, Beclan looked back only once to the life he had lost. As they passed the fork in the road that led to the Mahieran estates, he turned in the saddle. The road lay empty, just trampled and rutted snow. Dorrin said nothing; the boy needed time to make his own peace with it all, if he could.

On the last day of their journey, she brought up his new status. "I can't send you to another household as squire, Beclan, yet you need that training like any other lord's heir. So you will also continue as my squire on the same footing as before. I will explain to Gwenno and Daryan what I feel they need to know. Beyond that—it's as before, is that clear?"

"Yes, my lord."

"You will be learning more about this estate in particular, but you will not have authority as my kirgan until your term as my squire is complete."

"Yes, my lord."

"As I am commanded to keep you with me for supervision of whatever magery you develop, remember what I told you—I will be taking you with me to Lyonya at the Spring Evener to King Kieri's wedding."

His head came up. "But—surely they invited the king. If Mikeli's coming, I can't, can I?"

"Your father will represent him; he's planning to bring Rothlin. It was the king's decision. You will be introduced to Lyonyans as Kirgan Verrakai, my heir." She waited a moment for that to sink in. "I'm sure the court in Lyonya will have an abundance of eligible young women."

"I'm not interested in—" He paused. "I thought I couldn't marry because no one in Tsaia would want to risk it—but—"

"Lyonya does not have the same attitudes to magery," Dorrin said. "Falkians don't. Elves don't." She watched that idea seep in, producing a flush of color to his face and then the first genuine smile she'd seen on the journey. "And you'll need an heir yourself someday."

Already he sat taller in the saddle.

CHAPTER TWENTY-SIX

In the days approaching the Spring Evener and their wedding, Arian found time, even with the wedding preparations demanding her attention, to visit the ossuary several times. She no longer feared the place or Kieri's sister's spirit. She had walked the perimeter—dry whitewashed stone walls, the stone floor cleaned of the muddy footprints Kieri had made. The Seneschal answered her few questions and left her alone as long as she wanted.

She wasn't sure why she found the ossuary so attractive or why she took the time to listen to his sister's cryptic utterances. But she knew exactly why she stared at his sister's bones and those few pathetic shards that had been her child. In her own body . . . another child . . .

Beware.

She was being careful. Two Squires now followed her everywhere and guarded the door of her chamber at night. She wore mail under her clothes, though how that could be done as the child grew, she was not sure. Carrying a child was one thing, but the extra weight of mail . . . well . . . that was later. For now, she had not changed in size, and she practiced daily, as Kieri did.

The day before the Evener, she came out of the ossuary, looked around in the sunshine of an early spring day, and spotted Aliam and Estil Halveric coming across the courtyard.

Estil grinned. "There she is—well met, Arian. And you're with child!"

"Indeed," Arian said.

"You know," Estil said, "I thought it would be you from the time I saw you ride that horse for him."

"And you were miffed that he looked at the horse," Aliam said. "I remember that."

"Not miffed, exactly, but which is more important to the realm—the right horse or the right wife?"

"If the wrong horse throws you and breaks your neck—" Aliam began; Estil swatted his shoulder. He laughed; so did she.

"What did you see, Estil, that you thought I was right for him?" Arian asked.

"I have daughters and granddaughters," Estil said. "And some amount of taig-sense. I flatter myself that I can recognize a young person of character. And one in love." Arian felt her cheeks heating. "And yet, one mature enough to wait . . . not a youngster grabbing for what she wanted."

"Thank you," Arian said.

"Who will be your midwife?" Estil asked.

"Estil!" Aliam said.

"It's never too early," Estil said.

"I don't know," Arian said. "And I don't want to hurt anyone's feelings—"

"The only hurt to worry about is you, yourself, and your child," Estil said. "My daughter Martyl's quite good, but she's never helped a half-elf . . . do you know if there's anything special about birthing in the half-kin?"

"No," Arian said. "I never thought to ask."

"Well . . . Kieri's first wife had no problems, I understand, but she had no elven blood herself. We must find you some half-elven mothers, Arian, to talk with and find out."

"Not before the wedding, though," Aliam said. "Enough talk of birthings. There's a wedding to celebrate and feasts to eat. And I see the steward's by the entrance wishing we'd either come or go."

"Come, of course," Arian said. "I know where your guest room is; don't think you can escape staying here!"

They met Kieri coming out of his office in the lower main passage. "You made it!" he said. "I was afraid the rains these past five days had mired you in mud to the horses' bellies."

"Not so bad," Estil said. "And I would not have missed your wedding if I'd had to swim in mud to get here."

"Did the other kings come?" Aliam asked.

"No. Torfinn sent congratulations and a heap of furs to make us cloaks. Elis is here, as her father's representative."

"I was half expecting the old lady," Estil said.

"She died in their war," Kieri said. "A loss; I think she was honest, and she was also a link to the Kostandanyans. However, their king sent his eldest son, wedding greetings, and a jar of something that stinks abominably."

"Are Ganlin and Elis still so close?"

"No, as I suspected. They had different aims when they went in, and after Torfinn came to assassinate me and Elis became the nominal Pargunese ambassador, her focus shifted to that—to her father and to Pargun. She's a brilliant student, the Knight-Commander says, completely focused on her work. Sure to be knighted, in time. The Knight-Commander's comment on Ganlin was, 'She may or may not get her ruby, but she will definitely get her man.'"

"May I see your dress, Arian?" Estil asked.

"Of course," Arian said, glad of a chance to see Estil alone. Though not more than a decade older, Estil had been wife, mother, grandmother . . . and Arian had no one close to talk to about that. Up in her chambers, the wedding dress on its stand gleamed in the sunlight streaming in the windows, stiff with embroidery.

"A queen's robe indeed," Estil said. "Where did you have this made?"

"I didn't—my father sent it. I suppose it was elf-made." Arian touched one of the embroidered flowers, the brilliant colors shown off by the silvery sheen of the underlying fabric. "I expect he won't be there—the Lady doesn't like him—but I'm touched that he thought of me."

"Were you close to him, Arian?"

"When I was little, he stayed with us at times—for as much as a year. I loved him; I love him still. He sang to us—to me in particular—and he took me out in the forest and introduced me to the trees and ferns and so on. I had inherited more taig-sense than most half-elven, he said. He could call birds from the trees—it was wonderful, I thought."

"And then he left?"

"Not all at once, but in the longest absence . . . I thought he had gone forever, and my mother died . . ."

"You were still a child?"

"No—old enough to go to Falk's Hall. I blamed myself for not being home, but I knew even then it would have made no difference. But my father—he's the one who suggested I go to Falk's Hall, not stay in the village. He paid my fees. He had been gone—a year? Two?—around the time I was twelve. But then he was back for a couple of years, and then less and less. He looked worried from time to time. When I got my ruby, he showed up again and gave me a sword."

"That one?" Estil asked, pointing.

"Yes. He was happy, you know, when Kieri and I—when we discovered we were both—well. But then the Lady was angry, and she closed me off from the taig—"

"She had done it to me," Estil said. "Though my taig-sense was never as strong as yours . . . She apologized after the daskdraudigs; she thought it was her doing that I didn't sense it. But I'm not sure—I was so worried about Aliam, I might not have."

"How is your house now?"

"Strange," Estil said. "The elves helped . . . and the Lady . . . but it feels uncanny at times. It was better after Cal put Old Halveric's skull back in place in the attic. It's not that I don't like elves, you understand, but Old Halveric is one of us . . . the old people, I mean."

"I know," Arian said, thinking of the ossuary. "Have you ever seen the royal ossuary?"

"No. I thought it wasn't open to outsiders."

"You're not outsiders. Kieri says you're family. And the ossuary has become very important to him."

"His father's and his sister's bones, of course." Estil nodded.

Arian wondered whether to broach the subject she had not mentioned to anyone else.

"What is it?" Estil asked. "What's wrong? Kieri?" She put her hand on her chest as if it hurt her.

"No—he's fine. I think. But . . . but at Midwinter . . ."

Estil moved to the window seat and sat down. "Come, tell me what troubles you on the day before your wedding to the best man, bar Aliam, I ever knew. And you with child—is it that? For women do have strange feelings sometimes, especially with their first."

Arian perched on the bed. "I do not think it is being with child. In fact, I know it's not all that. Midwinter, you see, the king spends the night alone, fasting, in the ossuary, with the door closed. Kieri was not afraid, of course, but something happened in there. In the morning, when it was time to greet the sun's coming, and the Seneschal opened the door, he wasn't there."

Estil's brows went up. "What do you mean, he wasn't there? How big is the ossuary? Could he have fallen asleep behind something?"

"No. I had come behind the Seneschal. The ossuary was empty, silent . . . dark. No sign of him. The Seneschal called again and then again. I called—I felt my heart pause." Arian heard the upward shift of her voice, expressing the horror and panic she had felt. She took a deep breath before going on. "There's no other entrance that anyone knows about, but somehow . . . Kieri said it all changed, in the dark. And he was walking about, blessing the bones, when he felt along a wall, and instead of dressed stone he felt dirt and roots."

Estil stared. "But . . . he didn't feel any kind of entrance? Lintel, threshold?"

"No. He said perhaps he was not really attending, but he realized he was standing on dirt. With . . . with things crawling on him. He tried to feel his way back to the ossuary, but for a long time all he found was dirt and roots and creatures of the dark. Then he came to stone again—the outside of the ossuary, we think. At first he could find no way in, but then the stone yielded and he fell into the same room he'd left. But he looked—he was filthy, his feet all muddy and bruised and his clothes stained."

"Gods above," Estil breathed. "He told you all this?"

Arian nodded. "That night, after the betrothal."

"Have you been in there?" Estil asked.

"Yes—several times. It feels . . . friendly. Kieri's sister's bones . . . speak. To both of us."

Estil frowned a little. "I think we need to have a longer talk, you and I—and with Kieri, too, most likely. But can you tell me what your worry is about tomorrow, if not the things brides usually worry about?"

"The Lady is coming. I do not know what . . . what she might do . . ." Arian realized then that Estil probably knew nothing about where the Lady had been early in the war or any of the rest of it, busy in her own domain trying to repair the damages of the daskdraudigs and reorder her household. "We do need to talk, Estil Halveric, but let me set aside my worries for a day of joy. I feel better for being with you even this long."

"You're wearing mail, you and Kieri both," Estil said, leaning back to glance out the window into the palace forecourt. "So you think there is danger? Is the border not safe, after all?"

"His sister's bones warn of treachery," Arian said. "I will wear mail even under my wedding dress."

"Will Kieri tell Aliam, do you think, or must I convince him to stand close? And who is to be your maid?"

"I have no sisters—the other women Squires who are here drew lots, and Suriya is to be my senior attendant. Then three Siers' daughters and granddaughters of appropriate age."

"With respect . . . have you someone to stand as your mother if your father will not be here?"

"N-no," Arian said. "I think, because I'm Kieri's age, no one thought I needed one."

"My dear, every bride needs a family. I know Kieri has taken Aliam as his ceremonial father. Would you do me the honor of allowing me to stand as your mother?"

Arian felt tears stinging her eyes and blinked them away. "I—yes. Yes, I would. You do remind me of her."

"Good, then. I do not know the full protocol for a royal wedding . . . but I do know Kieri. He will have pared the ceremony to the bone and left marks on the bone."

Arian laughed as suddenly as she had cried. "I should have run to you when the Lady put the geas on me to leave; you knew him as boy and man."

"We could spend days," Estil said. "But I hear voices in the passage. We have had all the privacy we shall have for the rest of today and tomorrow. There's a reception this evening, I suppose."

"Yes, indeed. As before the coronation."

"Then I must go and change into something suitable," Estil said, and stood.

"And I," Arian said.

A soft tap at the door. "My lady? It is time—"

For the next several turns of the glass, Arian was immersed in the preparations for the reception.

Kieri waited for her at the head of the stairs; they came down into the entrance hall together, flanked by Squires. The steward, old Sier Hammarin, and several Squires were still organizing the line of guests. Arian glanced around. Siers and their families . . . a scattering of elves, most unfamiliar to her . . . Elis of Pargun, standing with the Knight-Commander of Falk, wearing once more the pale blue gown she'd worn last summer as a princess. Ganlin of Kostandan, also in last summer's dress, on the other side of the Knight-Commander with the Kostandanyan representative, her older brother.

Other foreigners she did not recognize, though she knew that among them were a delegation of senior Girdish from Fin Panir, the Sea-Prince of Prealíth, and a woman from Dzordanya who bore the title of Mother of Mothers of the Long Houses. Members of the Council, including those Kieri had added in the past year—two merchants, now, and Aliam as military advisor.

And from Tsaia, in Mahieran rose and silver, the king's uncle, Duke Mahieran himself . . . and in a far corner Dorrin, Duke Verrakai. Arian felt the sudden tension in Kieri's arm. He said nothing, but she heard a soft rumble in his chest.

Missing, so far, was the Lady—or any other senior elf. Well. Nothing to do but smile and hope this was the worst of the evening. She and Kieri took their places at the foot of the stairs, and the line began to move toward them. The foreigners were ushered to the fore . . . Dorrin lagged Duke Mahieran by what Arian thought of as a sword-safe distance.

"Sonder, Duke Mahieran of Tsaia," announced Sier Hammarin, "bearing his king's honors. And his son, Kirgan Mahieran."

The Duke bowed to Kieri, then to Arian, and handed over a box wrapped in rose satin tied with silver ribbons, with two silver bells dangling from the ends. "My lord king," he said. "King Mikeli sends greetings and wishes for your joy and prosperity." He nodded to his son. "My son and kirgan, Roth-lin." For a moment his eyes twinkled. "Roth heard from Kir-gan Marrakai about the beauty of Lyonya's daughters."

"Be very welcome here," Kieri said. "You will convey to your king my greetings and hopes for his health and prosperity. I hope your journey was easy."

"Indeed, it was, sir king." He dipped his head again and went on into the next room.

"Dorrin, Duke Verrakai of Tsaia," Hammarin said. "And her heir, Kirgan Verrakai."

Dorrin bowed as low as Mahieran had, but when she stood again, she was smiling broadly. "Sir king—Arian—I am so happy for you both. You do not perhaps know my squire and also my kirgan, Beclan."

Arian kept the formal smile on her face with an effort. Be-clan . . . Verrakai? This must be the same Beclan, Beclan Mahieran . . . and now Kirgan Verrakai?

"Be welcome here," Kieri said, as if he had expected them both. "We must talk. There are concerns about the border. The day after tomorrow?"

"As it pleases you," Dorrin said.

"Then that morning," Kieri said.

The rest of the line surged forward when Dorrin moved away, and for the next turn of the glass Arian accepted bow after bow, hand after hand. Elis of Pargun, Arian noted, was a very different young woman now that she had purpose and a structure in which to exercise it. Perhaps her gravity came from knowing all but one of her brothers were dead and her father had been gravely wounded, but it suited her. Ganlin, too, had changed: she walked without any hint of a limp and seemed completely relaxed and happy. The Sea-Prince had green and blue ribbons in his three long dark braids and a curved dagger thrust into a jeweled sheath. The Dzordanyan Mother of Mothers of the Long Houses was a tiny woman swathed in dark green. Her face, what little could be seen of it, was heavily wrinkled, but when she took Arian's hand, her grip had strength.

By the time the guests had paid their respects, the other rooms were buzzing with conversation over a background of music. Arian and Kieri circulated among the rooms and guests, pausing to compliment the musicians. After a time, Arian's feet hurt and she sat down among a group of older women, Siers' wives, and Sier Davonin.

At once one of the servants brought her a plate of food and a goblet of water flavored with cherry preserves. Sier Davonin leaned over. "My dear, forgive an old woman's presumption, but are you ensuring you eat enough roots?"

"Roots?"

"Didn't your mother tell you? Just as trees form strong root systems before they grow tall, so children must root deeply before they grow larger. The first days are most important."

"I ate plenty of redroots all winter, Sier Davonin."

"That's good," Davonin said, patting Arian's shoulder in a motherly way. "Now, am I right in thinking this child must have been engendered near Midwinter?"

Arian nodded.

"Then you know to eat spring greens."

"Yes."

The Siers' ladies chimed in then, and she felt trapped in a maze of maternal advice, but Kieri, who had been talking to Duke Mahieran some distance away, suddenly excused himself and came to her rescue.

"At least we do not have to begin our wedding at dawn," Kieri said. "Come, Arian, we should make another triumphal round, don't you think? You ladies will excuse us . . ."

"I've told Elis she should talk to Duke Mahieran," Kieri said when they had moved away. "She can reassure him about Pargun's intentions. And she will need to know the Tsaians and deal with them as well as us."

"Has Pargun ever had an ambassador to Tsaia?"

"Not in years. The Verrakaien used to claim they had contact with the Pargunese—fine fellows, they'd say—but the Pargunese claimed they were afraid of assassination if they sent anyone of consequence, and Mikeli's father would not accept anyone trivial. He had lost his own father to the Pargunese and had little patience with them. Elis is the right person to change Tsaian minds, and I'm sure the Pargunese are no threat to them at this time."

"Ganlin?"

"Her father's accepted that she wants to be a Knight of Falk—I suspect that means he's accepted she won't find a husband in Kostandan; her brother tells me that they hope she makes a good marriage alliance here or in Tsaia. If you look over there—" Arian followed his glance and saw Ganlin, flushed and pretty, listening to Rothlin Mahieran. "—she's already found one handsome young man in line for a throne. Her brother would rather she met Mikeli and wants my advice on how to arrange it."

"What about Dorrin? And isn't Beclan really—?"

"That's a ticklish business just now. Duke Mahieran gave me a précis—apparently an earlier letter didn't get through. Dorrin had to adopt Beclan as her heir—he had to change his name—to ensure he was out of the succession for the Tsaian throne and had close supervision of his magery."

"*Beclan?* Magery?"

"Through his mother, Mahieran's wife, they think. It's too complicated to explain fully now. We'll talk to Dorrin after the wedding. Sonder's staying a full tenday; there will be time. Beclan's upset about the adoption—and no wonder—but I see he's already attracted his own following."

Sure enough, several Siers' daughters were clustered around Beclan, who no longer looked tense or miserable. In fact, he looked quite happy.

"New faces," Kieri said in her ear. "Always more interesting than someone's brother whose faults you've heard about from his sister. And he's now heir to the Verrakai title and estates . . . quite eligible."

"That's what I told him." Dorrin had come up on Kieri's other side. She was grinning. "I'm glad he's enjoying himself. He was an idiot, but he didn't deserve much of what happened. But that's for another day's discussion. I applaud Mikeli for allowing us both to come and for sending Sonder and Rothlin."

"That doesn't make it harder?" Kieri asked.

"No. Here, Beclan can meet with his father and brother. In Tsaia, anyone in the line of succession is barred from Beclan and he from them. When I'm summoned to court, he must come with me to Vérella, but cannot attend court or visit his family. Besides, he can see for himself that Roth has just one girl showing interest and he has several. That never hurts a young man's mood."

By the end of the evening, Arian was exhausted and longing for her bed. She fell asleep quickly, and the dreams that came to her—though she could not remember them in the morning—left her with a vague melancholy, not the mood she had expected on her wedding morning.

"That's a solemn look," Kieri said. She opened her eyes. In the early light she could not see the scars that he had feared would frighten or repel a bride. She ran her hand down his side.

"I dreamed something," Arian said. "I'm not sure what the dream was. Do you think the Lady will come?"

"The one thing I know—and the only thing I care about—is that when this day ends, we will be formally wed and you will be a queen in name as you are now in truth. Does that please you?"

"Yes," Arian said. "Absolutely." Her earlier feelings of insecurity, of concern about her ability to be queen as well as wife, had dissipated in the quarter-year since Midwinter. Now she looked forward to her planned trip to Tsaia. Besides her Squires, she would travel with Sier Davonin, the only woman Sier, and Duke Mahieran of Tsaia and his son and escort. She had hoped Dorrin would travel with them, but now it could be only as far as the border. Still—an adventure. She stretched and grinned at Kieri. "We will make good dreams together, Kieri."

"I think so, too," he said. "But at the moment, we had best make good figureheads . . . alas that there is no more time for dreaming on this wedding morn. You to your bath and dressing, my queen, and I to mine."

After that the day rushed on; Arian bathed and ate a little breakfast in her own chamber, before her Squires and Siers' ladies and Estil Halveric came to dress her. Kieri had insisted she have mail and go armed even for the ceremony and had given her a baldric of the finest leather, dyed green and stamped with the royal insignia in gold to wear instead of her sword belt.

When she was ready and the fussiest of the Siers' ladies had finally quit moving a tendril of hair from this place to that, she went out into the passage; Kieri emerged from his chamber at almost the same instant. The perfume of spring flowers filled the air; Arian was aware of the scent and of the Lady's glamour at the same moment. She and Kieri went down together, and she was not surprised to find the Lady waiting for them, along with other elves of her court. But her father stood with them . . . and that was a complete surprise.

"Blessings of the Singer on this day of joy," the Lady said. Arian could feel the flood of enchantment but was not overwhelmed . . . others, she saw, were deep in awe, almost drowning in the Lady's power. Behind the elves stood one who was not: Dorrin Verrakai, like Duke Mahieran, wore formal court dress but unlike him was not gazing at the Lady in rapt adoration. Instead, she had a speculative expression, as if about to test what the Lady could do. She gave Arian a sharp look, then a tiny nod. Arian wondered if Dorrin's taig-sense had strengthened over the winter.

As a path opened before them and they came out the palace entrance to the courtyard, more flowers appeared, this time out of the air, drifting like colored snowflakes. Among them were butterflies, the small wind of their wings keeping the flowers aloft.

The wedding itself meant repeating some of the same vows as at their betrothal, with mention of the child engendered in the betrothal. Arian's father and the Lady spoke the elven Witnessing together—another surprise—and the Captain-General of Falk invoked Falk's Oath and the High Lord.

The courtyard was packed with people—many of the same who had attended Kieri's coronation the year before. Beyond the Lady's glamour, Arian felt the taig's wholehearted joy and the joy of the crowd—they had not needed the Lady's glamour to force them to celebrate.

As the ceremony ended, a gust of warm wind swirled the flowers and butterflies into a tower of color . . . and then the flowers fell on heads and shoulders and the butterflies flew away. The Lady turned to Kieri and Arian. "I have made up my quarrel with your father, king and queen of Lyonya, and he his with me. Set your mind at rest about that."

Arian's father had a quirk to the corner of his mouth that Kieri knew of old—but he said nothing to contradict the Lady.

"I am happy to hear that," Kieri said.

"And I," Arian said. She was not sure the quarrel was over—elves were known for long-held grudges—but having her father at her wedding was worth taking their words at face value. She turned to her father. "Thank you for my wedding gown."

His smile this time was genuine. "It was my delight to provide it, Arian. And you are even more beautiful than I remembered."

Next morning, the palace was still nowhere near back to normal. Kieri and Arian went to the salle as usual, but Kieri left when a servant brought word that Duke Mahieran wanted to talk to him again.

"Every ambassador will want time with me today," he said.

Arian sparred with one of her Squires and with Aliam Halveric when he showed up, then went to breakfast with Aliam and Estil. To her surprise, Dorrin was there, with Beclan at her side, and—a greater surprise—Arian's father Dameroth also attended.

"You have heard of my difficulty," Dorrin said without preamble.

"I don't understand it," Aliam said. "You saved the king's life—how can he be so ungrateful?"

"I saved his life by what, under Tsaian law, is the most heinous of crimes: killing by magery," Dorrin said. "And to make it worse, in the eyes of some, the man I killed had been invaded—his own life taken—by my father. So I killed his body and my father's mind and spirit, and all by magery."

"They had rather their king died because you didn't?" Aliam asked.

"They had rather I had used another method," Dorrin said.

"I do not blame them, Aliam. I know enough of my family's history to understand their suspicions of me. They trusted me with their children to be my squires, and two of them were put in peril in my service. Not through my intent, of course, but it happened nonetheless."

"You may not blame them, but I do," Aliam said. "I've known you long enough, seen you in battle, which they have not, to know that you are utterly honorable. Kieri told them— I know he told them—about you."

"Yes, but they did not know me. And Kieri had enemies in Tsaia beyond just my relatives—though I think my relatives were the reason he had enemies."

"You flatter your family," Aliam said, this time with a smile. "Kieri is quite capable of making enemies on his own."

Dorrin chuckled. "I have seen that in the South. Still, it's a reason for some to be less trusting of his opinion. And what happened to my squires would anger any parent."

"Squires are young fools as often as not," Aliam said. "And yours didn't die . . ."

"No, but neither of them is what he was. Daryan will be all right, especially if his heart-thumb grows."

"Wait—I hadn't heard about that." Aliam leaned forward.

"A Kuakgan, a Master Ashwind, healed him but had the strength only to mend both heel-strings and one thumb. Apparently, there's a chance that the—" Dorrin glanced at the elf, whose brows had risen. Arian knew her father was startled and a little distressed. "My pardon," she said. "I know you elves do not like Kuakkgani."

"I dislike them less than many elves," Arian's father said. "The only one I ever really talked to has a Grove in southern Tsaia, near the border. Master Oakhallow."

"You know Oakhallow?" Dorrin said. "I met him after the battle last year, when Kieri was attacked on his way here."

"Do you know why he left his Grove?" Arian's father asked.

"He had word that Paksenarrion wanted him to raise the taig for Kieri."

"That young woman," Arian's father said, "has changed the world in ways we do not yet understand."

"For Sinyi as well?" Arian asked.

"Indeed. Freeing the banast taig alone would have changed them; finding the lost prince changed them. And what else may come . . . tell me, lord Duke, was it not at the paladin's instigation that your mage powers were freed?"

"Yes."

"And I heard that you also have the power of water, which no magelord has had since Gird's day, when the Sier of Grahlin died at the Battle of Greenfields."

"If you mean that I healed a cursed well, that was the gods . . ."

"Lord Duke, if you will accept the word of one who was alive to see your ancestors arrive in Aarenis, it is wise to accept reality . . . and you may think that strange from a Sinyi. After all, we are known for enchantments that fool men. But beyond all enchantments is the world the Singer sang into being—or if it suits you better, that the Namer made by naming it, or the Maker made by hammering it out like iron on an anvil, as the dasksinyi believe. In that reality, lord Duke, your powers are as real as mine, and if you do not admit what you are, you will bring more trouble into the world, which I deem you do not wish."

"Indeed," Dorrin said, "the world has troubles enough without my adding to them. I do not wish to cause harm, sir elf, but I am not all-wise—"

"Which to know is good, but to excuse inaction is not good. We Sinyi are not accounted wise by any our enchantments do not fool, so I cannot guide you except to share my own experience. My daughter Arian here—who has never known her whole name because her mother forbade it—has met Wisdom itself. She has met Dragon and flown with him."

"You did not tell me that," Dorrin said to Arian.

"I met the dragon after I left you," Arian said. "The night the dragon's young burned tracks across Lyonya. He asked if I were wise and named me Half-Song, then bade me touch my tongue to his."

"You touched a dragon's tongue! Isn't it fire?"

"It is what the dragon wills it to be," Arian's father said. "A dragon's nature is fire, and fire transforms. So Dragon can be in the shape of anything with a mind."

"It did not even sting my tongue," Arian said. "And I felt safe inside it."

"And so you were . . . as safe as with me, or safer," her father said. "But lord Duke, when you seek wisdom, it is to Dragon you must go if human wisdom will not serve. You must learn and master your powers, for though I am no foreteller, yet I do foretell this: what the paladin wakened in you has wakened more than you know and will bring either good or ill depending on you yourself."

Dorrin grimaced. "It has chosen a poor vessel—"

"Nonsense. It has chosen a magelord of the purest blood, and one free of evil taint by her own choices and the gods' aid. Just as the gods chose that raw country girl as paladin when she had shown herself able . . . so you. That is why I wanted to meet you and speak with you. I have knowledge you may need."

"Do you know what that crown really is?" Dorrin asked.

"*Really* is?" Arian's father looked away then back at her. "I know something about it but not everything. You will have heard by now, I suspect, that the dasksinyi say the jewels came from no source they know, and disclaim any part in its making—as do we Sinyi. It was made by men—perhaps with aid I do not know—and men of your blood: magelords."

"It speaks to me," Dorrin said. "I told the king and the Marshal-General that: they could hear nothing. Do you know if it has a demon in it, or one of my family's mind, to speak?"

"I do not know all its nature," Arian's father said. "What I do know is that it has chosen you, by all accounts, and yet it is possible that another could find and abuse its powers."

"They tell me not even Paksenarrion can now move it from the treasury in Vérella," Dorrin said. "If she can't, who else could?"

"So I also heard," he said. "However, one other might do so. Part of the set was stolen from Fin Panir and is now in the hands of the man you knew as Alured the Black, now calling himself the Duke of Immer."

"I met him in Siniava's War. I did not know he had the necklace," Dorrin said. "Why does that give him the power to move the other pieces if he can reach them?"

"I am not sure," he said. "But I know it might if he shares your bloodline. He badly wants to prove himself descended from the kings of Old Aare, and it might be so . . . I did not memorize the pedigree of every human in Aare and Aarenis from the migration until now." He sounded resentful. "Then he need only kill you, and the crown might yield to him."

"Oh." Dorrin looked as startled as Arian felt. "You think he knows that?"

"I think he sees you as his rival, because he knows where the jewels were for so long. He must suspect that you inherited the power to use them."

"Is it possible that he has spread lies about Dorrin in Tsaia?" Arian asked.

"It is certain," he said. "She became Constable, and she warned Tsaia's king of danger from this fellow—he would see her as a personal enemy, anyway. And he has met you, has he not?"

"Yes," Dorrin said. "The last year of Siniava's War, Kieri allied with him—we thought he was just another half-civilized brigand."

"At heart he is all brigand. My point is that he knows your face; he can send his assassins after you. That crown in Alured's hands could ruin not just the south but the north as well."

"You were there, you say, when my ancestors came to Aarenis . . . from Old Aare?"

"Yes. We had left Aare—"

"Elves were in Old Aare?" She had not considered that they existed anywhere but where they were now.

"Yes. And it is something we do not talk about with anyone else: it involves the Severance. Then we came to the north, and a few humans were there already—they sailed over, and some farmed and some fished. We moved on to the forests, which we prefer, and found the mountains already inhabited by dasksinyi. They let us live in the forests but said we would be happier over the mountains, so most of us came—and all, in the end. We told the dasksinyi about the magelords of Aare, and they helped us set wards to keep them back if they ever came so far north."

"I never knew that," Dorrin said.

"Nor I," said Aliam.

"And you would not, if I were not minded to save my daughter great grief, and the world as well. Listen, then: when the magelords came, with those things you found, they used that power to break the wards we set and reset them for their own purposes. The Sinyi were evil, they said."

"Why?"

"Why did they say that? An old quarrel. Some elves mistook all humans for Kuakkgani, for one thing. For another . . . the rise of the magelords seemed to mean a loss of our power, and we had been proud of it a long, long time."

"The dragon told me that you asked dragons to limit their children."

"We did, since they could not control them, and each clutch a dragon laid could produce hundreds. Neither we nor any other creature could survive if they bred freely. Dragon saw the sense of this and agreed to limit their young to those they could train."

"Will you tell me what you know of my family?" Dorrin said.

"I do not know how much to tell," Dameroth said. "And some of it I did not see myself but heard from others, and not Sinyi alone. I cannot tell you what the jewels are, only that they are unlike all others known to me and full of power. We believe they were made by magelords."

"Made? Not found? They looked like ordinary jewels, not made things . . ."

"If neither we nor the dasksinyi know where they could be found, then I think they were made later."

"By my ancestors?"

"By them or others like them. And I do not know how, except I suspect that the higher mageries you have—with water and healing—have something to do with it."

"I don't think that my being a target for assassination by Alured is going to convince Duke Mahieran that I'm not conspiring against the king."

"No, almost certainly not. I find human politics unpleasantly similar to Sinyi court maneuvers, and I am too familiar with such things." He made the elven gesture to avert evil. "But I believe you must find a way to . . . to make use of whatever those jewels are, or destroy them. And in the meantime stay alert for danger." He turned to Arian. "And you, beloved daughter, flower of the forest that you are: be wary, child, for yourself and for the child you carry. This realm has been robbed before."

"Kieri's sister's bones talk to him," Arian said.

He shuddered. "Do not, please, talk of such things. It is not in our nature to think what our remains might do. When we are gone, we are gone."

"She also warns, Father. She warns me as well."

"Thank the gods you were ranger before Squire and Squire before queen, then. You will know how to protect yourself . . . if you are not taken by surprise."

"Do you know what happened to his mother?" Arian asked. "The bones say treachery; Kieri suspects someone . . . No, let me be clear; he suspects elves, because he was told she expected an elven escort that never came."

Dameroth seemed to fade and solidify again before their eyes. "I cannot . . . I cannot say. I was away . . . sent on an errand to the western kingdom. I have had thoughts, but they are only thoughts at this time. I asked and was told one version and then another. It is not something to ask the Lady, I can tell you that."

"Does she know?"

"I don't know. And I must not say more, not here—"

"Not even if it means the life of your grandson?"

He faded and solidified again. "My heart . . . I would not see you hurt. I worry . . . but here, so near what your king suspects and the bones of his ancestors, I cannot ... . It could endanger you more, if I were overheard or if I was wrong in my guesses. Another time, another place."

CHAPTER TWENTY-SEVEN

KIERI PHELAN GREETED his old friend Sonder Mahieran warmly. He suspected the Tsaian duke would want to talk about Dorrin and whatever had happened with her squires . . . especially how Sonder's son Beclan had become Dorrin's adopted heir. He would hear it again from Dorrin, he was sure, but he wanted Mahieran's side of the story.

Instead, Mahieran began with conventional courtesies. "I'm glad to see you married again, sir king," he said with a bow.

Kieri did not correct the formality. If this went as he expected, they might both be better within its limits. "I never thought to, my lord Duke," he said, relaxing into his chair and waving Mahieran to another. "But once this happened," he waved his hand at the room and all it represented, "I knew I must. Then, with Arian, I knew I wanted to."

"She's half-elven like you?" Mahieran looked hard at Kieri.

"Yes." Kieri knew he had changed in his year in Lyonya—he had lost the few gray hairs among the red; he knew he looked younger. Was it enough for Mahieran to notice?

"I've always wondered how the joint kingdom works, sir king," Mahieran said, settling more firmly in the chair across from Kieri. "Lyonya's never been a problem to our realm, but I confess I still find elves uncanny. Naturally so, of course. Not like . . . um."

"It works like a cart with one square wheel," Kieri said. "They're so beautiful, so elegant, and being long-lived, they give the sense of age we associate with wisdom. It's easy to think of them as Elders . . . but in practice, they're as full of foolish pride, stubbornness, and downright obstructiveness as any human."

"But wasn't your mother—?"

"An elf, yes. As is her mother, still alive."

"How old are they really?" That was what humans always wanted to know about elves.

"I don't know. I can't ask—it's the height of rudeness. Even my grandmother."

"And she rules them, I know. How is she to work with?"

"Mostly she's not here," Kieri said. "Especially when I need her to answer a question." He looked at Mahieran. Of course the man would be interested in Lyonya's method of governance; it had been a mystery to all outside the realm. But he would rather get to the topic he was sure Mahieran most wanted to discuss—his son. "I was glad to see your sons looking so well," he said, forcing the topic.

Mahieran shifted in his seat. "I suppose we must get this over with, sir king. Before anything—I agree that Beclan's . . . difficulty . . . was not due to any negligence on Duke Verrakai's part."

"Good," Kieri said.

"Still, if I had not sent him to her as squire, none of this would have happened."

"Are you sure?" Kieri said. "That close in succession, he would be the logical target for renegade Verrakaien anyway. Not Camwyn, not you, not Rothlin—all of you at court, constantly observed. Beclan is just the age—and was in just the position—where an enemy might seek to enthrall him, gain control of him, wherever he was."

Mahieran frowned, tapping his fingers on the arm of the chair. "I had not thought of that."

"How active have you been searching for such enemies since Mikeli's coronation?"

"We . . . haven't, really. Duke Verrakai was supposed—"

"To rebuild and manage Verrakai lands, act as Constable and chivvy you peers into doing proper training to meet your obligations to the crown, patrol the whole kingdom constantly, root out every evil—?" His tone made his opinion of that clear.

Mahieran flushed. "It's *her* family. No . . . I see your point. We expected too much."

"You did indeed," Kieri said. "Falk and Gird together, when alive, could not do all you demanded of her. And what I know of Dorrin is that she won't ever complain at being asked for more."

"Mmm. I just wish I didn't have to be grateful—"

"Grateful?"

"She saved my life and Beclan's—she saved the king's last summer and healed Marrakai from his head injury. Reason enough for gratitude. And yet . . . my wife never liked her."

"Ah. I suppose the court ladies found her intimidating."

"Unnatural, is what they said. You know she wore male court attire at the coronation—?"

"I heard, yes," Kieri said. "Seemed sensible to me."

"And no one's ever seen her in a skirt."

"I haven't," Kieri said. "But what of it? The Marshal-General never wears a skirt."

"It bothers the women," Mahieran said. "We've all seen women in trousers, of course; women ride astride, after all, and train in arms. But—she's different."

"What does your wife think now?" Kieri asked. "Dorrin saved your life, Beclan's, the king's . . . Surely she's softened her opinion."

Mahieran paled; for a moment Kieri thought he was angry and wondered why. "Then you have not heard all the gossip, sir king."

"I'm certain I have not. What troubles you now?"

"Celbrin," Mahieran said, tight-lipped. He told the story of the attack in the remote cottage in more detail than Kieri had heard before. "And when we got back to the house, Celbrin would have attacked Duke Verrakai if Beclan had not intervened. I was too weak. Next morning she left before I was aware, riding to Vérella to complain to the king about Duke Verrakai."

"Mmm," Kieri said. "And her complaint would have been—?"

"That Duke Verrakai was unnatural, a man in a woman's body, invaded in childhood and thus a tool of evil." Mahieran scrubbed at his face with both hands. "I didn't know—I couldn't have known—she was Konhalten, you see, but a branch that wasn't so attached to Verrakai. My father hoped by our marriage to wean more of them away . . . She's never shown any sign—"

"She hates Verrakai? Including Dorrin?"

"No! No . . . that's not it. She's—she must be—the source of Beclan's magery. She must have it herself—untrained—Duke Verrakai said she might not have known and never used it."

"Dorrin says your *wife* has magery?"

"No, no. She hasn't detected it, but—when I looked more deeply—Celbrin's father's grandmother was Verrakaien. It could be there. And Celbrin, since—since we asked—she's—she's not like she was."

"And of course that presents concerns not only about Beclan but about Rothlin as well," Kieri said, without inquiring what "not like she was" really meant. "And your daughters."

"Yes. Roth's third in succession. He doesn't think he has any magery, but neither did Beclan before this. The only person who might detect it is Duke Verrakai. And worse—this is not the first marriage that brought Verrakai blood into Mahierans. What if somehow *I* have the taint and never knew it? If my brother Beclan's children—if all the Mahierans—are tainted? It could bring down the throne, Kieri." Formality had vanished in Mahieran's distress.

"Who knows all of this?" Kieri asked.

"Mikeli, of course. The Marshal-Judicar—he's new since your time: Donag was killed in the assassinations last spring. Oktar's knowledgeable, but I'm not sure he's as committed to the realm as Donag was. He's insisting we must all be tested— all the peers who have intermarried with Verrakai any time in the last ten generations. Essentially all of us. And Mikeli and Camwyn."

"That will upset applecarts all over Tsaia," Kieri said. "Not a good time for that, with the trouble in the south I'm hearing about."

"No. What's odd is that Oktar has defended Duke Verrakai—said Beclan's capture wasn't her fault, for instance. You'd think he'd condemn her first. But again—he can't detect magery that's not being used, so it comes back to Duke Verrakai to test them."

"And you sent your son to her."

"Mikeli commanded it. The only way, he said, to save Mahieran's claim to the throne and not throw the whole realm into chaos was to disclaim Beclan and ensure he was where his magery would do no harm. He'd thought of condemning him for oathbreaking, but that would mean spilling all in public."

"How is he, do you think?"

"Better than I could have hoped. Alive, sane, and far more mature than a year ago. We're forbidden contact while in Tsaia. I can send messages to Duke Verrakai—transfer funds and so on—but Beclan may not speak nor write, nor receive letters directly, at least for now. All my communications with Duke Verrakai must be screened by the king and the Marshal-Judicar." He paused. "But I came here, instead of Mikeli, so that Beclan could meet with me and his brother. Mikeli told me so himself."

"He always had a generous heart, that young man," Kieri said.

"Yes. I am, however, to have a witness at such meetings— not within earshot, necessarily, but in sight."

"That's hard. But here, Sonder, we have many who can be witnesses and not talk later."

"You're suggesting—?"

"Only that I will make it as easy for you as possible. This was not your fault, or Beclan's, or Dorrin's . . . not even Celbrin's, if she didn't know of her magery." Kieri paused; when Mahieran nodded, he went on. "What about Dorrin's former heir, that other Verrakai? What does he think?"

"Ganarrion Verrakai, yes. Says he's delighted; he never wanted to run an estate anyway. He was acquitted of treason, you know; he's serving again in the Royal Guard, and that's what he wants to do."

"But doesn't that mean he also knows about Beclan's magery? Do you really think you can keep that a secret?"

Mahieran shook his head. "Not forever, certainly. We're saying publicly that because there's the barest chance Beclan was contaminated by the renegades, he had to be cast out. That we believe his being able to defeat all those grown men was by Gird's aid but we're taking no chances. It's proof that the king is as hard on his own family as on anyone else."

"And your wife—what about her?"

"She's . . . confined right now in our house in Vérella. She's angry, of course. And though my father made the match for me, as hers did for her, I loved her. She's the mother of our children; she's been a good wife, a good consort. I don't want to hurt her, and I already have."

"As she hurt you, Sonder. I doubt she wanted to." Celbrin had been one of those who thought Kieri unworthy of his ducal rank—he'd overheard her, years back, telling someone he was an upstart from nowhere—but he'd also known her fierce loyalty to her husband and children.

Mahieran shook his head; his shoulders had slumped. "And if she proves to be more than just the bearer of magery to Beclan? If she is inhabited, or . . . I don't know what . . ."

"What does your new Marshal-Judicar say?"

"That she must be tested. That is all he will say. Oh, and he would bring the Marshal-General into it, which Mikeli—and I—would rather not."

"You must," Kieri said. "Sonder, the Marshal-General will know in the end—better from you than from your enemies. With her on your side—"

"If she is on our side—"

"She is on Gird's side, and though I am a Falkian I honor the old man with the club. Some of his followers have gone far astray but not, I think, this Marshal-General. Will Celbrin listen to her?"

"Yes, I think so. She wants nothing to do with a paladin, however, and that frightens me." Mahieran stared at the floor a long moment, then lifted his gaze again to Kieri. "So much has happened since your paladin came and proclaimed you heir to this realm. Every life she touched has changed, and not all for the better."

"So my wife's father said—and predicted that we have not seen the end of it."

"Another elf?" Mahieran asked.

"Another elf," Kieri said, nodding. "And in the best tradition of so many families, Arian's father is at odds with my grandmother."

Mahieran chuckled at that. "My mother and Celbrin's were never best friends either. I wish you more joy of the elven conflict than I had of the human one." Then he sobered. "What are we to do, then, Kieri? How are we all to get past this and into a season of peace?"

"Tell your king, Sonder, that we will do all we can to help— assure him that although I am now king in another realm, I respect and care for him as I always did, though my people are now my greater responsibility. You and I will go on doing the best we can. There is no other way."

"You are right, Kieri. Sir king, I should say."

Kieri waved his hand. "You and I can use titles to cool our tempers if we must, but for me you are the friend you were when I was first at court. I cannot solve your problems, nor you mine, but let us be friends." He offered his hand, and Mahieran shook it.

When Mahieran had left the room, he went up to his own chamber and looked out the window to the south. Far up the Royal Ride, he saw a group riding a pattern, the horses weaving in and out of a ring. Rothlin, Beclan, and a bevy of young women, he was sure. Ganlin and Elis rode the two Pargunese Blacks.

YOUNG LADIES OF good family being deemed sufficient witness by their father, Rothlin and Beclan took advantage of the fine day after the wedding to canter up the Royal Ride on horses borrowed from the king's stable, surrounded by those young ladies who felt their riding skills sufficient to make a show.

Ganlin of Kostandan stayed close to Rothlin—stirrup to stirrup—on a big Pargunese Black her older brother had brought from home. She rode superbly, and sunlight favored her golden hair. Elis of Pargun also rode a Pargunese Black but made little attempt to approach Rothlin or Beclan; she seemed absorbed in the riding itself. Beclan found himself surrounded by Siers' daughters and granddaughters— Halveric, Belvarin, Tolmaric, Davonin. His original intent, to beg his brother for news from the family, proved impossible.

Skilled young riders on such a day . . . they must race; they must ride dance figures; they must leap the logs set so handily along one side of the ride. They challenged one another; they admired one another's horses—and, as they were all well aware, they admired one another. They came back in the afternoon, sun-flushed and laughing, the horses properly cooled out before being handed over to the palace staff. Roth, Beclan noticed, helped Ganlin dismount from her tall horse. Elis of Pargun did not wait for assistance, nor did any of the Lyonyan girls. Elis took her own horse into the stable, clearly not part of their group. He knew she was Pargun's ambassador to Lyonya—that her father was king of Pargun—and did not understand her lack of interest in Rothlin.

But he had no interest in Ganlin or Elis, both older than he; he thought the Lyonyan girls, with their lilting accent and their interest in him, by far the prettiest and best.

On their way to bathe and dress for dinner, Rothlin said "You're doing well, brother."

The misery came back for a moment, but after that day in the sunshine and the company of those who admired him, it vanished again. "I hope to do better," he said.

"Those are fine girls, Beclan. You need to start thinking—"

"I'm too young to marry!" Beclan said.

"Yes, but not too young for your duke to be thinking of succession. If you have a favorite, tell her now."

"And you?"

Roth grinned. "Well . . . you saw Ganlin. A princess, which means sufficient rank for anyone. Her father would like her to make a good marriage, away from Kostandan. Her brother told me that. I suspect her father would like her to marry Mikeli, but Mikeli's not likely to marry outside the realm. And Ganlin likes me. She's at Falk's Hall now, but she may not stay to get her ruby. She might rather have a husband. She said that."

Beclan opened his mouth to remind Roth that other girls had befriended him as a way of getting close to Mikeli, but his brother looked too happy and he could not bear to start a quarrel.

CHAPTER TWENTY-EIGHT

Valdaire

ARVID SEMMINSON FINGERED the familiar pockets in the black cloak he'd taken from one of the thieves, checking each blade and the Thieves' Guild icon on its chain he'd put in the narrowest. Dattur thought he was being a fool. But Dattur did not fully recognize the danger the letter from the Marshal-General presented in the wrong hands. With the letter, the Valdaire Guildmaster could send a real thief to a grange, and the Marshal would probably trust him.

He was not merely seeking vengeance against Master Mathol, he told himself. Not at all. He needed to retrieve that letter and, incidentally, his own Guildmaster medallion. He would not involve Dattur. He would do it himself.

His transformation from Ser Burin, the merchant, to Arvid Semminson, trained enforcer and assassin, took place in the stable. He wore a black leather coif padded over the head for protection from blows. The pair of stiffened leather "donkey ears" that funneled faint sounds to him through holes in the coif were tucked in a pocket of his doublet. Midnight blue trousers instead of black—that could not be helped. An undershirt, mail, and a black shirt over it. His weapons all where they should be, every blade honed and polished. Black gloves with a suede palm for more friction. Soft climbing half-boots, cross-gartered to the knee. And the black cloak, something any thief would recognize, its hood pulled well forward, hiding his face.

By dawn, he was nestled in the second attic of the Thieves' Guild house. It would have been dramatic to confront the Master at the turn of night, but Arvid knew that Guildmasters rarely slept at night. From full dark on, the Master would be alert and busy, taking reports from thieves on the night shift. No, he would wait until broad day. By day most Thieves' Guild houses had only a small door guard on duty, with a senior to answer inquiries from the city guard. The day shift would be out in the streets, picking pockets and stealing small items, while the night shift slept. It usually took two—at most three— turns of the glass for the Master to count and clerks to record the night's takings and assign bonuses and punishments where they were due. By midmorning, the Guildhouse was as quiet as it would ever be.

Arvid waited, a donkey's ear touching the ceiling below him, until the unmelodious sound of snoring from the thieves asleep in the room directly below replaced talk and movement. Then he removed the donkey's ear, put it back in his pocket, and moved carefully back to the attic access. Not the obvious trapdoor—it would squeal like a wounded pig if moved—but the concealed one used by the roof guard. The now-dead roof guard.

Once in the house itself, he walked normally—light sleepers might wake, and within the house only children practiced sneaking. Valdaire's Guildhouse was larger and more populous than any in the north, with a steady stream of visitors from other southern cities as well as those from the north, so a stranger's face would cause no alarm to most. As he descended the main stairs, he saw no one, as he'd expected. The house's narrow front belied its true shape—a wedge much wider in the back. The Guildmaster, Arvid recalled from his earlier disastrous visit, had his apartment in the center back. Would he be in his sitting room still or abed?

Hardly having to think, Arvid stepped over squeaking floorboards, touched the walls here and there to prevent traps from springing . . . the signs were obvious to him, and the house felt more homelike, less dangerous, for these things. In other buildings, he was never sure where the traps were—even *if* the traps were.

The Guildmaster's personal guard, the last defense but one, had trusted in the security of the house; Arvid killed him as he dozed on his bench and rolled the corpse under the Guildmaster's desk. Then he searched the parlor-office. He found his own Guildmaster medallion and the Marshal-General's letter in a little carved box shoved into one of the pigeonholes along the wall. He tucked them into one of his pockets. He found paper, pen, and sealing wax, then wrote the traditional words. From the casket that held the night's takings, he took the traditional assassin's fee, leaving the rest. Then he moved to the door of the bedchamber.

The last defense would have stopped most, but not a Guild enforcer, who—if a Guild turned against its Master—must be able to remove him. Arvid disarmed the trap, removed, capped, and pocketed the poisoned darts—another perquisite of an assassin who killed a Guildmaster—and opened the door.

The Guildmaster lay on his back, mouth open, snoring, in a nightshirt of pale blue silk. In the curve of his arm lay a child whose face was streaked with tears.

Sick fury came over Arvid. He had intended to wake the Guildmaster, the point of a blade to the man's throat, to be sure he knew who was about to kill him. Now memories he'd refused for decades washed over him; cold sweat drenched him.

The child stirred, moaned a little; the Guildmaster's arm tightened on the child. He grunted in his sleep, and then his eyes opened.

Before the Guildmaster could draw breath, Arvid struck, a blow with his fist to the man's throat that stopped all sound but the creaking of the bed as he thrashed for breath. "I am your death, Mathol," he murmured, as tradition demanded. The child woke, choked back a cry, and stared at Arvid.

It was his own face. It would always be his own face, no matter what child—dark, fair, tall, short, thin, plump. Arvid fought his roiling stomach and tried to smile at the child he knew he should kill. This one was small, dark of hair and eye, thin. So had Arvid been. Born a thief, brought up as a thief, subject to the whim of the Guildmaster. So had Arvid been.

The child stared back at him, not crying out, not pleading for mercy. Boy? Girl? Arvid could not yet see; the child's fists were clenched now on the bedclothes, mouth shut tight. A well-schooled child of the House. The child would die si-

lently—and it would be a mercy after what the child had endured.

Kill the child and you kill yourself. The voice rang in his
head. Arvid shivered, cold to the bone as if he lay once more
naked in the winter rain. He had to; he knew he had to, yet he
could not. Not that child, not that day.

"Be quiet," he said to the child. The child nodded and made
the sign for "sealed lips." Arvid glanced around the room and
spotted what might be the child's clothes on the floor near the
door. "Dress yourself," he said. The child slid from under the
covers. Arvid did not want to look; the sight of the child's face
and shoulders had brought torment enough, but the child's
training would hold him quiet only so long as Arvid looked
and acted like a thief of the House.

The child was a boy. He scuttled across to his clothes and
pulled them on hurriedly.

"Sit there," Arvid said, pointing to the floor by the bed, and
the boy sat down. Arvid took the Guildmaster's medallion,
then wrestled his seal ring off his dead finger and tucked it into
one of his own pockets. He kept a close watch on the boy, but
the boy did not move; he might have been carved of wood. Yet
the eyes were intelligent, alert, noting every detail of Arvid
and what Arvid did. Training, yes, but also more to remind
Arvid of his young self.

Arvid came back around the bed. "Do you know who I am?"

"A Master's Death," the boy said softly. "Who sent you?"

"We never tell," Arvid said. The boy would expect that.
"You will come with me."

The boy's eyes glistened for a moment; he blinked the tears
away. "You will kill me," he said.

"Perhaps," Arvid said. "But not in this room. And not in the
next, if you do what I say."

The small shoulders sagged. "Yes, Master."

Arvid's heart nearly stopped at that, a solid pain in the chest,
but he held out his hand. "Come, boy." He could feel through
his glove the trembling of the boy's fingers. In the next room,
he laid the paper he'd already written on top of the other papers, melted wax with a candle, and stamped the Guildmaster's own seal into it, all while trying to think how he could get

out of the place with the boy, both of them alive and with a chance to escape completely.

His original plan had been to retrace his steps up through the house to the roof, then climb from roof to roof and finally down to a street and away. This would not work with a bare-foot child in tow, even assuming the child to be perfectly docile.

Out the front? By now—Arvid estimated the time he'd spent in the house so far—it would not be far from midday. The younger children sent out to pick pockets early would be re-turning to report soon. He could hear nothing, but the Master's apartment was deliberately placed in the quietest, least-trafficked area. And the boy—would the boy yell? Did he feel real loyalty to his House? Were his parents still here?

"You have a choice," he said to the boy. "I have orders—" Never mind that they came from a god he had never meant to serve. "—to remove you from this House for a time. Alive or dead. If you wish to stay alive, you will stay silent and do ex-actly what I tell you. If you wish death, it will come."

Again the boy's eyes glistened, and again he blinked the tears back. Arvid's heart contracted. So young and so brave. *So were you. Take care of him.*

"I . . . don't want to die . . . if it hurts," the boy said.

"Then will you do as I say?"

"Yes, Master."

"I will tell the door-wards that the Master bade me take you out to the street, far from the house. That you are being pun-ished and are not to be allowed back in until dawn tomorrow. Say nothing but cry if you can, or at least feign crying."

"Yes, Master."

"I may have to jerk you about," Arvid said.

"Yes, Master."

The look on the boy's face, mingled terror and hope, made his own eyes sting. "Over my shoulder you go, then," Arvid said. The boy's body hardly seemed to weigh anything.

He met only one other thief before the door; that one chuck-led and said, "What'd he do, throw up again?"

Arvid nodded and went on without speaking. At the front of

the house, the door-wards eyed him with more curiosity for his burden than for himself. "Boy needs another dose?"

Again Arvid nodded and in a mix of Common and thieves' cant described what had earned the boy punishment.

"Master should just strangle him and get another," one of the door-wards said. The other looked shocked and made the gesture for silence. "Take him a good long way, then," the first said. "Little rat isn't grateful for a warm bed and a bellyful needs to learn what the real world is like."

They opened the doors to let Arvid out. He went down the two steps to street level with intentional roughness, smacking the boy on the rump. The boy's arms flopped against his back. As they cleared the Guild perimeter, two shop fronts down the street, Arvid set the boy roughly on his feet—as the man he pretended to be would—and grabbed his arm. "Come on, then," he said. "And don't snivel."

Other thieves would be watching, recognizing the punishment. Arvid walked fast, half-dragging the barefoot boy and paying no attention to his stumbles or muffled yelps of pain. He ignored as well the angry looks of street merchants and their customers in the first market square they passed through. He was trying to think how to work around to the inn without revealing where he was going. By now he knew the city fairly well, but there were areas where someone in thieves' black, out by daylight, would be stopped and questioned.

"Stop, you!" The voice was loud enough to turn heads. Arvid looked back to see a burly man in Girdish blue—a Marshal, he guessed—striding toward him at the head of a small group of men. He could run, but only by carrying the boy, and that would slow him. And now in midday, the streets were busy—a running man in thieves' black with a child in tow would surely be a target. Already others were slowing, stopping to watch.

"What?" Arvid said, moving until his back was to a shop wall, not a window.

"Let go of that child," the Marshal said. He was armed with a sword; his companions brandished the wooden clubs they called hauks. The child, apparently thinking this was a good time to follow orders, produced a couple of genuine-sounding sobs. Fresh tears streaked his face, along with mucus from a runny nose.

"I'm taking him to safety," Arvid said.

"And I'm an elf with a purse full of fairy gold," the Marshal said. "Do you think I'm stupid enough to believe that?"

"He don't hurt me," the boy said. He grabbed Arvid's hand with his free one. "He like me."

"You've cowed him," the Marshal said, without taking his gaze from Arvid's face. "But you won't cow us."

Arvid had the sense of someone laughing at him from far away. What now? He had done what Gird wanted. *Not exactly.* As well as he could have. *Maybe.* And now Girdsmen were going to attack him for that? Yet he knew what they would be thinking. The Marshal took a step forward. "Let go, I tell you. Or you're a dead man."

"I need to show you something," Arvid said. He lifted his hand slowly; the Marshal sucked in a noisy breath. "I have a letter from the Marshal-General. I would show it to you." Behind the Marshal and his men, a small crowd gathered now, nudging elbows and muttering.

"You must think me an utter fool," the Marshal said. "You? A letter from her?"

"Yes," Arvid said. He saw the Marshal's intent waver slightly at the confidence he showed. "Take me to your grange, where we can talk privately."

"A thief wants to go to a grange!" one of the other men said. "Now that's a surprise."

"Quiet, yeoman-marshal," the Marshal said. "And you— will you release that boy to us if I agree?"

"I will take him there myself. He is unused to being out of the House and does not know you."

"Do you know him, boy?" the Marshal asked the boy. "What's his name?"

"He knows me only as an enforcer," Arvid said. "Enforcers are not part of the regular community."

"If he makes a move to draw a weapon, kill him," the Marshal said to his followers. And to Arvid, "Come along, and be gentle with the lad."

"Up you come," Arvid said, picking the boy up, this time cradling him in his arms.

The grange opened on a narrow side lane. Arvid followed the Marshal inside and found himself in what seemed at first a sort of cave. Behind him the door banged shut; he heard the thud of a bar falling into place to hold it closed.

Then light rose from the far end—from a niche in the far wall—brighter than any lamp he'd ever seen. The room was large—large enough to hold a hundred men—high-ceilinged, stone-floored, with a wooden platform knee high and several strides long and wide at the far end, and weapons racked along both walls. Light filled it now, leaving no corner in shadow. His skin drew up in prickles. The men around him, angry as they seemed, were only men, but a power he had never encountered filled the place.

The boy nestled in his arms, relaxing muscle by muscle. Whatever Arvid felt, the boy felt something comforting.

"Bring a blanket for the lad," the Marshal said, still watching Arvid. One of the men moved quickly down the length of the room and disappeared into a passage at one corner. He returned in moments with a blanket. "We will lay him on the platform," the Marshal said, "and see what we see."

Arvid carried the boy to the platform and laid him on the folded blanket. "Be at ease," he said. "They will not hurt you."

"Go up on the platform," the Marshal said. "That corner: stand there." It was as far away from the boy as the platform allowed and closest to the niche in the wall that gave the light. To the others he said, "Dern, open the shutters. Cal, sit with the child. You others, stand behind him and be ready to strike if he does anything." The Marshal then walked around the platform to the niche. High overhead, shutters creaked open and daylight poured in; the uncanny light contracted until it lit only the niche itself.

"What was that?" Arvid said when he felt he could steady his voice.

"Gird's light," the Marshal said. "Not too surprising it came when you entered. Gird is not fond of evil."

"Boy's been hurt," the man looking at the boy said. "What you'd expect of them filth."

"You?" the Marshal asked Arvid.

"No," Arvid said. "I was taking him away from that."

The Marshal put his hand into the niche and withdrew what looked like a piece of stick, ragged at one end where it had broken. "This is a relic of Gird," he said. "Do you know what that means?"

"No," Arvid said. He was sweating again. "Don't you want to see the letter?"

"If there is a letter, it's a fake," the Marshal said. "She would not give a letter to a liar, murderer, and thief."

"She did," Arvid said.

"We shall see," the Marshal said. "Hold this and tell the truth if you are able. If you do not, you will be hurt: Gird's relic knows truth and hates lies."

Arvid took the wood—uneven, like a branch once stripped of bark and smoothed by many hands. It felt slightly warm from the Marshal's grip.

The Marshal stepped up on the platform and faced him. "Do you deny that you are a liar?"

His usual cleverness of tongue deserted him. "I have lied," he said. "But I do not always lie." The wood warmed in his hand, but not to discomfort. Then the warmth receded.

The Marshal's expression was unreadable. "Are you a thief?"

"I was trained as a thief," Arvid said. "I was—am—a member of the Thieves' Guild; I was trained as an enforcer after my years as apprentice thief. I do not steal now but at great need— like getting this boy away." Again the wood in his hand warmed, and again the warmth receded.

"And are you a murderer?" the Marshal asked. "Have you killed humans who did not menace you?"

"I have killed," Arvid said. "I have killed on order of my Guildmaster—"

"That is murder," the Marshal said.

"Then yes, I am a murderer," Arvid said. He felt a weight on his shoulders pressing him down and down, but he braced his legs and back against it.

"Did you not realize that before?"

How could he possibly explain, and yet he had to try. "Marshal, the Thieves' Guild has its own laws, and someone to enforce them, just as the city has its laws, and someone to enforce them. In Thieves' Guild law, to kill a man at the Guildmaster's order is to be an executioner, not a murderer. Someone else killing a thief, that's murder."

"And you kept believing that?"

"Mostly, yes." Until . . . until last year. Until Paksenarrion's ordeal. Until he felt compelled to save her—first her body, he thought, and then her life. Until he had killed to save her from that crazy, angry woman. Until she had said Gird might have plans for him and for the Guild. "It was Paksenarrion," was all he could say aloud. The wood warmed in his hand again and this time glowed so brightly that he could see the bones of his fingers as shadows in red flesh. It didn't hurt.

"Well." The Marshal rocked back on his heels. "The relic shows you telling truth. And you were touched by a paladin, were you?"

"Yes," Arvid said.

"And how has it been since then?"

"Since? I—" Tears rose again, this time overflowing; he could not stop them or the sobs that made his voice ragged. "I—I tried—I can't—I am not the same. I can't—do—what I did. I can't feel—without that other. And the voice—"

"Voice?"

"In my—in my head. Saying things—"

The Marshal's bushy gray brows had risen almost to his hairline. "You hear a voice, do you? Gird's voice?"

"I don't—I don't know—" *Yes, you do,* the voice said. *You know who I am. Tell him.* Arvid struggled again with his own voice and said, "He says he's Gird." Light flared between his fingers again, brighter even than before. The boy was sitting up now, resting against the man's knee, mouth open, staring. "It can't be Gird, can it?" Arvid asked the Marshal, hating the pleading in his voice. "I know she said—but it can't be—"

"If it's not Gird, who do you think is making that light?" the Marshal said. "Here in Gird's grange, who but Gird could make Gird's relic do that?"

"I don't know," Arvid said. His hands shook.

"Let me see the letter," the Marshal said. He put out his hand for the relic.

Arvid handed over the relic and fumbled the Marshal-General's letter out of a pocket, annoyed with his trembling fingers. He was an adult; he was a— *Fool.* He tried to shut the voice out of his mind, close every door and window there, but though the voice said no more for the moment, he knew that presence remained.

Instead, he watched the Marshal. The man read with pursed lips, intent. Once he looked up at Arvid, then back at the letter. Then he sighed. "Well," he said. "It appears that this is in fact a letter granting safe passage to a man doing some task for the Marshal-General. Whether that man is you . . . I do not see a kteknik gnome at your side."

"He's at the inn where I've been staying," Arvid said. "Dattur is the name he gives humans. Mine is Arvid Semminson."

"How did the Guildmaster of thieves come to have possession of this letter?"

Arvid told the story of his arrival in Valdaire, his approach to the Guildmaster, his capture and near death, then his return to the city.

"Why did you risk that?"

"The pass to the north was closed—I could not go back. Dattur and I had some gold—we took it from the men who tried to kill us."

"Are they dead?"

"Yes, but I didn't kill them. The ground collapsed." The Marshal gave Arvid a sharp look but did not ask more. "And then here, I set up as a small merchant. Dattur does tailors' work for a rockfolk shop. That's given us enough to live on for the winter."

"And the Guildmaster who captured you?"

"Dead," Arvid said. "And by my hand."

"At whose command?"

"My own. I counted it self-defense; you may not."

"I count it vengeance. A sword has fangs: it bites those who wield it." The Marshal sighed. "You are in more trouble than you know, Arvid Semminson. I believe you are speaking truth, but the truth too has fangs. You cannot walk the streets in safety today, not like that—" His gesture took in Arvid's choice of clothing and more. "I trust you left no clues behind you, but still—"

"I left clues," Arvid said. "I intended them to know who had done it."

"Then you will stay as my guest until nightfall, then leave the boy safe here and go."

Arvid shook his head. "I cannot—"

"You cannot take him into your quarrel, man. You are a danger to him whether you mean him harm or not. He is a child. We can care for him, find him a home, see that he is not hurt again."

"They will come looking for him; they will blame him, too." Arvid dug the heels of his hands into his eyes, trying to make a darkness in which he could think. "I didn't think—I didn't expect a child to be there—"

"And you got him out safely. A good thing. But not thinking—not ever a good thing." The Marshal's voice softened. "You need a cup of sib and a chance to sit down. Come on back to my office."

"The boy—" Arvid glanced over; one of the other men was talking to the boy in a low voice, but the boy was watching Arvid.

"We'll talk about that, too." The Marshal stepped off the platform and put the relic back in its niche. It did not glow. Arvid turned his back on it with difficulty—would it start glowing again?—and walked over to the boy. The man looked up, ready to be angry; the boy smiled.

"Says his name is Arvid, too," the man said. "Not a common name here. Is it up north?"

"Common enough," Arvid said. "Maybe his family was from the north."

"Says his mother worked in a tavern. Doesn't remember a father. She died of fever five winters ago." He stared at Arvid as if he thought meaning could cross the space without words to carry it.

"You've been in Aarenis before," the Marshal said. His look was also challenging.

"Yes . . . are you asking if I'm his father?" Arvid glanced at the boy; he was staring at Arvid, wide-eyed.

"It's a question," the Marshal said.

"I don't know," Arvid said. In the boy's face he saw hope and longing . . . a father come to find him, rescue him . . . it was a bard's tale, that notion. *Really? And did not I come to find and rescue you?* Arvid jerked as if someone had stuck him with a hot pin, and the Marshal shook his head.

"You never thought of that?" the Marshal asked.

"It wasn't that," Arvid said. "It was . . . I don't want to talk about it."

"You need sib," the Marshal said again. "Come with me."

Arvid followed him out of the cavernous room, feeling the boy's gaze following him like a ray of sun on his back, warming. Too warm. Too much.

In the Marshal's office, a small plain room with a table and two unpadded chairs, Arvid sat where he was bidden. He wanted to be alone. He wanted silence. He wanted, most of all, himself as he had been, without that annoying voice in his head, without the problems that had beset him since he first saw a stubborn yellow-haired girl with a sword. *No, that's not what you really want.* He would have argued, but the Marshal was handing him a mug.

"Sib and some herbs. Nothing to harm you, but you're shaking like a man in fever."

He was shaking, the sib sloshing in the cup, and he hadn't realized it. He took a gulp—lukewarm, as if it had been in the pot for an hour or so. "I—I can't—tell—"

The Marshal hitched a hip onto the table and sipped from his own mug. Arvid looked down, trying to will his hands to quit trembling. He had always had steady hands; a thief needed steady hands . . . and now they shook. "I can guess some of what's happening," the Marshal said. "But not all. You are the one who saved Paksenarrion's life; Gird is trying to save yours."

"I didn't need saving!" That came out in a rush. "I was fine."

"Gird thinks differently. Which means the High Lord thinks differently."

"I was Guildmaster in Vérella," Arvid said. His voice still shook, and he hated that. He took another gulp of sib. "I thought that was Gird's reward."

No.

"And they betrayed you to the Guildmaster here," the Marshal said. "And yet you escaped. Will you tell me Gird had no part in that?"

Arvid remembered every detail of that miserable day. "No," he said. "I can't—the voice came—and the rain softened the thongs just enough—but surely he could have just cut them—"

"You think Gird should have made it easy for you?" the Marshal said, brows raised. "Did he make it easy for Paksenarrion?"

"No," Arvid whispered. Those days and nights too came back to him, far more vivid than he wished. "No," he said again. "And I thought . . . it was cruel."

"Umm. And for all your bravado, Arvid Semminson, all your years as a Thieves' Guild enforcer, are you telling me you do not like cruelty? It must have been hard, when you were young, to pretend not to notice, not to care."

When he was young . . . He shook his head. He did not want to be that child again; he wanted the confident man he had been. "I don't know why it bothered me," he said. "It wasn't supposed to."

"Did you ever worship the Bloodlord?" the Marshal asked.

"No. I couldn't. When my master died—the Guildmaster who first gave me my assignment as enforcer—and the next began to bring in the red priests, I was often away. I—I made reasons to be away." He finished the last of the sib. "I just want—I just want to be who I was. I don't care, really, about being Guildmaster . . . but I can't—I can't live this way, on a rope between two poles."

"No one can," the Marshal said. "And you can't go back, Arvid. You can't be who you were. You have already changed too much, and the hands holding you now will never let you go."

Arvid felt the tears on his cheeks before he realized he was going to cry. The Marshal took the mug from his hand and set it on the table. He was mercifully silent, leaving the room for a moment and returning with a towel. He laid it in Arvid's lap and sat down in the other chair. Arvid picked up the towel in shaking hands and mopped his face. Tears poured out, as if from a spring. He no longer knew what they meant, if it was grief or joy or anger or pain that brought them forth, but he could not stop them. Finally, they ceased. His belly hurt; his head felt near bursting. He could not breathe but through his mouth, and he took in long breaths, trying to reach calm.

And calm held him. No voice in his head, just calm. He rested in it like a child . . . like the child he had once been, like that boy in his own arms. He blinked, clearing the last tears from his eyes, wiped his face again, and looked over at the Marshal. Instead of the scorn he expected, he saw only compassion.

"Paladins," the Marshal said, "always cause trouble."

"What?" That was not what Arvid expected to hear.

"You could even say the gods always cause trouble—certainly Gird did, though we celebrate the trouble he caused. Paladins, though—we don't really know how they started, but it's clear they come into the world to change it, and that's always trouble for someone. Usually a lot of someones. What I heard all last year, from the time the first spring caravans came down, was how things had changed in the north. All because of her."

Arvid thought about it. His life hadn't changed after meeting her except for a sort of tickle in the mind, a curiosity about her. Had she worn the necklace? Had he changed her? He'd been sorry when he heard she'd been cast out of the Fellowship, but he hadn't bothered looking for her.

"Surely you recognize what happened," the Marshal said. "Who found out Phelan was king? She did. Everyone the paladin touches changes, and change often hurts. Most of us in Valdaire knew of Duke Phelan even if we hadn't met him. We knew his reputation; we'd seen him; his soldiers were here all winter every year, campaigned all over Aarenis in summer. I'd met his Captain Arcolin; he offered to the grange every year. Now Phelan's a king, Arcolin's a lord, that woman captain—the Falkian—is a duke: they all changed. Had to. You changed, too."

"I didn't notice," Arvid said. "After I met her—nothing changed for a while." But looking back now, he could see images of himself . . . He had left Brewersbridge as smug as ever, but . . . the cruelty bothered him more. He had carried out assignments . . . mostly . . .

"Would the man you were ten years ago have bothered to save her after the ordeal?"

"I don't know," Arvid said. His younger self, well armored against compassion, confident in his superiority to the common herd of thieves, something he still felt, but . . . but differently . . . "I suppose not," he said. "I would have left the city, found some errand to pursue, but I would not have cared about her. But then I hadn't met her."

"And meeting her changed you," the Marshal said. "I would say the change began with your first meeting—she intrigued you, she surprised you, isn't that right?"

"Yes. But she wasn't a paladin then."

"True. She was one of Phelan's soldiers—she came to the markets whenever the Company was in Valdaire, just like the other soldiers. I saw her; everyone saw her. None of us knew what she would be; we saw only the surface. But that has changed *me*: knowing that someone I saw more than once, that I dismissed as just another non-Girdish soldier, could become a paladin of Gird. I am less certain of my judgment of those I see." The Marshal grinned suddenly. "And that's why you're still alive today. My old self might well have killed you for what I supposed you were doing to that boy who bears your name."

"I'm no paladin," Arvid said. "Nor like to be."

"Maybe," the Marshal said slowly. "But what the gods plan for you could surprise both of us." He was silent a long moment; Arvid concentrated on his own breathing and saw with relief that his hands no longer trembled. "You're calmer," the Marshal said then. "But you have not eaten—you and the boy both need lunch. I'll send him in and bring you something."

"I have money," Arvid said, reaching for his pocket.

The Marshal shook his head. "Not today. Today you will share our lunch."

The boy Arvid came to the Marshal's office hand in hand with one of the men, his hair still damp from a bath he'd been given, wearing clean patched trousers rolled up, a shirt that nearly came to his knees, and heavy wool socks on his bruised feet. He smiled shyly at Arvid. "M'ma named me . . . did she name you?"

"No, lad," Arvid said. "My own mother did, and she died long ago."

"Do you remember her?" the boy asked.

"Not well," Arvid said. "I was young, about your age, and her face faded over the years."

"My ma sang songs to me," the boy said. "She said my da sang to her. So she gave me his name and said he'd given me his voice."

Arvid's throat closed. He had learned to sing as a child, not from his parents but as part of the Guild's training: children who could sing could beg by singing and distract listeners from pickpockets and cutpurses. He'd had a good voice, he'd been told, and he'd been put up on a table to sing for the Guild itself more than once.

And as a man he'd sung sweet melodies to more than one lass, courting songs and bed songs both. How many of those happy nights had left sons and daughters scattered here and there? He'd never asked. He'd never cared enough.

"Are you my father?" the boy asked. The way he stood, the expression on his face, the tone of voice, all pierced Arvid's heart.

"I don't know," he said, fighting the lump in his throat. "And I am sorry I don't know. I do not know of any child I might have sired, but—Arvid—in my life I might have sired more than one. I am sorry I cannot tell you for certain."

The boy looked at him—no anger, no fear, no condemnation. Not the way Arvid had looked at his own father; he had been an angry boy, a troublemaker, his father insisted. "It is not your fault," the boy said. Arvid shivered. Of course it was his fault that he did not know if he had children. Whose else could it be? But the boy went on. "But if it does not displease you, sir, because you rescued me, and did not kill me, and because we have the same name, I would . . . I would pretend that you are, in my own mind. Not to trouble you . . ."

He did not deserve this . . . this forgiveness, if that was what it was. This acceptance. And the boy himself did not deserve a liar, a thief, a murderer bent on vengeance as a father. But the boy stood there, watching, and he had to say something, something that would not quench the spirit in the boy's eyes.

"It would not trouble me," Arvid said. "It would not trouble me to have a son like you, and if you are truly my son, then I am content, and if you are not, then . . . then I will do for you what I think a father should do." What he could do with gold, he would do. What a father should be—he did not know.

"You aren't really a thief," the boy said with certainty. "You wear black; you know thieves' talk; you killed the Guildmaster, but you aren't really a thief."

He had been telling people for years that he was not a thief—telling himself he was not a thief—and all along he knew himself thief to the bone . . . but the boy's words felt as heavy as stone.

"I was a thief," Arvid said to the boy, his heart hammering. "But perhaps you are right, and I'm not a thief now."

"Here we are," the Marshal said, bustling in with a large round loaf and a hunk of cheese that filled the room with its pungent scent. One of the other men brought in two stools; the boy stood and backed into a corner. The Marshal moved the empty chair over and then waved the boy into it. "You there, lad, and we'll have plenty of room. Bring us some water, Cal."

Bread, water, and cheese made up the meal; the boy ate silently and fast, a style Arvid recognized from his own youth. Thief children weren't ever plump. The Marshal and Cal—introduced at last as his yeoman-marshal—ate noisily, talking through mouthfuls of food about some grange business Arvid didn't understand. He scarcely listened. He himself ate slowly—he was hungry but distrusted his stomach after the day's already abundant emotion. One bite of the cheese was enough; he ate bread and drank water, grateful for them.

Finally the Marshal belched and sat back. "And now, what to do with you and the boy," he said. "Best thing for him is to find him a family, keep him safe and fed, and teach him a trade."

"I want to stay with him," the boy said, pointing to Arvid.

"Lad, he's in danger himself; he can't keep you as safe as a good solid family can."

"They'll be looking for him," Arvid said to the Marshal. "They know him, and they'll take him back if they can."

"Out of Valdaire somewhere? On a farm?"

"Maybe. But the risk's there until he's man-grown." Arvid looked at the boy. "It's true what the Marshal says, young Arvid. I cannot keep you safe while I'm being hunted—or not as safe as someone else could."

"Any chance you're his father?" the Marshal asked.

Arvid spread his hands. "As I told the lad, I simply do not know. I have been in Valdaire before, before Siniava's War as they call it in the north, and . . . it's possible. But I made no promises and heard no word." That was the way he'd always liked it: share a happy night or two, having made it clear he had no interest in staying, and walk away whistling. "I do have some gold, and that can go to help."

"I'm not worried about that," the Marshal said. He chewed his lip a moment. "See here, Arvid, the boy is not the only problem we have. Or that you have. You need to choose a path and stick to it—"

"You mean leave the Guild," Arvid said.

"I mean join the Fellowship, become a Girdsman," the Marshal said.

"I'm not—I can't—you don't understand," Arvid said. "I'm not your kind of person. I can't . . . I can't just put on a blue shirt and change everything."

You're right about that, laddie.

Arvid twitched. "I don't . . . I don't want to be—" How could he say it without offending them—and why did he care? "Ordinary," he said at last. "I'm—"

The Marshal's eyes twinkled. "Oh, no, you're not *ordinary.* You're intelligent and charming and gifted, and if you're not the guest over there at the Dragon who took down four—or was it five?—thieves all by yourself, I'd be very surprised. A gifted sneak, the way you got into and out of the Thieves' Guild house today. A fine voice—I'm sure you sang to the girls you slept with—and graceful. Sophisticated, no doubt. And you think of us—of the Fellowship—as a collection of grubby, dull, not-very-bright peasants, don't you?"

"Not . . . exactly. Not Paks. Not the Marshal-General."

"And I'm sure she's grateful for that." The Marshal shook his head. "Arvid, back in Gird's day it's true that his followers were nearly all poor countryfolk, mostly unable to read or write—Gird himself wasn't a scholar. That was a long time ago. Yes, we have many members who are farmers and many who are crafters and merchants—and many who are in every other occupation—other than the Thieves' Guild."

"Yes, but you're . . ." "Good" was the word hovering over his tongue, and the Marshal seemed to read it out of the air.

"Good, I suppose, is what's bothering you. Stuffy and priggish, maybe? Narrow-minded, perhaps?"

Arvid was aware of the boy's eyes shifting from face to face like a child watching a pair of jugglers perform. Inside his head, he was aware of a vast amusement. "Well—I—yes, sometimes. And I'm not—I mean, you know I've done things you wouldn't approve of."

"And so have I done things I don't approve of," the Marshal said. "I'm not perfect—don't pretend to be. I'm perhaps less interested in fashion than you would be if you didn't prefer black—"

Arvid could not help grinning at that. "Perhaps."

"Well, I was plain as a barrel and shaped like one from childhood, Arvid. No use trying for elegance. But I recognize it when I see it, appreciate it, and know good quality from bad."

"In other words . . . you think I take pride in what I should not take pride in."

"No. Not at all. I think you don't take pride in what you *should* take pride in . . . in addition to your knowledge, your skills, your handsome face."

"And that would be?"

"I told you. You aren't cruel. That's a start. And you've saved two lives—Paksenarrion's and this lad's—that you didn't have to. Build on that."

CHAPTER TWENTY-NINE

Lyonya, Chaya

FIVE DAYS AFTER the wedding, most of the guests had started home. Arian took advantage of the relative quiet to invite Estil Halveric and several Queen's Squires to spend a quiet afternoon relaxing in the queen's chambers. Arian felt tired; her muscles ached. She wasn't sure if it was from the crowds and ceremonies or if this was something that happened in pregnancy. Her Squire's uniform had been uncomfortably snug for the past couple of days; after a brief session in the salle that morning, she'd left it off, putting on softer, looser clothing since she would be among friends.

In the midst of a discussion of the new candidates for King's and Queen's Squires, Arian felt something inside, not quite a cramp but a strong sensation. She put a hand to her abdomen.

"What is it?" asked Estil Halveric.

"I think it must be the baby moving," Arian said. "Or maybe something I ate—but it's—strong."

"It's early if you conceived at Midwinter," Estil said. "Though I don't know with half-elves—"

"Very early for half-elves," Kaelith said. "Half-elven babies are almost three tendays longer from conception to birth; I'm surprised you're feeling movement now. Halfway between the Evener and Midsummer to as late as Midsummer is what I'd expect."

Arian sat back. "Well, we've all been eating rich foods the past few days. Maybe it's just that. It just feels . . . different."

The conversation they'd been having about Dorrin Verrakai shifted to what Kaelith remembered her mother telling her about the difference in pregnancies between half-elf and human. The pastries on the tray disappeared one by one as the afternoon passed. Arian felt anchored to her chair, as if the child within were much heavier than it could possibly be. Suddenly she felt another movement—sudden and strong enough to be painful.

"Arian?" Estil said, watching her.

"It's—I think it must be something I ate. Too many pastries." The pain eased; Arian settled back against the pillows. Her mouth wanted another of the jam-filled crispy ones, but she wouldn't risk it.

"I don't like your color," Estil said. "I'm going to call—"

"No," Arian said. "I'll be fine. If it's too many pastries or whatever, it will go away in a few turns of the glass. I don't want to be hovered over."

"You shouldn't take any chances now," Estil said.

Arian saw the look that passed from Estil to Kaelith and back. She started to speak, when the pain returned, much stronger, along with nausea. She felt cold, sick—she struggled up from the chair, but her knees gave way and she fell into the table of pastries. She could just hear Estil's exclamations, feel someone holding her shoulders, as her sight dimmed and pain racked her belly. Simultaneously, the taig cried out. She tried to reach for the little spark of life within her, but could not. Panicked, she struggled against the hands that held her. Her stomach heaved and she vomited; her bowels loosened, and even as she fought for the light, she fell into darkness.

"It was no normal miscarriage," Estil said to Kieri. White to the lips, he crouched beside the bed where Arian lay, cleaned now and put to bed with warm stones at her feet. "I've seen that . . . that's belly cramps and bleeding and then the little lump—"

He held up his hand. She fell silent. Across the room, Aliam sat in the chair Arian had fallen from; the carpet still had a damp patch, though the smell had gone. He shook his head slightly. Well, then. She would not say more, but more must be said sometime. Soon.

Kieri lifted one of Arian's hands and kissed it. She did not respond. "Will she live?" he asked without looking around.

"She is alive now," Estil said. "That is the best sign."

His head went down to the bedclothes, then rose again. "I . . . do not want to lose her."

Estil could think of nothing to say.

"If childbearing is too much for her . . . I will find another heir."

Estil glanced again at Aliam, who shrugged. "Kieri," Estil said in the gentlest voice she could. "It is not her body."

"But so much pain—"

"Kieri, this is important." He looked up at her finally, and she sank down to the floor, where she could lay a hand on his arm, look him in the face. "This was not just a miscarriage. It is not any weakness of hers. I know women's bodies as you cannot, even after knowing Tammarion. Arian should bear children as easily as any. This was treachery, Kieri. She was poisoned, or the babe was."

"But she—how—who would—?"

"I don't know. You don't know. But what happened—the smell of it—was not natural. You have had warnings, she told me, from your sister's bones, and she had one from her father."

Color came back to Kieri's face; he still held Arian's hand, but he looked at Estil. "Warning, yes, but . . . but she has had Squires with her, or me, every moment. How could it have been done? Through magic?"

"Maybe," Estil said. "But my guess would be in food. Something she ate."

"Today?"

Estil shook her head. "Not today, or not merely today. Very likely food for the wedding feasts, though it could have been earlier. Something that would not kill her of itself, but would kill the child in her . . . any child she might engender. It would not have been done before your engagement was known."

Kieri's brow furrowed. "The announcement was at Midwinter, but people knew before that. The Lady knew . . . but I cannot imagine her doing this, and anyway, Arian left Lyonya immediately after that confrontation."

"But when she came back . . ."

"The Pargunese had invaded." He looked thoughtful now. "I suppose . . . when we came back to Chaya . . . the fourth or fifth day after the first invasion. I cannot now recall exactly, but we told the Council and I took her into the ossuary."

"How did the ancestors react?"

"With joy. And with a caution. But everyone seemed happy, even the Lady. I sensed no resentment of Arian . . ."

"It may not be of her, Kieri. Think how much effort went into removing your mother and you and then keeping you away from the throne for so long. This is not a new menace. If it is elves—"

"If *what* is elves?" The Lady stood in the doorway, the elvenhome light shimmering around her. "What has happened to my daughter Arian?"

Kieri whirled to face her. "Did you kill the child?"

"What?"

"*Did you kill our child?* Were you lying when you said you wished us the joy of children?" His voice was harsh, a voice Estil had not heard him use before. "Do you now come to gloat over your success?"

"No!" A wave of elven power overwhelmed Estil; she felt herself floating on it, but Kieri, standing now, repelled it. He was alight, and so was the Lady, but their lights did not mingle. "I wished no harm to you, Grandson, or to Arian or to your child. I came when I felt the taig's grief." Kieri said nothing, merely staring at her. "I swear it," she said. "On the Singer's own name, I swear it."

"Someone did," Kieri said, "and I let a son of ours die through not protecting her." The Lady moved forward, but he held up his hand and she stopped. "Though I believe you, I do not want you closer to her," he said. "Not now."

"Not to heal her?"

"Can you?"

"Perhaps. Perhaps the two of us. I know it will not heal her grief, but she is cut off from the taig now."

"By you?"

"No, Grandson. I would not do that again. By whatever it was that took the child and by her grief. She needs its strength to heal."

"Estil?" Kieri said.

Estil raised her head, realizing then that she had slumped to the floor. The pressure around her eased as Kieri reached down and helped her up. She looked into the Lady's eyes from the bubble of Kieri's power and saw what she had not seen before, not even when the Lady had come to them at Halveric Steading. Deep, deep within, some fracture, some wound that had never healed. But not malice, not for Arian, not now. "Arian needs our comfort first," she said. "And the Lady is right; she will need the taig, but later."

"What would you do for her, if the Lady or I were not here, Estil?"

Love her. But that wasn't what Kieri meant. "Sib when she wakes. There's another root I'd add to the mix. Then the healing herbs. Strengthening foods. Sunlight." Estil looked at the Lady again. "Gracious one, at this moment she needs a human's care. Her taig-sense will return as her body recovers and complete the healing."

A long pause, then the Lady bowed slightly. "As you are mother and grandmother, Estil Halveric, I trust you." She withdrew.

Kieri turned to Estil. "And you think the poison came to her in something she ate?"

"It's the easiest way," Estil said. "Something she ate or drank."

"So . . . someone in the kitchen?"

"Not necessarily. Someone supplying the kitchen. You've had guests, haven't you, since Midwinter? And all those come for the wedding . . ."

"Yes . . . so the steward should know who's supplied the kitchens—"

"She should not eat anything from anyone you cannot trust, Kieri. Food fresh from the ground, that you or she or someone you know has picked."

"Who else might have been poisoned? She has eaten with others, I know that."

Estil shook out her sleeves. "If this was put in food others ate, someone else may have lost a child. Have you heard anything?"

"No—but with the wedding coming up, they might not have told me."

"I'm going to the kitchens," Estil said. "I will be back shortly—less than a glass. Your cooks and other servants will talk to me when they might not to you."

The news had already spread, Estil saw, as she hurried through the palace. Worried faces, whispering in corners. She overheard one servant say, "It's maybe spring fever . . . You know Perin just lost hers . . ." Estil slowed; the two servants nodded respectfully to her.

"Do you really think it's spring fever?" Estil asked. "When my dairymaid lost hers, two years agone, we thought it was from eating sourgrass."

"Sourgrass is up, to be true," one of the servants said. "But Cook only uses sourgrass late in the year, when it's safe, and not much then. Perin wouldn't have touched it; she wanted that child."

"How far along was she?" Estil said, leaning on the wall as if she'd been hoping for a good gossip, as indeed she had.

"Near half-term," the other servant said. "Showing and kicking. And you know—" She turned to the other servant. "Maris, she thought she'd caught, and she had a terrible time just two days ago. All day in her bed or the jacks, she was."

"Had there been other fever in the household?" Estil asked. "Or out in the city?"

"Nay. We's been lucky this year, all year. Thought it was the king's luck, him being the true heir. But then comes war and this . . . Maybe he's not so lucky, after all."

"The Pargunese would've come, king or no king," Estil said.

"Yes, my lady," they both said.

Estil saw at once she'd spoken too firmly; she tried again. "Forgive me. It's that I've known him since he was a starveling boy; he was like one of my own."

Their faces relaxed. The older one spoke. "Oh, my lady, tell us . . . We heard some tale of it but nothing specific. What was he like as a boy? Was he always so handsome?"

"No—he was just a ragged waif," she said. Their faces softened with the same sympathy she'd felt. But she could spend no more time feeding their curiosity; her own might save Arian's next child. "I'm sorry," she said. "I must not stay here chatting. Where are Perin and Maris? I want to talk to them, see if there's any connection between their loss and the queen's."

"I'll take you, Lady Halveric," the older servant said. "Gadlin, you'd best be at work when t'steward comes." She winked. Estil glanced back and saw the steward hurrying down the passage.

"Perin's my third cousin," the servant said over her shoulder as she led the way. "I'm Bettlan, milady. Perin's that upset . . . she won't likely talk to you unless I'm there, and she's a cryer, Perin is."

"I understand," Estil said. "I lost a child once."

"Ah. Be gentle with her, is all."

"I will be."

"And you think it's not spring fever."

"I think a fever would have taken more people," Estil said. "And there'd be fever in Chaya, with all the visitors who've come."

"So . . . ?"

Could she trust this Bettlan? They were out in the west court now, heading to the row of cottages that backed on the palace wall, where some of the servants lived. Estil touched Bettlan's shoulder; she stopped and turned. "Bettlan, if too much is known too soon, we may never figure out the truth. Can you keep a quiet tongue?"

Bettlan scowled. "I'm no blabber despite your finding me talking with Gadlin. If it's a secret you want kept, I'll keep my tongue behind my teeth."

"Fine, then. I think these babes were lost to poison, poison their mothers ate in food here, in the palace. There's been treachery in the air since the king's mother rode away with him expecting an escort who never came. Do you understand?"

"But they said elves—" Bettlan rocked back on her heels. Her face paled. "You mean it's them . . . they . . . they wouldn't have . . . the Lady . . ."

"Say no more, Bettlan. We don't know who; we're not accusing elves or humans yet, and it would be dangerous to guess wrongly. But we know whatever it is began long ago and old malice is still active. The king's escaped by the skin of his teeth again and again. His first wife and children were lost because of it. And now this—it cannot be coincidence."

"You'll be wanting to know if Perin ate anything the queen ate . . . and if anyone else did . . . you'll be wanting a friend in the kitchen, milady. My tasks aren't there, but my brother married an undercook."

"Not yet," Estil said. "Let me talk to Perin and Maris first. It may be there's another connection besides food. Food is just the most obvious and easiest."

Bettlan nodded without saying anything and walked on, Estil following.

Perin, wrapped in a knitted coverlet, was lying in the front room of the cottage, turning the heel of a sock. She looked pale but said she merely felt weak. Sure enough, when Estil mentioned the miscarriage, Perin began to cry.

"An' they just tol' me this mornin' 'bout the queen's losin' hers. Makes us sisters of a kind, not that I'm claiming that." Her sobbing intensified.

Estil asked her questions, the sort any Sier's wife with long experience of births and deaths might ask, and Perin calmed. Finally, she asked what Perin ate and drank in the last tendays of her pregnancy, from Midwinter Feast on.

"Midwinter Feast . . . it was truly that, milady." Perin smiled. "Same food for all and plenty of it. I was run off my feet, just about, carrying out the trays to the big tables. We took turns eating, same as the others."

"And did the king and queen—?"

"Only a few bites—they had to make their way through the city, you know. And they started late—some kerfluffle about the king and the ossuary. How he found mud in there I have no idea, but everything started a turn of the glass late. They each grabbed a pastry or two, and then they were off."

"I don't suppose you remember which pastries."

"Indeed I do, for I made sure I had some of those. Eating the king's food on Midwinter's good luck. Ham and mushroom and then a jam-filled one. I think the queen had two of those."

So. Quite possibly it had started that far back, unless— "Perin, do the servants usually have the same food as the king's table?"

She nodded. "Some of it. Not if the cook makes something special, you know, just for him. When the Pargunese were here, he might come in later than mealtimes and the cook would fix a small portion. But usually we had at least some of what the high table ate."

Estil repressed a shudder. How many other babies might die? And who would be so callous?

"Perin, how many other women are expecting, do you know?"

"No, milady, I don't. I know Maris—but not who else might be."

Estil went next to the kitchen gardens. The taig had warmed them for the wedding, she knew, and though the plants were small, rows of them were ready. She spoke to the head gardener, explained that the queen needed fresh greens, and picked a small bundle. She dug into the soil for a bit of briarroot, hacking it off with her belt-knife, and then went back into the palace through the kitchens to borrow a few pans. There she met the head cook, Tilgar, energetic and commanding; the kitchens were as clean as her own, shelves tidy and organized, workspaces not in use scrubbed and clear for the next task.

"It's ill-wishing," Tilgar said. "Some evil person's ill-wished this house. Perin, Maris, Dolin—"

"And Tilith, Cook," one of the undercooks said. "In the stables. M'sister Ranny told me this morning."

"Must be a tippin hid somewhere about," Tilgar said. "Probably some visitor brought it. I'd be looking for a Pargunese. If they'll burn forest, they'll kill childer."

"Your kitchens are so clean," Estil said. She got no further.

"Someone said it was *food*? From *my* kitchens?" Tilgar scowled. "There's no tippin here, I'll be bound. Scrubbed to the walls before we started on the wedding feasts, every shelf and cranny. And my own staff put away all the gifts of food; they'd have shown me anything strange that could be a tippin. If you think that I—"

"No, of course not," Estil said. She had not meant to bring it up so soon, but Tilgar's defensiveness had attracted the undercooks, all now staring wide-eyed at the two of them. "Nor your assistants. But someone could have put something in a food gift, couldn't they? And so far as we know, only those who ate the food here have lost their babies."

Tilgar was silent a long moment. "I don't see how," she said slowly. "Gifts . . . a lot of food did come in. There were a few things we threw out—damaged on the way here, it seemed. I wouldn't use anything bruised or touched with mold, of course, for a wedding feast. It's true we've used bruised fruit other times to make preserves—no harm there, as I'm sure milady knows."

"Indeed," Estil said. "I cut off the worst bits and put them in the kettle with the rest. A soft apple's not poison."

"But not for a wedding feast," Tilgar said again. "Everything must be perfect, is what I learned and what I do. Anything doubtful went out to the hen yard or sties." She shook her head. "I'll stand surety for my staff to the king himself. I trained them; I know them; they'd not poison a beggar, let alone the king and queen. If it is—if it's proven it came from my kitchens—then I want to know how, because I'm sure as sure that it wasn't any of my people."

"I believe you," Estil said. "But in the meantime, I told the king I would oversee Arian's meals myself. Would you lend me a few pots and pans?"

"You will watch us wash them, clean as they are," Tilgar said. "That way you will know they're not tainted."

"Thank you," Estil said.

ARiAN WAS AWAKE when Estil returned to the queen's chambers; she looked pale and miserable but was able to keep down the infusion Estil prepared for her. Kieri, seated now beside the bed, looked almost as haggard.

"Whom do you trust, Kieri?" Estil asked. "And you, Arian?"

"I did trust them all," Arian said. "But Kieri says you think it was poison intended to kill the child."

"Other women in the palace have had miscarriages in the past day and night," Estil said. "All fed from the king's table. No one has reported any such deaths in Chaya."

"We cannot trust anyone, then. Anyone in the kitchen, any who serve at table—"

"More likely someone who supplied foods for the feast days than your staff, Kieri," Estil said. "I've talked to your head cook; I am sure she is not guilty and that she would have noticed anything obvious in her kitchens. As a precaution, though, Arian should eat and drink only those things grown here and prepared by a few she can trust. I picked these leaves and roots from the garden myself, carried them in myself, prepared them myself. I can stay for a while but not permanently. What about your Squires? Surely some among them you know well enough."

"Yes," Arian said. "I have several friends I know would not do something like this."

"They can help me, then," Estil said.

"Can you tell what kind of poison?" Kieri asked.

"No. I'm not even sure when it was done. The most likely time, I would think, is in preparation of the wedding feasts. I suspect that something was brought in, either regular tribute or as a gift, and used in those dishes. That means some of your wedding guests could be poisoned as well, and one of them could have brought in the poison. Or the poison could have been brought in earlier, some time after the betrothal."

"I continued my duties as Squire—including trips away—until half-Evener," Arian said. "Could I have eaten poison then? Somewhere else?"

"Not with the women here having the same symptoms within a day of your loss," Estil said. "You and they must have had poison on the same day. Maybe several different times. There are such poisons . . . each harmless by itself but dangerous in combination. Or it might have been just one."

"So—any day she wasn't here, she wasn't poisoned?"

"Very likely."

"Garris will have a record of that; he tracks all the Squires' movements."

"And your steward, I presume, will know what days the palace had visitors and who they were, as well as foods supplied."

Arian, Estil noticed, was crying silently, tears running down her face. Kieri followed Estil's glance and took Arian into his arms.

"There, love. We will yet have children, you and I, and now

that we know someone is willing to poison not only you but others, we will find out who and why and end that cruelty."

"He was so small . . ."

"I know." He kissed her hair. "But you must rest and recover. Do what Estil tells you, will you. I must go and start the inquiries. I will come back often to tell you what I've learned."

She nodded and released his hand. Kieri stood slowly, stroking her head one last time, and then strode from the room.

Estil called in the Queen's Squires Arian had named and explained what she thought had happened. "And I need you to bring me the ingredients I ask for, fresh from the garden."

"What about flour?" Suriya asked.

"I'll send you to Sier Halveric's house with a note," Estil said. "I doubt the flour and meal and so on are contaminated, but we must take no chances. I know the Halveric cook; she's very careful at market, and there's been no trouble there I know of. You can ask."

"I'll pick whatever you like," Binir said. "The palace has its own dairy and poultry houses—what about butter and eggs? Those are strengthening."

"Gather the eggs yourself; eggs can be pricked. Here's what I need for supper." Estil wrote quickly, a list for Binir and another for Suriya, with a note to Remmis, Sier Halveric's cook. As she wrote, she said, "Notice if anyone asks too much or spreads rumors or the like. It's unlikely, but possible, that you will meet someone who is part of this."

Arian slept again; Kieri came and went, not waking her. By the time Arian woke, Estil had a broth simmering on the fire and bread from Halveric House to eat with it. Arian had an appetite, and her color improved as she ate.

"What have you learned?" she asked.

"That two more women in the palace lost a child—one yesterday and another while you slept. That makes six, counting you. It must be you were poisoned at the same time or times."

"And you still think it was by food . . . ?"

"It seems the most likely. It is the one thing you all had in common. And from Garris's information it is mostly likely that it happened at either Midwinter Feast or the feasts around the wedding. Or possibly both."

"Someone would have had more time to plan for the wedding," Arian said.

"True, but didn't you tell people here that you would announce your formal betrothal at Midwinter? That would give some time."

"Will it—will the poison stay? Will it kill the next child? Every child?"

"Surely not," Estil said. "I never heard of such . . . I do know if someone's used birthbane, she must not conceive again for two cycles."

"I want children," Arian said. Tears marked her cheeks again, but she did not sob. "And Kieri—"

"I believe you will have children, healthy children, but first you must recover from this. You must be completely healthy."

"I'm being childish," Arian said.

"No, that you are not. You are a woman of character and courage, but no one loses a child easily."

TRACING THE FOOD seemed at first to be impossible. Gifts of food—always common at feastings—had been accepted without question, and those suitable for use in the coming feast had been used.

"I know who brought food," the steward said. "But many sent the same things—onions and redroots, grain, dried fruits, apples, pears, honey in the comb, mushrooms—and all were stored with like kind and no regard to who sent them. Of course the cooks looked to see if anything seemed to be spoiled or if any of the wild foods brought in were of poisonous varieties, but beyond that, we have no way to know, for things in bulk storage, which came from where. So much, in preparation for the wedding—we put things where we could." The steward shook his head. "It's evil, is what it is, sir king. Poisoning anyone, but the *queen*? And then any other woman who might be with child and had a taste of the same food? And not just our own people, our guests. Evil. I thought the Pargunese were bad, but this—"

"It is indeed evil," Kieri said. He had not thought of the guests—and he should have. "We'll have to tell people." All those guests—how many had been pregnant? Had celebrated the happy day that night and then eaten more of the feast the next day, as he and Arian had?

"If only we had a way of identifying which foods were contaminated," the steward said. "Then we could throw those out and check everything coming in."

"Hmmm," Kieri said. "I wonder if strong taig-sense could do that . . . Foods were once alive."

CHAPTER THIRTY

PHYSICALLY, ARIAN FELT perfectly healthy, as strong as before the miscarriage. Her sense of the taig returned, as Estil had promised it would. Emotionally . . . she wanted to flinch from every glance, jump at every noise. She was the queen, she should be comforting the others . . . and as soon as she'd been able to walk that far, she'd gone to visit the other women in the palace who had lost their babies. Those had been such painful meetings that she felt exhausted after each and lay abed, unsleeping, the night after.

Her planned visit to Tsaia's court had been put off, of course. Duke Mahieran, who was supposed to be her escort, had stayed, sending his kirgan back to explain the delay to the king. Dorrin Verrakai had also stayed, with Beclan. While Beclan was in the salle for a workout, Arian and Dorrin sat in the rose garden; the roses had leafed out, and a few early ones showed buds. One bud had opened, adding its fragrance to that of the violets that nestled under the rosebushes along one wall.

Before Arian could ask, Dorrin explained her perspective on the situation with Beclan. "I'm sure you noticed how awkward it was, but in the end, it's for the best," she finished.

Arian nodded. "I did not think it fair, but if you do—that's what matters."

Dorrin stretched her long legs to the spring sun. "Arian, has your taig-sense helped you discover what poison they used?"

Arian said, "No. Nor Kieri's, either. We don't know if it's because the poison is in us still, though I can still feel the taig at large. Nor have the elves been able to tell us anything."

"From what Kieri said, he does not entirely trust the elves."

"That's so. But you have magery—can you tell?"

"May I touch you?"

Arian stared, then realized that she had not seen Dorrin touch anyone without permission other than shaking hands with Kieri, a warrior's gesture. "Yes," she said, and held out her hands. Dorrin took them; Arian could feel nothing unusual. Then Dorrin opened her own hands and sighed.

"I have been able to heal some things," Dorrin said. "But I felt something in my hands when I did. I felt nothing this time except a kind of heaviness. If the elves can't help you, have you considered a Kuakgan?"

"A Kuakgan! Elves don't—we don't have them here."

"I would have thought, with the taig—Paks asked a Kuakgan to raise the taig for her—"

"Elves say they're bad. You know about the old quarrel, the Severance."

"Yes. The elves' side of it, which I think does them no credit. Why should it keep you from seeking help wherever it might be?"

"Kieri did tell me that when the war started and the elves did not come to aid, he thought of calling in a Kuakgan."

"Did he?"

"No—I think he would have, but the dragon took me to free the elves from underground."

Dorrin's brows rose. "There's a story I want to hear someday. But for now—what about a Kuakgan? They know the plant world—wouldn't this likely be a plant poison? Mushrooms or something like that?"

"I don't know any Kuakkgani. They do pass through sometimes, but—"

"You do know that back before Midwinter, one healed my youngest squire, Daryan?"

"Yes, Kieri told me."

"I met him, worked with him a little, and I have also met one with a settled Grove, Master Oakhallow. I could send word to him—but as they are sensitive to the taig, perhaps we could use that—"

"We should be able to," Arian said. "Has Kieri met either of them?"

"Oakhallow, yes—last year, when he was coming to Lyonya, but very briefly," Dorrin said. "You and I might do better than

Kieri would. Let me have your hand again. You are better at contacting the taig than I am, but I think I can find the Kuakkgani more easily."

Arian reached out to the taig, pushing her awareness westward; she felt Dorrin within that contact as a bright thread. She could not tell the outcome. Dorrin suddenly pulled her hands away, shaking them.

"What's wrong?"

"I don't know—maybe nothing. Didn't you feel it, like a sting?"

"No."

"Another mystery. You taught me to feel the taig, but we do not feel it the same. I wish I knew more about how magery works, human and elven."

Arian felt chilled; the sun had moved, and the palace shadowed the rose garden. When she looked up, clouds were moving across the blue and the air felt damper.

"Rain coming," Dorrin said. "Let's go inside."

Next morning, the gentle spring rain that had begun in the night continued. Arian looked out at the courtyard and saw a cloaked and hooded figure walking toward the palace entrance. She could see nothing of the face, for the hood hid it, only one hand, holding a plain staff with the bark still on it and booted feet. Then the head tilted, and the hood fell back, revealing dark hair, a man's bearded face—and eyes that focused on her . . . She knew at once it was a tree-shepherd, a Kuakgan.

She went across to Kieri's bedchamber, where he was just dressing. "A Kuakgan has come."

"A Kuakgan? I wonder why." He twitched his shoulders, settling the mail shirt he still wore under his clothes, then reached for his tunic.

"Dorrin and I . . . she thought one might help us find the poison, since the elves didn't. We tried to call one."

"Good idea," Kieri said. "We'd better go down, then, and welcome him—or is it her?"

"Are there women Kuakkgani?"

"Yes. I haven't met one, but I've heard."

They went downstairs to find the Kuakgan standing in the hall, looking around while the steward and two King's Squires watched.

"He says you called him," the steward said to Arian.

"I did," she said. "With Dorrin's help."

"I am Master Oakhallow," the man said. He did not bow, but inclined his head. "I have met you before, O king, if you remember."

"I do," Kieri said.

"This is my semblance," Oakhallow said. "Do not try to touch me; it will vanish if you do. This was quicker than coming in the body, and I can learn what you need. Tell me why you called me."

Kieri gestured to the others, and they left the passage so Arian could speak privately to Oakhallow.

Arian explained as simply as she could. Oakhallow's semblance appeared to listen intently. When she had finished, he nodded. "It is likely a Kuakgan could help—I have some suspicion what might have been used, though not who used it. However, you need a Kuakgan's presence, not a semblance. There are other Kuakkgani nearer to you; they will come."

"They?"

"More than one person was injured; it will likely take more than one to untangle this." The semblance—so real that Arian was sure she saw its shadow and its impression on the carpet—bowed. "I must go. Help is on the way; you and the others will have joy in the future." The semblance turned and walked away: out the entrance, down the steps, across the courtyard, no one hindering.

Arian turned to Kieri. "I . . . don't know what to think."

"Nor I. But I feel more at ease. Help will come. That's better than anything my grandmother said."

A few hours later, when the rain had eased and watery sunlight made the pavement gleam, the steward announced another Kuakgan, this one a woman. Arian went down the steps to meet her. This one—shorter by a head than Arian and broader—wore the same kind of green-and-brown patterned robe, carried a staff in her heart-hand and in addition had a large satchel slung over her shoulder.

"I'm Pearwind," she said. "The taig has told me of trouble here and the need for tree-shepherds."

"You know Master Oakhallow?" Arian asked.

"Root to root," Pearwind said. "Though I have not been to his Grove. I wander, and so I have the name of wind; those with groves do not. Children dying, is it? And you are part-elven, I see."

"Yes," Arian said to both questions. "Children unborn, all within a few days. We think it was a poison in our food."

"Are all the mothers part-elven?"

"I don't know," Arian said. "Does it matter?"

Pearwind nodded. "Elves are susceptible to some poisons that do not affect humans, and the same is true of humans. Some poisons affect both. I will need to see all the women." Clouds were shifting overhead, moving apart. A shaft of sun brightened on them; to Arian's surprise, Pearwind's staff suddenly sprouted leaves and flowers . . . and then she realized the woman's hand had also turned green . . . and bees came, humming around the woman's head, settling into the flowers on the staff. "Oh dear," Pearwood said. "My kuakvaduonê would not be pleased about *this*."

"Kuakvaduonê?" Arian asked. She could think of nothing else to say, watching more and more bees stream in to cover the flowers . . . an entire swarm, it looked like. She could feel the taig trembling with excitement beneath the courtyard stones.

"Treeleader . . . teacher? She who made me Kuakgan and taught me. Sun . . . spring . . . it went to my staff . . ." Now the woman had a wreath of flowers on her head, and her robe no longer looked like green cloth with embroidered leaf shapes but like a robe of moss. A fern uncurled from her shoulder. "It's my first spring since—" Her lips sprouted tiny red mushrooms as her cheeks bloomed—sprays of flowers fell down past her neck.

Two more Kuakkgani came briskly through the palace gate. "We're here, miesiga masica," one said. And to Arian: "Do not touch her, lady; she needs *our* help."

Arian was not tempted to touch a woman so obviously turning into a pear tree. The Kuakkgani—one man, one woman—clasped hands around the first and sang in a language Arian did not know. Slowly but steadily, the flowers and leaves receded, first from her face, then from her hair and her arm . . . Her robe no longer seemed moss, and finally her staff returned to bare wood, except for the swarm of bees. The male Kuakgan reached out his staff and hummed; the swarm edged over onto his staff. He looked at Arian.

"You have a garden here? Are there any empty skeps?"

"I don't know," Arian said. "I'll ask."

"Show me the largest garden," he said. Arian led the way; at the far end of the kitchen garden, a row of skeps housed the palace bees. The palace beekeeper quickly fetched an empty skep from storage and set it up. The Kuakgan sang the bees into their new home, bowed to the beekeeper, and turned to Arian. "Master Oakhallow said you had need."

"Yes," Arian said. She explained again.

"I will make certain that Pearwind is settled, and then we will see the women."

"What happened to her?" Arian asked. She was still not sure she'd seen what she'd seen.

"It is her first spring after becoming a Kuakgan," he said. "She has never dealt with rising sap before." He gave Arian a sideways glance. "And she will not want to talk about it."

Once they were back inside, the older woman, who named herself Larchwind, lifted a small furry ball from her satchel.

"It's a pin-pig," she said, setting it down on the carpet, where it lay still for a moment. "They don't like to be held, but they're helpful in finding poison, which you suspect, I understand."

"Yes," Arian said. As the little animal uncurled and stood, it did have a vaguely pig-shaped body, though no larger than a kitten in size. Pale spines lifted from red-brown fur. After a bit, it minced about the room on tiny feet, its pink nose snuffling busily. "I've never seen one."

"They're rare outside Dzordanya. Now—tell me your symptoms, please."

Arian did so, all the while watching the pin-pig quarter the room. Finally it came back to the Kuakgan, let out a high-pitched squeak-grunt, and lay down with its nose on the Kuak-gan's boot. She leaned over, picked it up, and returned it to her satchel.

"It's not in the carpet," Larchwind said. "I didn't think it was, but she enjoys running about. Now—I will need to touch your hand." Arian nodded and held out her hand. Larchwind used her heart-hand, she noticed. After a moment, Larchwind sat back. "A plant, definitely, but your body has refused nearly all of it. I expect we'll find the same for the others."

They went downstairs and met the other Kuakkgani and Kieri just coming into the kitchen; the cooks and other kitchen workers were all wide-eyed, and more so when Larchwind set the pin-pig on the floor.

"She is clean and will cause no damage," Larchwind said. "But her nose is sensitive—more than ours—and she may find something we would not. Do not fear."

The pin-pig trotted around the main kitchen and, with Larchwind crooning to it, investigated each pantry and store-room, one after another. The other two Kuakkgani touched wooden bowls and utensils—"listening to the wood," they told the cooks when asked. When they'd left the main kitchen, the head cook sent her helpers back to work.

The pin-pig's sustained squeal interrupted everyone. Kieri, Arian, and the head cook, along with the other two Kuakk-gani, hurried to find Larchwind and the pin-pig.

The pin-pig stood in a corner of the spice pantry, all spines bristling out, little nose pointed upward. Larchwind, hum-ming, was touching first one shelf, then another. Arian breathed deeply; mingled fragrances of spices and herbs tingled in her nose.

"What's all this?" Kieri asked the cook, waving around the small room.

"All things we season with," the cook said. "Jars down there are sauces and pickles and such, and then up on the shelves are the dry things—roots, barks, leaves, seeds and nuts and buds and stalks—once they've dried. Some dry in sun, some in here out of the sun. Everything in its place; I won't have a jumble, sir king. Some must be stored in wooden boxes—the right kind of wood—and some in stone and some in clay, and some must lie open."

"Where do they all come from?"

"Mostly from the garden and the royal forest, but some are bought from far or as gifts."

"This, I think," Larchwind said. She lifted a narrow box with a carved lid and held it down to the pin-pig, whose spines flattened, then erected again. "Thank you," Larchwind said to the pin-pig. It was silent and after a moment curled up in a ball. Larchwind scooped it up in her free hand and slipped it into her satchel again.

"But it's—it's the farron. Farron's not a poison." The cook looked ready to faint.

Larchwind opened the box. Inside were two compressed lumps and a tangle of strands, all a rich magenta at first glance. "Farron, right enough . . . but not just farron. Look here—" She took out one of the lumps. Originally shaped in a rectangular block, one end had been broken off—and there, in the middle of the exposed break, was a streak of lighter color.

"That's . . . that's not right," the cook said. "It should be the same all through unless it's gone bad. But farron doesn't go bad; it keeps for years, and we're careful. You can see by the box there's been no moisture in it."

"Do you know where this came from?" Kieri asked the cook.

"Not exactly," the cook said. "As I told Lady Halveric when she asked, so much came in before the wedding, from so many people. I remember the steward bringing it down: there were four cakes of farron, a very expensive gift. They looked best quality, untouched—you can see here, on the outside, the color, the smooth surface. They were dry, or I swear I wouldn't have kept them, expensive as they are."

"What is that other color?" Kieri asked Larchwind.

"Not farron," she said, frowning. "It's melfar, related to farron but not safe to eat. It's known to cause sheep and cattle to lose their young."

"Could someone have gathered the wrong one by mistake? Do they grow together? Look alike?"

"No, sir king. Though related, the flowers are a different color, and they are never found in the same place. More to the point, you see that the melfar is hidden, wrapped round with the purple farron."

"So . . . it was intentional."

"It must have been," Larchwind said. She turned to the cook. "Have you ever seen melfar or its flower parts?"

"No, but I've heard of it. I know farron is always purple-red."

"You said there were four cakes of it," Kieri said to the cook. "Did you use the other cakes in the wedding foods?"

"Yes, sir king . . . it's traditional for both spring feasts and weddings, and this was both . . . I only thought to make it better, I swear—" The cook started sobbing and through her sobs went on: "I—I put a whole cake in the fruit filling for the pastries—for the color and the flavor both—I didn't see anything wrong with the color, but we were so busy . . . and another in the steamed grain . . ."

"I'm not blaming you," Kieri said. "But we must find out who sent it or—if that person should have transported it innocently—who made it."

"Melfar is not common," Larchwind said. "Nor is farron. Whoever made those blocks had to know where both grow, obtain enough of each, and then make the blocks. I suspect— but do not know for certain—that this person gathered the flower parts personally, as farron is expensive."

The steward looked in his records for anyone who had donated farron. That took hours of poring over the records, donor by donor. Finally he gave Kieri a name. "Only one gift of farron: four blocks of farron were donated along with a barrel of apples by Selmud Granil, a farmer on Sier Tolmaric's steading."

"A farmer?" Kieri said. Sier Tolmaric was not the richest of the Siers; those holding a farmstead would have less, and a barrel of apples sounded more reasonable than four cakes of expensive spice.

"Perhaps he carried it in for his Sier," the steward said.

"I will speak to Sier Tolmaric."

SIER TOLMARIC, SUMMONED to Kieri's office, stared in apparent shock and dismay. "You think my farmer did *what*?

Selmud? He couldn't have. First, he couldn't buy that much farron—he hasn't the money—and second, he hasn't been off his land all winter."

"He came to Chaya with the apples," Kieri said. "He could have visited the market."

"I don't believe it. Do you know what farron costs? He doesn't have it, I tell you! And if you're wondering if I sent such a gift: no. I could not afford it either. I sent meat on the hoof for the feast. Bullocks and sheep."

"Then how—"

"Someone slipped it into Selmud's contribution without being noticed," Sier Tolmaric said. "It's vile, is what it is. Whoever did this was willing to poison many people to harm one."

Kieri wished he could see the inside of Sier Tolmaric's head; the man seemed outraged at the poisoning, only reasonably indignant that his farmer had been suspected. Was that true?

"It was the elves," Tolmaric said. "It must have been. None of your human subjects would do such a thing, sir king. And it's elves who don't care about humans—about human children. They've not done one thing to help, have they? Just like before. And making sure a human would be blamed—it's just like when your mother was killed, sir king. Just the same."

And just what Kieri could expect to hear from Tolmaric after his earlier outbursts about the elves. Tolmaric had reason—or thought he had reason—to dislike and distrust elves. It was true the elves hadn't offered any help—hadn't identified the poison, hadn't shown any interest in doing so. But was that guilt?

"Sier Tolmaric," he said, trying to keep his voice calm, "I know you have long-standing resentment of elves—and a reason for it—but in this present instance, I must be very careful. The gift was listed as coming from your steading and a particular person. I believe you when you say he could not have afforded such a gift; I believe that you yourself had nothing to do with the poisoning. But from your innocence to the guilt of elves is a long, long stride. I am not willing to accuse them. Yet."

hoped for, all those years since your sister died—yes, half-elf, but a man who could—who would—stand up for us. You lived as a human all those years, not influenced by elven magery." Tolmaric's expression was pleading, and his hands reached out.

CHAPTER THIRTY-ONE

KIERI WAS STILL struggling for words to convey to Tolmaric the complexity he himself perceived, when he felt the taig shudder as if it felt a blow. Almost at once, the room filled with the glamour of the elvenhome and the force of the Lady's anger.

"You invited Kuakkgani!" she said without waiting for a greeting. Waves of power washed toward him; he ignored them. He was aware of Tolmaric standing open-mouthed to one side, and hoped the man would keep silent. "You know what I told you," the Lady went on. "We do not allow Kuakkgani in this land—they are disgusting!"

"You did not help us find the poison or the poisoner. The Kuakkgani did," Kieri said. "Our child died, and others as well, and you did nothing."

"There was nothing to do but grieve," she said. "The child was already dead." Her voice had softened a little but still held an arrogance that angered him.

"*Nothing* to do?" Kieri said. "When the Kuakkgani were able to find the poison quickly, to prevent more being poisoned, women whose unborn children would have died if it had not been discovered? If you had been willing to help, others now grieving might have life still within them. But you were not even within call."

"The Kuakkgani are—" A string of elven he did not understand but for "filthy" and "against the taig."

"Grandmother," Kieri said, and paused.

She glared at him but said nothing.

"Let us be clear," he said. "You are the Lady of the Ladys-forest, and where elven matters in the elvenhome are concerned, I have nothing to say. But where humans in Lyonya are concerned, and where my own children are concerned, I am the king, and I will choose what seems best to me. You knew about the poison and the grief we felt. You offered no advice; you offered scant comfort. Thus I did not seek your opinion and do not seek it now."

"But they are—"

"They have found the source of the poison: someone put cakes of farron mixed with melfar among the gifts brought for the wedding feast."

"Melfar!"

"I see you know what it is."

"Yes . . . but who? Who brought it? What grudge do they have against you?"

"The person among whose other gifts it was listed did not—*could* not—have brought it. Someone else put it with his. We know that much. And we are beginning to suspect what manner of being might have done so."

"What manner of—you cannot mean you suspect elves!" Her eyes glowed, almost dragon-like, Kieri thought. Her power intensified; Tolmaric crumpled to the floor, hands clutching at his head.

"Are you sure it was *not* elves?" Kieri asked. "Your own daughter attacked and killed, your grandson stolen away . . . You must have enemies, Grandmother. Certainly gnomes, and for all I know among the elves, too. Orlith's murder—"

"That was a human. That must have been a human! Maybe that man!" She pointed at Tolmaric. "He has always hated elves; he probably killed Orlith to keep you from learning more, and he could have poisoned Arian and the other women to blame it on us."

Don't be ridiculous came into Kieri's mind, but the Lady would not hear that, he was sure. Instead he said, "Sier Tolmaric is an honorable man and has reasons for his dislike of elves—the torment you inflicted on his father and grandfather. His family is poorer because of that, and the scathefire ran across his lands while you were away and could not help defend us."

"I apologize for that . . . I have already . . ."

"To him? For his losses? Are you going to grant him what I

asked: land to replace what was lost? You have answered nothing about that, and I have asked again and again."

"It doesn't mean he didn't do it," she said.

"He did not do it," Kieri said. "He did not kill Orlith because he was here, in Chaya, in the palace itself, when Orlith was killed, and he had no reason to poison us and kill our child. The humans in my court, Grandmother, are not my enemies. I have enough elven magery to know that for certain. Some are stubborn, some are slow, not all agree with me . . . but they are not enemies."

"And you think we are."

"I think some of you may be. Or it might be other beings—iynisin, perhaps. I've met those before."

"It cannot be. Such do not exist here."

Kieri's patience frayed; he struggled with himself. "Something is wrong, Grandmother, and you must know it—and I need to know it. I believe you intend me no harm, but you keep secrets . . . you go away and do not come back . . . you do not answer my simplest questions. If you were human, I would think—" He stopped short. Could he tell her what he really thought, that she was impaired in some way, unfit to rule? She was the Lady; she was so old he could not imagine what her real age might be—old enough to see mountains grow and seas rise and fall, as the dragon said he was. An Elder of Elders, and his own grandmother . . .

"You would think what?" she asked. She seemed to grow taller, more beautiful, more powerful; her glamour wrapped around him, heavy as water. Then, even as he struggled against it, her eyes widened, focusing past him, and her mouth opened.

War-honed reflexes acted; he had ducked aside and whirled, reaching for his sword, when a sword hummed through the space where he had been. Another presence—elven?—and his first glimpse was of an elf he had never seen, as tall as the Lady. He had his sword out then, the green jewel in the pommel glowing. The elf now aimed his sword's point at the Lady and extended his other hand to Kieri.

"You will not move," he said to Kieri; to the Lady he said, "Flessinathlin . . . dear lady, has it come at last? And is this puny mortal your champion?"

Kieri felt a weight of malice added to the Lady's glamour . . . and felt that glamour fade. The elf's face, those perfectly shaped bones, that exquisite beauty, held an expression of such viciousness that the beauty seemed even more unreal. He had never felt such before around elves—strangeness, yes, but not this.

"You should not have divided your power," the elf said to the Lady. "Once you were stronger . . . but now? I think perhaps you are not. And this one is your grandson, so I hear. How delightful it will be when he is blamed for your death. All your fawning little subjects will take care of him for me, and then . . . even the Kingsforest cannot withstand us."

The Lady's larger semblance had faded, leaving her slightly shorter than the other. With a sensation much like a bubble popping on the skin, Kieri felt the elvenhome presence disappear. With that, he could feel the malice of the other elf even more strongly. Only—it was not Sinyi, but iynisin.

"We will not be interrupted by any of your subjects," the iynisin said to the Lady. "Or yours," it said to Kieri. "Not that they could do me any harm if they were here in a crowd."

From the corner of his eye, Kieri saw Tolmaric move slightly, shoulders tensing, one eye opening. *Don't*, Kieri thought at him. Tolmaric wasn't armed, and if the Lady's glamour had felled him, the iynisin's power would surely overwhelm him, too. Whether it was his thought or Tolmaric's or the iynisin's power, Tolmaric relaxed again, eye closing.

"How will you defend yourself, Flessinathlin-aorlin? Or will you yield to me freely, out of your wisdom? I will allow you a blade; I am not unfair . . . but it is you alone I face this time, and you alone chose to limit your power, so I lose nothing by that."

The Lady raised her right hand, and a sword appeared in it. "Do you think the Singer will lend me no aid?"

"Oh, not that sword, Fless. That one I can destroy with a touch." The iynisin's long dark blade thrust forward, just touching the Lady's, and her blade shattered like thin ice, the shards vanishing in a mist even as they fell. "You must do better, indeed you must. I have waited too long to make this easy for you." Its voice dropped to a croon. "No one will mourn the winter's fairest flower . . . no one will mourn her beauty or sing her praise song, and not even one tree will keep her memory green."

Kieri's heart contracted; he could not draw breath for a moment. The Lady looked so helpless, so forlorn, her hands empty of any weapon, her connection to the elvenhome broken. He heard, as if far distant, someone knocking on his office door, but he knew whoever it was would not be able to come in.

"Reach for it, Fless," the iynisin said. "You still have power enough, I deem. It will weaken you a little, but you will still be able to lift the blade and use it . . . for a while. Or would you rather take your grandson's blade from his hands and leave him no protection at all when you fall at my feet?"

Kieri hoped she would not do that; he knew he could move and was only waiting for the best moment. He could feel the iynisin's pressure still. The Lady glanced at him; he dared not wink, but let one corner of his mouth twitch—a smile, if she understood. Her expression did not change. She held her hands palms up in front of her. Slowly, across her outstretched palms, a sword grew into being, first the outline, starting with the tip, and then the substance. This one Kieri felt sure was old—a sword she had drawn to her from somewhere else, somewhere deep in memory, for it appeared the way someone gazing with concentration along its blade would see it. It was like no sword Kieri had seen: the blade dark, glinting in reds and golds, a vapor rising from it. The hilt—but her hand was closing over it before he could see its design clearly.

The iynisin laughed. Kieri thought it was to break her concentration, for the laugh sounded forced. The sword continued to solidify; Kieri felt power in it as well. The hilt of his own sword heated in his hand, as if in response.

"You chose well, Fless," the iynisin said then. "But it will not help you as much as you think."

The Lady lifted the blade from her other hand, brought it to position . . . and the iynisin attacked. She parried, parried again as the iynisin redoubled, moved a little to her heart-hand.

The iynisin laughed again. "If you think I'm going to turn

my back on your grandson, Fless . . . no. I know his past. And he is fighting my power—he might get loose. Turn as you please and know that you cannot outwit me." The iynisin moved down the room, opening a distance from Kieri without turning away from him.

Kieri tried to create a semblance of himself on which the iynisin's attention and power would fix and allow him to move outside it without notice. Though the elvenhome had been severed from the Lady, his sword and dagger, he knew, put him in contact with some elven powers and with the taig . . . and they did still. He ignored the duel for the moment and reached for the taig and for the bones in the ossuary. He felt his father's alarm, his sister's anger, and then the door split, the grain opening silently to the width of a thin person. Through the opening, he saw Squires and two elves, swords gleaming. He tried, but could not coax or force it to open wider as they began to squeeze through, first an elf, then a Squire, then—

"You force me to this," the iynisin said, and lunged at the Lady, sweeping her blade aside. Kieri moved but knew he would be too late to save her if she could not parry.

"No!" With that word, one of the elves moved so fast Kieri saw only a blur, throwing himself between the iynisin and the Lady . . . and taking the thrust meant for her, even as his sword struck the iynisin's dagger arm.

The Lady thrust across the fallen body of the elf; for an instant her sword seemed red flame, but the iynisin backed out of range. Kieri advanced, feeling the eagerness in his own blade and the same excitement he'd always felt in a battle. He knew his Squires were in the room now; he knew the other elf was also advancing . . . the iynisin was outnumbered, trapped in that end of the room.

But he wasn't. He had used the same magery Kieri had attempted; he wasn't where he seemed to be, and Kieri barely parried the blow that came at him suddenly from the side. His blade squealed, a sound he'd never heard from any blade, and a blow hit his shoulder—only the mail he wore saved him. For an instant the blow numbed his arm. He almost dropped his sword but managed to keep his grip and stay upright.

"Finally," the iynisin said. "A challenge." It stood now over

Tolmaric, near Kieri's desk. "And an elf-hater to provide the blood; how very appropriate." As the tip of its sword touched Tolmaric's neck, Tolmaric convulsed. His eyes opened; he gave a strangled cry, and then his clothes turned black, as if rotting in water; his body sank in on itself, gray and withering.

And the iynisin grew—divided—became three, and then five, all identical, all with sword in hand, all with that arrogant, cruel smile. Were they semblances or true multiples? "It is only fair," it said. "You surely see that—" And it charged.

No time to think; no time to do anything but meet the attack. Kieri parried the first blade that came at him with his dagger, the second with his sword. He could do nothing about the others; he heard the clash of blades all over the room. Someone bumped into his back, and "Sir king!" that person gasped. How one of his Squires had reached him, he did not know, but for the moment, fighting back to back, he had one less thing to worry about.

He parried, the iynisin blades screeching as they touched his flashes of light he did not understand running down his blades. He tried to attack but with two opponents had no opening, and he was now close against the hearth on his dagger side. He slid a foot forward, hoping his Squire would follow the shift in his weight, and edged very slowly along that wall.

Kieri was aware of Kuakkgani nearby, but they came no closer. He took another blow that did not penetrate his mail but drove him back a step. He was tiring now. He blinked a trickle of sweat out of his eyes, reached to the taig for strength—and it came, a cool green stream. In that moment, he found an opening and lunged, thrust, redoubled, and then parried the second iynisin's downward swing with his sword as the first screamed and backed away, staggering.

One down? No, for the iynisin came at him again, slower but still dangerous. He was past the fireplace now; he advanced another step and swung to put his back to the wall; his Squire—Tamlin—did the same, which forced their opponents to face them. Now Kieri could see past the iynisin—in fragmented glances—to see another Squire enter the room and then another figure, this one in blue.

His heart skipped a beat. Arian: yes, in mail and a helmet,

but—Arian! And Dorrin. He missed his parry; the iynisin blade squealed on his mail, and it burned as if fire had heated it. Pain focused him again; he parried strongly, thrust, and for the first time his blade went home in the iynisin to his left just as Arian's transfixed the same iynisin from behind.

And Dorrin's blade, glowing blue, took off the head of the other in a level swipe. The head disintegrated before it hit the floor, a black spray splashing the Squire next to Kieri and then vanishing; the Squire's clothes blackened and frayed, as if burning. He cried out.

Kieri raised his sword in salute as he looked around the room in time to see two of the remaining iynisin flow into the third . . . who was pulling his blade free of the Lady.

"As I said, Flessinathlin: you will die, and he will be blamed." Then the iynisin vanished.

Kieri stared; the Lady of the Ladysforest, his grandmother, lay in a welter of silver-flashed scarlet, surrounded by the bodies of three elves. Dorrin moved first, blade still in hand, and Kieri followed, with Arian at his side. The taig was silent—shocked into stillness, he thought with the corner of his mind that could think, though horror almost overwhelmed him.

As he knelt by her side, he heard the door creak open, the hurried footsteps as those outside came in, as they gasped and exclaimed, elven and human voices mingling . . . but all he could see was the Lady's face, the light fading from it, and all he could really hear was the sound, too familiar, of a mortal wound that made her struggle to say aloud what words her lips tried to frame.

She seemed so small . . . he started to take her hands, realized he still held his weapons, and set them down, careless of the mess on the floor. He was the king . . . could he heal her? But when he touched her hands, touched the wounds, he knew he could not. The king's touch had no power over elves or the injuries dealt by iynisin.

"Grandmother," Kieri said. Her gaze focused on him; her lips moved again. "Grandmother, he lied. All will mourn you, winter's fairest flower. We will mourn your beauty lost, and we will sing your praise song, and a multitude of trees will keep your memory green. I swear this, Grandmother, Lady of the

Ladysforest, as I live, and on the oath we swore together a year ago, and on the blades you had forged for me."

"Grandson . . ." Her voice was a mere thread of sound but still as pure a music as one string of a harp, skillfully plucked. "I . . . fear . . . for you . . ."

"Do not," Kieri said. "Your enemy fled rather than face me, at the end."

"I . . . was wrong . . . too often. Not . . . telling . . . you. Iynisin . . . hate . . . life. Singer . . ." Her eyes dulled, the silver sparks in her blood dulling as if tarnished.

Kieri felt the taig shudder as if every tree had been shaken to its roots at once. Arian leaned into his shoulder; together they tried to calm the growing storm of grief and fear. Behind him, he heard the eerie keening of elven voices. Kieri laid his grandmother's hands gently on her bloody dress. He looked up at Dorrin, standing with blade still drawn on the other side of the Lady.

"Dorrin?"

"It might come back."

If you loved ECHOES OF BETRAYAL,

be sure not to miss:

LIMITS OF POWER

by

ELIZABETH MOON

The thrilling penultimate novel
in the Paladin's Legacy series.

Coming in Summer 2013.

Here's a special preview:

"YOU KILLED HER!" That first voice, instantly joined by others, rose in a furious screech of accusation. "*You* killed her! You killed *her*!"

The angry voices penetrated Kieri's grief and exhaustion, and he looked back over his shoulder to see at least a dozen elves, some with swords drawn, his uncle Amrothlin among them. Behind them, more Squires pushed into the room.

"I did not," he said. "I tried—"

"She's dead! You're alive; you must have—!"

"I tried to *save* her," Kieri said. "I could not." He stood up then, automatically collecting his weapons as he rose.

"Let me see that!" Amrothlin strode forward, pointing at Kieri's sword. "If it has her blood on it—"

"Of course it does," Kieri said. "You saw: my sword lay in her blood, there on the floor." He had knelt in her blood, he realized, and his hands were stained. No wonder Amrothlin suspected him, though the blood that spattered his clothes had come from others.

Amrothlin reached out his hand. "Let me smell it. I know her scent; I will know another's scent, if indeed another's blood is there. Give it to me."

"No," Arian said before Kieri could answer, blocking Amrothlin with her arm. "You will not disarm the king," she said. "Not after what has happened."

"You!" Amrothlin glared at her. "You half-bred trouble-maker, child of one who should never have sired children on mortals—"

"*Daughter* of one who gave his life to save the Lady," Arian said. Kieri saw the glitter of both tears and anger in her eyes. "There he lies, and you would insult him?"

"And you know you cannot hold this sword," Kieri said, forcing a calm tone through the anger he felt. How dare Amrothlin insult Arian—and where had he been all this time? Was he the traitor? "You remember: it's sealed to me. Smell if you wish, but do not touch it."

Amrothlin glared at them all, then fixed his gaze on Arian. "What should I think when I find three mortals around my Lady's body with swords drawn and her blood run out like water from a cracked jug? I see no other foe here. It is you, I say, and this—this so-called king."

Kieri glanced past Amrothlin. The ring of elves stood tense; behind them were Squires who hesitated to push them aside, and behind those the hooded figures of two Kuakkgani. He met Amrothlin's angry gaze once more.

"I am the king," he said, keeping his voice as steady as he could. "I am the king, and my mother was your sister, and this Lady was my grandmother. So we are kin, whether you like it or not. If you can indeed detect identity by the smell of the blood, then you will smell another immortal's blood on this—and on the queen's sword and Duke Verrakai's as well."

"Do you dare accuse an elf?" Amrothlin asked. He still trembled like a candle flame, but his voice had calmed.

"The one who did this could appear without walking through a door. Its mien seemed elven at first and also its magery, a glamour of the same sort as the Lady was wont to cast. Yet it was like no elf I have known in its malice and determination to kill the Lady. I believe you name such iynisin; in Tsaia we called them kuaknomi."

Amrothlin glared. "We do not speak of them." He looked over his shoulder, then back to Kieri. "Who was here at the time?"

"Later," Kieri said. Voices rose in the corridor: angry, frightened, demanding. Time to take command. "Uncle, this is not the time for questions. I am the king, and I am not your enemy, nor the Lady's. People are frightened; I must speak to them."

Before Amrothlin could answer, he raised his voice and called to those beyond the room. "The danger is over for now: I, the king, am alive, and the queen is safe here with me. Those of you in the corridor: fetch the palace physicians for the wounded. The rest disperse, but for the Queen's Squires assigned to the queen today and one Kuakgan. Put by your swords." The elves by the door looked at Amrothlin, who said nothing, and then at Kieri again and finally put up their swords. Two Queen's Squires made their way into the room and edged through the elves to Arian's side.

Dorrin had already moved to one of the wounded Squires. "This one first, sir king. Both are sore wounded, and though I tried, I cannot heal them."

Kieri knelt beside her. When he laid his hand on the man's shoulder, he felt nothing but a heaviness. "Nor I," he said, standing again. "I must be more worn than I thought."

The noise outside diminished. "I will tell the whole of it to Amrothlin," Kieri said to the elves. "Two may remain; the rest of you go and make what preparations you need make for the Lady's rest." He knelt beside the other Squire yet felt no healing power in himself. Sighing, he stood again.

Amrothlin's stony expression did not change, but he did not contradict Kieri; with a wave of his hand he sent most of the elves away. Now the carnage showed more clearly—the pools of blood, the stench of blood and death, bloody footprints on the fine carpet, what looked like scorch marks, the dead: the Lady, Dameroth, another dead elf whose name Kieri did not know, Tolmaric's twisted and shrunken body, and the two iynisin Kieri and Arian and Dorrin had killed. Arian's clothes were as bloodstained as his own, and Dorrin, though she had not knelt in any blood, still had splashes on her shirt and sword hand.

"More dead elves," one of the other elves said, bending to examine them. Then he stiffened, turning back to Amrothlin.

"My lord! These are not elves! They are . . . what the king said."

Amrothlin, still looking at Kieri, said, "Is this what you fought? Did you kill it?"

"That is another it split from its body after it killed Sier Tolmaric," Kieri said. "Look at Tolmaric, look at its body, and if you can explain how that was done, I will be glad."

Amrothlin turned and walked over to Tolmaric's remains. "This was human?" He sounded more worried than angry now.

"Yes. The iynisin did that with a touch of its blade to his throat. He was already bespelled by the Lady, as I said, and helpless."

"Where were you?"

"There." Kieri pointed. He told of questioning Sier Tolmaric, the Lady's interruption, and then the appearance of the iynisin—he insisted on using the name, though Amrothlin flinched every time—and its taunting of the Lady and attack. "I had just taken such a blow on my shoulder as almost threw me down. It was almost invisible; I could not see to parry the blow—and then it made for poor Tolmaric and did *that* to him, whatever that is. Then from the iynisin came two more, and each of those split into two."

"A formidable foe indeed," Amrothlin said. "Few of . . . such . . . can do that, and only with fresh blood and life taken." He moved over beside the elf looking at the other body. Kieri saw his shoulders stiffen. Amrothlin crouched beside the body and touched the blood staining its dark clothes, then sniffed at his fingers. He stood and faced Kieri again. "You brought this on us."

"What?" That accusation made no sense to him.

"You could not survive such a one unless it willed it so. The—these beings—" Even now Amrothlin would not use the word. "You know their origin? Traitors who once were elves, in the morning of the world, and who turned against all because of *those*." He pointed at the Kuakgan now standing near the door. "You called Kuakkgani here; that must be why the evil ones came. We do not speak of them. We do not acknowledge them."

"And yet these iynisin exist," Kieri said, once more using the elven name for them. "And they—or one—killed the Lady. Are all of them that powerful?" This, he was certain, was one of the secrets the elves had withheld from him; how could they think that not speaking of danger meant it did not exist?

"So you say, that she was killed by such." Amrothlin made an obvious attempt to calm down, but did not answer Kieri's question. He sniffed his fingers again. "It is more likely a lord of the Severance could kill her than a half-human like you," he said. "These dead are certainly ephemes, split from such a one. And that—" He glanced at Tolmaric's remains. "That is what any living thing looks like that they destroy to make ephemes." He nodded to Kieri, now apparently calm. "I accept your story of the fight, but still—it is your fault that the Lady came here unescorted and such evil followed her. You knew what she thought of the . . . the Kuakkgani." He nearly spat the last word, his voice full of venom again.

"What *I* see is that you are determined to blame the king," Arian said. Kieri had never seen her so angry before. Flanked by her Squires, she stalked over to him. "Where were you when I was poisoned and my child never had a chance to live? The Lady did not come. None of you came. It was a Kuakgan who found the poison concealed in a block of spice: you elves did nothing. And you blame us for that?"

Amrothlin stared at her, speechless in the face of her anger.

"So now," Kieri said, taking over once more, "let us clean up this mess and confer." The palace physicians bustled into the room; he pointed to Binir and Curn, the two wounded Squires. Linne, another of the King's Squires, handed him cleaning materials for his sword; he began wiping it down. Arian handed her blade to one of her Squires. "Who is now the ruler of the elvenhome?" Kieri asked Amrothlin. "Will it be you, her son, or had she named another in her stead?"

Amrothlin shook his head. "There is no elvenhome."

"What—? Of course there is . . . must be." At the look on Amrothlin's face, Kieri said, "How can it be gone?"

"Do you not *see*?" Amrothlin gestured to his own grief-stricken face. "Do I look the same? Do you feel the influence of the elvenhome? It was hers—*her* creation—and it died with her. She alone sustained the Ladysforest; she had no heir. We are unhomed, Nephew. We are cast away, and nowhere in the world will we find a home now."

"That cannot be. The taig is still here." Kieri could feel the taig, the strength of it, even in its grief.

"The taig, yes. It is the spirit of all life. Where there is life, there is taig, greater and smaller. The taig nourishes elvenkind, and elvenkind nourishes the taig. We encouraged it, taught it, lifted it toward more awareness, according to the Lady's design. But it is not the elvenhome."

This was the longest explanation Kieri had ever heard about the relationship of elves and taig. "Then what *is* an elvenhome? Did the Lady then maintain the elvenhome with her own power? By herself?" And if so, how could such a power be stripped away?

"At first, yes," Amrothlin said. "But after we left the great hall below, in the time of the banast taig . . ." His voice trailed away; he looked down and away. "I cannot talk of it now, Nephew, please. Her power diminished, and now she is gone; the elfane taig is gone; I must prepare to lay her body to rest."

Kieri felt tears rising in his eyes and blinked them back. "Why didn't you ever tell me? Why didn't Orlith? If I had known—"

"You would have tried to interfere," Amrothlin said, his voice harsh again. "And what could you, a mortal, do? *You* had no power to lend us. You could but cause the Lady more anguish, to know that you knew her shame."

"And this is better?" Kieri asked. The familiar irritation with elven arrogance overrode even his fatigue. He waved at the room, at the bodies and the blood and the stench of death.

"Her pride cost you dear, Uncle. You were so sure we could not help, you did not even seek understanding, let alone alliance—"

"How could such as you understand?" Amrothlin said. He looked more weary than angry now, his grace diminished. "What we live—what she lived—is beyond your comprehension. It is no use to explain; you do not have the mind for it."

Kieri's anger grew, but he knew that for a postbattle reaction as much as a fair response to Amrothlin. He glanced around the room. Everyone but the physicians working on the wounded Squires was looking at him. This was not the time to continue a quarrel with Amrothlin.

"Are any others wounded and in need of care?" No one answered. Arian's Squire returned her blade, now cleaned, and Arian slid it into the scabbard. Kieri had almost finished with his own.

"We will need to make a bier to move her," Amrothlin said. "And . . . and the others."

"Is there any menace in Sier Tolmaric's remains?" Kieri asked.

"No," Amrothlin said. "The evil destroyed him but does not remain. Do what you will with . . . that." He gestured toward Tolmaric's body but averted his gaze. "But beware the iynisin ephemes. Even their blood taints anything alive or that once lived. You must burn such things in a safe place away from here."

"Sier Tolmaric was a brave man from a family that had suffered much at elven hands," Kieri said, ignoring the rest for the moment. Amrothlin's arrogance grated on him. "Had the Lady not pressed her glamour on him, he might have fought at my side."

"What injury had he from elves?" Amrothlin asked, brows raised.

Kieri regretted mentioning it; this was something else that would be better discussed later. But if he wanted answers to questions, then he must answer those asked of him. "When my mother was killed, and I abducted, Tolmaric's father and grandfather were taken away by the elves—possibly by you yourself. Were you involved in that?"

Amrothlin scowled. "We thought humans involved, of course. How else?"

"Perhaps today you see another possibility," Kieri said. "Elves took some of his family, and they came back damaged, with no apologies or recompense made. Nor, though I asked the Lady, was any recompense made for his losses from scathefire. Nor was that family the only one injured in your search for my mother's killers." He slid his sword home in its scabbard, picked up the dagger, and wiped it down. "But we will talk of this later, when you have taken the Lady away. For now, tell your people what happened—what *really* happened— and give those who died whatever honor you can. Where will you lay the Lady?"

"In that valley where the elvenhome below was," Amrothlin said. "She loved that valley. It is not in Lyonya as you know it, but you would be welcome to come there."

Kieri shook his head as he slid the dagger, now clean and oiled, into its sheath. "With this menace hanging over us, I cannot leave, Uncle. It would be better, indeed, if you found a place for her nearer to Chaya, since you lack the protection of the elvenhome. Why not the King's Grove, where the symbol of our alliance is? You say, I understand, that your people have no existence beyond death—though truly I do not understand how you can know that—"

"We were told," Amrothlin said in a low voice.

Kieri wanted to ask, *By whom?*, but this was not the time. "Linne, please tell the steward or Garris—whomever you find first—to summon the Council to the large dining room. They may already have heard, but I will formally announce Sier Tolmaric's death there. And we will need a bier for Tolmaric's body." He looked at Amrothlin again. "The palace can furnish biers for your dead. I will want two elves at the Council. You, unless your duties to the Lady's body require you here, and whomever you choose."

"Yes," Amrothlin said. His sword hand moved weakly, as if he could not decide on a gesture. "Yes, to all. Is there—is there any place we could take the bodies to wash them? I do not wish to parade the Lady through the streets to our inn."

"Of course. We will use the salle for them. Arian?" Kieri turned to her. "What is your desire in this?"

"That it not have happened," she answered, her voice choked with grief. "But it did. I would stay with my father's body, if you can spare me." Her expression was grave and resolute.

Kieri nodded. "Of course I can. You are his kin; it is your right."

"You said you were hit on the shoulder," Arian said. "I see the cut in your clothes—"

"And the blade did not touch my skin thanks to the mail. I will have it seen to when I can, but not now." He laid his hand on her shoulder. "I will come, Arian. But first I must speak to the Council, and then I will come to the salle."

"Then I take my leave," Arian said. "But you will be seen by physicians, Kieri—I insist on it." She gave a little bow and turned away, going back to her father's body. Kieri watched the set of her shoulders. He had lost his parents so long ago . . . he knew the pain of having none but not the pain of recent loss. And with the loss of their child . . . she had lost so much in so short a time.

He moved away from the iynisin's body to Tolmaric's. He could hardly recognize this ugly twisted relic as human remains. "You were brave," he said to Tolmaric's spirit in case it lingered. "You were not afraid to speak out the truth you knew and would have fought if you'd had the chance. I am sorry I could not save you from this fate. I swear to you, I will do my best by your family. Your sons and daughters will have a father in me."